Experience the passion and excitement of
the Irish Eyes romances . . .

IRISH DEVIL
by Donna Fletcher

*In a land of heavenly landscapes and hellish warfare, a Lady
and Lord discover a love both have desired—and denied—for
too long . . .*

TO MARRY AN IRISH ROGUE
by Lisa Hendrix

*In the quaint town of Kilbooly, two people are about to meet
their match. "Hendrix is a talented newcomer." —Susan Wiggs*

DAUGHTER OF IRELAND
by Sonja Massie

*An American businessman draws the ire of a traditional Irish
beauty—and a fiery passion neither can ignore . . .*

Midsummer Lightning

Kate Ivers

JOVE BOOKS, NEW YORK

This is a work of fiction. Names, characters, places, and incidents are
either the product of the author's imagination or are used fictitiously,
and any resemblance to actual persons, living or dead, business
establishments, events, or locales is entirely coincidental.

MIDSUMMER LIGHTNING

A Jove Book / published by arrangement with
the author

PRINTING HISTORY
Jove edition / August 2000

All rights reserved.
Copyright © 2000 by Kathy Chwedyk.
This book may not be reproduced in whole or in part,
by mimeograph or any other means, without permission.
For information address: The Berkley Publishing Group,
a division of Penguin Putnam Inc.,
375 Hudson Street, New York, New York 10014.

The Penguin Putnam Inc. World Wide Web site address is
http://www.penguinputnam.com

ISBN: 0-515-12884-8

A JOVE BOOK®
Jove Books are published by The Berkley Publishing Group,
a division of Penguin Putnam Inc.,
375 Hudson Street, New York, New York 10014.
JOVE and the "J" design
are trademarks belonging to Penguin Putnam Inc.

PRINTED IN THE UNITED STATES OF AMERICA

10 9 8 7 6 5 4 3 2 1

Acknowledgments

Heartfelt thanks to Jake Elwell, Gail Fortune, Christine Hahn, Eleanor Lerner, Joyce and Elizabeth Romke, Noreen Weldon, and the staff of the Algonquin Area Public Library, who made this book possible.

Special thanks also to Jennifer Coleman, my personal guru of contemporary culture, who dragged me kicking and screaming into the nineties just in time to celebrate the millennium.

One

Whitlock Castle
County Cork, Ireland

Kelly Sullivan knew she was scaring the woman at the front desk by the way the woman's mild blue eyes widened and her voice acquired the soft, soothing tone one uses when confronted by people who might be crazy or dangerous.

It only made Kelly madder.

She had been stood up at the airport—actually stood up!—by the interim manager of her company's newest acquisition, Whitlock Castle. As Lawrence Hotels' transition team head, Kelly was accustomed to being treated with more respect by people who wanted to keep their jobs once the new regime took over.

Conor O'Meara should have been at the airport with bells on, wearing his best suit and obsequious to the point of licking the soles of her shoes and strewing rose petals in her path. To do otherwise was a deadly insult to Kelly and the corporation she represented.

Unmistakably, what we had here was the classic gesture of defiance.

In standing Kelly up, Whitlock Castle's manager had followed in the footsteps of the sea captain in old movies who mouths off to the hairy guy holding the big, sharp knife to his throat while the rest of the pirates swarm over the side of his ship.

A grand gesture, but not a very bright one.

After being awake for twenty-one hours straight, Kelly was definitely *not* in the mood for clumsy mind games. She had given him thirty minutes, then she set off for the castle on her own. Kelly would be damned if she was going to wait around for this clown.

Upon arrival at the castle she might have been mollified to learn that he was involved in a fatal car crash on the way to the airport. From the primitive conditions of the roads, she suspected car crashes were a leading cause of human mortality on the island. But when the middle-aged woman cheerfully informed her that Conor was working on the immersion tank—whatever the hell *that* was—and would be with her directly, Kelly could feel the veins stick out on her neck.

Fortunately for the desk clerk, it was against Kelly's principles to chew out blameless receptionists, administrative assistants, and customer service representatives when what she really wanted was to tear a strip off their supervisors' hides. Instead, Kelly stood at the front desk and tapped her professionally manicured nails against its leather-padded surface to relieve her frustration.

She said a crisp, "No, thank you," to the nervous woman's timid suggestion that she sit down and wait for the boss in comfort. The woman's movements became jerky and her shoulders hunched. Kelly was not proud of the mean satisfaction the woman's anxious glances gave her.

"Here he is," the desk clerk said a full ten minutes later, sounding relieved to hand the crazy woman over to a man. "Conor, Miss Sullivan to see you."

Conor O'Meara, as it turned out, was drop-dead, movie-star gorgeous, even in slightly oil-smeared, well-worn blue jeans and a beat-up jacket. Kelly's eyes narrowed. Here she was, dressed in her most intimidating power suit and high heels to establish her credibility as a power to be reckoned with, and he looked like a youngish stand-in for Mel Gibson in one of those interminable sequels to *Lethal Weapon*.

As a single woman on the shady side of thirty who rarely dated because being on the fast track didn't leave much time for a love life, Kelly normally was the first to appreciate a well-toned male body, even if in her experience it too often came with a brain pan roughly the size of a walnut as standard equipment. The jerk who stood her up at the airport was definitely an exception. It was all she could do not to bare her teeth at him.

Conor O'Meara had black hair with a bit of curl in it. Dark blue eyes. A handsome, open, friendly face. Really *nice* shoulders. and that *smile*.

Most women probably melted at the sight of it; he might as well learn right now that Kelly wouldn't be one of them.

Kelly composed her face in what she hoped was a cool, dignified expression. She did not offer her hand.

"Welcome to Ireland, Kelly!" he exclaimed, just as if meeting her was an agreeable but unexpected pleasure. "I was going to the airport to fetch you as soon as I got the immersion tank working. Did you have a nice trip?"

For a moment Kelly was utterly speechless.

"No, *Mr. O'Meara*," she said pointedly, making it clear that she was Ms. Sullivan to him. "I did *not* have a nice trip, thank you *very* much!"

"I am sorry to hear that," he said. "Well, you're here now, and that's all that matters."

Kelly had made her displeasure known, and it was time to pick up the shreds of her dignity and move forward. But like the old guy with the dead albatross around his neck, she couldn't seem to let it alone.

"O'Hare was a zoo, as usual," she complained. "The flight over was so bumpy I couldn't sleep. Then *you* stood me up, and I had a *hell* of a time getting here. There would have been an hour wait for a rental car, I couldn't find a taxi, and the bus only went as far as this little village that wasn't even on the map. It took me forever to find someone to give me directions. I finally had to go to the pub and interrogate drunks, and I thought I'd never get away. I've never met so many chatty people in my life! For the final leg, I hitched a ride with a farmer on his way to somewhere near here with a load of chickens in the back of his truck."

"That would be William MacNamara," Conor said helpfully.

He had listened to the whole recital with this tolerant little half-smile on his lips that made Kelly want to rip his face off.

"You should have *been* there," she snapped.

The smile hardened.

"I was supposed to drop everything and rush to the airport in my Sunday suit with my hat in my hand."

Kelly just glared at him. He made it sound like the most unreasonable of demands, yet that was *exactly* what she had a perfect right to expect.

"If it was such a hardship for you to find your own way, why didn't you ring me here to let me know you were waiting?" he asked, continuing in that maddeningly reasonable voice flavored with a soft west-county lilt. "You could have had a cup of tea in one of the restaurants. The plane from America gets in early if it catches a tail wind. It wasn't officially due until twenty minutes ago, and I couldn't get there any sooner."

Did he think that was an excuse? He should have been on the phone monitoring her flight with the airline if he thought she might arrive early.

"Because you had to fix the immersion tank," Kelly said, not minding that her tone dripped with sarcasm. Her head was throbbing. She cheerfully would have sold her own mother for a cup of coffee.

"Yes. Three of the rooms are rented to American tourists, and they get cranky when they don't have hot water for the loo in the mornings. Yanks are an impatient lot."

His tone was perfectly amiable, but it got his point across. He was the cool, calm voice of reason, and she was a hysterical . . . woman. Kelly was furious with herself for giving him this opportunity to score one on her. She *never* lost her cool. It irritated the hell out of her that she had lost it completely on her first meeting with an interim manager. The front desk clerk was looking at Kelly as if she thought Kelly might have a gun in her briefcase.

"Come along. Your room is ready, *Miss Sullivan,*" Conor said, reaching for her suitcases. He apparently wasn't as dense as he seemed. Kelly instinctively grabbed the biggest one just so he would know she wasn't a wimp. Then she could have kicked herself for being so childish. The dumb thing was *heavy*. Conor raised one mocking eyebrow, but made no comment.

Kelly turned away from the desk to follow him, resolving to step smartly along if it killed her. Then she stopped dead in her tracks.

She had seen many reception areas and hotel lobbies, but none like this. Her mouth dropped open.

"Holy cow," she breathed. She heard Conor give an involuntary snort of laughter.

Had she been so angry about being stood up that she stomped right past *this* without noticing it?

The entrance hall seemed to go on *forever*. The whole length was lined with classical, pinkish marble columns on both sides. Above a black marble fireplace was a huge, dramatic oil painting of the castle itself. The furniture was upholstered in slightly shabby, peach-colored velvet. The floor, an elegant inlay of different colors of wood, gleamed with lemon wax. She could smell it.

There was nothing coordinated about the hall. There were no snazzy designer touches or color schemes. Every object in the room was an individual work of art.

Tears stung her eyes. She couldn't speak for a moment.

"It still affects me that way," Conor said quietly, "and I've lived here all my life."

"I didn't expect anything like this," Kelly said, awed. "It's so . . . civilized."

"You'd be expecting suits of armor? Trestle tables? A

boar's head or two on the wall?" he suggested. "Dirty straw spread around the floor for bedding?"

The amusement in his voice saved his comments from being offensive.

"Something like that," she admitted.

"This isn't a castle built for defense," he explained in the smooth tones of someone delivering a familiar speech. "It was built in the 1800s by an elderly English noble who thought a fashionable Gothic castle would please his discontented young bride. It didn't work. She ran off to Dublin with a man her own age. My great-grandfather bought it from his estate."

"Well, what an airhead!" Kelly exclaimed, pleased by the slight echo of her voice. She walked into the middle of the room and turned around in a slow circle to take it all in. "She should have stuck around and tried to work it out with him. The guy must have been *crazy* about her."

Conor gave a low, appreciative chuckle, and the sound sent a vibration along Kelly's nerve endings. She must be in worse shape than she thought.

"There might be hope for you after all," he murmured.

Kelly decided to pretend she didn't hear that.

The black marble fireplace mantel was carved in an elaborate scroll motif, and Kelly couldn't resist putting down her suitcase and tracing one of the curves with a reverent finger. It was cool and smooth to the touch.

"I've never seen anything like this in my life," she breathed.

"There aren't many left," he said, his smile fading.

Conor wondered how old she was. With Yank women it was hard to tell. They all had the same sleek, relentlessly groomed look. He suspected they sacrificed virgins to stay that way.

This one certainly looked capable of anything.

Her dark suit fit her like a glove and emphasized her small waistline and long, slim legs in that oddly sexless way peculiar to the females who deliver the RTÉ News on the telly.

Her hair was a sleek, shining blonde bubble that ended in smooth curves along her jawline, and not a strand was out of place.

She should have been half dead from jet lag. Instead, she showed up here, making demands and scaring poor Aunt Margaret half to death.

It would have given Conor the greatest satisfaction to throw this bossy little Yank out on her bum. Instead, for his father's sake, he had to be civil to her. Sean O'Meara was in the hospital in a coma, and it was up to Conor to handle his interests with Lawrence Hotels.

Selling the castle had to be done, even though leaving it would be like cutting off his right arm.

Conor gritted his teeth and opened a pair of intricately carved wooden doors.

Kelly stared for a moment at the dramatically curved twin staircases and the domed ceiling of ornate plasterwork that had always reminded Conor of the icing on a wedding cake.

"Awesome," she said appreciatively, heading for the small jewel of a lift that resembled an elaborate birdcage with its elegant brass scrollwork.

"Sorry. It doesn't work," he said, pointing to the Out of Order sign affixed to the front. She looked at him as if she hoped he was kidding. "Your room is on the second floor. There are no other guests up there, so you'll be having the loo to yourself."

"No private baths," she said flatly.

"I'm afraid not."

"And I would guess the second floor in Ireland is what we would call the third floor in the States," she added with a sigh.

"You would be right," he said.

If she hadn't been so demanding, Conor might have felt sorry for her. The ceilings were high, so the flights of stairs were long ones. She must be exhausted from the six-hour international flight, but her progress up the steps was brisk. Only the slight sag of her shoulders gave her fatigue away.

Without looking directly at her, Conor reached over and took the heavy suitcase from her hand.

"Thanks," she said, sounding a bit embarrassed.

Conor nodded.

"This is very nice," Kelly said, perking up a bit when they got to the second floor and he ushered her into her room. "Great fireplace."

"We like it," he said. The fireplace mantel was made of wood carved in classical lines and painted white with gold leaf trim. In its own way it was as beautiful as the black marble fireplace in the entrance hall.

The walls were painted a clear shade between blue and green. The white four-poster bed was covered with a soft peach-colored coverlet trimmed with lace, and matching lace curtains framed the lower panes of the peaked Gothic window. Stained glass in the upper panes featured little Celtic symbols. A vase of freshly picked daffodils resided on the bedside table.

"*Very* nice," Kelly repeated with real respect in her voice.

She sat down in a big armchair by the fireplace and took off her high-heeled shoes with a sigh of relief. At her elbow was a low table laid out with dainty porcelain teacups and small matching plates.

"I love it," she said, picking up a little cup. "It looks just like a set from *Pride and Prejudice*."

As if on cue, Conor's aunts bustled in with a pot of tea and a plate of biscuits, bless their hospitable little souls. Aunt Margaret, who had been minding the front desk when Kelly came in, was watching the American woman with a slightly anxious expression. From the wary look on Aunt Rose's face, Conor knew Margaret had told her all about Kelly's little tantrum at the front desk.

"*Miss* Sullivan," Conor said, stressing the title. "I would like you to meet my aunts, Miss Margaret O'Meara and Miss Rose O'Meara."

"A pleasure," Kelly said, extending her hand to them. "Please call me Kelly." She looked at Conor with eyes the innocent blue of a summer sky. There was a slightly mischievous quirk to her lips. "No need to be so formal."

The ladies shook her hand in turn.

"This is a lovely room," Kelly said.

"We normally don't rent it out to guests," Rose said. "Sean, our brother, likes to offer it to couples from the village for their wedding nights."

"I heard about his stroke," Kelly said. "How is he doing?"

"I was with him early this morning," said Conor, thinking that it took her long enough to be asking about his poor father. "No change yet, but we're still hopeful."

Rose poured out the tea and handed Kelly a cup.

"Caffeine! *Bless* you," she said fervently as she took a sip. "This is just what I need."

"No cream or sugar?" asked Rose.

"No, thank you," Kelly said. "I drink it black."

"Yanks," Conor said tolerantly as he put some cream in his own cup and filled it with tea.

Conor passed Kelly the plate of biscuits. She selected one and nibbled it daintily.

Kelly closed her eyes in appreciation.

"God, these are pure sin. I can taste the real butter and brown sugar in them."

She made it sound as if butter and brown sugar were controlled substances. Margaret laughed, pleased with this testimony to her baking skills.

"Have another," Conor said.

"Are you kidding? These things are lethal!" She left half the biscuit on her saucer. Conor picked up three and wolfed them down.

"We should get back to work," Conor said, standing up after the four of them had spent a few more minutes in stilted conversation, "and you'll be wanting to rest."

"I'll be at the front desk if you're needing anything, Kelly," Rose said, standing.

"Thank you."

"Come along, Margaret," Rose said when her sister would have lingered. Conor could tell that Margaret, no longer intimidated by the American woman, would have stayed to pry her life's story out of her with the slightest encouragement. Kelly gave Margaret a friendly smile as Rose firmly took her sister's arm and ushered her out.

"Do you have any questions before I go?" Conor asked Kelly, glad that she could behave properly when she chose.

Kelly looked around.

"Uh, where's the—"

"Down the hall to your left," he said, amused. "First door on the right."

"No, not *that*," she said. "I meant the phone."

"You can use the telephone at the front desk."

"No phones in the rooms?" she said, appalled.

"People come here on holiday to get *away* from telephones."

"No phone," she said, as if finding that fact hard to take in. "I can't call my office. I can't plug in my computer and access my e-mail."

"You can use the telephone at the front desk," Conor repeated, trying not to smile at the note of panic in her voice. "You've brought an adapter for your computer?"

"Yes, of course. I'd better go back downstairs and make some phone calls. I've got to call—" she broke off with a gasp. "Wait a minute! It's still the middle of the night at home. I can't call anybody!"

Conor couldn't help it. He burst into laughter.

"What's so funny?" she demanded.

"Poor, frustrated little Yank," he said soothingly.

"You don't *understand*!" she wailed. "I'm cut off from the mother ship!"

"Just like all the other Yank tourists," Conor said. "You'll either settle down in a few days, or you'll be begging me to drive you to the airport so you can take the first flight back to your idea of civilization. Either way, you'll survive."

"I'm no tourist," she declared, sticking her chin out. "And I'm no quitter."

"I'm not thinking you are."

Kelly looked around again.

"No television either, huh?" she asked in a small, pathetic voice.

"There's the telly in the guest parlor," he said, "but no Jacuzzi or swimming pool, I'm afraid."

"I know that," she said, annoyed. "But I thought you'd at least have *phones*—"

She broke off.

"Never mind. It's the jet lag talking," she said, rubbing a hand over her face. "Just let me get a shower and a little nap, and I'll be fine. But right now I'm tired and cranky and I need some privacy, okay?"

"Okay," he said, wondering if she was up to more bad news.

"What?" she asked after a moment.

"There's no shower," he said, smiling when she gave him a look of utter disbelief. "Remember, down the hall to your left, first door on your right. And you might want to wait a half hour so the immersion tank has enough time to heat the water."

He gave her an ironic little salute and left.

No shower, Kelly thought crossly as she walked down the hall barefooted and wrapped in her teal terry-cloth robe. Hideous visions of an old BBC special on castles and a latrine that consisted of holes cut into wooden seats over a moat full of dead rats danced in her head.

Stop it, she told her imagination. It's not that kind of a castle.

To her relief, the bathroom smelled of potpourri, and the huge claw-footed tub was wonderfully inviting. One of Conor's aunts apparently had just filled it with hot water and lavender-scented bath salts for her. The O'Meara ladies knew a thing or two about basic hospitality and creature comforts. Fluffy white towels were stacked on a little table near the tub.

The toilet flushed, too. You had to pull a chain. It was pretty droll.

No little jars of shampoo or paper-wrapped bars of soap

were provided, though. Kelly hadn't expected them. She took her plastic pouch of toiletries out of her cosmetic case and put it on the white marble pedestal sink.

The steaming water was sheer heaven. Kelly couldn't remember the last time she took a bath. Normally she was in too much of a hurry to let the tub fill. With a shower, you turned on the water, gave yourself a good scrub, and you were on your way. Her flesh turned bright pink and she sighed with pleasure.

She was tempted to soak until the water cooled, but she was dangerously close to falling asleep. Would she slide down in the tub and drown? It would certainly distress Conor's aunts to find her corpse all pruny and stiff in the tub. What *would* they do with the thing? They'd call Conor for his advice, of course. The thought of Conor seeing her bloated size twelve naked body got her moving.

Jet lag did really weird things to your head.

Kelly washed her hair and rinsed it by submerging her head in the bathwater, gave herself a thorough scrub with a loofah, and was soon back in her room. She used her blow-dryer on her hair and thanked God for low-maintenance, fifty-dollar haircuts. Then she fell bonelessly across the bed and into blessed oblivion.

TWO

Rose rapped on Kelly's door and cautiously stuck her head in the room when she got no answer. Kelly's suitcase was open on the bed as if she had been interrupted in the process of unpacking. Bits of colorful fabric surrounded it and caught Rose's attention. Handkerchiefs, she guessed? Scarves?

Rose said, "Kelly?" in case the girl was in the room somewhere.

She glanced again at those tantalizing little bits of fabric, and then her eyes focused and popped wide open. To make sure her eyes weren't deceiving her, Rose picked up a wisp of red lace between her thumb and index finger.

Jesus, Mary, Joseph and all the saints!

It was the skimpiest brassiere Rose had ever seen. And this tiny matching triangle of red lace and elastic was a pair of panties!

She was scandalized. Absolutely scandalized.

Beneath her proper street clothes, that girl from America wore underwear that would be fitting for a lady of the streets. All of this must be worth a small fortune, Rose thought as she picked up a blue silk all-in-one trimmed in ivory lace.

She heard a noise and dropped a pink garter belt beside an unopened package of real silk stockings. In black, of course.

"Were you looking for something?" Kelly said from the doorway. She was wearing blue jeans that were a little too tight, if you asked Rose, and a red sweatshirt with the name of what Rose guessed was some Yank sports team on it.

Rose didn't know what to say. The girl was looking at her as if she had caught Rose picking her pockets.

"I came up to tell you dinner is on the table," Rose said. She wouldn't apologize. She had a right to know what was going on in her own house.

Women who wore underthings like that *expected* them to be seen. Rose had watched enough American films on the telly to know her kind, she thought as her spine grew rigid and she started to precede Kelly from the room.

"Wait," Kelly said, picking up the half-empty plate of biscuits. "We don't want to leave these around for the little critters. Conor may as well have the rest of them."

Rose stiffened.

Now she was accusing them of having the sort of dirty place that would attract rodents. And she was expecting Conor to eat biscuits right out of her hand, no doubt.

Rose decided to nip this Conor business in the bud. She didn't want the little floozy to think she was going to display her tight American jeans in front of *her* nephew!

"Conor isn't here," Rose said.

"Oh? Where is he?"

Pushy city woman! No doubt she'll be making Conor account to her for every last minute of his time just because her people were buying the castle.

"Conor's a grown man, and where he'll be going is his own business," Rose said virtuously, even though she knew perfectly well Conor went to the hospital to sit beside his poor father. "I don't stick my nose where it doesn't belong."

As soon as the words were out of her mouth, Rose could have kicked herself.

"Really?" Kelly raised one eyebrow, but she didn't make the obvious comment about Rose taking a look inside her suitcase.

She didn't have to.

Rose compressed her lips and refused to say another word.

Conor looked up when Rose and Kelly walked in.

Both of the women had set looks on their faces as if they'd had words.

"You're back," Rose said to Conor.

She sounded almost annoyed to see him.

"Yes. I came back from the hospital early because the nurse wanted to give Da his bath."

"How is he doing?" Kelly asked.

"Still no change," he said, smiling at her when she took the chair next to him. She looked younger and altogether more approachable in jeans and sweatshirt. Her hair was a soft, clean golden halo around her pretty face.

"Why don't you say grace before the food gets cold, Conor," Rose said pointedly. Conor gave her a bewildered look. She sounded so harsh.

Conor obediently bowed his head and shot a look of inquiry at Margaret. She shrugged.

Kelly had reached for a piece of soda bread and hastily drew her hand back. Apparently she wasn't accustomed to saying grace before meals.

Conor recited the meal prayer and offered Kelly the platter of roasted pork one of his aunts handed him. There was more food than usual, and Conor assumed the big meal was in honor of Kelly's arrival.

Why, then, was Rose directing such sour looks in Kelly's direction?

Margaret made a valiant attempt to carry on a neutral conversation, but she finally gave up in the face of Rose's and Kelly's silence. Conor wasn't much help. He felt like a soldier crossing a mine field, afraid to move for fear of getting his head blown off.

Kelly apparently wasn't hungry. She took one small slice of pork and scraped all the gravy off it. She contented herself with a little dab of potatoes and no butter or gravy on them. She cut her meat into tiny little pieces and chewed each bite about a hundred times. She ate all her boiled cabbage, but she moved it around on her plate with a fork quite a bit before she did. She ate only half a slice of soda bread.

Incredibly, she politely refused a piece of Aunt Margaret's blackberry trifle.

If Conor had eaten like that as a child, his parents would have told him to stop playing with his food. He could tell by the expression on his aunts' faces that they didn't know what to make of this. Neither did he, for that matter.

"Thank you. That was wonderful," Kelly said at the conclusion of the meal. She sounded as if she meant it. "May I help you with the dishes?"

Conor had to give her credit for trying to be nice. Sweet, friendly Margaret responded eagerly to this overture.

"Not on your first night with us, Kelly. Most of our guests like to relax in the parlor after dinner," Margaret said cheerfully. "We have a nice fire going in here because it still gets a bit chilly at night, and of course there's the telly."

"I'm not a guest exactly," Kelly pointed out.

"Take the night off," Conor said grandly. "Tell your boss I said it was all right."

"If you don't mind, I'd like to call my office and use the telephone jack at the front desk to plug in my modem," Kelly said. "I really must check my e-mail."

"I'll show you where it is." Conor regretfully put down the spoonful of trifle that was halfway to his mouth.

"No, I can find it. Go ahead and finish your dessert," Kelly said. "I'll just run upstairs and get my laptop."

"I'll just run upstairs and get my laptop," Aunt Rose mimicked in a high-pitched voice when Kelly was out of sight.

"Rose, what is *wrong* with you?" demanded Margaret, giving voice to the question Conor was about to ask.

"Miss Kelly Sullivan is what's wrong with me," Rose

snapped. "Here, Conor. Her Highness brought down her leftover biscuits for you to eat."

She put the plate in front of him with a thump that made the biscuits bounce.

"Good," he said, reaching for one. "I wonder why she didn't eat them herself."

"Our homemade biscuits aren't good enough for the likes of her," she sniffed. "She ate like a bird at dinner, too."

Conor had started to bite into one of the biscuits, but at Rose's words he put it down.

"Aunt Rose, why don't you tell me what Kelly has done to offend you," he suggested. "She got off to a bad start, but I think she's been trying to make up for it."

"Well, it's plain she has *you* fooled," Rose said defensively. "You should see what she had in her suitcase."

"What?" asked Margaret, her eyes round as saucers.

"Drugs?" asked Conor, grinning and taking a bite out of the biscuit. "A gun? A bomb?"

"Yes, make fun of me," Rose snarled. "She has—scandalous underwear!"

Conor choked on the biscuit and coughed until his eyes watered. Margaret pounded him on the back.

"Scandalous underwear!" he repeated, wiping the moisture from his eyes.

"Tiny little scraps of material no decent woman would be caught dead in, and all of it made of *real silk* in black and red and blue with lace trimming! Why would any woman be having such things if she didn't intend for them to be *seen*, I'd like to know."

Conor was speechless at the idea of Kelly in "tiny little scraps of material no decent woman would be caught dead in." He really didn't want to think about this or, rather, he *did*, but not in front of his aunts.

"She doesn't seem like that kind of girl," Margaret protested.

"Hah! She's that kind, all right," Rose scoffed. "You should have *seen* it, Margaret. She has one of those garter belts made almost all of lace, and black silk stockings. Her underpants are little see-through triangles, and not a proper pair of white cotton panties in the lot!"

Conor started coughing again.

Rose pointed her finger at him.

"Don't you be laughing, Conor Patrick O'Meara! That girl is going to try to get her hooks in you, make no mistake! She's going to use you and make a fool of you."

"That's *enough*, Aunt Rose!" Conor said. "I seriously doubt that a city woman like Kelly would be interested in me."

"That makes no difference," Rose insisted. "These little jezebels chase after anything in trousers. They can't help themselves. I've seen it all on the telly."

"This is *nonsense*! Why would you be looking at Kelly's underwear? You can't be snooping around and looking at people's underwear."

"Snooping! How *dare* you accuse me of snooping? It was right on her bed where anyone could see it!" Aunt Rose said, turning bright red. "We have a right to know what's going on under our roof!"

"What Kelly has in her luggage is none of our business!" he insisted. "I don't want to hear another word about this."

"None of our business! You'll be thinking it's our business when she has a parade of men going up those stairs at all hours of the day and night to visit her!" Rose retorted. Mercifully she had lowered her voice. "Maybe you'll be the first one to be going up to her room."

"Rose!" cried Margaret, shocked.

"I am *not* going to listen to any more of this," Conor said. He ate the rest of his dessert in silence and left the kitchen immediately to keep from saying something he'd regret.

Miss Kelly Sullivan from America setting a trap for *him*! *That* would be the day, he thought.

He gave a guilty start when he came face to face with Kelly herself in the hallway. *Idiot*, he thought, knowing he was blushing.

"Hi," she said. "I'm having a little trouble plugging in the modem. Do you have time to help me?"

"Yes," he said.

She gave him an odd look. He knew he was breathing too heavily.

Conor followed Kelly to the front desk and saw she had her laptop computer plugged into the electrical outlet, but the modem cord that would fit into a telephone jack was loose on the desk. He could see her problem. The desk was a wraparound type, so she couldn't reach under or over it to disconnect the phone and plug in the modem cord. Fortunately, his arms were long enough to accomplish the task.

"There," he said. He couldn't look her in the face.

"Thanks," she said. "I'll modem into Lawrence's system with a toll-free access number, so you don't have to worry that this will show up on your phone bill."

"All right," Conor said, noticing that she was deliberately blocking the computer monitor with her body so he wouldn't see what she had been typing.

Her report to her superiors, no doubt, telling them that the lift didn't work, there were no telephones in the rooms, and the bathrooms had no showers in them.

Conor wished he hadn't thought of showers. People got naked in showers. He became aware that Kelly was looking at him strangely again.

"Thanks, Conor," she said in obvious dismissal. "I appreciate it."

"You're welcome," he said hastily, determined to get away from her before he made even more of a fool of himself.

Kelly had been annoyed when she saw Conor's Aunt Rose pawing through her lingerie, but now she thought it was pretty funny.

It cracked her up that Rose obviously thought she was some sort of scarlet woman. No doubt both Rose and Margaret wore knee-length bleached white cotton underdrawers and hid them under the workshirts on laundry day to protect old Conor's virgin eyes from the racy sight of female un-mentionables.

What a bunch of characters!

Rose kept scowling at Kelly as if she expected her to jump on the kitchen table and do a striptease.

Margaret kept popping out to the front desk to see if Kelly wanted tea, and she made a point of introducing the bed-and-breakfast guests to her when they came in from their evening of pub-crawling.

Like Kelly really wanted to interrupt her work to make stilted conversation with a bunch of German tourists!

It was sweet, though. Margaret the mother hen obviously was willing to overlook Kelly's little hissy fit that morning.

Then there was Conor.

Yummy Conor.

Everything he said in that beautiful voice of his made Kelly's pulse race. She had to keep reminding herself that while it was in her company's best interests for her to maintain a civil relationship with Whitlock Castle's interim manager, she and Conor were *not* on the same side. Her job was to find out where the bodies were buried. Period.

Finally everyone else went to bed, and Kelly was alone with her computer at last. By then, she had composed replies to the dozens of e-mail messages she retrieved on her first contact with the Lawrence Hotels computer system, and she'd finished writing her first report from Ireland.

Kelly scrolled through her report one more time. There wasn't much information to convey to the home office yet, but that didn't matter. The point of this exercise was simply to keep her name in front of Matthew Lawrence, the CEO, and remind the members of her transition team who was boss now that she wasn't going to be in their faces for a while. Kelly couldn't afford to give anyone, especially the CEO, a chance to forget about her. Matthew was notorious for his short-term memory.

Bradley Kovacks, Kelly's chief rival for the promotion to

Vice President of Guest Services, would do his best to insinuate himself into the CEO's good graces while she was out of the country. Kelly's appointment as head of the high-profile Whitlock Castle transition team indicated that she had the inside track for the promotion, but Matthew would think nothing of switching his support to Bradley if it seemed like a good idea at the time. Kelly couldn't afford to let down her guard for a minute.

Kelly had to say her report struck just the right note. She glowingly described the castle's gorgeous entrance hall, told a few humorous anecdotes about her adventures in getting to the castle under her own steam that emphasized her stamina and athletic prowess because Matthew was convinced jocks made the best leaders, and pointed out a few issues she intended to investigate immediately just so old Matthew would know she is working her butt off out here and *loving* every minute of it.

The overall tone was upbeat, enthusiastic, and superficial—just the way Matthew Lawrence liked *all* his business communications.

Kelly spell-checked the report, closed the file, opened her communications program, dialed up the Lawrence Hotels mainframe, and crossed her fingers.

There were chronic problems with the computer system, but the new Manager of Information Services wasn't likely to do anything about them. Matthew had fired the last Manager of IS who had the gall to tell him the system was obsolete and needed to be updated to the tune of several million dollars. For now, everyone was pretending that the computer system was working just fine. Naive souls who called IS to report a problem soon got the message that they had committed a grave vocational error.

It all reminded Kelly of the fable about the emperor's new clothes.

To her relief, she got on-line first try. She was pleased to see an incoming post with an attached file from Matthew's assistant. This was an excellent sign—it told her that the

Whitlock Castle project was still at the head of Matthew Lawrence's priority list.

Her job was going to be almost too easy, Kelly mused. Whitlock Castle was such a wow that it would take a complete idiot to screw this project up. It was going to make a fabulous luxury hotel.

She went off-line and called up the file. Her smile of expectation faded, though, as she skimmed the long document.

It couldn't be. It just couldn't be.

Matthew, it seemed, had received a brilliant inspiration. What the southwest of Ireland needs, he decided, is a medieval theme park with Whitlock Castle as the centerpiece. Therefore, Kelly is to take bids on demolishing the present interior so Matthew's architects and designers can rebuild it as a fake Norman stronghold complete with suits of armor, banqueting halls, minstrel galleries, and a torture chamber in the dungeon to amuse the kiddies.

He hadn't forgotten the black marble fireplace, brass Art Nouveau fixtures, and other beautiful objects. Those were to be crated and sent to Chicago so Matthew could install them in his new condo or parcel them out for use in various other luxury hotels in the chain. Those he couldn't use would fetch a nice price on the antiques market.

Kelly was very, very afraid.

Whitlock Castle was going to be another Spruce Goose.

And Kelly, heaven help her, was going to be the official scapegoat when it laid an egg.

Had Kelly tempted fate by thinking only a complete idiot could screw this project up? It seemed that one had come forward to do just that.

Unfortunately, he owned the damned company.

Kelly printed out the file and crammed it into her day planner. She would read the instructions point by point tomorrow and hope she wouldn't be required to execute any of them.

Matthew was nothing if not volatile. There was every chance he'd change his mind, but Kelly knew better than to try to influence him. He did not tolerate opposition, and he was quick to replace any manager he perceived as "obstruc-tive" or "inflexible." If he wanted a medieval theme park, Kelly would deliver.

No way was Kelly going to hang her butt on the line for Whitlock Castle, much as she'd hate to see Matthew ruin it.

She had worked too hard for that promotion to risk losing it now.

Three

The first thing Kelly noticed in the morning was the absolute silence. That, and the sunlight streaming through the lace curtains to tease at her eyelids.

It was a bit disorienting. No traffic sounds outside her window. No sound of her upstairs neighbor's feet pounding against the ceiling. She often suspected he wore combat boots to bed. No slamming doors. No people talking in the hall. No whine of the elevator in her building.

She looked at the clock and frowned. It was nearly nine o'clock. For years she had awakened at six-thirty sharp, no matter what day it was or how late she had gotten in the night before.

Of course, in Chicago it was three o'clock in the morning.

She lolled in bed for a moment, but she soon decided she needed to get to work. She was a professional, she reminded herself as she left the warm bed to put her bare feet on the cool floor.

Gathering toothpaste, makeup, and clothes, she grumbled halfheartedly to herself about the inconvenience of having to wrap up in a robe to go down the hall to the bathroom. She hoped she hadn't forgotten anything. She peeked out into the hall to make sure Conor O'Meara and his aunts weren't lurking about and went off to make herself presentable.

Twenty minutes later she was in the kitchen, relieved to see that it was Margaret presiding at the stove instead of Rose.

"Good morning, Kelly," Margaret said cheerfully. "Sit down. Your breakfast will be ready in a minute."

"Thanks, but I never eat breakfast," Kelly said. She smelled bacon and sausage and eggs. Firmly she told her stomach that this stuff—regardless of how good it smelled—was *bad* for it. Her stomach just growled at her. "I was hoping for a cup of coffee, though, if you have some."

"Oh, but breakfast is very important," Margaret objected.

"Just coffee will be fine," Kelly said.

Margaret took a ceramic mug from the cupboard to fill with coffee for Kelly.

"Here you are, then," she said, putting the hot, fragrant brew in front of her. "Here is some warm milk," she added, reaching to the counter for a small pitcher, "and the sugar is on the table."

"I drink it black, thank you," Kelly said, taking a sip of the coffee and opening her day planner. In the house where Kelly grew up, the breakfast table had been a place for reading the paper and making to-do lists. Chattiness in the morning was a major faux pas. After asking Kelly a few questions and getting monosyllabic, preoccupied answers, the older woman took the hint and lapsed into silence.

From the corner of her eye, Kelly saw Margaret sigh and put the skillet aside. An unwelcome thought occurred to her.

"You didn't make all that just for me, did you?" she asked.

"It doesn't matter," Margaret said politely. Then she looked beyond Kelly and her face lit up.

It was Conor, of course. He was probably spoiled rotten with two maiden aunts to fuss over him.

"Good morning, Kelly," he said from the doorway. "Aunt Margaret."

He went to the stove and kissed his aunt on the cheek.

"Good morning, Conor," Margaret said warmly.

"Black pudding, white pudding, bangers, rashers," he announced, peering into the skillet and the other covered pans on the stove. "Is there enough for a poor, hungry laborer?" he added soulfully.

"Of course," Margaret said, piling a plate high with various types of sausages, bacon, and eggs for him.

"I didn't expect to be back in time for breakfast," he said tucking into his meal with a sigh of contentment. "I went to the farm to get my chores done straight from the hospital, so I thought you'd be finished serving by now. Aren't you having any breakfast, Kelly?"

"I never eat breakfast," Kelly said, trying not to sound defensive. Now she *knew* Margaret had put out this spread just for her after cooking a meal earlier for her regular guests. Kelly couldn't think of a thing to say that wouldn't make the situation even more awkward, so she said nothing.

Conor looked from one woman to the other and raised his brows. Kelly looked down at her day planner.

"Are you sure?" he asked. "Aunt Margaret makes a wonderful breakfast."

"I'm sure," Kelly said. No way was she putting *that* in her stomach. It would take a solid month on the stair machine to rectify that kind of damage. "The coffee is wonderful, though."

Conor gave her a skeptical look.

"So, what do you plan for this morning?" he asked after he had chewed a bite of sausage and Margaret set a cup of tea before him. He reached for the hot milk and sugar.

"Are you available to give me the grand tour? I have the floor plans your father provided, but it would help if you could go along to answer questions. I'll have a lot of them."

"Aunt Margaret, is the immersion tank working?"

"The water is lovely and hot," Margaret said, smiling at Conor as if he personally had invented steam.

"I'm available, then," Conor said.

"Don't you have maintenance people who can be trusted to take care of that sort of thing?" she asked, frowning.

"Yes. Me."

"Conor has an engineering degree from the university in Cork," Margaret interjected proudly.

"That's handy around a place like this, I'm sure," Kelly said. She made a note in the day planner and looked up at Conor.

"Bread?" Conor asked, handing her a slice from his own plate as easily as if he were hand-feeding a child or pet—or a lover.

"Thank you," Kelly said, thinking maybe they'd stop trying to force food on her if she'd eat something.

Jeez! They even fry the bread here!

She tore the bread in two and ate half. She left the other half on the table in front of her. When Conor had finished eating, she took the last swallow of her coffee, closed her day planner and stood up.

"Thank you for the coffee and toast," she said.

"You're welcome," Margaret said, looking at the bread Kelly had left in front of her. Conor casually reached over, picked up the bread and stuffed it in his mouth all at once.

"Well, thanks again," Kelly said lamely.

Conor had finished chewing by the time she got to the door.

"You'll want to change your clothes," he said when he caught up with her.

Kelly looked down at her neatly tailored gray wool dress pants, white blouse, and navy blazer. If anything, she was dressed more casually than usual. She gave him a questioning look.

"You'll get those fine things dirty if you're thinking of looking at the rooms that have been closed off," he warned. "I'll wait for you here."

He obviously expected her to run upstairs and change, just because he told her to.

"No. I'm fine as I am," she said firmly.

Conor shrugged.

"All right. We'll start with the top floor and work down," he suggested.

Kelly thought she'd better establish the pecking order right now.

"We'll start with the lower floors and work up," she said, taking the folded floor plan out of the day planner.

Without comment, Conor took his plate to the sink, thanked his aunt again for breakfast and led Kelly to a stairway going down to the lower level. It wasn't really a basement. It reminded her of a garden apartment. The ceiling was low, and only part of the floor was underground. Windows to the outside started at about shoulder level, giving her a nice view of the plant stalks in the beds outside.

"Oh, *man*," she said, awed, as she stopped before a gear box affixed to a thick vertical pole and an arrangement of metal fixtures. "Is that the mechanism for the elevator?"

"It's powered by an aerohydraulic engine," he said, sounding impressed that she recognized it. "The gears and chains are in the box, of course. It came from a 19th-century estate house in Paris."

"Impressive! What would it take to get it fixed?"

"Money," he said with a sigh. "Lots and lots of money."

"Bummer," she said softly.

That depressing topic exhausted, Conor gestured toward a row of shelves with neatly labeled jars on them.

"My aunts grow vegetables and can them for the winter," he said. "Care for some grape jelly?" he added, reaching for a jar. "It's the best in County Cork. Aunt Margaret has a medal to prove it."

"No, thanks. I never eat stuff like that."

He put the jar back on the shelf and turned around to face her.

"What *do* you eat?" he asked, sounding offended. "Last night at dinner you were cutting your food into little pieces and playing with it, but you weren't doing much eating. This morning you passed up a full Irish breakfast. Maybe it's my aunt's cooking you don't like."

"I'm sure your aunts are great cooks," Kelly said. "I'm trying to lose weight. Cutting everything up like that fools my stomach into thinking it's getting more than it actually is."

"Why do you want to lose weight?" he asked, giving her figure a frank inspection. There was nothing rude about it. He was just looking for information.

"I'm overweight by ten pounds, if you must know," she said. *Right. Just as if those extra pounds weren't out there for the world to see.*

"That's ridiculous," he scoffed. His snort of disbelief made her smile. "You look fine to me."

Kelly was immensely flattered. The tone of his voice made it clear that he meant it. It was time to get off such a personal subject.

"This place would make a great wine cellar," she said, looking around. Too bad it was going to be a tacky kiddie dungeon instead, she thought with regret.

"Also a convenient place for hiding the bodies of people who annoy you," Conor said with one of those charming smiles that made his eyes crinkle at the corners.

He just *had* to go and say that.

"Useful," Kelly murmured. She opened her day planner to make a note, and some of her loose sheets slipped out.

She made a dive for the papers; Conor was quicker.

He dropped to one knee, gathered the papers, and started to hand them up to her. To Kelly's dismay, he casually glanced at the top page, did a double take, and snatched the papers back.

When he finished reading the top page, he stood up and stared at her. His mouth was white around the edges.

"Go ahead. Read all of it," Kelly said between clenched teeth. He would have found out when the demolition crews arrived, anyway.

Conor stood and read the whole printout of the attached file from Corporate. It seemed to take forever. When he finished, he handed the sheets back to Kelly. They were a bit crumpled.

"Matthew Lawrence promised my father the castle would stay the way it is except for some superficial renovation before it was reopened as a luxury hotel. They shook hands on it," Conor said bitterly. "And my father trusted him. Are you going to let him do this?"

"There's nothing I can do," she said evenly. "The stipulation about the castle remaining intact was not stated in the contract, so it's perfectly legal for Matthew Lawrence to do whatever he pleases with it. I read my copy of the contract again myself last night to make sure. I'm sorry."

"You're sorry," he said, glaring at her. "Is that the best you can do? You're in charge of the bloody transition!"

"Matthew Lawrence has given me specific instructions about that transition, and he is paying me good money to carry them out," Kelly said, trying to keep her tone unemotional. "That's the bottom line, as far as I'm concerned."

"There are ruined castles all over Ireland with gutted interiors that would serve his purpose," Conor snapped. "Why didn't he buy one of *them*?"

"Because this is the one he wants! If it's so damned important to you, why are *you* selling it?" Kelly snapped right back.

Their words hung in the air between them.

"We are selling it," Conor said, breaking the silence at last, "because we have no choice."

"Look, this is none of my business," Kelly said hastily. She didn't want to hear about any sad family tragedies. She felt bad enough as it was.

"I want you to know." His eyes pinned her where she stood. "We have been the guardians of Whitlock Castle for four generations. Everything we've earned or hope to earn has gone into the upkeep of this place. I'm the only able-bodied member of the family left. If there was any way in *hell* I could keep it, I would. But I can't do it alone. Selling the castle is the only way we can pay my father's medical bills and provide security for him and his sisters in their old age."

"Conor, I'm sorry."

"I just wanted you to understand. Come. You might as well see the rest."

Grateful for the change of subject, Kelly pointed to another door.

"What's in there?"

"Water turbine generators. They're powered by the river."

"Get *out*! And they *work*?"

He nodded, and gestured for her to follow him. They walked down another flight of stairs to access a sub-basement.

The thick door revealed three gleaming black, hive-shaped generators humming like huge industrious bees.

Kelly's eyes bugged out.

"This is *amazing*," she said. "And these things supply all your electricity?"

"They do, yes," he said with a nod. "My great-grandfather installed these in the mid-twenties, right after he bought the place. It was in the early days of the Republic, and grand days they were."

He sounded as if he'd been there, but of course he hadn't.

"My great-grandfather left most of the original Gothic architectural details so beloved by the English nobles who were in power here for so long. One of the things he added were the Celtic stained glass panels above the Gothic windows. Consistency was not something that concerned him a great deal. He was a devout Catholic, but he hosted a Celtic festival with strong pagan overtones every year on June 23, Midsummer Eve."

His voice had taken on the cadence of the professional tour guide. He had led tours of the castle many, many times, Kelly realized. It should have become his, in turn. Instead, it would be destroyed by foreigners.

"Conor, I'm so sorry," Kelly said again. If he kept on like this, she was going to cry.

"You have to stop them, Kelly."

"Me! How can *I* stop them. I'm on *their* side, remember?"

"I saw the tears in your eyes when you were looking at the entrance hall."

"Give me a break. I had been up for twenty-one hours straight," she muttered, embarrassed. "I wasn't myself."

"You're not a money-grubbing butcher like your boss, Kelly. I'll never believe that."

"Hey! Believe it!" she objected. "If a medieval castle is what Matthew Lawrence wants, I'll deliver. I'm in line for Vice President of Guest Services, and I'm not risking that for anything or anybody."

"Oh, I see," Conor said with a challenging look in his eye. "You're a hard-hearted businesswoman. Sentiment has nothing to do with it. Or justice."

"Damn straight."

"Whitlock Castle is just another acquisition to you. A stepping-stone to this *title* that is so bloody important. Nothing more."

"That's right."

"We'll see about that," he said, seizing her hand and practically dragging her up the stairs.

"What are you doing?" she demanded, trying to snatch her hand away. He was too strong, and she had to climb the stairs or fall on her face.

"I'm going to show you the price of your bloody title."

"Killing me won't save the castle," Kelly gasped.

Conor didn't answer and he didn't stop, even though he knew she was out of breath and a little frightened. He just kept hauling her up the stairs. When she stumbled, he grabbed her around her waist and hauled her up a few more steps until she pushed him away and resumed climbing on her own.

He'd carry her on his back if he had to.

Seven circular flights of stairs later, he grabbed her by the shoulders and propped her up against the thick oak door that led to the tower room. She sank to her hands and knees, but snarled at him when he started to reach for her.

"Are you ready to go on?" he asked impatiently when she got shakily to her feet, using the wall for support.

"Yeah," she said sarcastically. "My legs are like rubber and my lungs may never be the same, but don't let *that* bother you. What in the *hell* do you think you're doing?"

Instead of answering her, he took her by the arm, spun her around, clapped one hand over her eyes, and opened the door with the other.

"Hey!" she shouted. "I've had about enough of the caveman routine!" She elbowed him hard in the ribs, but he didn't let go. Instead, he propelled her into the room.

"What are you going to do?" she asked him with bravado. He could feel her trembling, and her voice was about an octave higher than usual. "Shoot me and hide my body in a closet? Matthew will just send someone else."

"Close your mouth and open your eyes, for once!" he shouted as he took his hand off her eyes. "*Then* tell me you don't care what happens to this place."

Kelly's day planner dropped from her nerveless fingers and landed with a thump on the floor.

"Oh, my God," she breathed.

She covered her mouth with both hands.

"Oh, my God," she said again.

Tears welled in her eyes when she turned to glare at him.

"Damn you, Conor O'Meara," she said hoarsely.

Conor walked backward to the door and leaned against the frame, watching her. She had a soul, after all.

He remembered how he felt the first time he saw the tower room as a child. The bed was huge and hung all about with deep rose velvet curtains embroidered with green and gold Celtic symbols. On low pedestals around the room were displayed classical statues of white marble and bronze. An Oriental carpet in tones of rose, gold, and cobalt blue covered part of the inlaid wood floor. Marble columns flanked the bed.

His great-grandfather's Irish harp set with amethysts and moonstones stood in one corner on a low table along with the uilleann pipes and a bhrodran.

The walls were covered with tapestries depicting heroic scenes from Irish mythology. The tops of the windows were decorated with ornamental plasterwork in the shapes of Art Nouveau nymphs with sculpted hair that curved out gracefully from their enigmatically smiling faces and draped over the peaked tops of the windows.

"It was my great-grandfather's room, or 'the lord's chamber' as he liked to call it," Conor said. "He traveled all over the world to find these furnishings. They tell me I was conceived in that bed."

"It's beautiful."

"It should be. The bed frame and the posts were hand carved during the Renaissance for one of the Medicis. The counterpane came from France. It took the nuns two years to complete the embroidery. The marble fireplace mantel came from a villa in southern Italy."

Kelly lifted her hand and held it in a patch of sunlight, a constantly changing pattern of blue, pink, green, and smoky yellow against her fair skin.

"I've never seen anything like this," she said, referring to the tiny panes of pastel-colored glass that were set, jewel-like, in the windows.

"It was made in the Tiffany studios," Conor said. "Maybe your boss would like to take it all out and put it in his new condominium along with the black marble fireplace."

"Don't," said Kelly softly.

"My aunts bring fresh flowers up here several times a week," he said, indicating the brass vases of daffodils. "We think of it as a kind of shrine."

"You win, Conor," Kelly said quietly. "I'll talk him out of it, or I'll die trying."

Four

Kelly rolled her eyes, pointedly looked at her watch and gave another long, audible sigh.

Even so, the weathered, auburn-haired clerk at the counter continued her animated conversation with her current customer about somebody's wedding while a few shoppers attracted by the conversation joined in with comments.

If she moved any slower, she could be declared legally dead!

When the clerk finally bade her customer a lengthy farewell and promptly started discussing another fine point of the bridal arrangements with the next woman in line, Kelly's temper snapped.

"*Excuse* me!" she snarled. "I'd like to get out of here sometime before midnight, *if* you don't mind!"

The clerk looked startled, and then her pale blue eyes narrowed. Lips set, she did start to move a little faster.

To Kelly's surprise, the other customers gave *her* disapproving looks.

"Yank," one muttered contemptuously, as if that explained everything.

The woman in line behind Kelly abandoned her friendly

attempt to start a conversation with her and resolutely turned around to talk to the customer behind her.

Well, *good*, thought Kelly, feeling defensive. These people had *no* concept of personal space.

Kelly looked down at the toothpaste and newspaper in her hands and wondered if she could afford the luxury of stomping out of the store in a huff without buying anything.

Nope. She needed the toothpaste, and this seemed to be the only store that sold it. When her turn at the old-fashioned cash register came, the clerk added up Kelly's purchases and bagged them in complete silence. Everyone else in the queue was silent, too. It was weird.

The clerk acknowledged Kelly's quiet "thank you" with an unsmiling nod. The silence held until Kelly opened the shop door and went out.

Her shoulder blades started to twitch as soon as she was on the sidewalk. The clerk and her customers probably were talking about what an impatient Yank witch she was.

As if she *cared*, Kelly told herself.

Shrugging off the feeling of vague discomfort, she frowned at the overcast sky. It had looked so bright early this morning when Margaret gave her a lift to the village on her way to the hospital to take her turn sitting beside her brother's bed that Kelly hadn't brought an overcoat or an umbrella.

Rats! Naturally she was wearing a lightweight wool blazer and slim skirt with a formerly crisp white blouse and a wilting silk scarf at her throat. She hoped the town boasted a competent dry cleaner.

Lord, what a place! Primitive was a *kind* description. The village was quaint and charming, yes. But Kelly found herself missing the anonymity, gridlock and—compared to Ireland—lightning efficiency of the Chicago Loop. It was weird to have to depend on the O'Mearas for transportation instead of anonymous cabdrivers. And apparently having the audacity to expect a clerk in a store to stop gossiping with the locals and do her job was a grave breech of etiquette.

Kelly had cased the village pretty well on foot before the weather turned on her, and she now had a good idea of what sort of professional services were available locally. Unfortunately, Margaret wouldn't meet her at the pub on her way back from the hospital for at least an hour.

Kelly thought about doing a little shopping while she was waiting for Margaret, but she was too restless. Now that the wheels had been set in motion, she was eager to get back to the castle and set up her spreadsheets. She had a good idea of what sort of wages the local workforce expected for domestic services, and tomorrow she had appointments set up with both a demolitions expert to give her a quote on gutting the interior if it came to that, and a carpenter to give her a quote on refurbishing some of the woodwork that had been damaged by dampness.

Kelly sighed and walked over to the pub to get out of the drizzle. It was a quaint little place with a weathered, hand painted sign that probably was once green. Once inside, she was uncomfortably aware that all conversation had stopped and every male eye was turned on her.

Just peachy, she thought crossly. She felt exposed, like she had just walked past a construction site in a bikini top and a pair of Lycra shorts.

"You'd be Conor's Yank," the barkeep said with a friendly grin.

Conor's Yank, indeed!

"I'm staying at Whitlock Castle, yes," she said.

"Eh, the lad said you were a pretty one," he replied with a knowing wink that made Kelly wonder what *else* Conor had said. "What will you have? A glass of Guinness?"

"Lord, no!" Kelly exclaimed, revolted by the mere thought at this hour. It was barely ten o'clock! The barkeep laughed. "Coffee, if you have it."

"Coffee, it is," the man said.

"Put it on my tab!" a familiar voice called out from the end of the bar.

Kelly's breath caught.

Conor.

The little frisson of pleasure that went through her body at the sound of his voice annoyed the heck out of her.

She grabbed the coffee the bartender had poured for her, walked to the end of the bar, and joined Conor after some of his companions winked and grinned and made room for her.

"It's a little early for this, isn't it?" she said, looking straight at the beer in Conor's hand.

"Never too early for a pint," he said as his buddies cheered. "I saw Aunt Margaret at the hospital and offered to meet you in her place so she could go straightaway to the castle. She has lunch to get for some guests who wanted to take their meals with us, and she has to relieve Aunt Rose so she can take her turn sitting with Da."

"Good. I've got things to do back at the castle, anyway," she said firmly, seeing that he had caught the barkeep's eye and was about to signal for another pint. "Are you ready to go?"

It was not a question. It was an order.

Conor sighed, but Kelly hardened her heart.

"How is your father?" she asked.

"The same," Conor said. "But as long as he's still breathing, there's hope. Thank you for asking."

"Sure," she said, feeling uncomfortable. All the platitudes that came to her mind seemed inadequate.

"We've been hearing a lot about you," one of Conor's companions interjected, smirking. "*Céad Mile Fáilte,*" he added appreciatively, not quite under his breath as he looked her up and down. The lads laughed and whistled. Kelly gave him a quizzical look.

"It's the traditional Irish greeting," Conor said, frowning at the guy while some of the other men laughed in an insinuating way. "In Irish. It means a hundred thousand welcomes."

"Uh, thanks," Kelly said warily, wondering what the hell *that* was about.

Kelly had spent years clawing her way past the glass ceiling at Lawrence Hotels, a bastion of sexism and old-boy politics if there ever was one, but this experience did not quite prepare her for dealing with Conor O'Meara and his beer-swilling pals. They looked at her as if maybe they found her name and phone number scrawled on the wall in the men's washroom.

"We'd better go, then," Conor said, signaling the barkeep for his tab. He gave Kelly a curious glance when she offered to pay for her own coffee.

It almost felt like a . . . date. Not that Kelly had any recent experience with *those*. She went out with male coworkers to talk shop occasionally, but most of them were either married or political rivals, like Bradley Kovacks, so they went dutch. Kelly was always careful to maintain her distance so there would be no misunderstandings.

Only an *idiot* got personally involved with a coworker or business associate, she told herself a little desperately when Conor smiled at her.

She felt a bit self-conscious at the thought of riding up to the castle alone with him. Once he had shown her the tower room the previous day, they completed the tour of the house in virtual silence as if the understanding between them was too fragile to take the strain of further conversation. She had spent the rest of the day setting up appointments and generally staying out of his way.

The light pressure of Conor's big, warm hand at the small of her back was a polite, courtly gesture that still managed to convey ownership. Childishly, Kelly walked a little faster to break the contact.

The sky was still misty and pregnant with rain, Kelly noted with a sigh when she stepped outside.

"Which one is yours?" she asked, indicating the cars in the small gravel parking lot behind the pub.

"None of them. I took my boat down river to the hospital because Aunt Margaret wanted the car today. This way."

He pointed.

Kelly's mouth dropped open when she spotted the little metal motorboat anchored in the muddy river bank. She gave Conor a look of disbelief.

"It'll be a bit of a wet ride," he said with a charming, apologetic smile.

"A little rain won't kill me," she said, irked by the implication that she was some whiny bimbo with big hair who was afraid her mascara was going to run.

"Are you sure?" he asked, giving her low-heeled, leather pumps a doubtful look. "We could go back in the pub and see if one of the lads could give you a lift to the castle."

"No, thank you," Kelly said hastily at the thought of being confined in a car with one of the leering boys at the bar. "Listen, Conor. I was born in Chicago. You haven't *lived* until you've tried walking up Lake Shore Drive with the rain coming down in sheets and the wind screaming off Lake Michigan at about sixty miles an hour. *That's* wet. This pitiful little drizzle doesn't impress me in the least."

"Is that the truth?" He had the gall to look amused.

"Absolutely," she said with a bright, insincere smile. "We'll just think of it as an adventure."

"If you insist," he said with a shrug. Then he scooped Kelly right up in his arms! He did it in one smooth motion, without bracing himself or grunting. Like it was no big deal.

"What are you doing?" she squeaked out of sheer surprise that he could lift her. Kelly didn't think any of the guys she knew in the States could have managed it, at least not so easily. She was trying really, really hard not to be impressed.

"I can't bring the boat to you," he pointed out. "Your shoes are worth saving. Mine aren't."

"Put . . . me . . . down," she said, stressing every word. There wasn't a chance in *hell* he could carry her all the way across the slippery mud to the boat. He was out of his mind to even *think* about it! She firmly repressed the pure, feminine fluttering that grew in the pit of her stomach and brought sudden heat to her face.

"Are you afraid I'll drop you in the mud?" Conor asked, grinning.

"*Damn straight!*" she snapped. And no doubt he would swear up and down it was an accident.

He burst out laughing and took a step toward the boat, so

she squirmed and kicked her feet for emphasis. She had to get him to put her down before they left the gravel parking lot or surely she'd end up in the slime.

"Conor, *please*!" She hated the note of panic in her voice.

Some of the men loitering beneath the overhang by the pub cheered and shouted encouragement at Conor.

"Whatever you say," he replied.

Still grinning, Conor simply let go of her! Kelly threw her arms around his neck to save herself. Before the scream was all the way out of her mouth, Conor slipped both hands under her armpits and held her in front of him so they were nose to nose. It was another impressive demonstration of his strength. Her feet were dangling off the ground.

Another cheer went up from the peanut gallery.

"So it's an adventure you'll be having, is it?" he asked softly.

"*Cute*, Conor," she said dryly, refusing to acknowledge the thrilling way his rock-hard shoulder muscles bunched under her clutching fingers. "If you're finished showing off for your drinking buddies, I'm ready to go now."

His lips twitched.

"As your ladyship commands."

He could say the corniest things, Kelly realized, but his lovely west-country lilt only made them sound seductive.

Kelly tensed, expecting Conor to drop her with a thud to get another cheap laugh out of the boys. Instead, he let her down gently on the gravel with a minimum of body contact and indicated the waiting boat with a gallant wave of his arm. The slimy sea of mud stretched from the parking lot to the riverbank.

"It's not too late to be changing your mind about letting me carry you," Conor teased when she took a deep breath and braced herself to take the plunge. He held his arms wide, presumably so she could throw herself into them.

She gave him a withering look and took her first step off the gravel. When he offered her his hand for support, she swallowed her pride and took it. The sensation of sinking into the cold, slippery mud was every bit as unpleasant as she had anticipated.

Trying to ignore the disgusting squelch of her shoes in the slime, she carefully picked her way to the boat and got in. She gasped when her bottom connected with the wet aluminum seat. She could feel the sharp slap of cold all the way through her lined wool skirt.

Kelly looked back over her shoulder at Conor. He was just standing there, trying unsuccessfully to suppress a smile. She wanted to slug him.

"Coming?" she asked sweetly instead.

"There's a likely lass," he said admiringly with a crooked smile that shook all of Kelly's carefully constructed defenses.

Then he pulled up the anchor, pushed off from shore, and leaped gracefully into the boat. Kelly ducked her head and cowered out of sheer reflex. Conor touched her shoulder lightly to balance himself and stepped over the middle seat to take control of the motor.

"Put this on," he said, reaching beneath his seat and handing her a life preserver. It was the kind that had to be strapped on across the chest.

Kelly wrinkled her nose. It had a moldy smell, but she didn't hesitate. The water was dark and choppy.

"What about you?" she asked, noticing that there was only one life preserver in the boat.

"Don't worry about me," he muttered, giving the engine three pulls before it coughed into reluctant life.

"Can't you make it go any faster?" she asked when they were under way. At this rate, they might get to the castle by dinnertime!

"This is as fast as she goes."

When they had chugged on in silence for a little while, the mist became a gentle rain; Conor removed his battered jacket with all the self-possession of a courtier and passed it to her. She put it on like a veil to protect her head and shoulders. She must have looked ridiculous, but what the heck? The whole situation was ridiculous.

"We'll be there soon," Conor said, looking apologetic again.

As well he might, Kelly thought crossly.

Kelly was trying to pretend she was annoyed with him, but Conor knew better. He didn't doubt she was uncomfortable. It was a wet, cold day and she wasn't dressed for it. But the expressions that chased themselves across her face as she stared at the waves of green grass, stone cottages and freshly plowed fields left him in no doubt that she was moved by the beauty around her.

"It's fabulous," she said, awed. She had given his jacket back to him as soon as it had stopped raining hard, and her fair hair glistened with droplets of moisture.

"It is that," he agreed, careful not to let her pretty face distract him from his occupation of scanning the water for hazards.

They went around the bend, and Conor's heart lifted at the sight of his castle crowning the hill, even though it would soon be lost to him. This sorrow had been like an open wound for the past month, but somehow it was bearable while Kelly was in the boat with him.

How strange that the bossy little Yank's presence should lift his spirits during the worst time of his life.

"There. Up ahead," he said.

Kelly glanced over her shoulder, did a double take, and then cheered Conor immeasurably by swinging her lovely long legs all the way around so she could face forward. When she looked back at him, her eyes were shining.

"God, it's *wonderful*! I can't wait to get my hands on it!" she exclaimed in a burst of enthusiasm that made his blood run cold.

That's just what he was afraid of.

Five

If Conor hadn't grabbed her arm when she tripped over a rock, Kelly might have rolled back down the hill.

She wouldn't have noticed.

Her blazer was probably trashed, the heels of her brand new shoes were mired in mud, damp hair spray glued her bangs to her forehead, and her panty hose adhered to her wet, clammy legs like pieces of plastic wrap. She didn't care.

To hell with dignity!

Whitlock Castle loomed out of the mist in front of her like something out of a dream.

Nothing had prepared her for the sight of gray stone walls soaring straight to the sky on the hill above the majestic River Lee. She loved the invigorating smell of the salt air that whipped against her body.

"We'll have to install better steps with landings in a couple of places," she said between gasps. "This single run of stairs is like climbing a mountain."

Conor grabbed her elbow again as she almost tripped over another loose piece of stone.

"Careful," he warned. "It's a bit rough here."

A bit rough, indeed!

She slanted a look at Conor. He wasn't even breathing hard.

Kelly's lungs, on the other hand, were about ready to burst from the climb.

They were almost to the castle now, and Kelly was panting like a dog. Conor smiled, took her hand and hauled her up the rest of the steps as if she weighed nothing at all. She tried not to look too grateful.

She was *mortified*.

Hundreds of dollars a year for a health club membership, religious workouts on the stair machine, aerobics classes three days a week, meticulous attention to a spartan diet and for *what*? After climbing the stairs from the river to the castle, she was wrecked. Her legs were still sore from climbing the long flights of stairs inside the castle yesterday.

Conor, on the other hand, was striding along as if he were on a Sunday stroll. He had such long, long legs.

"Sorry," Conor said apologetically, slowing down so she wouldn't have to trot beside him to keep up. "Should we stop for a minute?"

"No. I'm fine," she lied. She was getting a stitch in her side, but she was not about to admit it. The heel of her shoe lodged between a crack in the broken pavement. Conor caught her arm to keep her from tipping over while she stood on one leg and pulled the shoe out of the crevice with her other hand. To get it loose, she had to bark up the leather on the heel. She tried not to wince when she put her foot back into the clammy shoe.

"I love the flowers, especially the purply-pink stuff growing on the hill," she said, pausing to sniff the yellow head of a daffodil. It had been snowing in Chicago when she left, so these early spring flowers seemed like a wildly extravagant gift to her winter-weary senses. "Whoever landscaped this place did a great job."

"Thank you. My aunts and I planted the daffodils and primroses. God planted the heather."

"Oh. So *that's* heather," she said.

The smile in his eyes told her she had said something remarkably foolish. Even so, she couldn't help smiling back.

Down, girl, she told herself firmly. This guy was looking entirely too good to her.

"This is really a great castle," Kelly said aloud, looking up at the gray walls appreciatively.

"We like it," Conor said, pleased with her enthusiasm. "We'll go around to the other side, so we can go in properly through the front hall."

Kelly almost argued with him. It was a *long* way around, but she didn't want to give him the satisfaction of seeing just how bad off she was.

The front of the castle was well worth the walk, even though Kelly almost whimpered when she came to the steep flight of steps to the entrance.

Gluts protesting loudly all the way, Kelly scaled another summit. The beautifully carved wooden door was flanked by big, peaked Gothic windows. Amber, carnelian red, emerald green, and cobalt blue stained glass gleamed in the upper panes.

How could she have failed to appreciate all this the day before yesterday when she arrived? Of course, then she had been half-dead from jet lag and intent upon getting into the castle as soon as possible so she could give Conor O'Meara a piece of her mind. And she had spent all yesterday inside.

Kelly followed Conor's example and scraped the mud off her shoes on the rubber mat outside the door as well as she could. He took his shoes off and carried them.

"What a great door knocker!" she said, impressed by the grinning gargoyle. It looked like weathered iron. "Is it original?"

"It's always been here," he said. He reached around her and pushed open the door.

The first thing Conor heard was two women bawling their eyes out.

Every muscle in his body tensed. Aunt Margaret still had her hand on the telephone.

"Da?" he said, walking up to the front desk to put a consoling arm around each of his aunts when Aunt Rose gave up trying to speak through her sobs and nodded wearily. "Is he . . ."

"Awake," Margaret managed to croak. "He woke up and asked for us."

"If it isn't just like the stubborn old fool to be waking up at a time when none of us is there," Rose said gruffly as a tear leaked down her cheek. "Well, we can't all be traipsing off to the hospital and leaving the guests to fend for themselves."

Conor exchanged a long look with his aunts.

"I'll stay," he offered. "You and Aunt Margaret should go."

"No, Conor," Margaret said, trying with an effort to pull herself together. "You're his son, and your place is with him. You and Rose go."

"And why should I be going and leaving the work to you?" Rose demanded.

"You haven't seen him yet today," Margaret replied. "One of us has to see to the guests coming in this afternoon."

"So, what am I? Chopped liver?"

Conor turned to stare at Kelly. In his anxiety about his father, he had forgotten she was there.

"*All* of you will go. I can take care of the guests," Kelly said, stepping briskly up to the desk.

"Are you sure?" Conor said, hoping she was. "We can't ask you to—"

"Yeah, yeah, yeah," she said, flapping her arms at him. "You didn't ask. I volunteered. G'wan, get outa here!"

"Some of the guests will be expecting lunch because they're paying extra for their board, and we might not be back in time to cook dinner . . ." Margaret said hesitantly.

"I'll take them into the pub compliments of Lawrence Hotels. I've hardly put anything on my expense account because you've been feeding me and driving me around, so we owe you big. When are the new people arriving?"

"About three o'clock," Rose said, dashing tears from her

eyes. "The rooms are clean, but I haven't made the bed in one of the rooms—"

"Hey, I know how to change sheets," Kelly said. "I didn't do three hideous weeks in Housekeeping during my orientation period for nothing. Just tell me which rooms you want them in."

Rose bit her lip. Then she kissed Kelly on the cheek, surprising them both. Kelly's face went all soft around the edges. It was a lovely thing to watch.

"Room five for the Davises and their three children, then," Rose said, all business. "The cots and baby bed are already in the room. And Room three for the Clooneys. The bed must be made in Room three, and you'll need to pick some daffodils from the back garden for both rooms. You know where the linens are."

"And they'll be expecting tea when they arrive—" Margaret began.

"Okay, okay, enough already!" Kelly said, flapping her arms some more. "Like it takes a brain surgeon to boil water and pick flowers! Get 'em outa here, big guy, before I change my mind."

Kelly gave Conor a little shove to send him on his way, and he laughed out loud.

She was so cute when she was pretending to be tough.

When Margaret would have lingered to give Kelly more instructions, Conor took her arm and steered her and Rose away.

"Thank you, Kelly, dear!" Margaret said, turning around when she got to the doorway. "I don't know how we can ever repay—"

"Never mind all that—you guys just make sure you're back in time to do the full Irish breakfast thing, because I haven't a *clue* how to cook all that stuff!" Kelly shouted after them.

Conor knew he was grinning like an eejit as he led his aunts to the car, but that was all right because his aunts were grinning, too.

Da is awake.

God is good, after all.

Tears welled in Conor's eyes, but he tamped them down hard.

Somebody had to be able to see well enough to drive to the hospital.

"So, tell me about this pushy American lass with the fancy red underwear," Sean O'Meara said with a bright, expectant look in his faded blue eyes.

Conor's mouth dropped open.

"You old gossip!" he said, taken aback. "How did you hear about *that*?"

"Were you forgetting Ghillie has a sister who works as a nurse at this hospital? It's all over the parish, from what I hear," Sean explained, grinning. He looked pale and bloated and there were still a lot of tubes in him, but he was awake, lucid and laughing at the way his sisters fussed over him. "Tell me, Conor, me boy. *You* haven't been taking a wee look at this famous red underwear, have you?"

"No!" Conor said stiffly. "A gentleman doesn't talk about a lady's underwear in public."

"Sounds like sour grapes to me," Sean observed sagely to his blushing sisters.

"Shame on you, Sean," Margaret scolded, just as if she hadn't told all of her lady friends about the fascinating contents of Kelly's luggage. "Kelly has a good heart for all of her big-city ways. She insisted upon taking care of our guests at the castle while we're gone."

"Not what you would expect of a Yank with red underwear," Da said, waggling his eyebrows. "When are you going to bring the girl to meet your old father, Conor? You can't be keeping all the pretty lasses to yourself."

"I'll ask her if she wants to come tomorrow," Conor promised. "And I'll expect you to behave yourself. Not one word about red underwear while she's here. I'll be having your word on that."

Da gave him a look so full of mischief that Conor felt

tears start in his eyes again. He had begun to lose hope that he'd ever see his father smile again.

"And what does our Ghillie think of her?"

"Ghillie hasn't met her," Conor said. "Not that it would matter. Ghillie is just a friend, Da."

"Ghillie might have other ideas about that, so you'll be wanting to keep them apart unless you want to see a hair-pulling match. Ghillie's a little thing, but she's all wire and muscle."

No doubt Da would organize a betting pool with the lads at the pub on the outcome of the catfight.

A nurse came in the door and stood looking at them with her hands on her hips.

"All three of you in here at once!" she said reprovingly. "That's against the rules, and well you know it, Mr. O'Meara!"

"Eh, but it's a grand day, Nurse," he said, giving her an ingratiating smile. "Rules were meant to be bent a wee bit."

"They've been bent enough as it is," she said, although a little smile played at the corner of her mouth. Da had a talent for turning the hearts of officious women to mush. "You've overstayed your time, so you will have to go." She fixed a stern eye on Conor and his aunts. "You can come back in an hour—and you'll be visiting with Mr. O'Meara one at a time, if you please!"

The little flapping motions she made with her hands reminded Conor suddenly of Kelly.

"The sooner we go and let you rest, the sooner we can take you home," Margaret said cheerfully as she kissed her brother's cheek.

Home.

Conor almost gasped.

In his relief at his father's awakening, he forgot all about what was waiting for Sean O'Meara at Whitlock Castle.

If Da knew about Kelly's red underwear, it was only a matter of time before he learned that the Director of Guest Services for Lawrence Hotels had an appointment with the owner of the village's only demolition company at the castle tomorrow.

"You're the Yank," the beautiful, red-haired girl said accusingly after Kelly had interrupted her conversation with the city folks from Dublin to greet the visitor. "It looks like you're taking over already."

Kelly was puzzled by the hostile tone, but she was willing to be courteous. At moments like these, her old customer service training in dealing with cranks automatically clicked into place.

"May I help you?" she asked.

"I was looking for Conor."

"He's at the hospital with his aunts. His father regained consciousness today."

"Oh, but that's grand!" the girl exclaimed, looking pleased. "I didn't know. We've all been so worried!"

"Are you a relative?" Kelly asked.

"No. A friend." The wary look was back in her big green eyes.

She had been looking for Conor. Why was Kelly not surprised?

This girl was absolutely gorgeous from the soles of her new black hightops to the crown of her long, wildly curling red hair. Her slender but curvy figure managed to transform the inexpensive pink polyester flowered dress and faded denim battle jacket into a smashing fashion statement. Her sultry mouth was smeared in candy pink lip gloss and she wore demure pearl earrings on her small, perfectly shaped ears.

Kelly's hair was still drooping from the morning's excursion down the River Lee because there was barely enough time to change her clothes before she had to take the guests into the village for lunch, and never mind that Kelly's navy blazer and gray flannel trousers had designer labels stitched inside. The petite redhead would swim in them. Kelly's makeup had been eaten off hours ago at the pub, and she had been too busy making beds and seeing to the guests to put any more on.

Next to the dainty vision in pink, she felt like a moose.

"When will Conor be back?" the girl asked.

"Probably when the hospital kicks him out. Do you want to wait for him?" Kelly felt obligated to make the offer, but she hoped the girl wouldn't take her up on it. "It might be a while, but there's a TV—a telly—in the guest parlor right through—"

"I don't need *you* to tell me where the guest parlor is," the girl snapped. "I've known the O'Meara family all of my life." Then she made a curious little gesture that might have had an element of apology in it. "Tell Conor to ring me, will you please? He knows the number."

"Sure. And you are—?"

"I'm Ghillie. Conor's probably mentioned me."

"No, but I'll have him call you," Kelly said, giving Conor's girlfriend one of those teeth-breaking smiles reserved for people you instinctively know you're going to dislike on principle.

Six

It was late when Conor and his aunts came back to the castle, and Conor was disarmed to see Kelly curled up asleep on one of the sofas in the lobby.

"Hi!" she said when she sat up, looking adorably rumpled and heavy-eyed. She shook her head to get her hair out of her eyes. "How is he?"

"Badgering the nurses and begging the doctor to let him come home," Conor said, smiling. "Sorry we're so late. We were starving so we stopped by the pub to get something to eat."

"That's okay," she said, yawning.

"Did you have any trouble while we were gone?" Margaret asked.

"No. None at all," Kelly said, rubbing her eyes. She stood up and stretched a little. "The guests were happy to go to the pub for lunch, and everybody wanted to go out on their own for dinner so I was off the hook. They're all looking forward to the famous full Irish breakfast, though, so be warned."

"Thanks for waiting up for us," Conor said.

"I didn't. I'm waiting for a call from my office." Kelly seemed to be searching for something and with a little smile of relief pulled her day planner from between the cushions of the sofa.

"Don't they know how late it is here?" Conor said, frowning.

"Yeah, it's four o'clock in Chicago so I only have to wait up another hour at most. My team is having a meeting, and they'll patch me in on a conference call."

"We're for bed," Rose said, yawning as she and Margaret stumbled for the stairs. She looked from Conor to Kelly, and her brow furrowed a little. "Don't stay up too late, Conor. You have to be up early."

"Yes, Aunt Rose. Good night." He kissed both aunts on the cheek. "Good night, Aunt Margaret."

"Sleep well, dear," Margaret said sleepily.

Kelly had gone to sit down at the desk next to the telephone. She braced her head on her arm, but she straightened with a start when Conor stood behind her and put his hands on her shoulders.

"It was a kind thing you did today," he said, bending down to whisper in her ear. He was playing with fire, and he knew it. But he had been thinking about her all day. Her hair was warm where his lips brushed against it, and she smelled like meadow flowers on a soft day.

She burst into laughter.

"Hoisted a few pints of Guinness, did we?" she asked, pushing him away as if he were an over-friendly dog.

"Half and halfs," he admitted.

"Well, I guess you're entitled," she said good-naturedly. "Why don't you go sleep it off— Conor!"

He was nuzzling her again.

"I'm not sleepy. I feel like talking. And dancing."

He pulled her out of the chair and into his arms, whirling her around until he got a little dizzy. He was drunk on beer and Kelly's laughter.

"Go to bed, Conor," she said as she steadied him with a firm hand. He kissed her full on the lips. His aim was impeccable, he was pleased to see.

"Conor!" she cried out in surprise.

"You're a darling woman, Kelly Sullivan."

"Yeah. All the sloppy drunks think so." But she was smiling. She put her hand against his face so his nose was squashed against her fingers when he would have kissed her again. She had such soft, sweet lips. "Cut it out, Conor, I've got to gather my mental forces for the meeting."

"And I distract you?" He asked hopefully. When she sat down at the desk, he started nuzzling the soft nape of her neck again.

"Yeah, you big goof! How can I concentrate with you slobbering all over me?" She was trying unsuccessfully to look vexed.

"I never slobber. Sweet, pretty Kelly," Conor murmured. "It was nice of you to mind the place so we could see Da."

"I enjoyed it, actually," she admitted. "Everybody was really nice, and they said they hoped your father would be well soon."

He was nibbling again, but instead of pushing him away, she gave a resigned sigh of what sounded suspiciously like pleasure.

"Oh, I cleaned out Room four and moved the Davises into it because it has all that cool Egyptian Art Nouveau stuff in it and their children remembered it from last year and wanted to stay in there," she said. Her voice was pitched higher than usual, and she was talking a little too fast. "The people who were in there last night left today, so it seemed silly not to let them have it."

"You wouldn't have had to bother," Conor murmured as he kissed her temple. "We could have seen to it tomorrow."

"I know. It was fun. I hadn't done any hands-on in a long time."

"Hands-on?" he whispered, kissing her cheek. "I'm liking the sound of that. You smell so good."

Kelly was blushing. He could tell because her ears turned pink.

"And you smell like a brewery!" she told him. "It was a kick to see the Davis kids get all excited about the Egyptian room. When I got into management at the corporate level, I was suddenly going to work in a regular office instead of a hotel. I missed seeing the guests come and go."

"It's what I'll be missing most when the castle is gone," he said softly.

Kelly disarmed Conor by covering one of his hands with hers.

"You pretend to be so tough," he whispered.

"I *am* tough," she told him. She sat up a bit straighter and adopted a businesslike tone. "Anyway, I wrote everything down and left it in a note for your aunts—" He had started nuzzling again, and she broke off and swiveled around in the chair to face him. He went down on one knee and put his hands on the arms of the chair so she couldn't escape from him.

"Conor," she said when he moved in on her. His questing lips were inches from hers. "I don't think this is a good idea."

"Why not?" he asked, smiling. "You don't have a husband in America you didn't tell us about, do you?"

"No. Of course not. But . . . this . . . makes things complicated." Even so, her cheeks were flushed prettily, and she had tilted her face up in unmistakable—if reluctant—invitation.

"It makes things simple," he corrected just before he kissed her. "And right."

"We can't *do* this," she said shakily when they had to break apart to breathe.

"Sure we can," he said, knowing he was grinning at her like a lovesick eejit. She was so sweet and shy underneath all the cool, competent blathering.

"Conor, *no!*" She pushed the heels of her hands hard against his chest when he would have kissed her again. "I *mean* it, Conor!"

He blinked, and the pleasant haze surrounding his brain cleared a little. She really did look distressed.

"I apologize," he said, although he wasn't the least bit sorry. He stood up to give her some distance. "I got carried away—because of Da and all."

"Understandable," she said with a wave of her hand. She turned the swivel chair around to face the desk again. "Your girlfriend was here looking for you."

"Who?" he asked absently. He didn't know what she was talking about.

Kelly looked over her shoulder at him with reproachful eyes.

"Curly red hair? Green eyes? Legs a mile long?" When Conor continued to look vague, she snapped, "Dresses kind of faux Euro-trash with an *attitude*?"

"Ah, that would be Ghillie," Conor said slowly. "She's an old friend."

"Yeah? Your old friend wants you to call her. She said you know the number."

"I do, yes," he acknowledged. "What did she say?"

Not that he cared in the least what Ghillie had to say while his lips were still tingling from kissing Kelly.

"Only that she wanted to talk to you."

"She just wants to know about Da."

"It looked to me like she was sizing up the competition," Kelly said with an edge to her voice. "She was pretty unfriendly."

Conor thought she was probably right. Ghillie had heard about Kelly's red underwear, and she had some misguided idea that Conor needed saving from the sex-crazed American city woman.

In your dreams, boyo.

The thought of Ghillie and the rest of the nosy village folk brought Conor back to earth with a thump.

"Da is going to be released from the hospital later this week," he said cautiously.

"Okay," Kelly said slowly in that wary tone of voice that means, *Is this going somewhere*?

"If he finds out what your boss wants to do to the castle, he might have another stroke."

"He won't hear about it from me," Kelly promised. "The man from the demolition company is coming tomorrow, and once he's out of the way we'll only be seeing carpenters and contractors and people like that until my cost studies are completed."

"That should be safe enough," said Conor, still feeling troubled. "I hope no one from the village mentions it to him. One of the first things he'll want to do when he gets out of the hospital is go to the pub to see all his friends."

"You worry too much," Kelly said, softening, "even though I've got to say people around here are incredibly nosy."

Conor nodded glumly. He could just imagine what she would say if she knew her underwear was the talk of the parish.

"You're probably right," he said, unconvinced.

"Look," she said, smiling at him. "You're dead on your feet. And you're going to have the mother of all hangovers if you don't get a couple of aspirins down you. Why don't you go to bed?"

"Kiss me good night?" he suggested hopefully.

"I really don't think that's a good—"

Before she could finish her sentence, he gave the back of the swivel chair a twist so they were face to face. Then he pulled her right out of the chair and into his arms.

"Pleasant dreams, Kelly," he whispered, and kissed her as if his life depended on it.

You might as well be hanged for a sheep as for a lamb, as the English used to say. If Kelly was going to be slapping him silly, it might as well be for a good reason.

Instead of slapping him, though, she melted in his arms and kissed him back. Ah, but she was a lovely, soft, darling girl.

"*Definitely* not a good idea," she murmured when he finally released her and she fell bonelessly back into the chair as if her knees were weak. She looked up at him. "You don't have to look so disgustingly well pleased with yourself, Conor O'Meara!"

"I'm not. Just grateful," he said. "Everlastingly grateful. I'll see you in the morning."

He blew her a kiss and headed for the stairs without bothering to wipe the silly grin off his face.

Have you lost your ever-loving mind, Sullivan?

Kelly put her head down on the desk and groaned.

Conor O'Meara didn't have a politically correct bone in his whole gorgeous body!

And, good God almighty, could he kiss!

Kelly was wrecked. Absolutely wrecked.

So, naturally the phone rang and it was her crisp, efficient assistant letting her know they were ready to do the conference call.

"Oh, hello, Julie," she said, forcing perkiness into her voice. "Yes, things are going well. . . . Sure. I'm all ready. Go ahead and patch me in."

She took a deep breath, opened her day planner, and hoped she wasn't going to sound too much like a ditz with Conor's kisses still messing up her mind.

Seven

What must she be thinking of me, Conor wondered with some trepidation as he walked into the kitchen the next day.

He almost had decided to hide at the farm all morning, but he needed coffee very badly and there was none left in his spartan kitchen.

I actually had my tongue in her mouth, he remembered with a groan. He hoped she had breakfasted and was already secreted in her room with her laptop and her spreadsheets so he wouldn't have to face her.

Like hell, boyo. You're dying to see her. Like a drunk wanting his next drink, he thought in disgust.

What had started out with a bit of healthy male interest in a good-looking female stranger was turning into an obsession. Despite a killing hangover, he had been up before sunrise, rushing through his chores with a song on his lips like a bloody fool so he could get to the hospital to see Da and back to the castle in time to see Kelly. Fortunately, the windy ride in his boat had cleared his throbbing head a little.

Kelly was there, all right, he noticed as soon as he walked into the kitchen. She had on a soft blue sweater and a slim navy skirt that bared her legs well above the knee. She wore dainty silver hoop earrings and a demure silver chain at her throat that caught the light.

She smelled of meadow flowers, as usual.

He probably smelled like a dog that had been too long in the rain.

Aunt Margaret was presiding at the stove and Kelly, instead of sitting at the table nursing a cup of coffee and frowning at her day planner as usual, was saying something that made her laugh.

Oh, God. Maybe Kelly was telling Aunt Margaret about the way he got befuddled and had his hands all over her as soon as his aunts were out of the room. But his aunt greeted him cheerfully, as usual, and her eyes were innocent.

Conor took a deep breath and told himself not to be a fool. The last two people Kelly would tell about his drunken pawing last night would be his aunts—and if she did, Aunt Margaret would *not* be laughing.

He straightened up and bid Kelly a bashful good morning when she turned around and smiled at him with a teasing look in her eyes.

She was laughing at him. He was going to die of humiliation.

"Hi, Conor," she said, lifting her eyebrows. "Feeling a bit under the weather today, are we?"

"If you've any compassion in your heart, me lass, you'll be passing me that pot of coffee," he said, putting his head in his hands to hide the fact that he was grinning through his pain like a lovesick fool at the mere sound of her voice. He looked up when he had his face under control.

"It's not his fault," Margaret said, giving him a sympathetic look over her shoulder. "Our Conor's not used to the drink like some of the lads. They kept pushing half-and-halfs on him last night, and being the well-brought-up lad he is, he had to keep buying them rounds in return."

Well. That's reduced him to the level of callow youth, he thought in despair.

Kelly smirked and poured him a cup of the steaming coffee.

When she set the coffee down, he took her hand and kissed her long, graceful fingers behind Aunt Margaret's back. He couldn't help himself.

"Bless you," he said humbly.

Mercifully, she just rolled her eyes at him instead of smacking him against the side of the head and making his pain worse.

"Gotta serve this while it's hot," Kelly said gaily as she took two filled plates from Aunt Margaret and sailed out the doorway.

"She's serving the guests in the dining room?" Conor asked in amazement as soon as she was gone in a tantalizing flash of short skirt and long leg.

"Rose was after going to the shops early for vegetables so Kelly offered to serve breakfast in Rose's place and mind the guests again today, bless her, so Rose and I could go into the hospital together. She said she'll be having some men up to the castle to see about doing some work, anyway, so she'd be here all day. Isn't that lovely of her?"

"Lovely," Conor repeated dully.

"Maybe you should be having a lie-down," Margaret said, giving him a concerned look.

"Too much work to do," he said. "Don't worry about me. I'll be fine."

The sound of shrill juvenile laughter from the guest parlor made Conor's eyes water. He clutched his poor, suffering head.

"The Davis children have taken a fancy to Kelly," Margaret said. "They follow her around like puppies."

"I'll bet she loves that," Conor said, taking a long, healing swallow of the steaming coffee. It burned all the way down and the caffeine went straight to his brain. He could have wept with relief.

"That she does," Margaret said, missing the sarcasm. "She has a lovely way with them."

A childish, high-pitched scream came from the other room along with the unmistakable sound of breaking crockery. Conor was on his feet, going to investigate, when Kelly suddenly appeared in the doorway and almost collided with him. Automatically, he took her shoulders to steady her.

Her breath caught, and she looked up into his eyes for a moment. Then she wiggled out of his grip and darted away from him.

"Small catastrophe," she said to Margaret as Conor sat back down. "Cassie accidentally knocked her plate on the floor. Do you have any scrambled eggs and bacon left? It would have broken your heart to see how her little face fell. She said she was saving the bacon for last, and now she won't have any."

"Aww, bless the darling little soul," said Margaret, who had a soft spot for children.

"I got the broken pieces and most of the spilled food up with a napkin and put it off to the side," Kelly said. "I'll clean the floor when they leave the table."

"You don't have to bother with that, dear," Margaret said. "I'll see to it when I get finished here."

"I don't mind. It's almost an honor to clean beautiful hardwoods like that," Kelly said.

Conor made a show of feeling her forehead for signs of fever. It was corny, but it provided an excuse to touch her.

"What a comedian," Kelly said wryly, giving him a playful little bump with her hip to move him out of her way when she took the fresh plate from Margaret and sailed back into the dining room.

"That girl's a worker," Margaret said admiringly. "She was up early and insisted on helping. I think the good Lord sent her to us to help us through our troubles."

"Unlikely. Lawrence Hotels sent her to close down the castle and make it ready for the new owners."

"Well, maybe God was working in mysterious ways again," Margaret said happily. Conor didn't try to contradict her. He only gave the heavily filled plate she set in front of him a skeptical look.

"You're thinking it will come right back up again," she said, effortlessly reading his mind. "But a lad who works as hard as you needs something in his stomach or he'll be fainting with hunger before noon."

"Yes, Aunt Margaret," he said meekly as he forked up a bite of crisp, perfectly done fried potato.

Kelly came back into the kitchen and poured herself a cup of coffee.

"So, how are you feeling?" she asked Conor conversationally.

"As if I might live," he said after he had chewed and swallowed a piece of banger with more appetite than he would have dreamed possible.

"I'm glad to hear it. Your father is still doing well, I hope?"

"Alive, awake, and pelting a poor body with questions about how things are faring with the castle," he said. He selected a rasher from his plate and handed it to her. "I can't eat all this, and it would be a pity to waste good bacon."

She looked as if she might refuse, but then her stomach growled audibly and they both laughed.

"Looks more like ham to me," she said as she took the rasher. She bit off one end and closed her eyes. "Oh, God," she breathed. "Is there any more of that?"

"It's not like that dreadful streaky stuff they have in America," Aunt Margaret said, enjoying the opportunity to feel superior.

"This is *so* good," she said, accepting another piece from an amused Conor. Then she pushed away from the table. "No. That's enough. I have to stop *now*."

"There's more here, Kelly," Margaret said, filling a plate full of remains of the breakfast she had cooked. Kelly's eyes opened wide at the way the food mounded over it. "This would just be to throw out, so take what you want and leave the rest."

"Oh, I *couldn't*," she said longingly as Margaret put the plate in front of her. It was the same assortment of foods she had been turning her nose up at for the past few days, but it looked like her resistance finally had been worn down. With a little cry of surrender, she took the fork Aunt Margaret handed her and fell on the food like a ravening wolf.

Looking smug, Margaret went into the dining room and started bringing back dirty dishes from the guests' table.

"Oh, I'll do that," said Kelly, getting up when the older woman came back with her arms full.

"Eat your breakfast before it gets cold," she told her. "This is the first decent meal I've seen you eat since you arrived."

"Well, thanks," Kelly said, returning to her plate with a little sigh. "Look out, arteries! Here it comes!"

When she finished eating everything on her plate, Conor handed her a half piece of bread from his. With a rueful little smile, she took it and sopped up the egg yolk and grease from her plate with it.

"It looks like I'm going to be back in my fat clothes for sure," she said ruefully after she had eaten every crumb of the grease-soaked bread.

"I'm sure you'll wear them with distinction," Conor said, grinning. His headache was not gone, but the look of bliss on Kelly's face after putting away enough food to satisfy a sumo wrestler went a fair way to easing the pain.

Kelly made a face at him and carried her plate to the sink. Margaret was up to her elbows in soapy water and humming to herself as she did the washing up.

"You don't have to do that, dear," the older woman said, gratified, when Kelly picked up a towel and started drying.

"It's the least I can do after that breakfast," Kelly insisted. "The sooner we get this stuff over with, the sooner you and Rose can go to the hospital. I don't have anything to do, anyway, until Mr.——" she broke off and turned a guilty look toward Conor, who had stood up in alarm. "Uh, I forget his name, but he's going to look at the woodwork in some of the parlors and give me an estimate on how much it would cost to repair the spots where the damp has rotted it."

Conor gave her a grateful look.

"That would be Mr. Parker," Margaret said comfortably as she concentrated on getting a spot off one of her dishes.

"Didn't you go courting with him when you were young, Aunt Margaret?" Conor asked.

His aunt gave a reminiscent sigh.

"Yes, before that hussy Molly Bliven stole him from me," Margaret said. "But I have no regrets. I'd have had to leave the castle, and it would have broken my heart."

She met Conor's eyes guiltily.

"*Then*," she said firmly. "It would have broken my heart *then*. But now I'm more than ready to have younger hands take over the work so I can enjoy my retirement."

It was a kind lie, and Conor knew it. His aunts would miss the castle as much as he would. Da was the one who had to retire, and that for the sake of his health. No man deserved to take the rest of his days easy more than he did.

Conor just prayed that his father was out of danger and he *had* some years left to enjoy his retirement.

Rose came back from the shops just as Margaret and Kelly finished putting away the dishes.

Kelly excused herself and went into the dining room to deal with the slightly greasy hardwood floor after she poured Conor a second cup of coffee.

Conor's soulful blue eyes had met Kelly's with a look of gratitude that made her want to wind her arms around his neck and kiss him right on his unshaven jaw.

Don't go there, she warned herself. She had to get away from him. Now.

The Davises and the Clooneys had gone out to enjoy their day touring the village and surrounding countryside, so she was alone in the dining room as she worked on the floor.

"We're going now, Kelly," Margaret said gaily from the doorway.

"Good luck!" Kelly called out. For some reason, the natives said "good luck" instead of "good-bye," and Kelly had adopted the habit.

"You don't need to bother with that," said Rose, coming to the doorway with her coat still on and the car keys in hand. "I'll do it when I come back."

"No problem," Kelly said, standing up. "See, I'm finished already."

When she returned from putting the cleaning supplies away, she almost ran smack into Conor.

He put his arms around her and bent to press his forehead against hers.

"Thank you," he said.

"For what?" she asked, feeling self-conscious. It was easy enough to face him with Margaret around, but now she was alone with him. She wondered how much he remembered of last night.

Did he remember that she willingly let him kiss her so thoroughly?

Don't go there, she warned herself again. For *God's* sake, don't go there!

"For not telling Aunt Margaret I made a fool of myself last night. For helping her with breakfast. For cleaning this floor while I sat in the kitchen nursing my thick head. For not telling Aunt Margaret the demolitions man is coming this morning."

He stopped and gave her a shy, vulnerable look.

"Mostly for kissing me back last night instead of giving me a clout on the side of the head and screaming the house down," he said ruefully.

"Oh," she said in a small, mortified voice. "You remembered that."

"*Remembered* that? I've been thinking of nothing else all morning."

"Me, too," she admitted with a sigh. "Look, we're going to have to stop beating ourselves up over it and get on with our lives or it's going to be really awkward for me to work here the next few months. There was no harm done, so we'll just chalk it up to a few too many pints."

She wiggled a little to indicate he should release her now, but he merely tightened his arms.

"No hard feelings?" he asked.

"None at all," she said, trying to sound breezy and confident even though Conor was staring at her lips with all the longing of a starving man. "*Conor*! Stop looking at me like that!"

"Like what?" he said teasingly. His lips were getting closer, inch by inch.

"You *know* like what!" she exclaimed, leaning back. Even so, she couldn't do anything about the little bubble of laughter that escaped from her lips.

She was about to recite the part of the PC code that forbids friendly physical contact between representatives of opposing corporate entities when she heard the bell at the front desk.

"Ah, saved by the bell," she said unoriginally, grateful for the interruption that allowed her to step away from Conor without betraying the fact that she would like nothing better than to finish what they had started last night. "That would be the demolitions man."

It wasn't.

"There you are," said Ghillie, turning around from ringing the bell impatiently again and frowning at Kelly. "Conor didn't ring me last night, so I figured you didn't tell him I was here."

Before she could respond to this petulant accusation, Kelly felt Conor's warm hands on her shoulders as he moved her to the side so he could approach his visitor.

"Kelly told me," he said, stepping in front of Kelly as if he intended to defend her from some threat. "We got home too late for me to be ringing anybody."

Today Ghillie was wearing a pair of snug jeans with a black Lycra shell that showed off her slender, well-toned body like a leotard. Her hair was flying loose all around her.

Her arms wore goose bumps from the cool morning air, but she looked ravishing.

"Well, if you'll excuse me," Kelly said, raising her eyebrows at the redhead, who was pouting up at Conor. The girl's eyes were shooting green sparks, and Kelly figured it would take a stronger man than Conor O'Meara to resist her.

Kelly didn't want to see it.

Conor started to go after Kelly when she left the room, but Ghillie snagged the sleeve of his shirt.

"Let her go, Conor!" Ghillie snarled. "Don't you know what she's done? She has Mr. Feeney, the demolitions man, coming up to the castle today to give her an estimate on wrecking the interior. She'd probably have the whole castle knocked down if it wasn't against the law!"

"I knew about it, Ghillie, and I'll thank you to be minding your own business," he said sternly.

"How dare you say that to *me*, Conor O'Meara," she said reproachfully. "As if I were a stranger to you. You loved me once."

"That was a long time ago, my girl," Conor said.

"I know I hurt you when I left," she said softly as she reached up to touch his cheek. "I wasn't ready to settle down to a husband and family then. All I could think of was the dancing. But all that is behind me. We were *meant* for each other. I know that now."

Conor looked into that beautiful face and wondered how he could have mistaken his youthful infatuation with Ghillie for love. With the memory of Kelly's kisses searing his brain, it was all he could do to stop himself from flinching when Ghillie raised on tiptoe and kissed his cheek.

"Ghillie, darling," he said, trying to be kind. "You wouldn't be thinking of marrying me if that dancing troupe had worked out."

"That's not true," she snapped.

"It is, and you know it," he insisted.

"What about the Yank?" she asked. "Don't you *care* that she wants to tear the place down? It should belong to you. And our children."

Conor gave Ghillie a look of utter exasperation. He would always love Ghillie like the little sister he never had, but the last thing he wanted to do was marry her!

He knew well that it was her injured pride talking. She was back from Dublin, disappointed because she hadn't found a place in another troupe despite going to audition after audition until her savings ran out and she had to return to her parents' home in disgrace.

Somehow she'd convinced herself that her only choice was to marry the boy back home who had sworn he'd die a bachelor if she didn't marry him.

If God ever made a bigger fool than Conor O'Meara, Conor didn't know his name.

When Ghillie came back to County Cork and found out Conor hadn't married, she'd hinted that the grand courtyard at the castle would make a beautiful setting for an outdoor wedding, as if her ma wouldn't make a powerful fuss over Ghillie not being married in a proper church.

Aunt Margaret and Aunt Rose were no help with their well-meaning encouragement of Ghillie's determination to marry him.

They remembered how he mooned around like a lovesick fool after the stagestruck Ghillie took the bus for Dublin without a backward glance.

Like Ghillie's parents, they thought the girl was home for good, having gone to the city to have her career before settling down with a good man to have his babies, but Conor was not fooled.

A girl with Ghillie's beauty and talent would not be content to settle down to country life now that she'd had a taste of the city.

If he gave in and married her, someday she'd be sorry she threw herself away on him.

Thank God, Conor no longer wanted her.

But he couldn't be telling *her* that. Not while she was still hurting from the disappointment of being turned down at all those auditions.

"Ghillie, I know you want to help," he began, trying to distract her from the subject of marrying him and—heaven forbid—bearing his children. *Why* did his head have to be pounding with the after-effects of the drink when he needed his wits about him? "But interfering in something you don't understand is not going to do us any good."

"I wish the Yank had never come here," Ghillie said vehemently. "It's all her fault."

"The castle would still have to be sold, Ghillie. If Kelly hadn't come, someone else would have come in her place. And her company might not decide to use the demolitions man, after all. Surely it will cost less to repair the castle than to gut it and start over, and Kelly will do her best to convince her boss of that."

"Why should you trust her? She's just another bossy, impatient Yank. She was in the shops yesterday, scolding poor Noreen Cleary for not working fast enough to suit her. She did it in front of a whole shop full of people as if Noreen was nothing more than a servant who wasn't good enough to clean her ladyship's boots."

"Now that is an exaggeration, I'm sure," Conor said reproachfully.

"You think because she has blond hair and city clothes and a pretty face, you can trust her," Ghillie snapped. "Men are such fools."

"Yes, darling," Conor couldn't help saying deliberately. "You should know."

"Oh, Conor," Ghillie said tearfully. "I don't want to fight with you."

She put her arms around his waist and sobbed on his chest. He couldn't do anything but pat her awkwardly on the back.

"Don't let *her* come between us," she cried passionately.

"It's all right, Ghillie, it's all right," he murmured, trying to quiet her. He knew it was a mistake but he kissed her on the forehead. She seemed so upset.

As soon as he did, he heard a small sound behind him. His heart sank when he turned to look into Kelly's solemn blue eyes.

"What are you doing there?" Ghillie snarled at her.

"Nothing," Kelly said, holding her hands up as if in surrender. "Nothing at all. You didn't see me."

"Kelly," Conor called after her when she hastily ran out of the room.

Ghillie grabbed his arm when he would have followed Kelly. She was stronger from the dancing than she looked, so it took him a minute to pry her clutching fingers loose.

"You don't need *her*," she said as her green eyes smoldered up at him.

Ah, there you'd be wrong, my girl, he thought ruefully.

Eight

He came up behind her while she was in the beautiful parlor that Conor's great-grandfather had christened the Peacock Room because of its brilliant stained glass window depicting the exotic bird in all its teal, jade, amber, and cobalt blue glory on a field of gold and russet.

It wasn't the most spectacular room in the castle. Just a little nook, really, with barely enough room for Kelly to sit enthroned at a graceful, gilded writing desk and work with her laptop on battery power. But her heart had recognized this place at once, and she could have wept for joy the first time she saw it.

God! What was *happening* to her? It was as if this room had been waiting just behind her eyelids all her life for her to come to Ireland and claim it as her own.

Along with Conor.

It was about ten o'clock, and he had just come in from the hospital.

"You can't avoid me forever," he said from behind her.

Kelly sighed and turned around to face him.

Conor was wearing snug, faded jeans and a soft, loose blue shirt that emphasized his broad shoulders and was open at the throat to show a glimpse of his dark, curling chest hair. Over the shirt he wore a leather vest.

He was so handsome, and he wasn't half trying. No wonder women made fools of themselves over him.

Kelly would *not* be one of them, damn it!

"I don't know what you mean," she lied, forcing a cool, polite smile to her lips. "I've been awfully busy—"

"Is it because I kissed you?" he persisted. "or is it because of Ghillie?"

"Neither. Both," she gave a futile little shrug. "I don't know."

He waited patiently for more.

"Your relationship with Ghillie is none of my business," she said at last.

"True," he said, giving her that polite, skeptical little smile that always made her want to scream. "I am not courting Ghillie."

"Good for you. Now if you'll excuse me—"

"Kelly," he said, taking her hands in his. "There's no reason for you to avoid me. The other night I had too much to drink and made a bloody fool of myself, and there's an end to it."

He kissed her fingers.

"If you want it to be," he added, giving her a smile that made her blush when she would have withdrawn her hands.

"God, you are *too* good at this," she said, rolling her eyes and giving a self-conscious little laugh. "Let *go*, Conor." She gave another tug on her hands and he tightened his playful grip on them.

"Why?" He was openly laughing at her now.

"I need them to type, for one thing."

"Oh, that," he said, releasing her and causing her to have mixed feelings about it. "What I'm trying to say is I'll keep my hands off you if that's what you want."

"That's what I want," she lied.

"All right then," he said, as if that settled the matter. "That looks interesting. Can you give me a look, or is it a secret thing?"

For a minute she didn't know what he was talking about, but then she realized he meant the spreadsheet she had been working on.

"Sure. Why not?" she said, trying to mentally shift gears back to work.

She expected to have to explain the function of the spreadsheet to him, but she soon realized that he was no novice when it came to computers. Of course. He had a degree in engineering. He would have had to use a PC at some point.

The spreadsheet was a masterpiece, if she did say so herself.

It was in black, blue and white—Lawrence's corporate colors—with no graphics except for the corporate logo. Kelly had passed on the special effects and screaming fonts in favor of simple lines and an elegant, legible typeface that she thought would appeal to the bean counters. She had been filling in the quotes as she got them for demolition, cleanup, salvage, and rebuilding the castle as a fake Medieval stronghold on one side; on the other side she listed the costs of preserving the castle in its present state with minor remodeling to bring it up to corporate standards.

She had even built in comparisons for the size of the staff needed to maintain and service both concepts, using calculations based on the local rate for labor. The fake Medieval castle would have smaller guest rooms and lower rates to reflect the family audience; the luxury hotel would make it possible to keep the rooms their existing sizes and charge a higher rate to reflect a more upscale customer expectation. Because there would be fewer rooms, the luxury hotel could be adequately serviced with a smaller staff.

Kelly had demonstrated that there would be fewer telephone lines required if the castle remained intact, which would be another huge cost savings.

Bottom line—it would cost an outrageous amount of money to rebuild the castle as a fake Norman stronghold, and the corporation wouldn't recoup its investment for at least three years. If the castle was merely updated and operated as a luxury hotel, Lawrence could expect to be in the black within a year or two.

It was all right there in black and white—or would be, when Kelly got the rest of her quotations.

"This should convince them," Conor said with satisfaction. "You've done a wonderful job. Congratulations."

"It's not over yet," she said, rubbing her eyes. It had been a long day. "It may boil down to how badly Matthew wants the black marble fireplace in his condo."

She could see Conor flinch at the thought of hacking up the castle to provide Matthew Lawrence with conversation pieces for his trophy home on Lake Michigan. She couldn't blame him.

Kelly knew that through the generations the O'Mearas could have sold off bits and pieces of the castle's furnishings and architectural features to raise ready cash but refused to do so. The castle was a sacred trust that had been handed from father to son for seventy years.

If they couldn't hand it on to the next generation of caretakers intact, Conor had told her, then they deserved to see it passed into the hands of strangers. It was a matter of pride.

The O'Mearas would not commit the outrage on Whitlock Castle that had been perpetrated on other great homes.

If it happened—if she couldn't convince Lawrence to take on this sacred trust by preserving the castle—Kelly would never forgive herself.

The thought of the Peacock Room—_her_ Peacock Room— wrecked, and its furnishings and stained glass window parceled out to the highest bidder was unendurable.

"Whatever happens, the castle will be no more lost to me than it was before you came," Conor said softly, as if he had read her mind. "I do appreciate the way you've been helping us."

Kelly looked away, embarrassed. The lovingly oiled wood of the wainscotting glimmered in the shadows, illuminated only by the stained glass lamps and torchères Kelly would have bet her paycheck were genuine Tiffanys. She had tended the mellow wood herself because Conor's aunts were so busy on the lower floors with the cooking and the guest rooms and she considered it a privilege to do so.

"It's the least I could do," she said, trying for a tone of indifference. "Your aunts insist on feeding me, and I have to do something to repay them."

"Serving the guests at breakfast?" he said quizzically. "Polishing the furniture? Cleaning the loos?"

"Only *one* loo," she pointed out. "It seems silly for your aunts or the girl from the village to clean the bathroom when I was the only one to use it until yesterday, when they finally put a couple more guests on that floor."

"It's a kindness. Aunt Margaret and Aunt Rose can't take the steps like they did when they were young. And poor Mary has so much work to do, I'm surprised she shows up day after day."

"The least I can do," Kelly repeated. "But if you put any real slobs up there, you're on your own."

"You are determined to have us think you're a hardhearted city woman," he said, sounding amused.

"I *am* a hard-hearted city woman," she insisted, "and don't you forget it. Oh!"

"Is something wrong?" Conor asked.

"No," Kelly said, jotting down a quick note in her day planner. "Jeez. There is so much stuff to do, it's a wonder I'm still sane!"

Conor's mention of the steps reminded her that the man from the village who was supposed to give her an estimate on fixing the vintage elevator had failed to show up. She'd have to call him. Again. And she'd have to see if a modern reproduction of it could be made and installed on the opposite side of the building. She would get a quote from Sam, an elevator builder from New Jersey she worked with sometimes, and ask him not to tell anybody at Lawrence about it. With the castle full to capacity, one elevator would not be enough.

"Why don't you scram so I can get some work done," she told Conor, trying to sound tough again.

"It's a pleasure to have you here, Kelly," Conor said,

touching her shoulder to stop her from turning away from him. When she gave him a suspicious look, he went on, "Leaving the castle will be the saddest thing I'll ever have to do in my life, but having you here has made it bearable."

"Aw, Conor," Kelly said with a sigh. "Don't go all mushy on me."

"Sometimes you're like a person from another world," he said seriously. "Then it seems as though you've been here forever."

"Don't be a dope," she scoffed.

But it seemed like that to her, too.

Leaving Ireland was going to be like leaving a chunk of her soul behind.

Kelly's affection for Ireland and its people suffered a serious setback two days later when she accepted Rose's offer to give her a lift into the village so she could pick up a few necessities. All this "soft" weather had convinced her that her dry cleaning bills were going to break her budget if she didn't buy *something* that was wash and wear.

After that, she and Rose were going to the hospital so Kelly could meet Sean O'Meara at last. This was the first day visitors other than family were allowed into his room.

"Oh. My. God," Kelly said, awed, when she stepped into the shop.

"What is it?" asked Rose, looking a bit alarmed.

"That," Kelly said, pointing to a gorgeous purple cloak on a display. "I've got to try it on."

Noreen, the clerk with whom Kelly had words a week ago, had given her a cool nod when she and Rose entered the shop, but her face softened when she turned to follow the direction of Kelly's pointing finger.

"Well, the city woman has taste," the clerk quipped to the customer she was helping. "My sister made it," she added when Kelly smiled at her. "And I'll be telling you now that you won't see another as fine for many a day."

"I believe it," Kelly said, handing her purse to Rose. "Do you mind?"

"Of course not," Rose said. "I'm not in a hurry. Take all the time you need."

The older woman walked over to the display with her.

"The color would suit your blond hair and blue eyes," Rose added with an indulgent smile.

"It's the only one we have," the clerk supplied helpfully over her shoulder as she assisted her next customer. "My sister likes to take her time with each one."

Kelly held the fabric to her cheek.

"It's so soft," she crooned, carrying it to the small fitting room. It was pure wool, of course. On her way she picked up a plain beige skirt so free of wrinkles that it couldn't be anything but polyester. "I might as well try this on, too, while I'm at it." The skirt had an elastic waistband. Kelly's mother would be appalled at the sight of her daughter in such a pedestrian garment, but it might come in handy if Kelly continued to indulge in the famous full Irish breakfasts.

There was no mirror in the fitting room, but Kelly didn't need one to know the cloak looked fabulous on her. She could tell by the sensual feel of the fabric against her arms and the way the color swirled around her body.

The polyester skirt fit pretty well, too.

She had already decided to buy the cloak, but she couldn't resist the temptation to wear it into the shop to see it in the full-length mirror. She would probably wear it out of the shop and watch her reflection in every window on the way to the car.

She hadn't even looked at the price tag, but that was irrelevant. It was hers, and she was going to have it regardless of what it cost.

She had just reached for the handle of the fitting room door when she heard a disastrously clear voice address Rose.

"How are you getting along up at the castle with the Yank with the red underwear?" the woman asked.

"Uh, well enough," answered Rose from the other side of the door where she was holding Kelly's jacket and purse for her. The silence that followed told Kelly a signal had been passed between the women, but the damage had been done.

Kelly's good mood vanished and was replaced by sense of hurt and humiliation.

Apparently Rose O'Meara and probably Margaret, too, had been gossiping about the lurid contents of Kelly's suitcase.

She felt naked and betrayed.

How *could* they strip her of her dignity and pride before a bunch of cackling gossips?

She took the beautiful, flamboyant purple coat off and folded it over her arm. All her pleasure in it was spoiled. She opened the door and looked into Rose's stricken face.

Kelly couldn't speak. She simply returned the purple cloak to the display and gave the lovely fabric a last, regretful caress.

She should have known it wasn't for her. Not the cloak. Not the castle.

Not the man.

The shop was silent. Everyone in it was either pretending to examine merchandise or watching her with ill-disguised curiosity.

Kelly was an outsider here. She would always be one. She had come to think of the O'Mearas as her friends, but all the time they had been ridiculing her behind her back.

Rose started to speak when Kelly took her purse back from her, but Kelly turned away.

There really was nothing she could say that wouldn't make things worse.

Nine

"If you'd rather go home—" Rose began, giving Kelly an apologetic look.

"Home?" Kelly said tonelessly. "I'm a long way from home."

"To the castle, I meant."

"I know what you meant," Kelly told her. "No. I'll go to the hospital to meet Mr. O'Meara. I'm a professional. I can do this. Even though I know everybody in the village is laughing at me behind my back. A hundred thousand welcomes, my ass!"

"It was no harm meant," Rose said apologetically.

She ended with a sniff, and a fat tear ran down her cheek.

"Stop it, Rose," Kelly said, hardening her heart. "Do you want to get us killed? Keep your eyes on the road, for God's sake!"

When Rose sniffed again, Kelly gave a long sigh.

"Oh, for crying out loud!" she snapped. "Pull over, then, and I'll drive. I don't know why *you're* so upset. *I'm* the one who has to watch all Conor's buddies leer and punch each other every time I go into the pub."

"What do you take us for! We didn't tell any of the men," Rose said indignantly, ignoring Kelly's order to pull over.

Then she had to spoil it by adding, "except for Conor, of course."

"Of course," Kelly repeated, closing her eyes. "I should have known you'd tell good old Conor."

"Well, he has a right to know what's going on beneath his own roof," Rose said, her face crumpling.

"No wonder the guy has been so—"

"What?" Rose demanded sharply. "If Conor has been bothering you—"

"Nothing!" Kelly wasn't pleased with the O'Mearas right now—*any* of the O'Mearas. But she wasn't about to tell Rose that Conor got tanked up and French kissed her within an inch of her life the other night. "I'll bet you couldn't wait to give the old biddies all the gory details."

"I didn't know you then," Rose said defensively. "What was I to think when some worldly city woman comes into the castle with her short skirts and her high heeled shoes and has my poor nephew practically swallowing his tongue."

"Hah! Conor the Lady-killer? Don't make me laugh! He probably has more notches in his bedpost than—" She broke off. "I've seen the way that redhead looks at him!"

"Patricia?" Rose guessed. "Has she been up to the castle?"

"Jeez. How many of them *are* there? This one's Ghillie."

"Ghillie is a nickname. Her real name is Patricia O'Brien."

"I'm not surprised she needs an alias."

"She's a dancer."

Kelly raised her eyebrows.

"Exotic?"

"Irish," said Rose, scowling. "She ran away to Dublin to be a dancer and broke Conor's heart."

"Knowing Conor, it didn't stay broken for long," Kelly said, recalling the way Conor could melt a woman with a look. He had very good hands—and he didn't waste them playing football.

"He's popular with the girls, is Conor," Rose said

proudly. "There isn't a more handsome lad in all of County Cork."

Probably not in the world, Kelly thought. But she'd be damned if she'd gratify nosy old Rose by saying so.

Kelly was beginning to feel like a rat by the time they got to the hospital. Rose was the picture of dejection the whole way.

"You'll not be upsetting my brother, will you, because we've had words?" Rose asked, sounding anxious.

"Of course not," Kelly replied with a sigh. "The fewer people who know about this, the better."

She had to grit her teeth, though, when she and Rose were halfway in the door to Sean O'Meara's hospital room and Kelly heard one of the middle-aged nurses in the corridor cackle, "I'll bet me socks it's the Yank with the red knickers."

Rose flinched, but Kelly marched into the room with her head held high.

And stopped dead.

There, in the bed, was Conor in thirty years.

Because he had been felled by a stroke, Kelly had expected him to look older and flabbier and balder.

Instead, Sean O'Meara was a fine figure of a man with a lean physique, a handsome face and a respectable amount of his dark hair left.

"Ah, Rosie! I see you've brought a pretty lass to cheer up your old brother!" he said, giving her a wink from one of his merry blue eyes. He didn't look like an old man. Rather, he looked like a young actor who had been made up to *look* like an old man. His eyes were so bright and alive.

Conor obviously had inherited his heart-stopping smile from his father.

"Sean, this is Kelly Sullivan from Lawrence Hotels," Rose said stiffly.

Conor's father raised his eyebrows. His eyes were twinkling.

"Welcome to Ireland, Kelly," he said, exactly as Conor did the first time she met him.

"Thank you, sir," she replied.

"I hope my sisters have made you comfortable?"

Kelly exchanged a long look with Rose.

"Yes, very comfortable," she said, forcing a smile to her lips. "It's a beautiful place."

Mr. O'Meara grinned as if she'd just complimented him on a beloved child's intelligence and handsome looks.

"That she is," he agreed. "It's a great comfort to me that Mr. Lawrence will be keeping Whitlock Castle in all her glory for people to enjoy. He's getting a real bargain there. I could have gotten a better price elsewhere, but I wanted Whitlock Castle to go to a gentleman who would appreciate her."

"Yes," Kelly said, trying not to squirm. *Damn* her boss for lying to this nice man!

"How long will you be here?" he asked. "Will you be staying through the Midsummer Festival?"

"Is that the festival in June that Conor mentioned? No. I'll have to go back to Chicago by then."

"There's a pity," said Mr. O'Meara, looking disappointed. "We'll have lots of dancing and singing and Guinness, of course, and lots of bangers, although my doctor says I'm not to have such things."

The corners of his mouth drooped a little. Kelly could sympathize. As one who had recently discovered the delights of Irish sausages and bacon, she imagined Sean O'Meara was not going to like the low-fat diet any responsible physician would insist he adopt.

"Let's not have any grumbling," Rose said, patting her brother's hand. "You're lucky enough to be alive."

"Well, and so I am," he said, cheering up at once. "Are you sure you can't be staying for the festival, Kelly? It's a grand time. And it will be the last one. Conor is going to be the Summer Lord this year."

"That he isn't, Sean," Rose said, frowning. "He stood right in this room and told you as much yesterday. He doesn't want to parade around in the courtyard in a pair of tight pants with his chest all bare and decorated with a lot of heathen jewelry, and I don't blame him."

Tight pants? His chest all bare? Kelly's blood pressure rose just thinking about it.

"*I'd* do it one more time, but the doctor says he doesn't want me overtaxing myself," Sean argued. "It'll be for the last time, and if I know my son he won't be disappointing the whole village." He gave Rose a wistful look. "I want the boy to have a chance to be lord of the festival before the castle passes from the family."

"You need to be thinking about getting well, Sean," Rose said without meeting her brother's eyes. "We don't need the foolishness of a festival when we've so much to do with moving and all. I've been thinking we shouldn't have the festival this year."

"Not have the festival," Sean said in disbelief. "You'll not be meaning it, Rosie! The whole village will be counting on it."

Rose bit her lip.

"We have to be out of the castle by the end of the summer, and we've got your care to be thinking of, too."

"So, now I'm a burden to you," he said sadly.

"No such thing, and you know it, you old fool," Rose said gruffly. "And there's all the expense. You know we never break even because you won't hear a word about charging for the booths or selling the beer at a profit."

"But everyone knows what beer costs, Rosie! The lads will be tarring and feathering me if I try to build a little extra into it for myself. The whole village looks forward to the festival all year, and I hate to think of disappointing them."

"Foolishness," Rose said, compressing her lips.

Sean gave Rose a hard look. He might be flat on his back in a hospital bed, but it was plain he didn't intend to let his sister run roughshod over him.

"We'll talk about it when I'm home," he said in a tone of voice that told them the subject was closed for now. Rose shut right up, much to Kelly's surprise. This was a clear demonstration of that Irish machismo Kelly found alternately so annoying and so appealing.

Just then a young nurse poked her head in the door and excused herself when she saw the patient had visitors.

"What is it, Flora?" he asked.

Trust Conor's father to know the name of every pretty nurse on the floor when he had been only a few days out of a coma.

"I can come back," the girl said politely, although she looked at Kelly with undisguised interest. No doubt she, too, had heard about the red underwear.

Great. Just great.

"My sister Rose," Sean said affably, "and Kelly Sullivan from America."

The girl nodded to both of them, but her eyes lingered on Kelly.

"What have you got there?" Sean asked, indicating the papers in the nurse's hand.

"These are the instructions for your diet," she said, handing them over to Rose when the older woman reached for them. "The nutritionist would like to meet with you and your sisters tomorrow to explain."

Rose gave a snort of impatience.

"Look at this," she said. "No fatty meat, no eggs. Bake rather than fry. Avoid bacon and other red meat. Limit sweets and alcohol."

"What is left?" Sean asked plaintively. He gave them his disappointed baby look again.

"All kinds of stuff," said Kelly, smiling at him. "Whole wheat pasta, rice, beans, tofu, lovely fresh vegetables and fruits, yogurt, low-fat cottage cheese—" She burst out laughing at Sean's look of absolute horror. "Never mind. It's not nearly as bad as you think. This is what I've been eating for years."

"I suppose that means I can't have Margaret's biscuits," he said with a sigh.

"You can," Kelly said soothingly. "Just not so many of them."

"But I don't know how to cook these things!" Rose wailed.

"Nothing to it," Kelly said. "It's as easy as boiling water, most of it."

Sean looked relieved.

"This might not be so bad if you're willing to help us, Kelly."

"Absolutely," she said. "Now we'd better leave so you can rest." She had noticed he was looking fatigued.

"It was a kind thing you did in there," Rose said grudgingly when they were in the car.

"What?" Kelly asked.

"A body would never know you'd like to wash your hands of the lot of us."

"I hope I know better than to take it out on *him* because *you* are a nosy gossip."

"It won't do to upset him in his condition." She was silent for a moment as she negotiated traffic. "Did you mean it about helping us with the cooking for his diet?"

"Of course."

"I'd be grateful," Rose said humbly.

Kelly gave a deprecating little snort. She wasn't doing it for Rose, and she almost said as much.

"What about this festival?" Kelly asked instead.

"What about it?" Rose sighed. "As usual, my brother will host this great, noisy pagan festival making lots of extra work for us all and costing us money we can't afford to lose."

"It seems important to your brother," Kelly pointed out.

"And if it beggars us, we'll have the festival, then. It'll be hardest for poor Conor."

"The festival?"

Rose gave her a look that said she was dumber than dirt.

"Leaving the castle. It was to have been his. Can you imagine what it will be like for him to preside as the Summer Lord, knowing it will be for the last time?

"You think it would be better for him not to do it at all?"

"Of course, I do," Rose said bitterly. "But what *I* think doesn't matter. It'll be what Himself says that'll set the tune we'll all be dancing to."

Rose gave Kelly a sideways look.

"He fancies you, does Conor."

"Yeah, I look pretty good to him when he's been hoisting a few pints," Kelly said dryly.

Conor must think she was a pathetic bimbo. How could he respect her now that he knew she wore Victoria's Secret's finest for nobody?

When Rose dropped her off at the house, she got her laptop and headed off to one of the parlors on the fourth floor. She figured no one would look for her up there.

The light was beginning to go, and the display on her computer monitor glowed eerily. The parlor was one of the most beautiful in the castle, but it was rarely used because it was such a climb to the fourth floor. Kelly rubbed her tired eyes and just sat for a minute, appreciating her grand surroundings. The fine coating of dust and other signs of mild neglect just added to the atmosphere of elegant decadence.

The sun was sinking in the west, sending an orange glow through the ivory lace sheers and setting the ornate plaster border of medallions and leaves into sharp relief. Such delicate, meticulous work would crumble to dust at the touch of the demolition man's instruments. The fireplaces and light fixtures and lamps and perhaps the carved wooden moldings might be saved, but it would be far too much work to painstakingly cut around each panel of ornamental plasterwork and lift it out.

There were classical murals painted on the walls from Greek mythology. Perseus slew the Medusa on one wall. Cupid and Psyche went hand in hand to their bower. Around the ceiling a parade of Satyrs chased garland-crowned nymphs.

Kelly remembered how Conor had told her the stories of both myths in his bard's voice.

And because she couldn't bear to look at the beautiful, doomed room anymore, she went out into the night.

Ten

It was cold in the gardens, but Kelly needed the wind and the salt air to clear her head.

Who died and made *her* the savior of the world? She didn't *want* the job. It was too important. Life was simpler when all she had to worry about was keeping old Bradley from stabbing her in the back.

Now she was ready to jeopardize her job and her shot at VP for a bunch of people who couldn't keep their mouths shut about her personal business.

But although she was seriously irritated with them for blabbing her sordid little secret all over the parish, she had to do everything she could for them.

They were so *sweet*, you know?

Margaret, the mother hen.

Conor of the killer kisses.

Even Rose was beginning to grow on her, and Sean O'Meara—an old guy with twinkling Conor-eyes and a weak heart—utterly charmed her.

She was just kidding herself when she insisted she was fighting for the castle alone, although she was prepared to defend it with her last breath.

This little sculpture garden behind the castle was another

one of those places her soul knew before she came to Ireland. It did no good to tell herself she didn't believe in all that New Age crap.

In the moonlit darkness she could see the small weathered figures peeking at her from under the trees and around the bushes. There were gargoyles and elves and amazing half-human, half-animal forms she couldn't identify, all mixed in with figures straight out of Greek and Roman mythology. Serene goddesses stood in their marble draperies in grottoes of stone. An almost embarrassingly anatomically correct naked marble man pursued a marble maiden who didn't look as if she was trying too hard to escape. His fingertips were just a handspan from touching her arm.

Just like Kelly—almost touching Ireland and knowing it could never be hers.

There was a mist in the air, as usual, but she welcomed it. It made her feel alive. Sometimes it seemed as if she had never been alive until she came to Ireland.

When she looked at the castle itself she thought of the man who had bought it in those first vigorous days of the Republic. But out here in the romantically moonlit sculpture garden with its newly blossomed bushes she thought of the Englishman who built the castle before Conor's great-grandfather was born.

The sculpture garden was his contribution to the home he built for his bride in the excessive style of all things Gothic. How he must have eagerly anticipated her delight in this romantic place.

There would have been deep red roses and flowering trees. The remains of a cobalt blue and sea green mosaic surrounded a yew tree in the center of the garden where the crumbling brick paths converged. There was a miniature Greek-style temple before the mosaic, left open at the top and sides to look as if it were already in ruins at its creation, with a pretty bench just wide enough for two to sit.

This was where Kelly sat now, thinking of its long-dead creator and his desperation to bind the glorious creature that was his bride to him.

In the end it was to no purpose. The girl ran away with a younger man, anyway. Perhaps she even met with him secretly in this absurdly romantic temple.

Did she laugh at her husband behind his back with her virile young lover, the way these Irish laughed about Kelly behind *her* back?

"I used to sit here in the dark and think of him after Ghillie ran off to Dublin," Conor said, materializing out of the shadows and sitting beside her on the little bench. "I imagined I knew just how he felt."

Kelly wasn't surprised to see him, nor was she surprised that he spoke of the English lord as if he knew Kelly was thinking of him. Every brick, plant and tree in this romantic garden spoke of that long-dead, besotted man.

"And now she wants you back."

Conor shook his head.

"I represent . . ." He made a frustrated gesture. "Her youth, I suppose, or security. Dumb old Conor, who used to follow her around like a lovesick dog and let her walk all over him."

"Oh, Conor," said Kelly, standing and touching his cheek. "You are such a sweet man."

He smiled up at her and put his hand over hers so she couldn't pull it away.

"That's a kind way of putting it," he said ruefully, gently pulling on her arm so she would sit beside him again. "Ghillie doesn't want me back, Kelly. She won't stay. Once the girls have a taste for the city life, they won't be satisfied with this again. If they ever were."

He took a deep breath to signal a change of subject.

"Are you all right?" he asked, putting his arm around her. She couldn't help snuggling into his warmth. "Aunt Rose told me what happened at the shop. She and Aunt Margaret are both very sorry for it. And I am, too, of course."

"*You*? Don't tell me *you* were spreading it around, too!"

"No. But I know how it feels. Like betrayal. I've had to deal with it all my life, and from the people who should have been on my side."

"I thought it was because I'm an outsider."

"Not at all. The only difference is they weren't slagging you to your face about it. When Ghillie refused to marry me and went off to Dublin instead, I never heard the end of it. It's hard to have your pride when half the town is laughing at you and the other half is badgering you to find another girl and stop looking so glum."

"People around here need to get a life," Kelly said, putting her head on his shoulder.

"Gossip *is* their lives," he said, laying his cheek against the top of her head. "Aunt Margaret and Aunt Rose are worried because you didn't come to dinner and they couldn't find you. They're afraid you'll never speak to them again."

"I will," she said. "Just not yet."

"Understandable. If you're hungry and not ready to face them, I can sneak some food out of the kitchen and bring it to you."

He was so earnest and comforting.

"I'm not hungry," she said. *Not for food.*

"Well, then," he said, withdrawing his arm and standing up. He probably thought she wanted to be alone.

He was *so* wrong.

When the words came out of her mouth, Kelly wasn't sure where they came from.

"Conor, come up to my room?" she asked.

His breath caught.

"You're not meaning it," he said softly.

"Look, I'm not pledging undying love here. But, yeah, I mean it."

She couldn't look him in the eye, but she wasn't going to take it back or try to pass it off as a joke. Because it wasn't.

"No, I won't come to your room," he said softly.

"You don't want to," Kelly said, trying to sound casual. "Of course. Well, forget I asked. I'll just go—"

"Oh, I want to," he said. There was a goofy little grin on his face that made Kelly want to cover it with kisses. "Sweet Jesus, how I want to. But I can't do it here."

Even in the moonlight she could see the sudden color sear his cheekbones.

"You mean, ah, perform?" Kelly asked delicately.

"Not in the castle," he said, "where my aunts could walk in on us, or one of the guests on his way to use the loo might see me sneaking out afterwards."

Kelly closed her eyes.

"I get the picture. All right. I understand. No hard feelings," Kelly said, not sure whether she was relieved or disappointed.

Disappointed. Definitely.

She was going to go off somewhere and quietly die of humiliation. She had just propositioned an interim manager, and he had turned her down.

But when she would have gone back into the castle, he held onto her arm and brought her close.

He tilted her chin up and looked straight into her eyes.

"Come to the cottage with me."

Kelly's heart hammered against her ribs.

"Now?" she asked.

"It's not a bad night. A little cold, but you can have my jacket." He took it off and draped it around her shoulders like a cape. "Please?" he whispered.

"Yes," she said, putting her hand in his.

It was a clear, cool night, and the stars seemed so big and bright and close she could almost imagine they were walking through them. Kelly could smell the daffodils as they passed the beds carefully planted along the path to the castle.

Kelly, girl, you are in *way* over your head, she told herself.

She didn't care. She wanted Conor O'Meara like she wanted her next breath.

Eleven

Conor had never brought a woman to the cottage before. He thought of telling her that because she seemed so nervous and was trying so hard to act as if what would happen here wasn't important.

But his tongue stuck in his mouth. She was so beautiful with her hair all blown in the wind and her cheeks all pink with cold. Her eyes were huge in her pretty face, and so vulnerable.

"Nice place," she said casually, but her voice quavered a little. She clung to the jacket when he took it from her.

A look of panic crossed her face.

"Don't worry," he said, kissing her cheek. "It's all I'll be taking off for now."

She laughed, then, and relaxed, the saints be praised, although it seemed like blasphemy to invoke them now. It was cold in the cottage, so he gave her a little time to get used to being alone with him by building up the coal fire.

He probably should do the gentlemanly thing and give her a chance to back out, but he wanted her too badly.

"That feels good," Kelly said, holding her hands to the warmth.

He stood and cupped her face in his hands.

"Will you have a glass of beer?" he asked, feeling that he should offer her some refreshment. It seemed the hospitable thing to do.

"Beer?" She looked as if she'd never heard the word before.

"It should be wine, I know," he admitted, "but I don't have any. If you don't want beer, I can make tea. I don't have coffee."

"It's all right," she said with another of those nervous laughs. "I don't want anything, just—" She broke off and gave him a look that raised his blood pressure. "We could *talk* first," she suggested in a small voice.

He sat down in the big chair before the fire and pulled her into his lap.

"You're such a darling little thing," he said.

"No one *ever* calls me a little thing," she protested, but she put her arms around his neck and hugged him like a trusting child.

"That's enough talk, then," he said. He stood up with her cradled in his arms and carried her into his bedroom with the pretty blue curtains his aunts had starched and ironed and the bed he had made in the morning for a change, thank God. Most of the time he didn't bother.

"This is a first for me," she said, sounding shy.

A *first*? Conor was so surprised he had to clutch her tightly to keep from dropping her. He could feel her smile against his chest.

"Being carried to bed, I mean," she said.

He let out a sigh of relief. Or disappointment. He wasn't sure which. She'd probably laugh at him for either thought.

"I'm going to make love with an interim manager," Kelly whispered, as if she couldn't quite believe it.

"Only if you want to," he said solemnly.

"I want to."

There. She said it, right out loud.

Kelly would never be able to tell herself later that he swept her off her feet although, literally, he had. If he had simply come up to her room, she could have dismissed it later as a crime of passion. An impulse. But there had been that long, romantic walk in the moonlight with his jacket and his arm around her shoulders.

Plenty of time to back out if she had wanted to.

He reached for the top button on her blouse. His hand was trembling. Kelly was so touched that she put her arms around his neck and kissed him. He responded with an enthusiasm that took her breath away.

"I've wanted you for so long," he said.

"You've only known me for a week," she pointed out.

"Yes. A week of torture, following you up the stairs, and you in these lovely little short skirts that ride up when you sit down and—" He broke off, staring at her. He had undone enough buttons to bare the upper part of her bra. Wouldn't you know it would be red.

"Maybe we should turn out some of the lights," she said, suddenly shy. Now was when he found out the awful truth about her body.

"Not on your life," he said on a long, ecstatic breath. "This is even better than I imagined when Rose was blathering on and on about—"

"Got it," Kelly said dryly. "Now you can confirm the rumor for the lads at the pub."

"Not me," he said, kissing her. "They'd want to see for themselves, and then I'd have to kill them."

He gave her another one of those deep, almost reverent kisses, and she felt a thrill at the possessive tone of his voice as his clever fingers made short work of the rest of the buttons on her blouse. He broke off the kiss to unhook the front closure of the red lace bra.

"It occurs to me," she said, loving the feel of his hands on her body, "that things are a bit one-sided here."

"They look perfect to me," he said kindly as he took the weight of her freed breasts in his hands.

"I meant that it's my turn," she said, unbuttoning his shirt. Such lovely muscles he had, all covered with a light dusting of dark hair. He was magnificent.

When she reached for his zipper, he picked her up bodily and deposited her on wobbly legs next to the bed.

"My turn again," Conor said as she looked at him in confusion.

How lovely she looked with the proper little navy blouse open to reveal her full breasts and the red lace bra hanging on to her by the straps alone. He wanted to rip the rest of her clothes off, but he took a deep, steadying breath and forced himself to go slowly. He knelt before her and reached up to caress her breasts. Then he brought his hands down slowly over her rib cage, her navel and her belly. He felt every muscle in her body quiver when he kissed her on the bare skin just above the waistband of the prim little skirt. She gasped when he moved his hands to her hips.

"You are so beautiful," he said as he unzipped the skirt and released it to pool around her ankles.

She blushed so much that the top of her breasts were pink by the time she stood revealed to him in pantyhose over a tiny triangle of red lace. He started peeling down the pantyhose, kissing her smooth skin as he uncovered it. She sat back on the bed when he reached her knees. He carefully lifted each foot, removed the shoe and kissed her ankle as he released the foot from the pantyhose. Then he stood and raised her, holding her tightly to him as he kissed her. Her feet dangled above the floor.

Kelly thought she might die of pleasure when her bare skin touched Conor's body at full length.

Conor gave a sigh of contentment and buried his face in her hair. His big hands cradled her bottom as he lifted her higher. Then he kissed her and put her down. When he reached for his zipper, Kelly covered his hands with hers.

"Let me," she said throatily. She pushed his shirt the rest of the way off his arms. Then she unzipped his pants. He was wearing white cotton briefs. It made her smile. She put her fingers inside the elastic at the sides of his waist, but before she could pull his brief down, he grabbed her upper arms and raised her to her feet, crushing his lips against hers. Then he put his big, warm hands inside the elastic of her panties and slowly removed them, sinking to his knees before her and kissing her thighs all the way to the knees.

Kelly gasped when he kissed her right above the place where the blonde curls started. His thumbs reached lower, spreading the soft skin and finding the little nub that throbbed for him.

"Conor," she breathed. "Conor."

Conor kissed the damp mound, stood and took her arms to press her down on the bed. He quickly got out of his briefs and, without taking his eyes from Kelly's flushed face, opened the drawer to his night stand.

"Oh, thank God," Kelly said when he opened the little cellophane package. He would have put it on himself, but Kelly took it from him.

"Allow me," she said.

"Whatever the lady wants," he murmured. He lay back on the bed and closed his eyes when he felt Kelly's fingers roll the sheath over his engorged organ. No woman had ever performed this intimate service for him. Kelly's hands were not quite steady, which pleased him.

"I'm not hurting you, am I?" she asked when he groaned.

"No. God, no," he breathed.

When the condom was in place, he grasped Kelly's waist and lifted her to sheath himself inside her. He couldn't wait any longer. Her eyes grew round with surprise and then soft with pleasure. It took every ounce of Conor's control not to explode.

Kelly began riding him, whimpering with excitement as the pressure built within her. The abrasion of his chest against her breasts and his deep, passionate kisses, the heat coming in waves from his strong body, the feel of his hands kneading her buttocks and, most of all, his long, thrusting, powerful strokes drove her higher and higher until the orgasm broke free and caused her to scream with her release as he exploded with her.

"Oh, God. Oh, God," she whispered when she had collapsed on top of him.

Conor absorbed her shuddering aftershocks by holding

her tightly in his arms and drowning her in more of those deep, passionate kisses. She gave a giddy little burst of laughter.

"I'll never be the same again," she said, nestling close.

"Neither will I," he said solemnly.

For tonight she was his, no matter what happened tomorrow.

"I'm not through with you yet," Conor whispered in a tone of voice that made Kelly's toes curl. With a graceful movement he reversed their positions and entered her. He was fully erect again and ready to go.

With excruciatingly slow movements he started entering and withdrawing from her, over and over, until her nipples were hard, hungry pebbles against his chest.

"Do you want me to stop?" he asked when her cry of surprise burst against his lips.

"No," she said, shocked to feel herself start building again. "No, please. It's just . . . I've never been able to . . . ah . . ."

He murmured something tender and unintelligible just before the explosion came. Kelly saw little pinpricks of light beneath her closed lids as the pleasure enveloped her. She couldn't speak. She couldn't move. She just returned Conor's deep, almost reverent kisses and fell into oblivion.

She was so beautiful, so generous; so strong yet delicate.

In the moonlight from the window, Conor drank in the sight of Kelly's lovely face at sleep. There was a smile on her face as if she was having pleasant dreams.

Conor had worn her out.

Well, laddie, you don't need to be so proud of yourself, he thought. *You almost went off like a boy with his first sweetheart before you barely had her clothes off.*

Conor was too euphoric to sleep. He folded back the sheet covering her.

Just a look, he told himself. Her breasts were so round and full.

Then a touch.

Then a taste.

Surely it wasn't chivalrous, but he would stop at that.

Any moment now.

Kelly opened her eyes wide and gave a loud gasp to find Conor leaning over her with her left breast in his mouth. One of his hands was caressing her thigh.

Now, laddie, there will be hell to pay.

"I'm sorry," he whispered as he kissed her lovely, sleep-warmed face. Amazingly, she still smelled like flowers. "I couldn't resist."

To his relief, she kissed him back.

Kelly knew she should be mad at him for groping her body while she slept. It didn't get any more politically incorrect than this. But her body was so aroused that she couldn't do anything but return his deep, feverish kisses as his hands roamed all over her languid body. To her surprise, he pulled her out of the warm bed to stand before him. Slowly he ran his hands down the sides of her breasts to her waist. Then he bent his head and kissed her, melding their hot bodies together. His full erection pressed against her stomach.

When he grasped her bottom in his strong hands and lifted her, she gave a cry of mingled surprise and pleasure and held onto his shoulders for dear life.

Conor shook his head to clear it a little when Kelly wrapped her gloriously long, smooth legs around his waist. His hands were still supporting her firm, round bottom, so he lifted her just a little higher and sheathed himself in her. She gasped with excitement and placed frantic little kisses all over his face.

He was afraid he might drop her, so he turned and braced her against the wall as they rode each other to shattering fulfillment. As he kissed her neck, she slid bonelessly down his body.

Kelly's knees were so weak she would have melted into a sweaty little heap on the floor if Conor hadn't held onto her. From the harsh sound of his breathing, she suspected that he wasn't much steadier than she was.

He sat her on the bed and sank to his knees in front of her, cupped her face in his hands and kissed her.

"All this time, I thought that position was a myth," she gasped when she could talk.

"So did I," Conor agreed shakily as Kelly lay back and scooted over in invitation.

Kelly cocked a suspicious eyebrow at him when he stretched out beside her.

"Oh, sure," she said, as she braced herself on one elbow to look at his face. "Like I'm going to believe you've never done that before."

"I'll be thanking you for the compliment. But it's true. I imagine few women are athletic enough to—"

"Hah! I'll bet your old buddy Ghillie has enough flexibility to tie herself in knots, besides weighing 90 pounds soaking wet."

Oh, that was bright, Kelly. Invite comparisons with Ghillie of the perfect dancer's body while you're naked.

Conor laughed and pulled her on top of him to kiss her lips in apparent delight. He settled her into the crook of his arm.

"As Ghillie and I had to be doing it in my car—"

"Your *car*?"

"Well, yes," he said, blushing a little. "We couldn't do it at the castle or her parents' house, and this cottage was rented to tenants, so there was no help for it. I had to drive forty miles for rubbers so I wouldn't be recognized buying them. I was nineteen. Thank God our parents never found out."

"I suppose these are from the same box," Kelly said skeptically as she gestured toward the bedside table.

"No. I burned the rest for fear my aunts or my father would find them. I bought these just for you."

"Well! That was confident of you."

"Hopeful," he corrected, kissing her again.

He pulled her into his arms so her head was pillowed on his chest. She yawned like a sleepy kitten and was soon fast asleep.

• • •

Kelly opened her eyes and squinted at the soft gray light of day streaming in through the windows.

Conor was still asleep, and Kelly couldn't help caressing the part of his muscular chest exposed by the sheet. As she watched in fascination, all of his stomach muscles tightened and he opened his eyes.

With a look of absolute adoration on his face, he reached for her.

Then a knock sounded at the door of the cottage.

"Who's that?" Kelly whispered.

Her eyes showed white all around as she clutched the sheet to her chest. "Maybe they'll go away if we're quiet."

"Conor!" called a voice from outside.

Conor sank his head in his hands.

"Not bloody likely," he said. "They have a key."

"Omigod," breathed Kelly.

The key turned in the lock.

"Conor! Are you here?" Aunt Rose called out sharply. Conor looked at the alarm clock by his bed and groaned.

Almost noon.

"The cows weren't milked," Aunt Margaret said, sounding concerned. "And there was no feed in the yard for the chickens. Poor boy. He must be sick."

Footsteps approached the bedroom.

"They're coming in here," Kelly whispered. She looked as if she wanted to die of embarrassment.

"That, they're not," Conor said firmly as he pulled on his jeans and padded across the floor in his bare feet.

Talk about coming to earth with a bang!

Conor closed the door behind him just as Margaret had been about to turn the knob.

"Conor," she said, scandalized by his state of undress. "What are you doing in bed at this hour? Are you sickening for something?"

Rose crossed her arms across her chest.

"Don't be a fool," she scoffed. "The truth is written all over his deceitful face. He's got a woman in there!"

"Come into the kitchen," Conor said, determined not to step from the door until they were well away from it.

"Who is it?" Aunt Rose demanded, her eyes snapping, "as if I didn't have a strong suspicion."

"None of your business," he said, taking Rose's arm when she would have gone into the bedroom to see for herself. "I'm a man grown, and no saint."

"And *she*—" Rose began belligerently.

"You'll leave her out of this," he said sternly. "If you've anything to say, you'll be saying it to me."

"Conor, how could you, today of all days," Margaret said, "with your father at the hospital waiting for us to fetch him?"

"I knew her kind the minute I saw her," Rose said maliciously.

"You'll be leaving your nasty tongue off of her," Conor shouted. "*I* am the one at fault here."

"*She*—" Rose began.

"I *mean* it, Aunt Rose," he said. "What right do you have to come here snooping—"

Margaret gave a sob and turned away.

Conor hated seeing either of his aunts cry, but he wouldn't let Rose talk that way about Kelly.

"We were worried about you, so we brought you some lunch," Margaret said, gesturing with the covered plate in her hands.

"Come to the kitchen," Conor said again. There was no way he was going to expose Kelly to Rose's spitefulness.

To his surprise, Kelly quietly opened the door to the bedroom and came out. She had tried to make herself presentable, but there was no concealing the fact that she had been loved thoroughly and well. There was whisker burn on her cheeks and nose. Her hair was all tangled. And there was a long run in her stockings. She was carrying one shoe. He'd have to help her look for the other one when he got rid of his aunts.

She was blushing furiously, but her chin was up. How like her to refuse to let him take the blame alone.

"Just as I suspected," Rose announced dramatically.

Conor gave her a warning look.

"What I'd like to know is when we'll be having the wedding," Margaret said.

"Wedding!" croaked Kelly. "What are you talking about? Nobody said anything about—"

Conor put his arm around her shoulders.

"We'll talk about this later," he said firmly as his eyes sent an unmistakable message to his aunts.

"You've compromised the girl, Conor," Margaret said gently. "You have no choice but to be marrying her."

Rose gave Kelly a poisonous look.

"She's had her eye on him from the beginning," she said darkly.

"No more of *that*," Conor said with steel in his voice.

He herded his aunts to the door.

"Go up to the castle. We'll be there soon."

Rose gave an affronted sniff and walked out the door with her head held high.

Margaret, looking troubled, started to speak. Then, looking down at the plate in her hands as if she didn't know how it got there, she hesitated and handed it to Conor.

"Don't look so worried, dear," she said to Kelly. "He's a good man, our Conor, and he'll do right by you."

She kissed her on the cheek and hurried out to the car.

"Well," said Kelly, letting out her breath in a little puff of air that blew her bangs out from her face. "That was awkward, wasn't it?"

"I've had better mornings," he said wryly, "but never a better night."

"Thanks," she said, giving him a sad smile. "Don't worry. I'll be gone in a month or so, and the Rosary Sodality will move on to other things."

"Or I can make an honest woman out of you." He tried to say it casually, but it was too important. It came out in a croak.

"Oh, Conor," Kelly said, putting her arms around him and

kissing his cheek. "You don't have to marry me just because we went to bed together."

This made his humiliation complete. She was talking to him as if he was a lovesick idiot, which, of course, he was. It wasn't just the way it was with them in bed. It was her kind heart, her intelligence, her energy, and her attraction to all that was beautiful that made him love her.

"That's me. Always the gentleman," he said, forcing himself to smile.

He went past her and into the bedroom to find his shirt and socks. The sheets would smell of her flower scent until he washed them, he supposed. He found the toe of her other shoe peeking out from under his chest of drawers.

Kelly was looking at his books when he came out.

"I haven't read Shakespeare since I was in college," she said, accepting her shoe from him with a nod of thanks.

"The bard is better company on a winter night than the telly," he said.

Kelly thought of him in this cozy room with a coal fire burning and a book in his hands. What would it be like to share it with him and make love with him in his bed every night? It was a full bed, not even a queen like she had in her apartment in Chicago.

Such a simple life.

How could she have thought she could fit into this world?

Kelly was very much afraid that she loved him enough to try, even if it would probably ruin his life and hers.

It's just sex, Kelly told herself a little desperately. It can't be love. Not yet. It was too soon. They had nothing in common. They came from separate worlds. It would never work out.

"Well," she said, forcing herself to smile brightly at him. "Ready to face the music?"

He took her in his arms and kissed her.

It tasted very much like good-bye.

She clung to him for a minute, and then she walked out into the gray, drizzly day.

"God. What were we thinking?" she said in despair. "We had to be crazy."

Conor took her hand. She wrested it away from him.

"Crazy is as good a word for it as any," he said bleakly.

"I went to bed with an interim manager," she said as if it was the most terrible thing in the world. "If this gets back to Matthew Lawrence, I'm dead meat."

Her bloody career. What a fool he had been, thinking that last night was as important to her as it was to him.

"And I did it without protection—twice," she said. "Like some adolescent bimbo overcome by lust. Whoever heard of a thirty-two-year-old unwed mother?"

"Then you'd be marrying me, of course," Conor said.

"Conor, where I come from you don't have to get married just because you got knocked up."

"I don't have much to offer a wife, so I'm not blaming you for running away."

"Running away?" she said, turning to him in outrage.

It started raining harder.

"Yes! Running away!" he shouted over the sound of the rain. "From me and what happened between us."

"Nothing happened," she said.

"*Everything* happened, and you know it!"

Her eyes were wild when she grabbed his shoulders and forced him to face her.

"All right!" she shouted. "*Everything* happened. But this isn't my world. I feel off-balance here. Wrong. Out of control. Every time you kiss me—every time you touch me—my brain short-circuits and my hormones take over."

"And you don't like it," he said.

She gave a bitter laugh.

"I *do* like it. Too much. It makes me feel alive, but it's not real. I'll never fit in. What would I *do* here? Join the Rosary Sodality? Keep a shop?"

"I see." He turned to face ahead so she couldn't see the hurt on his face. "You're too good for me."

"That's not true!" she snapped. "I'm *not* too good for you. I'm just different."

"And what we did last night was perfectly ordinary— something you've experienced hundreds of times with other men in America?"

"Yeah. Right," she said, giving him a look that said he was dumb as a post. "It was incredible, and you know it."

"I know it," he said, putting his arm around her shoulder and turning so he blocked the lashing wind from her as they walked through the rain. "Poor little Yank." He grimaced as a torrent of water washed under his collar. "Aunt Rose would say we're reaping the punishment for our sin."

"That's just the kind of thing I mean," Kelly said. "If we got married, thirty years from now they'd be telling our children how we did the wild thing in the cottage and got surprised the morning after by your aunts. I'd always be known in the village as the Yank with the red underwear who trapped you into marriage."

Conor shut his mouth firmly.

Why bother arguing?

Kelly Sullivan would never marry him.

His heart sank into his shoes.

How humiliating. He had been thinking in terms of marriage and forever last night when she gave herself to him so generously, and to her he was only what the Americans call a one-night stand.

Up ahead, the castle was in sight.

In spite of her wet and bedraggled condition, Kelly felt her heart lift when she saw it, as if it were home.

She was *so* confused. Her heart had melted when Conor shielded her from the rain with his body. She felt cherished, even though she could tell he was angry with her. Even now, in the lashing rain with the mud sticking to her shoes and splattering against her legs, he could make her pulse race.

When they got to the castle, Kelly would have gone straight to her room if Conor hadn't grabbed her arms and pulled her against his chest to kiss her within an inch of her life.

She tasted passion and anger and frustration, but because he was Conor he looked deeply into her eyes, cupped her face in his hands and caressed her cheekbones almost reverently with his thumbs before he released her. She bit her lip and ran up the stairs at a reckless pace, not caring if she broke her neck.

Conor had tasted the salt of her tears when he kissed her.

She might still go back to Chicago. He might never see her again once she did. But she wanted him. He would never be surer of anything in his life.

He also knew that the surest way to lose her forever was to hold on too tightly.

Conor squared his shoulders and went purposefully into the kitchen where he found his aunts putting dishes away. They'd gone silent and looked guilty when they saw him, so he knew exactly what they were talking about when he interrupted them.

"There you are," Rose said, primed for battle.

"I'll say this once," Conor told his aunts angrily. "What happened in that cottage is between Kelly and me. I don't want this making the rounds in the village."

"Conor, I—" began Margaret.

"And for *your* information," he said to Margaret, "she said no."

Margaret touched Conor's arm. He knew her gentle soul saw past the anger and straight to the hurt in his heart.

"She'll change her mind if she's the one for you," Margaret said softly.

Conor couldn't stand the pity in her eyes. He wondered if everyone in County Cork knew he was in love with Kelly Sullivan.

Twelve

"You're going to love this," Kelly promised Sean as she stirred a pot of oatmeal on the stove, causing Rose to sniff and look martyred. It was Sean's first full day home from the hospital, but it didn't take him long to size up the interesting dynamics that had invaded the castle in his absence.

Rose was cooking the traditional full Irish breakfast of bangers, rashers, and eggs for the guests. The American girl appeared to have designated herself caretaker for the bloody low-fat diet Sean was doomed to follow if he wanted to live.

He had been so tired and worn out and heartsick at the thought of seeing the castle go out of the family, he wasn't sure he *wanted* to live. But somehow when he woke up in that hospital with all the tubes in his arms and the pretty nurses fussing over him, he decided he might as well stay on this earth a while longer and see what more God was willing to provide in the way of entertainment. The arrival of his sisters and his son all tearful with joy made him wonder why he had been willing to give it all up. The nurses had told him how devotedly Margaret, Rose, and Conor had kept vigil at his bedside while he was in a coma. Sean guessed it took something like this to show a man how much his family loved him.

Even when he had failed them.

As for entertainment, here was this pretty American whose tender ministrations over his porridge almost made up for the loss of the rashers he could hear spattering cheerfully in Rose's skillet.

Rose, of course, was ready to scream at the intrusion of the Yank into her kitchen. Very set in her ways was Rose. All she had done was complain about the low-fat diet and how much work it was going to be, which shocked the little Yank, who assumed Rose cared more for her own convenience than she did for her brother's health.

She didn't know that was just Rose, frustrated because she felt powerless to protect her brother from whatever threatened him. Rose had a warm heart under that prickly manner, but Sean wouldn't tell Kelly. It was too pleasant to watch her busy herself cooking his breakfast, carefully explaining what she was putting into it as if *he* would ever have cause to do it for himself. His sisters would send him about his business with stinging ears if he took a notion to mess around in *their* kitchen.

The Yank probably didn't realize it, but Rose was being unusually forbearing despite all her disapproving sniffs in the Yank's direction.

Kelly shot Rose cool looks, not giving an inch.

Sean sat back and smiled.

Yes, the good Lord *did* have a bit more to offer Sean in the way of entertainment after all.

Kelly took the pot off the stove and put it on a thick cloth on the table so Sean could watch her prepare the rest of the porridge. She ignored Rose, indicating she didn't expect Rose to exert herself to take care of her own brother. Obviously the ladies had clashed before, and Kelly had made it clear she'd be taking no more harsh words from Miss Rose O'Meara.

"First you stir in the peanut butter," Kelly was telling him. "This'll be great. I got the recipe off the Internet."

It was a pleasure to watch her in her prim suit and her hair all pulled up with matching combs. She was a neat little creature. So far she had kept from getting a spot on her clothes.

"When it gets gooey, you put in some cinnamon." She paused to shake the spice in and released a tantalizing aroma into the kitchen. "Irish oatmeal is the *best*."

Ah, but she had a lovely smile. It *almost* made up for the rashers. "Now for some protein powder."

"Instead of meat," Sean said wistfully, allowing himself a soulful gaze at Rose's skillet.

"This is better," Kelly said reprovingly.

Rose sniffed again.

"Now you want to put in more cinnamon, and then you add the chopped apples."

"It smells good," Sean said.

Kelly rewarded him with an approving smile.

"And it's done," she said, pouring the porridge into two heavy ceramic bowls. "Except for a little cinnamon sprinkled on top."

She set one serving in front of Sean and handed him a spoon.

"Enjoy!" she said, smiling again.

Eh, a man would gladly eat rat poison if it was administered along with a smile like that.

"Delicious," he said after his first bite, watching the anxious little furrow in Kelly's forehead smooth out. Bless the girl, she really had a kind heart.

Then Conor walked in and her face changed altogether.

Ah, so it cuts both ways, Sean thought. He hadn't missed the way Conor's voice changed whenever he spoke the girl's name. She was a city girl, and a fancy one at that, and so she was bound to go back to America soon enough. But a man could dream.

"Here's your chicken, Aunt Rose," Conor said, lifting the plastic bag to show her.

Rose gave him a stiff nod.

"You *killed* it?" Kelly asked, looking shocked.

"Don't worry. The end was quick," he said mockingly as

he put the dead chicken in the refrigerator. "What have you there?"

"Kelly made some porridge for me," Sean said. "It's delicious."

"It smells lovely," Conor said, giving Kelly a look that made her blush. She dipped her spoon into her own serving of porridge and gave him a taste. "It's good."

"All this fuss over a bit of porridge," Rose muttered.

Conor turned at once and snatched a rasher with the speed and precision of a hungry wolf.

"Conor, that's for the guests," Rose scolded. She had been up before any of them, Sean knew, laying out the ingredients for breakfast, brewing the coffee, and lighting the coal fires in the common rooms. Her brow was moist with perspiration and the heat from the fire. Her skin was tough from being blistered with decades' worth of spattering grease from decades' worth of rashers.

And here was pretty little Kelly being praised to the skies for cooking a pot of porridge.

Sean could hardly blame Rose for being put out, but he knew that she would treat a direct attempt to soothe her ruffled feathers with contempt.

"Ah, I'd sell my soul for one of Rosie's rashers," he said with a sigh. He didn't miss the way his sister's face softened. "Do you think one wee rasher will put me back in the hospital?" He deferred to Kelly, since she had designated herself the keeper of the low-fat diet.

"I don't suppose so," she said.

Rose smiled and selected one of the rashers from the platter, then she blotted it on a paper towel as if her life depended on it.

There were few things in life more pleasant, Sean thought with satisfaction, than to have adoring women fussing over a man. Conor gave a snort of good-natured derision as if he knew exactly what Sean was thinking.

"When *I* snuck a rasher, it was for the guests," Conor pointed out, trying to sound wistful. The boy was good,

Sean had to admit, but he wasn't in his old man's class yet when it came to breaking down the ladies' defenses.

"You'll have your breakfast after the guests have had theirs," Rose said sternly, although Sean could see she was pleased at having the men's attention removed from Kelly's porridge for the moment.

Sean didn't miss the way that Kelly glanced at Rose to make sure she wasn't paying attention to her and took another piece of bacon that she quickly hid in the paper towel.

"Do you want me to take those in?" Kelly asked when Rose prepared the first two plates.

"I can be serving the guests myself, as I've been doing for thirty years and more," Rose told her.

"You're welcome," Kelly said pertly.

Rose just shook her head at her and glided into the guest dining room. As soon as she was gone, Kelly stepped up to Conor and fed him the rasher she'd stolen from the platter. He closed his eyes and ate it from her hand. Sean could see a pulse throb in Kelly's throat.

Sean stared at his porridge to give them a bit of privacy. The look on his son's face was so vulnerable. He had never seen him look like that, not even when he fancied himself in love with Ghillie.

There was so much tension in the air. So much expectation. If they weren't lovers yet, they would be soon.

He said a silent prayer that his boy's heart would not be too damaged in the process. For all his handsome looks and easy manners, Conor did not give his heart easily or freely.

Sean hoped Kelly understood that.

When breakfast was over, Kelly rinsed out the porridge pot and bowls so the gluelike substance would not stick to them, had her offer of help with the dishes rebuffed by Rose, and excused herself by saying she had to work on her spreadsheet. Conor caught up with her at the foot of the stairs and held a piece of bacon in front of her face.

Grinning, she ate it in small, dainty bites.

"You devil," she said, close to rapture. "You didn't blot it."

"And take away most of the flavor?" he said in mock dismay. He ended the sentence in a groan when she took the last of the bacon from his hand and slowly licked the grease from his fingers with those beautiful eyes staring into his.

"You're killing me, lass," he breathed.

She gave him a smug grin and evaded his attempt to kiss her.

"It's too bad I didn't get a chance to wash my hands after I killed the chicken," he said in a tone of regret.

Kelly's eyes widened with dismay, and she gave a sharp gasp as she looked up at him. He gave her a quick kiss on her parted lips.

"Gotcha," he whispered.

Then, whistling, he went on his way, repressing the desire to look back at the expression on her face.

Kelly gave an involuntary shiver and commanded her pulse to slow down before she had a heart attack.

The O'Meara men were lethal—both of them.

She shook her head to clear it of distracting thoughts. *Back to work*, she told herself firmly as she continued on her way to get her laptop. It was like a slap in the face to hear Ghillie's voice when she got to the lobby.

The red-haired beauty had stopped Conor on his way outdoors and was looking up into his face with her green eyes sparkling. Her long curly hair was gathered in a high ponytail to expose her long, graceful neck. If he chose to look—and what normal man wouldn't—the cleft between her firm, round breasts was clearly visible above the scoop neckline of her form-fitting, emerald green sweater. Her graceful floral skirt displayed her trim ankles and elegant calves. Her full lips were glossy with candy pink lipstick as she pouted up at Conor, who was smiling down at her in a friendly manner.

"I had to wait to hear from my sister that your father had come home from the hospital," she scolded flirtatiously. "Shame on you for not ringing me."

"You didn't have to wait long," he pointed out, mocking her tone. "He only came home yesterday, and he was asleep before I cut the engine on the car. He was too tired to be having company to visit."

Ghillie pursed those pretty lips.

"And since when, Conor O'Meara, am *I* company?"

"You're dressed like company," he said, smiling indulgently, "and looking pretty enough to give him another stroke if you're not careful. He's in the kitchen having a cup of tea, if you'd care to go in."

Conor looked over Ghillie's bright curls to see Kelly watching them, and the smile faded from his face.

Kelly felt like a fool at being caught eavesdropping.

Ghillie turned to see what had distracted Conor and gave Kelly a cool stare.

"Well, if it isn't Herself," she said with a bitter smile.

"Good morning," Kelly said, forcing herself to be pleasant. "Don't mind me. I'm just passing through."

She deliberately avoided looking at Conor on her way to the staircase.

I'm just passing through, she repeated to herself.

Thirteen

Amazingly, Kelly's life fell into a pleasant routine, even though she was sure she was still known as the Yank with the red underwear throughout the village.

Ghillie was a frequent visitor, ostensibly to Sean, who basked in the beautiful girl's attention even though he had to know her real object in hanging around the castle was to see Conor rather than himself.

Kelly didn't mind Ghillie so much because Conor all but ignored her. Ghillie would have had to be blind not to realize Conor only had eyes for Kelly. It alternately thrilled and horrified her.

Kelly had a well-developed incest taboo that kicked in automatically whenever she felt even the slightest attraction to a business associate or member of an interim staff. Conor had somehow short-circuited that taboo the minute she met him.

Her life in Chicago seemed more and more like a distant dream.

It took all the discipline at her command to concentrate on the dozens of e-mail messages she received from her office. All these memos and directives and the snatches of office gossip used to demand her immediate action. Now they were unwelcome distractions from her work at the castle and from the comfortable simplicity that was her life in Ireland.

With Sean, the patriarch, at Whitlock Castle, the O'Meara family circle was complete, and his unqualified acceptance of Kelly secured her place in it. The old rascal loved sitting on the sofa in the living room between Kelly and Ghillie, enjoying their subtle competition for his favor.

Margaret had welcomed Kelly from the first, but even Rose finally had unbent and accepted Kelly's presence at Whitlock Castle. She had even started consulting Kelly about how to adapt the usual Irish recipes to conform with Sean's diet.

Kelly was losing her edge and her objectivity about this project. It did no good to tell herself it was just another assignment, another stepping stone to the title of Vice President of Guest Services for which she had worked so hard. She thought of what used to be her primary goal and willed herself to care about it. She closed her eyes and visualized her dream office, one of the tangible results that would come with the title of VP. Visualization was an important part of success.

Mentally, she had already chosen the furniture—a glossy plexiglass conference table with leather chairs, the rich Eurostyle black desk with the matching in-out boxes, the 10-karat gold letter opener, the minimalist, almost spartan simplicity of white walls and Japanese prints in black and deep rose and white to pull it all together. She had already purchased the tall, graceful black porcelain vase for her desk that she would keep supplied with single stems of perfect roses, lilies, or orchids. Her desk drawer would contain boxes of jasmine tea for stolen moments of peace to add balance to her hectic, challenging days.

A gleaming red BMW would seal her status in the eyes of her peers, even though driving in Chicago traffic was her concept of hell, and most of the time she found it more convenient to walk or cab it around the city instead of getting her six-year-old car out of the indoor parking bay she rented by the month.

The visualization failed utterly to work its magic, for once. Instead, she wondered if the pub owner's wife had had her baby yet, if Sam from New Jersey was *ever* going to come through with his quote for the reproduction elevator, and if Conor would forget all about her after she had gone back to her old life. When once she had not permitted animal fats to cross her lips, she eagerly devoured the juicy breakfast meats, even after Conor explained in clinical detail exactly how they made black pudding.

She needed distance, she told herself a little desperately one night in bed as she failed to be soothed by the mingled scents of the lavender-, ylang-ylang-, and barley-filled dream pillow she had purchased in one of the village shops and the coal fire that had been carefully sealed with slag to contain the warmth for the chilly night.

It was March, about to turn into April. She had spent almost a third of her life—ten years—aiming with deadly accuracy at her goal of success in the hotel industry and now, when she was on the verge of realizing her ambition, it had lost its savor.

She had been gone from Chicago and Lawrence Hotels too long. Once back at Corporate, she would recover her edge. She needed to get away from Ireland, from Whitlock Castle, from Sean O'Meara's warm family circle.

From Sean O'Meara's handsome son.

But when the summons came, she was not prepared for it.

The evening that Kelly was told she had to leave Ireland, Sean, Conor, and both his aunts were sitting in the lobby area close to the front desk while Kelly read her e-mail. She was in the habit of checking her messages in the evening and composing replies right away so her office would receive them when Lawrence opened for business at 8 A.M.—which would be 2 P.M. Irish time. In Ireland it was now nine o'clock in the evening—3 P.M. in Chicago—and Kelly was staying close to the phone in case anyone from Lawrence called or wanted to patch her into a conference call or meeting.

Since Sean had come home from the hospital, he often stayed in the lobby area reading or holding court with the bed-and-breakfast guests to keep Kelly company, and she had found she enjoyed having him around. Because Sean was in the lobby, his sisters and Conor tended to gather there in the evening instead of using the family parlor. It was as if they needed to be with Sean every possible moment because they had come so close to losing him.

He was such a darling old guy, Kelly thought affectionately.

She and Conor had continued their conspiracy to shield his father from knowledge of Matthew Lawrence's plan to wreck the interior, which wasn't easy because Sean was vitally interested in the restoration work he expected Lawrence to undertake to transform the castle into a luxury hotel. He peppered Kelly and each craftsman she invited to the castle with questions and suggestions.

"Conor, I have some papers for you to sign," Sean said one evening, "but you're going to have to do it in the presence of the solicitor."

"No, Da," Conor objected, his face full of reluctance. "Surely there's time to spare for that—"

"There's not, boyo, and you know it," Sean said quietly. "I could be sent back into the coma any day. If that happens, you'd better have the legal right to take care of things here."

Kelly's heart thudded in her chest to hear the lovable man talk so calmly about his own mortality.

Obviously, Conor felt the same way.

"You've got years left—" he began.

"Only if God wills," Sean said. "I want you to read these papers over so the solicitor can answer your questions at the signing. We'll go tomorrow."

Conor lowered his head so his face was hidden from her, but Kelly's eyes misted in sympathy. Conor had no choice but to accept, for he must know his father was right. Conor needed to have the right to act as power of attorney in case his father fell into another coma and was unable to take care of his own and his family's business affairs. This was especially crucial at this stage of the sale to Lawrence Hotels.

Margaret and Rose remained silent. Sean clearly was handing over to Conor his responsibility for taking care of his sisters and, being women, they were to abide by their menfolk's decision.

The fact that two grown, intelligent, perfectly capable women in their sixties would see nothing illogical in sitting quietly while their brother presumed to give his thirty-year-old son responsibility for them was *so* Irish, Kelly thought. It obviously didn't occur to either woman to offer an opinion in the matter. The weird thing was, the O'Mearas were beginning to make sense to her.

Kelly was so engrossed in the drama that she jumped when the phone rang.

"Whitlock Castle," she said into the mouthpiece. The familiar voice at the other end of the line made her straighten up in her chair. "Matthew! How are things in Chicago?"

The sound of her boss's voice had the effect of a dousing in cold water.

She glanced over at the O'Mearas when three heads bobbed up to stare at her with identical expressions of curiosity on their faces.

Conor's eyes had narrowed in unwelcome suspicion.

He knows how much Matthew's voice makes my skin crawl, she realized, feeling exposed.

"I'm good," she answered in response to Matthew's inquiry. Had her boss always sounded so oily and sinister?

"Next week?" she said weakly, failing utterly to keep the reluctance out of her voice.

Conor's jaw hardened, and he made a movement that revealed his quickly checked impulse to come to her.

"I don't know if I can wrap up the project that quickly," she said, mentally chiding herself for sounding so wimpy. "I may not be able to get a flight out—"

"We'll take care of all that," Matthew interrupted silkily as if he were giving her good news. "The tickets will be waiting for you at the Aer Lingus reservation desk at the airport."

"Well, then," Kelly said, forcing herself to sound as if he had laid all her objections to rest. "I'll be there. I knew about the annual meeting, of course, but usually those of us who are out in the field are excused from it, so I thought—"

"Yes, I know," he interrupted again, "but I'd like you to bring me up to speed on the project personally."

The intimate way his voice deepened on the word "personally" made Kelly's heart sink.

She could feel Conor's eyes burning into the back of her head and risked a look at him.

All the veins in his neck were standing out.

"I'm having a little cocktail party here at the house on Saturday," Matthew continued. "I hope you can make it. Your parents will be here, too."

"Excellent," Kelly said, forcing enthusiasm into her voice. "I'll enjoy seeing Linda. It's been a long time." The mention of her boss's wife, Kelly hoped, would make it clear that her relationship with Matthew was strictly business as far as she was concerned, even though she knew that Matthew's marriage was on the rocks and had been for some time.

Kelly always made it clear in the least offensive manner possible that she didn't have affairs with married men, and if he got the impression that she had no other objection to a more intimate relationship with him, she was hardly to blame.

It was an uncomfortable tightrope she walked, actively campaigning for the promotion to vice president while pretending to misunderstand Matthew's overtures.

She felt like sagging with relief when she hung up the phone. Talking to Matthew, as always, had left her emotionally exhausted. Instead, she forced herself to smile at the four pairs of concerned O'Meara eyes staring at her.

"Mr. Lawrence?" Sean guessed.

"I should have told him you were here. He probably would have wanted to say hello," Kelly lied.

She had told Matthew when Sean came out of the coma, but he had greeted the information with indifference. The arrangement of flowers that had been sent to Sean's hospital room with the card signed with Matthew's name had been ordered by Kelly.

"When do you leave?" Conor asked quietly.

"Thursday," she said, forcing herself to meet his eyes.

"And you'll be coming back when?" he asked with an edge to his voice.

"The following Tuesday," she said easily. "Just time enough to recover from the jet lag only to have to go through it all over again."

"We'll take you out to dinner Wednesday night to the pub," Margaret said cheerfully. "To celebrate your birthday."

Her birthday. She had almost forgotten it.

Kelly's heart swelled. They were such sweet people.

"You'll be glad to see your parents," Sean said comfortably.

"Of course," she said, straining to smile at his innocence.

Her parents. They barely realized she was gone.

Later Conor came to her in the Peacock Room. He knew her well enough, it seemed, to know she went there when she was troubled. He leaned over the writing desk to face her, bracing his arms on either side of the laptop. His sleeves were rolled up, revealing the strong muscles of his forearms and the sculptured tension of his wrists. The room was in semidarkness because the only light came from the eerie glow of the computer screen and the muted radiance of the jade and peach-colored glass of a Tiffany lamp by the door. His eyes were alive with earnestness in his shadowed face.

"Don't go," he said simply.

She could have treated it lightly. Laughed it off with a joke or a cool comment. But he had sensed her distress and she would not insult him by trivializing his concern.

"I have no choice," she said. "A summons to Corporate is the same as a royal command."

"You are afraid of him." It was a statement, not a question.

"Just a bit uncomfortable," she said, not looking him in the eye. "About the time I left Chicago, he started making sexual innuendos, only you can tell he's not kidding, if you know what I mean. He's been known to get pretty ugly with female employees who won't play."

"I thought they frowned on that sort of thing in America," he said. "Aren't there laws?"

"Sure, if you want to commit political suicide," Kelly said bitterly. "If I play my cards right, I could nail that promotion this weekend."

"You would . . . give yourself to this man for a promotion?" Conor asked incredulously. The veins were sticking out on his neck again.

Kelly smiled wryly.

"No," she said taking a deep breath. "I'm not talking about 'giving myself' to him in the sexual sense. Just letting him believe I might. It's done all the time, no matter what the law says. Consenting adults, you know. Unfortunately, I'm an old-fashioned girl. I want to get ahead by *earning* that promotion, not by playing footsie with the boss."

"Nothing is worth that," Conor told her.

Kelly rubbed her tired eyes and came around the desk to peer into his shadowed face. He put his hands on her shoulders.

"Are you so sure?" Kelly asked. "Maybe you don't think a promotion is worth it, but what about Whitlock Castle? Can you look me in the eye and say saving Whitlock Castle wouldn't be worth any sacrifice?"

Conor's fingers tightened on her arms.

"Yes," he said without hesitation. "It doesn't matter if you don't actually go to bed with him. It's what it would do to *you*, if you let him believe you would."

"Oh, Conor," Kelly said wistfully. "When did you get to be so wise?"

"Don't go," he said again.

"Have to. Apart from the fact that I can't disobey a direct

order, it's the only way to solidify my political position. I haven't met with the members of my team in person for too long. If I fail to show up for the annual meeting, it will lead to serious doubts about my commitment."

"Tell them you're sick, then."

"Worst thing I can do. Sickness translates into weakness. Real executives don't get colds and the flu, although an athletic injury might be acceptable on occasion. Only if it's a skiing accident or something macho like that, though, and *only* if you show up for your meetings anyway and have rehearsed a funny story to tell while everyone admires your cast."

He looked absolutely appalled.

"Pretty shallow, huh?" she said. She looked down and busied her fingers playing with her pen. "Conor, there's something else we've got to consider."

"What's that?" he asked.

She looked up at him.

"If Matthew has any reason to doubt my loyalties on the Whitlock Castle project, he could replace me at any time. Whoever he chooses will not hesitate to gut the castle and follow Matthew's instructions to the letter. If that happens, there will be nothing I can do to save the castle. Matthew does not forgive disloyalty. Ever."

"I see," Conor said, sounding angry. "*You* have to have ethics, but he doesn't."

She gave him a bleak smile and picked up her pen again.

"That's about the size of it," she said.

Conor put his hand over hers to stop her restless toying with the pen, and she looked up at him.

"If that happens, I may never see you again," he said.

"Right," she acknowledged, realizing that her heart had plummeted somewhere in the vicinity of her shoes. She gave a shaky laugh. "And the Yank with the red underwear will pass into legend."

"Kelly," he said reproachfully.

"Bad joke," she agreed. "Want to hear something funny? I'll miss all of you, even Rose and the gossips. At least it's relatively harmless gossip. And I'll miss this beautiful place."

"We all will," he said grimly, "if your boss gets his way."

He framed her face in his hands.

"But if it happens," he said, "it's the way it was meant to be and it'll be no blame to you."

"Thanks, Conor," she said, smiling. She hoped it was too dark for him to see the tears in her eyes.

He nodded once and was gone.

Fourteen

Julie gasped and gave a throaty giggle when she felt Bradley Kovacks's warm lips on the nape of her neck. The risk of getting caught added to the excitement, that and the kick of having a handsome and single executive pay attention to her.

"How about a drink after work?" he asked as he nibbled on her earlobe playfully.

"Sure," she said softly. She giggled again. "Bradley! Someone is going to notice."

"They are all in a meeting, so we're all alone, babe. What's this?" Julie craned her neck up to look at his face. He was reading the materials over her shoulder.

"Hey! You can't do that!" she objected, frowning at him. She covered the papers and diskette with her hand.

"It's a quote from a guy who restores elevators," he said, picking up one of the papers for a closer look. "Why is Kelly talking to him?"

Julie shrugged.

"She didn't say. She just said to watch out for this and forward it to her. *If* you don't mind," she said, taking the document out of his hand and laying it on the desk.

"So, how's old Kel doing?" Bradley said, putting the envelope down.

"All right, I guess. We haven't talked much lately. Guess we've both been pretty busy."

"Yeah. She's been in Ireland, living in a castle, and you've been stuck here, doing all her work so she can take credit for it."

That wasn't exactly true. Kelly was pretty much a hands-on manager, but Julie was flattered that Bradley thought she was the woman behind the woman, so to speak.

"Well," she said, giving him a dedicated, can-do smile. "A girl's gotta do what a girl's gotta do."

"That's one thing I admire about you, Julie. You're a real team player. Too bad you're stuck over here making Kelly look good."

"It's not so bad," she said bravely. "For one thing, now that she's in Ireland I get to leave at five most of the time."

"I hope she appreciates you," he said.

Actually, Kelly was unusually generous with perks like lunches out and flowers on Julie's birthday. She didn't get all bent out of shape if Julie overslept or wanted to leave an hour early once in a while, but Julie couldn't resist encouraging Bradley to believe Julie sacrificed much more than she actually did for the company. Everybody thought Kelly was such a wow, but where would she be without Julie to do her grunt work, Julie wanted to know.

She glanced at Bradley in time to catch him looking at the quote again.

"Hey!" she said, frowning.

"C'mon. I just want to see if he's the same guy she used in Florida. I might be able to use him on one of my projects."

"I don't know—"

"Hey, what's the big deal? We're all on the same team, aren't we? Here. You can watch me to make sure I don't take anything." His voice was amused, as if he were humoring her. He braced his hands on each side of her and read over her shoulder.

Bradley read the quote all the way through, leaning over Julie so his cheek touched the side of her head. He smelled of some sexy, spicy cologne that made Julie's senses swim pleasantly. Bradley was always meticulously groomed and obviously had enough money to take out any woman he wanted. The fact that he might be interested in Julie made her think maybe she should pinch herself.

Any day now.

"How about that drink?" he whispered as his warm lips touched the top of her head.

"Sure," she said.

"How long did you say they were going to be in that meeting?"

"Another hour," she said, "at least." She gave him a questioning look.

"In another hour it'll be five," he said with a boyish grin. "Let's go now."

Julie loved riding with Bradley in his BMW. She inhaled the fragrance of the leather seats. He switched the radio from a sports talk show to her favorite easy listening channel. It was a bleak early spring day, but the world looked great to Julie as she cruised with the most handsome guy in the office down Michigan Avenue. Too bad her girlfriends at work couldn't see her now. Or, she amended, it was probably a good thing they couldn't since Matthew Lawrence didn't approve of interoffice affairs unless they were his own.

As Julie expected, Bradley selected a bar pretty far from the office.

It wasn't that he was ashamed to be seen with her, she told herself. It was because he didn't want to jeopardize their jobs at Lawrence.

"I hear Jennifer isn't coming back," she said when their drinks had been served. Jennifer was Bradley's assistant. "Do you need some help?"

He looked hesitant.

"I don't want you to think I asked you out so I can get you to do my grunt work," he said with an embarrassed laugh.

"It's okay," she said warmly.

"Well, Jennifer's a nice person, but she was never very efficient," he admitted. "Things are really a mess, and the temp they got for me just made things worse."

Julie made a sympathetic noise.

"But that's not your problem," Bradley said quickly. "I'll manage." He gave a wistful little smile. "You have enough to do. I couldn't ask you to—"

"Hey! What are friends for?" She smiled at him. "I can give you a couple of hours tomorrow."

She could actually give him more than that. With Kelly out of the country, she had been forced to invent busywork so she could look swamped enough to keep from getting hijacked to file invoices or cover the switchboard. Getting to sit near Bradley and maybe getting taken out to lunch as a thank-you was worth the price of having to put his files in order and type a few letters.

Julie had a thought.

"What if Jennifer doesn't come back after her baby's born?" she asked.

Bradley gave her a beatific smile.

"I guess I'll be looking for another assistant," he said.

Julie licked her lips. Wouldn't it be great to work closely with the most handsome man in the office every day? A man who was single and had a beemer?

Right now, Julie's world was a very cool place.

Bradley had no trouble at all reading Julie's mind. He grinned. Really, this was almost too easy. He predicted that within the week he'd know everything he wanted to know about Kelly's projects. And if Julie got the impression that he was going to use his influence to have her appointed as his assistant, all the better.

Right now, Kelly's position was too secure for him to threaten, even though it was plain from the quotation from New Jersey that she wasn't following the Lawrence game plan with respect to the castle in Ireland. He had to bide his time, even though his first impulse was to storm the oval office and wave the papers in the CEO's face. Old Matt had a thing for the golden-haired girl, and any attempt to discredit her was likely to backfire. But all Bradley needed was for Kelly to slip up once, and he'd be ready with the ammunition to nail her.

That promotion to Vice President of Guest Services was as good as his.

The O'Mearas made good on their promise by hosting a noisy birthday party for Kelly at the pub the night before she was to leave for Chicago.

It was like a family party—or at least what Kelly had often thought a family party might be like. Faces flushed with excitement, the Davis kids were running around the pub bumping into people. The bartender's baby was on Kelly's lap, making juicy little noises that Kelly thought were thoroughly enchanting. Kelly's eyebrows rose when Conor, Ghillie, and some other couples did some set dancing. This was as good as *Riverdance*.

"Do you dance, Kelly?" Sean asked with a smile.

"Not like that," she said. "He's really good."

"Conor? That, he is. So good that Ghillie wanted him to go with her to Dublin to audition for the dance company. He would have won a place, too."

Kelly gave him a curious look.

"Why didn't he? I got the impression she dumped him, not the other way around."

"And so she did, after he told her that it was no life for him, and if she wanted to marry him she'd have to settle down with him here. Conor was younger then. More stubborn."

"More stubborn than now?" she said in disbelief.

Sean laughed, then sobered.

"Everything is different now. Conor isn't going to inherit the castle, and the life of a farmer isn't for him, either, although he does the work without complaint, and hard work it is, too."

"You must be very proud of him."

"I am. He wouldn't expect his wife to give up everything

for him," Sean said. "He's grown up since then. But Ghillie isn't for him, much as we parents would have wished for a match between them once upon a time."

"I don't think she'd agree," Kelly said dryly as she watched Ghillie throw her arms around Conor and give him an ecstatic little kiss on the cheek at the end of the dance. Conor glanced quickly at Kelly, and she gave him a cheerful wave to show him she couldn't care less if he wanted to kiss every redhead in the place.

"Time for presents," Margaret said happily, motioning everyone, including the musicians, to the table.

To Kelly's amazement, the O'Mearas and even some of the townspeople produced gaily wrapped gifts.

"Oh, you guys!" Kelly exclaimed, touched. "You didn't have to do this!"

She gave a juicy sniff and stood when it appeared it was expected of her to say a few words.

"I don't know what to say," she began, and sniffed again. "Look. I'll be back in a week."

I hope, she added silently.

Conor took the baby from Kelly's arms. She felt strangely bereft without the soft, sweet-smelling little bundle.

"Open this first," said William MacNamara, the chicken guy, as Kelly thought of him after he gave her a ride to the castle on that seemingly long-ago day that she arrived in Ireland, dressed for power and with blood in her eye.

She gave him a suspicious look. It seemed the lads—as everyone called the motley assortment of jovial jokesters and begrudgers who habitually lined the bar—had chipped in for a present.

The way they jostled each other and watched her with ornery grins on their faces tipped her off to the contents, so she shrieked and put her hands on her hips in mock outrage after she opened the lid of the box and quickly closed it again.

"Let's see what you've got there, lass," Sean shouted, enjoying himself.

Kelly had intended to, of course, but she gave a show of reluctance that delighted the lads.

She gave them a wry look and pulled a pair of knee-length white cotton drawers out of the box. She flashed them around as if they were a flag and she was signaling for help from a sinking ship.

"Try them on," a couple of the guys chanted.

She slowly shook her head, and the laughter erupted again. Rose and Margaret's cheeks were stained pink.

Kelly felt as if she had just passed some peculiar sort of freshman initiation. It symbolized acceptance.

Incorrigibly, the lads lined up for kisses, and Kelly obliged. She started to kiss Conor, too, but the lads objected noisily.

"Conor O'Meara wasn't after contributing to the gift, so he doesn't get a kiss," William said sternly.

Conor gave her a sheepish smile and a shrug.

The O'Meara sisters gave her a dainty silver-tone Irish cross on a slender chain similar to those sold in the village at the gift shops. Sean gave her a can of the pinhead oatmeal she liked so much. To Kelly's relief, none of the gifts were too expensive. Ghillie gave her a small bottle of scent called Tara. Kelly was astonished to receive a gift from a woman who considered her a rival for Conor's affections. William the chicken guy stood in line twice when Kelly distributed thank-you kisses all around.

"It's the best birthday I've ever had," she sobbed sentimentally. The party certainly took the sting out of turning thirty-three.

Conor grinned and shook his head.

"That's enough beer for you until you've worked some of it off, darling," he said, taking her glass from her hand and ushering her to the dance floor. A waltz was playing, to Kelly's relief. She could handle that. Kelly put both arms around his neck when he would have held her in the typical ballroom-dance position.

"I bought you a present, too," he said. "I'll give it to you tomorrow, before you leave."

"You didn't have to get me anything," she replied.

"I wanted to. I'll be sorry if you don't come back."

Kelly edged closer so she could rest her head on his shoulder. Let him think she is a little drunk.

"So will I," she said.

Conor gave a gusty sigh.

"What will we do for excitement, then?" he asked. "We'll be sitting in the parish hall with nothing to say. The ladies will all come home from the Rosary Sodality an hour early for lack of gossip, and the men will have to end their card games and go home to their families while the night is still young."

"Awww," Kelly said with mock sympathy.

She had been so offended to be the talk of the parish. Now it seemed harmless and sort of innocent. Flattering, even.

"Oh! I'll be right back," she said suddenly, causing Conor to look down at her. "William is leaving, and I have to talk to him."

"William?" Conor repeated with a frown.

He looked insulted, but she didn't have time to explain. William was getting away!

"William!" she called, walking across the dance floor in pursuit.

The tall, rangy farmer turned with a smile on his face.

"William, I hear you're going to Shannon tomorrow to pick up your sister. What time? I'm looking for a lift to the airport."

"I'll be leaving at half past seven, but I'll have a load of chickens to take into the village on the way," he warned.

"Fine with me as long as you keep them in the back."

"I'll clean out the front of the truck special for you," he promised.

"I'll be ready," Kelly said. "Good night!"

She ran back to Conor, who had waited patiently right where she left him.

"All set," she said, settling back into his arms. "William is going to give me a lift to the airport."

"I thought I would—"

"You are too busy with your morning chores. Besides, he has to go, anyway. His mother told Margaret who told me that his sister is coming in on Aer Lingus tomorrow morning."

Conor burst into laughter and hugged her.

"Ah, Kelly," he said. "Congratulations. You've mastered the Irish way at last."

"I have to admit," she said, "the village grapevine can be efficient."

The next morning it seemed strange to dress in one of her best power suits and pack her briefcase. The waistband of the skirt was a little tight, she noticed ruefully. She would have been more comfortable in jeans, but she had to go straight into the office after she landed in Chicago.

To Kelly's surprise, Conor was waiting for her in the kitchen when she went to bum a quick cup of coffee from Margaret to sip while she was waiting for William. Normally Conor didn't appear until after he had done all his morning chores at the farm.

Sean was presiding over a pot of Irish oatmeal with a spoon in his hand and Kelly's heart swelled, even though she knew one of his sisters probably had prepared the oatmeal and he was just stirring it for effect.

"Here you are, lass," he said cheerfully.

You are *not* going to cry, she told herself, absurdly touched as she ate the oatmeal. She could brush her teeth in the airport washroom and put on more lipstick.

Conor handed her a tissue. She made a wry grimace at him as she patted her eyes lightly to keep her makeup from smearing. If her nose started running, she would have to do a major overhaul.

"You'll tell Mr. Lawrence hello for us," Sean reminded her. "And you'll come back to us safe."

"Of course," she said. She felt as if she were leaving her real family although she hadn't met any of the O'Mearas a month ago. "Eeek! Time to go!" She gulped down the last of her coffee and stood up. Conor grabbed a box, took her arm and escorted her to the door. He frowned when Sean would have followed.

"Don't be kissing her too long, lad," the older man said cheerfully. "We don't want William to be going to the airport without her."

"Thanks, Da," Conor said sarcastically.

At the door, he did kiss Kelly. Then he gave her the box that he had placed by the door.

"Happy birthday, Kelly," he said.

"Conor, you didn't have to do this," she said as a thrill of anticipation ran up her spine. The little green and gold seal of the village shop caused her to hope. She gave an involuntary squeal when she lifted the white tissue to reveal the soft, heavenly purple wool.

Of course. Rose would have told him about the cloak.

It was a struggle, but her better self triumphed. She gave a gusty sigh and put the lid back on the box and held it closed as if she was afraid something might escape from it.

"You have to take it back," she said.

"That, I will not," he said firmly.

"It's too expensive! You can't afford it!"

"I can, and I did," he said, prying the lid loose from her clutching fingers and reverently lifting the gorgeous cloak out of the box. "It was made for you, Kelly. How can you expect me to take it back and look like a fool before the whole village?"

"Naturally, they would know all about it," she agreed with a shaky laugh. "Oh, it's so beautiful! I can't resist."

Conor placed the cloak around her shoulders with a flourish and cupped her face in his hands.

"Exactly what I was thinking. Come back to us, Kelly," he said huskily right before he kissed her.

They broke off the kiss and stepped back self-consciously when the door knocker sounded. Conor frowned at the man he used to think of as a friend until recently.

"Good morning to you," William MacNamara said cheerfully. His hair was neatly combed, and he was dressed in a shirt and trousers much too clean and new for picking up his sister Maureen and delivering a load of chickens to the village. He gave Kelly an approving look. "It's the cloak from Noreen's shop, and well it becomes you!"

Noreen probably told the whole village he bought it, Conor thought sourly.

"Thanks! I'm all ready," Kelly said, smiling at him. Conor gave William a look that made him grin mischievously when he reached for the larger of Kelly's suitcases. William opened his eyes wide with mock alarm and held his hands up in surrender when Conor took a step forward. Conor picked up the heavy suitcase. William took the garment bag out of Kelly's hands, leaving her the briefcase.

"I'll have to be putting your things back with the chickens," William said, looking to Kelly for approval.

"Whatever," she said easily.

Conor stifled a grin.

He remembered the appalled note in her voice the day she arrived and told him how she had caught a lift to the castle with a guy transporting a load of chickens.

Conor swallowed the lump that formed in his throat as he watched them drive away

She was in his blood now. She didn't know it yet, but Ireland was in hers.

Fifteen

Maureen MacNamara was one of those wholesome, fresh-faced girls who looked out at you from the pages of all the Irish tourist publications. She had milk-white skin, rosy cheeks, dark blue eyes and blue-black hair cascading to her slim shoulders.

The famous black Irish coloring.

Like Conor's.

Kelly was very much afraid that Conor had ruined her for normal men, and Ireland had ruined her for normal life.

When it was time to wave good-bye to Maureen and William, who hung out with her until her flight boarded to keep her company, her heart plummeted as if she were on her way to prison instead of home.

She drew the comforting folds of the cloak closer. She couldn't bear it if she never saw him again.

The dirty snow-patched countryside from the vantage point of the interminable tollway totally sucked after Ireland.

The depressing, drizzling weather did not add mystery and lushness to the landscape like similar weather did in Ireland. She had forgotten that early spring was a cold, depressing season in Chicago.

And the *smell*! It made her eyes water. She had the taxi drop her off at her apartment so she could stash her luggage, and then she walked the few blocks to work.

Lawrence Hotels' corporate headquarters was on the top two floors of Lawrence's flagship hotel, the same place where Kelly had been a part-time desk clerk in college.

On her way to the elevator, she gave a nostalgic sigh as she passed the usual collection of travelers in the lobby. Life was so much simpler when all she had to worry about was making sure the guests were comfortable.

When she got to her floor, Kelly got out of the elevator and opened the glass door to the executive offices. The usual office racket suddenly assaulted her, and she wanted to turn around and go home. With a mental shrug, Kelly approached the receptionist's desk. The harassed-looking attendant gave her a perfunctory smile.

"I'll be right with you," she said.

The woman was unfamiliar to her. She must be new. Kelly was about to tell her she worked here and could find her way on her own when she noticed the receptionist was attending a fax machine that spewed forth sheet after sheet of paper covered with indecipherable writing.

Bradley's.

Kelly would recognize that awful scrawl anywhere. As usual, Bradley decided to blow off part of the day at home and fax this mess to his poor secretary to make sense of.

"I've got to get this to Julie right away," the receptionist explained conversationally.

Julie?

Kelly's assistant?

What was going on here?

Kelly frowned and started to walk into the Guest Services department, which was located just off the reception area.

"Wait! Wait! Wait!" the receptionist cried out in near panic. "You don't have a badge."

A badge?

Kelly didn't need no stinking badge!

"I *work* here," she told the girl before she walked into her department. Suddenly a loud, piercing, electronic shriek tore through the air.

"She went into Guest Services," she heard the receptionist say after the sound of running feet clattered on the polished tile of the reception area. "She wouldn't stop when I told her she needed a badge."

Two men from security came to each side of Kelly.

"Rick?" Kelly said, recognizing one of them. She laughed. "Are you going to arrest me, or what?"

By now a little crowd had gathered.

"Kelly," he said, relaxing. "It's okay," he added to the earnest young man on Kelly's other side. "She works here."

"That's what I told *her*!" Kelly said impatiently, gesturing in the direction of the receptionist's desk.

"She doesn't have a badge," the other man said suspiciously.

"Oh, for pete's sake," Kelly said, rolling her eyes. "Where's Julie?"

"She's okay, I tell you," Rick insisted.

Kelly could hear the receptionist breathlessly telling the tale to someone else.

"She went right by me," the receptionist said defensively. "She wouldn't stop, even when I *told* her she needed a badge."

Kelly saw a familiar face and could have wept from sheer relief.

"Julie!" she said, grinning. "Tell them I don't have a bomb."

"What's going on here?" Julie asked, giving the guy on Kelly's right a scowl. "This is Kelly Sullivan, a Director of Guest Services."

The man jumped away from Kelly as if she had burst into flames.

Matthew came striding into the department.

"What's going on here, people?" he demanded. Then he

noticed Kelly and grinned. "Hello, Kelly! No one told me you were here."

"I guess I should have picked up a badge," she said sheepishly.

"All right, people," Matthew said. "Show's over!"

It was said in a genial tone of voice, but his eyes were impatient. People scattered everywhere.

"Just get in?" Matthew asked Kelly.

"Right off the plane," Kelly confirmed.

"Good. Come on up to my office after you get your badge," he said as he walked away.

"Will do." Kelly turned to Julie. "I have some things to go over with you—"

"Maybe after lunch," Julie said, cutting her off. "Right now I've got to work on this proposal for Brad. He's working from home so he won't be interrupted. Excuse me. I have to pick up his notes from the fax machine."

Kelly stared open-mouthed as Julie brushed right by her. Then she went in pursuit.

"*Wait* a minute," she said with deadly calm, arriving ahead of Julie and putting her hand on the fax sheets the receptionist had placed on the desk for pickup. "Since when is *my* assistant too busy doing *Brad's* work to talk to me when I've just come back from being out of the country on assignment?"

The receptionist was listening avidly, but Kelly didn't care that most of the workers in the adjoining offices could probably hear her.

Julie's face was flaming. She didn't dare look Kelly in the eye.

"Jennifer is on maternity leave," Julie said, referring to Bradley's assistant. "I've just been helping him out."

"Okay," Kelly said. "We'll go to lunch and talk."

"I'm having lunch with Brad," Julie said, standing her ground. "He'll be here in a couple of hours." Julie snatched the papers out from under Kelly's hand. "I need to have the first draft of this finished before he gets here so he can go over it then."

Without a backward look, Julie flounced off.

Kelly stared at the receptionist, who jumped at being caught eavesdropping.

"How about that badge?" Kelly asked calmly.

Sixteen

Kelly frowned at the piles of unopened mail on her desk.

Julie should have opened all this stuff, taken care of any issues that could be resolved without Kelly's attention, thrown away the solicitations for wine clubs and magazine subscriptions, and forwarded to Ireland anything that required Kelly's approval.

By contrast, Julie's own workspace adjoining Kelly's was as clean as a whistle. Obviously, no one was home and hadn't been for some time.

Julie whizzed by once and escalated speed when she saw Kelly looking at her.

Kelly wasn't surprised—she had a few questions she wanted to ask her so-called assistant. Like, why was she doing work for Bradley while her own work was neglected?

Kelly had seen the phenomenon before—support staff members who kowtow to the men because they perceive them as being more important than the female executives at the same level. She just hadn't expected it of Julie.

She also noticed that Julie was taking unusual pains with her appearance these days. Today Julie was wearing a sophisticated cobalt blue coat dress with pearl-toned beads and pearl drop earrings. Her slim skirt was unbuttoned to well above the knee, and she was wearing high heels! It was the first time Kelly had actually seen her assistant's legs. Her hair was arranged in pretty curls at her temples. As long as Kelly had known her, Julie's work attire consisted of casual pantsuits with minimal makeup, no jewelry, and comfortable loafers.

Yet here she was, dressed like a model in a fashion magazine and scenting the air with some exotic department-store fragrance with every movement.

Pick your battles, Kelly told herself, striving for calm. If she played her cards wrong, she would come off as a paranoid nitpicker carping because her assistant—who would come off as a team player—pitched in to help one of Kelly's coworkers during Kelly's absence. The last thing Kelly needed was to be perceived as inflexible.

She pawed through the mail to see if anything looked important and found, as she feared, several issues that should have been dealt with a week ago.

Welcome back, Kelly, she told herself dryly.

Then she pulled herself together and went to see Matthew.

Matthew settled in his chair and smiled at Kelly, showing every one of his capped teeth. She narrowed her eyes at him when he put his hot, slightly moist hand on top of hers.

"You know Linda and I have decided to go our separate ways," he said.

Oh, peachy, she thought. This was not the kind of conversation anybody should have to deal with while she was suffering from jet lag. *Make the wrong response, Kelly old girl, and you're history*.

"Sorry to hear that." Kelly sat back and grinned at him. *Treat it lightly*, her instinct told her.

"So, who gets her office?" she asked audaciously.

Matthew gave an appreciative chuckle. Linda's beautifully decorated office was an object of desire and envy throughout the company.

"She'll still be in it for a while, of course, until we buy her out."

Kelly wasn't surprised. After all, Linda's daddy's money was a big factor in the chain's initial success, and Linda's daddy would make sure Linda's rights were protected. If Matthew wanted to run the show alone, he'd have to cough up enough cash to do it.

So, what did Kelly say to *that*?

She needn't have worried because Matthew went right on with a smoldering look—something Kelly didn't *even* want to see on an empty stomach—and a wistful remark that "Linda and I haven't had a real marriage for a long time now."

No kidding, Kelly thought. *How could it be with you chasing everything that doesn't bark?*

"We've only stayed together this long for the sake of the children," he continued, as if this wasn't the oldest line in the world. His youngest child was about to graduate from high school.

Maybe that's why Linda stuck around, Kelly thought. *You were sticking around because you needed Linda's Daddy's money to play the big-shot CEO.*

To the amusement and despair of the employees, Lawrence's so-called corporate culture changed every time the volatile and impulsive Matthew read an article in *Crain's Chicago Business* about a new management philosophy. The walls were full of slightly sinister slogans like "The Lion That Does Not Hunt Becomes A Rug."

It was a slogan kind of place.

All of this slick brainwashing masqueraded as motivational support and/or humor, but there was an underlying thread of meanness that ran through all these so-called office decorations. Before she went to Ireland, Kelly had never noticed the subliminal hostility that surrounded her here. Now it made her slightly sick to her stomach.

In Ireland she might not have liked what people said or did, but there was no ambivalence about it.

Jet lag, she told herself firmly. *It isn't that bad.*

She couldn't *let* it be that bad. This was her real life, after all. She felt a little like she did when she awoke from a beautiful dream to find herself still in bed with a cold or the flu, bathed in the sweat of her sickness.

Now she recognized the feeling that had twisted her gut on the way to the office. It was the same one that twisted her gut every Sunday night for years—Monday morning dread. In Ireland it had disappeared.

The nightmare continued.

A meeting of her so-called team showed how much damage her absence had done to her place in the pecking order. She had no real staff of her own except Julie, and the fact that Julie seemed preoccupied and ready to bolt back to Bradley's desk left that in doubt. All team leaders shared the same team. For example, a member of the graphics department might be assigned to your project. Your status and the status of your project was clearly defined by whom you got. If you got the head of the graphics department, you would get that department's best effort. This showed that the VP of that business unit perceived you as being the horse to hitch his or her wagon to. If you kept getting one of the worker bees or, worse, a trainee, it was time to take that business unit VP to lunch and schmooze like crazy—or start looking for another job.

A practiced glance at the room showed Kelly that everybody was there who should be. It was now three o'clock and Kelly was running on empty, but this was show time so she put on a perky face. Kelly learned a long time ago that these meetings had nothing to do with getting the actual work done and everything to do with selling your project and getting everybody to perceive your work as the most important challenge facing the company.

She'd better be *on* today. Five minutes after she called the meeting to order, Matthew walked in and sat down at the chair at the conference table Julie vacated for him.

Kelly gave Julie a sharp look. She could read her like a book, and she knew darn well she took an extra chair and placed it by the door so she could slip out as soon as possible. She was probably eager to get back to her precious Bradley. A minute or so later, Bradley himself walked in and seated himself beside Julie, distracting her attention from note-taking by making her laugh and handing her sheets of paper covered with his vile handwriting that he obviously wanted her to transcribe.

Kelly began her PowerPoint presentation, which consisted of a timetable lavishly illustrated with beautiful shots of the castle's gorgeous architectural details. She had taken the photos with her digital camera.

With luck, the pictures would work their subliminal magic on Matthew and make him think preserving the castle was *his* idea without her having to talk him into it.

It was a slick presentation, if she did say so herself, and Matthew was grinning like a proud papa. Kelly knew he gave himself a lot of the credit for her work because he liked to think of himself as the mentor who had shaped and groomed her for stardom in his private constellation.

"Julie," Kelly said gently at one point. "You'd better get this down for the timetable. It's important."

Julie's face was a study in guilt.

You'd better cultivate a poker face, old girl, Kelly thought, *if you want to play with the pros.*

"Sorry," Julie mumbled, sitting up straight and facing the projection screen.

Bradley gave Kelly an insolent smirk, which told Kelly clearer than words that he was surer of his position in Matthew's esteem than he was before Kelly went to Ireland. Otherwise, he wouldn't have risked Matthew's displeasure by crashing the meeting and deliberately laying claim to Kelly's assistant when he knew very well this was a gross violation of business etiquette. Beyond giving Julie a half-puzzled, half-disapproving look when she giggled self-consciously in response to one of Bradley's remarks, Matthew didn't seem to find anything odd in Bradley's presence.

Warning bells went off in Kelly's head as she proceeded with her material. They almost knocked her head off when Bradley raised his hand for attention.

"I'm just curious," he said with a self-deprecating smile. "It's not my project, so you can tell me to go scratch if you

want to. But why are you wasting your time with quotes on
restoring the interior when the plan is to gut the thing and
start over? And why aren't those figures in your spreadsheet? It seems like you've been spending a lot of your time
in Ireland on your own agenda, when you could have
wrapped up a simple project like this weeks ago."

The shocked look on Julie's guilty face told Kelly everything.

So the little traitor had been keeping Bradley posted on
every move she made. Fortunately, Kelly was ready with an
answer. She had known the question would come up eventually. She just hoped it would be later, after she had completed her analysis and polished the sales pitch that was
supposed to convince Matthew that her carefully orchestrated plan was *his* idea.

"Just covering all the bases," she said with a bland smile.
"The place was originally designed to have the flavor of a
medieval castle. The workmanship is superb. There's no
way it could be replicated today for less than a small fortune, *if* it would be possible. Why destroy something we
might be able to use?"

Kelly let her amused glance rest on Julie for a fraction of
a second. Her assistant quailed. Then Kelly favored
Matthew with a smile designed to look modest.

"I'm the daughter of an architect," she continued. "I have
a fair idea how much this stuff would cost to build from
scratch. It would be a mistake to be too hasty with the
wrecking ball."

Kelly almost sagged with relief when Matthew gave her a
look of approval.

Crisis averted for now.

The rest of the meeting went smoothly enough as the
team members gave their progress reports. Kelly knew how
to make each person feel as if his or her contribution was
crucial to the success of the project. The marketing manager's presentation made her cringe a bit.

Shades of Euro Disney!

But she could tell Matthew approved.

The sound of scuffling feet and chairs being pushed back on the carpet that signaled the end of the meeting was the most welcome that Kelly had heard all day, but she knew better than to think she could relax now.

"Julie," she said when her assistant and Brad started to walk out of the room together. When Brad would have stayed behind to wait for Julie, Kelly added, "I'll catch up with you in a minute," just as if she thought Brad was waiting for her. It was a subtle way of underscoring her authority and the fact that his monopolization of Kelly's assistant was inappropriate.

God, how she hated these games!

Brad had no choice but to go since Matthew had stayed behind, too.

"Jules," Kelly said crisply, "I'll need an up-to-date revision of the timetable by the end of the day. I noticed that the current one did not include a few things that were discussed in the last team meeting. It is important for you to stay in communication with all the team members at all times during this project and to keep me updated. I thought you understood that."

"Okay," Julie said, glancing uncomfortably at Matthew. She looked as if she was trying to decide whether she could afford to argue about it. No doubt Brad had other things he wanted her to do for him.

"That will be all," Kelly said firmly, making it clear—in front of Matthew—that this was nonnegotiable. "We'll talk later."

She turned to smile at Matthew as if she was in control of the situation.

More games, she thought with an inward sigh.

Julie knew she was between a rock and a hard place. She had kidded herself into thinking she could continue to support Kelly and still please Brad, but the meeting had put an end to that comfortable fantasy.

Kelly had made it perfectly clear—in front of the CEO— that her performance was unsatisfactory. Kelly had always treated Julie with a tolerant camaraderie that Julie took for granted until it was withdrawn. With surgical precision, her usually fair boss had cut her dead.

And Brad had betrayed her.

Now, when it was too late, the scales were lifted from her eyes.

He had told Kelly in front of her team that he knew every move she made on this project—and he could have gotten that information from no one except Kelly's trusted assistant.

Brad had to know that any reprisals would fall on Julie's head and not his.

Everyone in the company knew Matthew was unstable and impulsive. If he was feeling decisive, he would fire anyone at the drop of a hat. He once fired a receptionist of five years because she kept him on hold too long while he was calling in from an out-of-town business trip.

Julie felt utterly vulnerable. The sick feeling in her stomach forced her to take in deep breaths through her nose to keep from throwing up.

When Brad walked up behind her and started massaging her neck, she spun around and glared at him. She had been gathering her stuff from his former assistant's cubicle by his desk.

"How about a drink after work?" he asked as if nothing had happened.

"Go to hell," she snarled.

His smile wavered. Now that she was no longer thinking with her hormones, she saw him for what he truly was.

A rat.

A sneaky, smarmy, unscrupulous, game-playing, character-assassinating *rat*!

"Julie," he asked, looking incredulous. "What's the deal?"

"The *deal*," she said, putting her stuff into a cardboard box, "is I'm not having a drink with you."

"Look, Julie—"

"Out of my way, please," she said crisply. "Kelly needs

her timetable updated by the end of the day and, thanks to you, I'm way behind."

"Julie, what happened in there was—"

She gave him a mocking smile.

"I'm sure a spin doctor like you can provide a perfectly fascinating excuse for making me look bad in front of the person who gives me my annual review *and* the owner of the company, not to mention the various heads of every department in the company. Unfortunately, I'm going to be too busy saving my butt to listen to any more of your bullshit."

He made the grave error of putting a hand on her arm, and she shook it off angrily.

"Keep your slimy paws off me," she demanded through gritted teeth.

He looked as if he had been burned.

Good, Julie thought in satisfaction as the tears swam in her eyes.

It was past five o'clock, and Kelly willed herself to show no sign of impatience when Matthew lingered, prattling on about his stimulating golf game on a Scottish course. He was the kind of guy who would tour Europe and see nothing but meticulously manicured greens and the interiors of clubhouses.

Before she went to Ireland she would have found nothing odd about this.

She noted with some satisfaction that Julie was back at the desk by Kelly's cubicle concentrating fiercely on the project time line.

Kelly could be reasonably certain Julie would behave herself from now on, but the proverbial barn door was locked now that the cows were loose.

Thanks to Julie, Brad had blown Kelly's cover about not following Matthew's instructions to the letter. Fortunately, Matthew seemed to take this in good humor.

She had succeeded in her effort at damage control.

For now.

When Matthew finally moved on, Kelly walked out of her cubicle to look over Julie's shoulder.

"How are you doing with that?" she asked.

"Just about done," Julie replied. "There."

Julie sent the document to the printer and flexed her cramped fingers.

Ordinarily Kelly would have suggested a snack or dinner after being gone so long. She knew dinners on Kelly were one of the perks Julie appreciated about her job. They made her feel as if she worked *with* Kelly, not *for* her.

But strategically, Kelly knew, this would be a mistake.

Screw strategy, Kelly thought with genuine sadness. Still, she couldn't back down now.

Ordinarily, she would have taken the time line off the printer and put it directly into her briefcase, tacitly releasing Julie for the night. Instead, she waited for Julie to take it off the printer and hand it to her, slave to master.

Kelly kept her waiting as she read through it.

"You didn't put in the part about the kitchen staffing," she said after a moment. "I believe you were listening to Bradley instead of paying attention during that part."

Lips compressed, Julie paged through her notes.

"No, I've got it," she said. "I just overlooked it."

She gave Kelly a chance to say she could wait to do the revision in the morning. When it apparently was not forthcoming, she sighed and added the information.

"Do you see anything else?" she asked meekly.

"Nope. Looks okay except for that."

Not great. Not good. Just okay.

Julie sent it to the printer and gave the finished document to Kelly.

"Thanks," Kelly said, putting it in her briefcase. "See you in the morning."

Kelly did not allow her shoulders to slump until Julie had put on her coat and headed out the door.

She put on her own coat and followed a moment later, just in time to watch as Bradley, who apparently had been wait-

ing by Julie's car, tried to engage the unreceptive administrative assistant in conversation.

Julie blew him off and got into her car, squealing her tires
a bit in her haste to get away from him.

I'll bet that's a first for old golden tongue, Kelly thought,
mentally chalking one up for Julie. His jaw actually dropped
as he watched Julie drive away.

Kelly walked out from the building and smiled at him.

"Goodnight, Brad," she said pleasantly.

"Hey, Kell! Wait up!" called Kelly's buddy Beverly from
graphics. "Are you walking home?"

"Yeah," Kelly replied, waiting for the other woman to
catch up. She lived in a nearby apartment building.

"Good. I'll walk with you," Bev said cheerfully. "Lotta
creeps hanging around these days."

"You're telling me," Kelly agreed, giving Brad a nod as
she and Bev walked by him.

Seventeen

The walk home made Kelly think nostalgically of her travels with William MacNamara. What a bleak, scarred place Chicago was! Her father always said new construction, remodeling, and roadwork were signs of vitality in a city, but to Kelly it didn't look vital. It just looked damaged.

The sight of Lake Michigan off Lake Shore Drive failed to lift her spirits, even though it meant she was home.

Home?

It didn't feel at all like home.

It's the jet lag, she told herself a little desperately.

The smooth elevator ride to her tenth-floor apartment didn't cheer her. This time of evening the elevator was full of fellow office workers on their way home after a long day. Funny. She had lived in this building for three years and not one face looked familiar. Oddly, she found that disturbing. Before she could stop herself, she initiated a conversation with the woman standing next to her. The woman replied tersely to Kelly's remarks, all the while looking at Kelly as if she expected her to try to steal her purse. Vaguely embarrassed and depressed, Kelly got off at her floor and walked with footsteps muffled against the thick synthetic hall carpeting to her apartment. The building's interior was done in tasteful yuppie shades of gray, teal, and burgundy. Innocuous, pseudotrendy prints of irises and calla lilies lined the walls along with discreet framed advertisements for the bar/restaurant on the top floor.

Kelly toyed with the idea of going there to put off facing her empty apartment and decided against it. The place had a carefully orchestrated upbeat atmosphere that always depressed the living hell out of her. Somehow, although it was always crowded with singles her own age, being there was worse than being alone.

Sleep, she thought. A little sleep will fix everything. A little dinner will take the bad taste out of her mouth. A bath—shower, she corrected herself—will loosen her tension-taut muscles. Then oblivion.

She opened the door and stepped inside her apartment, recoiling a little as the stale air hit her in the face.

Cut it out, she told herself impatiently. *It always smells like this when you've been out of town for awhile.*

Still, Kelly looked at her home of three years with alien eyes. The carpeting was plushy and white. So were the walls. The furniture had sleek, contemporary lines and was upholstered in white leather. So clean, her mother had said with satisfaction after it had been delivered. Kelly's mother, a professional decorator by vocation, had helped her choose the prints from a gallery. They were innocuous in color and design. Slick. Impersonal. Trendy.

What *had* she been thinking when she chose this stuff?

This was *not* her apartment. It looked as if it belonged to a mental patient whose environment had to be carefully designed to provide no stimulation whatsoever.

No plants—they'd just wither and die when she was out of town on assignment.

No cat or dog—it wouldn't be fair to a pet to leave it alone all the time while she worked.

There was not even a magazine in evidence to mar the perfection of what looked like one of those fake model units elsewhere in the building.

Oh, God.

She got the panicky feeling that she was an ant in a little air pocket in an anthill, focused on a series of tasks that meant nothing, crawling intently along with millions of other anonymous ants on parallel missions.

She could spend the rest of her life in this sterile apartment or one like it, wasting her life playing silly mind games at Lawrence. She ran a hand over her coffee table and encountered not a speck of dust. The housekeeping service she had shopped for so carefully did an impeccable job, as usual.

The place was so immaculate, you'd think no one lived here at all.

On that depressing note, Kelly stripped off her suit and took a shower in the fiberglass stall, wishing it were a big, white porcelain, claw-footed tub fragrant with Margaret O'Meara's lily-of-the-valley bath salts and steaming hot water courtesy of cheerfully clanking pipes and Conor's geriatric immersion tank.

Kelly had slept for twelve hours straight when the alarm awoke her. She sat upright in bed, gasping, when she came awake to all that noise. Her stomach was growling, but she never ate breakfast before she went to Ireland and there was nothing to eat in her kitchen except a few pathetic tea bags, half a bag of dry gourmet pasta, and some stale rice cakes.

She promised her insistent stomach a bagel with fat-free cream cheese she could grab at the snack bar in the lobby of her building.

Today was the big company annual meeting, so she had to look good, but not too obviously dressed up. Gray pants, pressed perfectly so the creases were as sharp as sushi knives. Cobalt blue silk blouse the color of Conor's eyes.

Stop that, she told herself firmly.

A navy double-breasted blazer and a 14-karat gold choker with big matching hoop earrings completed the look.

She fluffed her hair so it wouldn't look so perfect, frowned, put on darker lipstick, and undid the two top buttons of the blouse.

Better.

Better?

Aghast, she buttoned the blouse back up.

She must be losing her mind!

With that cheery thought, she grabbed the briefcase full of paperwork she hadn't read last night and ran out the door and into the dreary cacophony of the street.

When she arrived at Lawrence, she had to turn the lights on in her department because she was the first one there. It was Friday, and since it was common knowledge Matthew and therefore most of the executives always came in late on Friday, almost everyone took the opportunity to dawdle. Kelly started on the paperwork she should have read last night. Julie, not entirely to Kelly's surprise, came in at 8:30 on the dot.

As if *that* made up for yesterday, Kelly thought cynically.

"Do you want some coffee, Kelly?" Julie asked.

"You haven't brought me coffee in the three years you've been my assistant," Kelly observed pleasantly.

Julie bit her lip.

Kelly sighed. She was *not* enjoying this.

She dove back into the paperwork and mentally rehearsed an upbeat little update on her project to deliver at the company meeting if she was asked. Traditionally Matthew gave an informal talk and everybody asked questions. Then there were refreshments. It was a team-building thing, the one time in the year when a cat could look at a king.

Bradley, dressed in the male equivalent of Kelly's understated but impeccable business casual costume, sat on the corner of her desk looking boyish and approachable.

Kelly raised her eyebrows.

"Lunch?" he asked winsomely. From the corner of her eye, Kelly could see Julie's shoulders stiffen.

Before Ireland, Kelly would have returned an equally sincere smile and accepted, but today she wasn't in the mood to look at his smarmy face while she ate.

"No," she said bluntly.

It was his turn to raise his eyebrows.

"Another time then," he said, gracefully levering his thigh from her desk.

"Sure," Kelly said with no conviction whatsoever. Julie watched him walk by with hostile eyes.

There was a time when she would have welcomed a chance to probe Bradley for information. Like any professional, she had her share of meals with people she couldn't stand, but Ireland had brought out something reckless in her nature that she was afraid she wore on her face like whisker burn after a night of passion.

With that thought, she felt a wave of longing for Conor so strong it left her breathless.

Her stomach growled.

She had never felt hunger like this in her life—for red meat and fried bread, for friendly faces and unbarbed conversation, for the smell of salt from the sea, for Conor, for *life*.

She wasn't getting any of that here, she thought with a sigh as she looked around her cubicle. Blue carpeting. Charcoal gray file cabinets. White walls. A Successories calendar.

Yuck.

"Winning With Teamwork," proclaimed Kelly's black coffee mug in worn gold letters. It had looked great when she got it at a team-building seminar, but the trim had tarnished in the microwave.

She had intended to eat a salad at her desk for lunch, but she decided she'd never survive this day on rabbit food. She left the building right behind Bev and some women from her department on their way to lunch. Kelly impulsively invited herself along.

"T.G.I. Friday's?" one of them suggested.

Grease! Salt! Kelly's mouth watered at the thought. While the other women ate salads with fat-free dressing on the side and warmed breadsticks, Kelly had skewered shrimp wrapped in bacon, a side of onion rings, and a salad with real buttermilk ranch dressing.

Her bemused companions watched, fascinated, as she washed all this down with a *real* Coke.

It was fabulous! She even ate the crumbs from the onion ring basket and licked the grease from her fingers.

"What?" she asked when she looked up to see the other women had broken off their conversation to stare at her in shocked disbelief.

When some explanation seemed to be expected, Kelly added, "I slept through dinner last night. Let's have another order of onion rings and share them."

They looked at her, kind of horrified and aroused, as if she had suggested having group sex with the guys from the construction site on the corner.

"Oh, you are *bad*," breathed one of them huskily as she put up an arm to signal their server.

Kelly waved good-bye to them in the lobby as she went her separate way to her cubicle, feeling sated and at peace with the world.

As soon as her assignment in Ireland was over, she promised herself she would look for a new apartment, maybe in a neighborhood with plenty of atmosphere like Rogers Park instead of another slick, anonymous high-rise.

And a new job, was the scary thought that surfaced unbidden.

What was she thinking? She had fought and clawed her way to the top of the flow chart of Lawrence Hotels. She was so close to making VP that she could taste it.

It was all she'd ever wanted, wasn't it?

Wasn't it?

Well, not exactly.

She started working at Lawrence Hotels in college because her daddy arranged for his buddy Matthew to give his little girl a job. Successful men did this all the time—wasted their secretaries' time writing chatty letters to their successful friends extolling their spoiled children's imaginary virtues to get the kid on the inside track for a summer job when college let out. Kelly ended up working the front desk at Lawrence's flagship hotel in the Loop. She didn't expect the job to be anything special. It was the rich girl's equivalent of working at McDonald's. Only this job involved working in the cool beauty of a classy hotel lobby with crystal chandeliers dripping overhead.

She'd loved it. Absolutely loved it, tired feet at the end of the day and all. The little groups of people spilling into the lobby with their children and packages from Marshall Field's delighted her. They spoke many languages. Some were haughty and polished. Others seemed pleased just to be in such a classy place, and Kelly could imagine them telling their children and grandchildren about their magnificent trip to Chicago way back in the nineties.

Sometimes they came to her frustrated and weary and ruffled, and it gave Kelly immense satisfaction to soothe them and straighten out their problems. Give them a bit of friendly attention and most people went away smiling. They mentioned her in the little questionnaires placed in their rooms, and she even got a pin and certificate to commend her for excellence in customer satisfaction.

At first her parents had been pleased by her obvious delight in her job, then a bit concerned. It was just supposed to be a summer job that would look good on her resume when she applied for a real job. Working at a fancy hotel in the Loop had a certain amount of prestige.

But the hospitality business involved long hours and not that much money. Not for a clerk at the front desk, anyway. They wanted so much more for their only child.

Unfortunately, Kelly was quite serious about the hospitality business, and she wouldn't be discouraged from pursuing it. To her parents' alarm, she actually switched her major to hotel management. Before that, they had groomed her for law and possibly politics.

By the time Kelly graduated with a degree in hotel management, their old buddy Matthew Lawrence was ready to take her under his wing. The staff at the Loop facility knew and trusted Kelly, although eyebrows were raised when Matthew arbitrarily promoted her to assistant manager only three months after she went to work for Lawrence full time after graduation. The college girl who had worked the front desk was now supervising the veterans.

Kelly *loved* being an assistant manager. She had her finger in everything, and customers left feeling they had been her personal guests. When her manager retired, Kelly was poised to assume his position only to find that—courtesy of Matthew's patronage—greatness beckoned. At the tender age of twenty-five, Kelly was accepted into the prestigious offices of Corporate.

Her parents sighed with relief. The inner circle of an international hotel chain would give their darling the proper scope for her talents.

Kelly knew an opportunity to ascend the lofty heights of Corporate was not to be missed. Only a fool would turn down a chance to influence Corporate standards on such a grand scale. And there was the money. Kelly had demonstrated her ability to work long hours. She was a *wunderkind*. But the door would not be open long. Matthew would not give her another opportunity like this if she threw his patronage in his face.

Kelly took the promotion to Corporate and had been there, honing her skills and working her butt off, ever since.

Now she was about to make VP.

Big deal.

She could look forward to another twenty years of walking on eggshells for fear of tipping the delicate balance of Matthew's approval. Of doing the mating dance that was office politics. Of dealing with scumbags like Bradley Kovacks who could smile and smile and be a villain.

Of lonely evenings coming home exhausted to a sleek and anonymous apartment and feeling tainted by the icky stuff.

She felt as if lead weights were attached to her arms and legs and quicksand was slurping at her feet.

No!

Conor was right.

She was *not* one of them.

She never would be.

Suddenly she felt free again as she hadn't since that day

she was climbing the hill to the castle with Conor, laughing in the teeth of an approaching storm as the salt air plastered her silly, strictly ornamental power suit to her body.

She couldn't wait to tell him. She counted the days, but any way she counted, there were too many of them.

Meanwhile, she had the annual meeting to get through. And her belated birthday dinner with her parents tonight. And the command performance at Matthew's cocktail party tomorrow night. And a few hours at the office on Saturday to go through her desk thoroughly and examine with a fine-tooth comb the correspondence that had accumulated in her absence.

If Kelly had not already decided to move on, the annual meeting would have nailed the decision for her.

Gone was the usual format of Matthew and his VPs taking turns recapping the fiscal year just past, giving an informal preview of goals for the following year, and taking questions. Instead, Matthew gave a talk that was meant, Kelly supposed, to be motivational, but it was mostly New Age jargon interspersed with vaguely sinister threats.

Translation: Lawrence Hotels is making changes, and only team players willing to give 110 percent need apply. If you're not happy, we don't want to hear about it. In fact, if you're not upbeat and enthusiastic and willing to give your all for the company, you're a loser and deadweight. Morale is wonderful. Morale couldn't be better. By gum, this is the best company in America.

Budget cuts? Well, sure. This is a *positive* thing. We're trimming the fat for a better future. Staff cuts? Well, yeah, but only as part of an efficient downsizing to better manage our resources.

When hands went up, Matthew frowned and stared hard at those who would have asked questions as if he was committing their names to memory for future reprisals.

Questions would be taken after all the speakers had finished, he said sternly. The fact that he was still smiling made this statement scarier than it should have been. All hands went down.

Kelly hadn't been around for the planning stages of this tightly orchestrated little demonstration of power, so she sat there, absolutely appalled.

Then came the pep talks. The VPs took turns standing up there and patting themselves on the back, extolling their achievements. Then the directors took their turns.

This was right up Bradley's alley, Kelly thought as she watched him go into his act.

Never mind that his Tokyo project was a fiasco because the Asian economy crashed just when it should have started paying off. He managed to make the experience sound like a triumph. In fact, he implied, the movement into that market just before the bottom fell out was a shrewd and canny business strategy.

By five o'clock, the speeches weren't over, and most of the hourly employees had to leave to pick up children from day care or catch trains to their respective working-class suburbs.

How convenient.

The rank and file would miss the question-and-answer period.

Kelly would have given just about anything she possessed for the luxury of shipping out with them, but that would have been unthinkable.

One department head after another pumped up Matthew's ego by telling him—Kelly had no delusions that their presentations were meant to impress anyone else—how tickled pink they were to serve on the Lawrence team.

Then it was over and the love-in began because no one was left except the members of the inner circle and their attendant sycophants. Julie, she noticed, stayed to the bitter end, seemingly hanging on every word.

All the more reason to keep an eye on little Julie.

Although she would barely have time to shower and dress for dinner with her parents, Kelly knew she had to stay until the end. She wouldn't want anyone to think she had a personal life that prevented her from giving 110 percent.

"I'll walk out with you," said Julie, suddenly appearing at her side when the love-in finally wound down.

Kelly gave her a suspicious look.

"Okay," she said, looking at her askance.

"Well," said Julie, emitting a long breath once they were outside the building. "After that, I'll never have trouble faking an orgasm again."

Kelly gave an involuntary snort of laughter.

Aw, Julie, she thought, mourning a perfectly good working relationship in her heart. They hadn't been close personal friends, but Kelly had enjoyed Julie's irreverent sense of humor and loopy way of looking at the world. She had been able to let her hair down with her occasionally.

But no more.

And she was not in the mood to play games.

"I guess that useful little skill is going to come in handy considering the company you've been keeping," Kelly said coolly, deliberately spurning what she had no trouble identifying as an overture of peace.

Julie bit her lip.

"I made a mistake," she said, looking crushed.

"You sure did," Kelly agreed.

"Pretty pathetic, huh?" Julie said bitterly. There were tears in her eyes, but Kelly remained unmoved. "The guy compliments me on my efficiency and tells me he likes my sense of humor and I'm on my back."

"Cripes, Julie," Kelly said, wincing. "Don't go there. Please."

"Don't worry. I meant that figuratively, not literally. You don't think he would lower himself to getting sweaty with a thirty-something, overweight divorcée with two kids who still lives with her mother because her salary barely keeps the kids in shoes and breakfast cereal, do you? Could I have *been* any more of an idiot?"

"Oh, cut it out," Kelly said impatiently, tacitly accepting Julie's implied offer of a ride home when she gestured toward the passenger side of her car.

"The thing is," said Julie, determined to unburden herself, "he's not like you."

"Thank you. And I mean that sincerely."

Julie gave a wintry smile.

"What I mean is, you're nice and all that, and I think you appreciate my work, but you don't really need me."

"So, it's *my* fault you let Brad see correspondence and reports relating to *my* project?" Kelly asked, lifting her eyebrows.

"No, of course not," Julie said impatiently. "But he kept complimenting me and telling me how underrated I was and how he couldn't get along without me—"

"Like I *don't* do those things!"

"Well, you *can* get along without me," Julie pointed out.

"And it's a good thing," Kelly said coolly, "because I'm going to have to come into the office tomorrow to go through the pile on my desk to see if anything fell through the cracks while you were impressing Brad with your efficiency."

"Well, he *was* impressed," Julie said, "or seemed to be. Maybe he's gotten good at faking orgasms, too."

Kelly winced.

"Maybe you don't think I compliment you enough," Kelly said. "But I've never had the impression you need *me*, either."

"What's that supposed to mean?" Julie snapped.

Irrationally, Kelly relaxed, glad to see annoyance replace that uncharacteristically hangdog look.

"You're not exactly meek and submissive," Kelly said. "You have a brain and you know how to use it. You function perfectly well in an emergency, and I never have to worry that things are going to go to hell in a handbasket if I'm not here to hold your hand. At least, I didn't have to worry until now. I didn't think you were so insecure that I had to keep telling you how wonderful you are, like you were a six-year-old. It would have seemed kind of presumptuous, like telling Cher she had a nice voice after she sang the national anthem at a ball game."

"Wow," said Julie, kind of awed. "You think I'm that good, huh?"

"Oh, like you're surprised," Kelly said. "You're so obviously overqualified that only an idiot—naming no names— would think you're working to your full potential."

"Oh," Julie snapped. "Now I'm not working hard enough."

"You're working very hard. But you've got to be frustrated working this hard just to make people like Brad—and me, for that matter—look good. The hotel business is my passion. So what's *your* excuse for putting up with this crap?"

"My children," Julie said bitterly. "And fear, I suppose. Sometimes it's easier to settle for what you have than to reach for what you may not be able to get."

Leave it to Julie to sum it up so eloquently.

"And that would be?" Kelly prompted, curious.

Julie gave a Mona Lisa smile as she hit the door lock button in front of Kelly's building.

"You, first," Julie said.

Conor, Kelly almost blurted out. *A life*.

"Have a nice weekend," Kelly said instead, and got out of the car.

Eighteen

Connie and Donald Sullivan exchanged a disapproving look when Kelly answered her door in an extremely eccentric purple garment that made her look like Sherlock Holmes on acid, when she knew perfectly well they were going to the Frontera Grill and might be seen by people they knew.

Worse, she reeked of some floral scent reminiscent of little old ladies with blue-rinsed hair on their way to church.

Kelly's mother, a lady so elegant and well-toned that she and her daughter were often mistaken for sisters, wore nothing but Shalimar. It had been her signature scent for years.

Connie forced a teasing smile to her lips.

"You could use a trim, dear," she said, touching Kelly's slightly split ends. Kelly kept her bangs out of her eyes with an inexpensive plastic band that more or less coordinated with the purple thing and the jade silk pantsuit beneath it. Connie gingerly fingered a fold of the purple cloak and noted the way Kelly's chin jutted out.

Too bad.

Connie and Donald Sullivan had not worked so hard to give themselves and their daughter the best of everything to enjoy the sight of their only child dressed like *that*. At least she was wearing gold jewelry and proper makeup.

"Don't you have another coat, Kelly?" Connie asked in a tone of gentle rebuke.

"Yes, but I want to wear this," Kelly said, picking up her purse. "Are you ready to go?" Without waiting for an answer, she led the way out of the apartment and waited for them to go into the hall so she could lock her door.

Conversation at dinner did nothing to reassure her mother.

Kelly's face glowed as she made a funny story of her adventures in Ireland. Her voice had even acquired a soft brogue.

This was definitely adding insult to injury considering that Connie and Donald had taken speech therapy at exorbitant expense to eradicate their Boston-Irish neighborhood accents when they first moved to Chicago in their determination to break off from their parents' poor immigrant roots and make something of themselves.

The evening went downhill from there.

Kelly ate a huge meal, embarked upon a chatty and completely inappropriate personal conversation with their server, and when the server had finally responded to Connie's and Donald's pointed frowns, kept on chattering inanely about Ireland, the damned castle and those O'Mearas, who sounded exactly like the sort of repressed, superstitious, backward people Connie and Donald had struggled so hard to get away from.

A young man named Conor played too prominent a role in these anecdotes for their peace of mind. Connie noticed the pitch of Kelly's voice changed when she said his name and her eyes sparkled.

A very bad sign.

So was the way Kelly was washing down her food with beer. The girl was consuming enough calories to keep the inhabitants of a small underdeveloped country alive for a month. Connie noticed that Kelly's slacks were a little tight in the hips.

Connie exchanged a where-have-we-failed look with her husband, who obviously was as dismayed as she was.

"They have this great thing in Ireland called the full Irish breakfast," Kelly went on chattily. "Rashers—which are bacon strips, only not like we have here; they're more like Canadian bacon—with potatoes and sausages and eggs and stuff all fixed in one skillet, grease and all." She gave them a droll look. "You don't want to know how they make the black pudding."

Connie closed her eyes in repulsion. She knew too well how they made black pudding. They packed the meat in its own blood and stuffed it into intestine casings, and here was her daughter acting as if it were some sort of gourmet experience.

"Sorry," Kelly said contritely when her parents failed to respond. "I've been babbling on and on and not giving you a chance to get a word in edgewise. What's going on with you two?"

"Not much," her mother said. "Business is good."

Kelly looked at her father.

"Same here," he said.

Kelly nodded.

"Kelly, about the party tomorrow night—" her mother blurted out.

Kelly raised her eyebrows.

"Yes? Do you want to pick me up and make sure I'm not wearing something that will embarrass you?"

"Certainly not. You're a grown woman. It would be ridiculous for us to take you to the party as if you were still a little girl."

"Yeah," Kelly said, grinning. "Still, why don't we go together? That way, I won't have my car so if I decide to pick up guys—" she broke off at the sight of her parents' pained looks. "Oh, lighten up!" she said, laughing. "Like I'd want to go out with any of the clowns from *my* office."

"That Bradley Kovacks is a nice-looking young man," Connie offered.

Kelly gave her an incredulous stare.

"That dirt-ball? I'd rather date old Matt!" She laughed to show how ridiculous the mere thought of *that* was, but her parents weren't smiling. "Oh, come *on*," she wailed.

"Matthew will soon be divorced," Connie said, "and I am sure you'll agree he is an attractive man for his age."

"You mean, I could be the next Leona Helmsley if I play my cards right? Gee, thanks. He's old enough to be my father. No offense, Dad."

"None taken," Donald assured her.

"Well, what about Bradley Kovacks, then? He has a position equal to yours," her mother persisted. "He dresses well, behaves well in public, and always speaks highly of you when we see him socially."

"Oh, *please*! I'm trying to *eat* here!"

"It looks to me as if you've succeeded," her mother snapped. "I've rarely seen you eat a meal with such enthusiasm."

Kelly did not even *pretend* these weren't fighting words.

"Happy birthday to me," she said with a sigh.

"Look, Princess—" her father began.

"Aw, Dad. Don't call me Princess," she said. "It sounds like I'm your dog."

"Your mother and I," he continued, ignoring her interruption, "only want what's best for you."

"Well, it's *not* Bradley Kovacks or Matthew Lawrence. Trust me on this."

"You're not getting any younger," her mother declared.

"Well—*news flash*!" Kelly said brightly.

"You were thirty-three this week," her mother persisted. "You can be flippant about your prospects all you want, but most of the men your age are marrying younger women."

"So, that must mean I'm just what old Matt is looking for," Kelly said sarcastically. "Well, I don't have to worry that he can't father children. He's got *three* of them almost as old as I am. As for Bradley, I'd rather join a convent. Give me credit for *some* taste."

Taste, her mother thought, disgruntled. Kelly's taste obviously ran to handsome Irish rogues with no ambition and no prospects.

•   •   •

On Saturday night when Kelly opened the door to her parents, Connie's eyes narrowed in concentration. Kelly pirouetted, knowing when she was being sized up.

She was wearing a short black Liz Claiborne dress, peau de soie pumps, diamond drops in a sleek, contemporary setting at her earlobes, and a gold choker with a diamond solitaire slide at her throat. She carried the short, honey mink jacket her parents gave her for Christmas in one hand.

She knew she must look good; she was flattered it took her mother so long to find something to criticize.

"I see you didn't have time to get your hair trimmed," Connie said at last, frowning.

Kelly shrugged. Not since she was a teenager could she remember her mother not finding something about her appearance to criticize before she went out, so this didn't bother her.

"No," Kelly said pleasantly. "I think I'm going to let it grow out."

"It looks a little ragged," her mother persisted. "And the rhinestone barrettes detract from your diamond jewelry."

"I have some plain gold-tone ones if you think they'd be better," Kelly said, willing to humor her.

"No. These are probably all right. We'd better go."

Kelly sighed. She was not looking forward to being a captive audience while Matthew and Linda pretended their deteriorating relationship was somehow chic and sophisticated enough to allow them to entertain guests in a civilized fashion while on the side they flirted with potential new lovers.

Kelly didn't expect to see anyone her own age there unless Bradley Kovacks showed up, and he didn't count. Of course, some of the old guys' wives might be her age.

When they arrived at the Lawrence house, Kelly braced herself for Matt's kiss of greeting. It lasted too long and was placed too close to Kelly's lips for comfort, even though she had turned her face away as soon as she saw his slightly moist lips headed in her direction. He also let his hands linger a little too long on her bare arm when he took her jacket. Putting his arm around her shoulders, he guided her into the living room, chatting all the while about golf to her father.

Oh, God. Golf. It occurred to her that not once when she was in Ireland did Kelly have to listen to any long, boring accounts of anyone's golf game. Of course, while talking about golf, the speaker got to get in that he had been golfing on some very exclusive course with someone very famous, who, the speaker would say in a self-deprecating way, he managed to beat. From there he would entertain his captive listener with anecdotes meant to illustrate how athletic he was, how clever he was, how many famous people he knew well enough to pay golf with, and how rich he was. For, although he had to complain about how expensive it was getting to play golf at this exclusive resort, his real motive was to make sure you knew he could afford it.

From there he would, in a pretense of good nature, talk about how much money his trophy wife had spent on jewelry and clothing at the pro shop and nearby boutiques while he was golfing.

Bo-ring!

Kelly decided to check on the food. Shrimp. That was good. She selected a few and added a spoonful of cocktail sauce to her plate. Pasta salad. Naaaw. Some celery sticks, cherry tomatoes. A finger sandwich. Very nice. She lifted a shrimp to her mouth and caught her parents frowning at her. She was supposed to be mingling.

"Hi, Kell," a familiar voice said.

"Hi, Bradley," she said without bothering to pretend enthusiasm as she turned to face him. "Nice party."

"Yeah. Did you come alone?"

"No. My parents gave me a lift."

He grinned.

"Sounds like fun."

"I haven't seen them much lately, so we have some catching up to do," she said easily. "Did you bring a date?"

Bradley indicated a voluptuous brunette in a painted-on red dress. Matthew Lawrence was practically salivating as he looked down her cleavage.

"My little goodwill ambassador," Brad joked, looking fondly at his date.

Better her than me, Kelly thought. The sad thing was, Brad was as close as she got to stimulating company all evening.

Before she met Conor, Kelly resigned herself to spending most of her social life with people much older than she was. She resigned herself to listening with every show of interest while they went on and on about their possessions, their stock market acumen, and their relentless one-upsmanship.

Linda was usually good for a laugh or two at these stifling affairs, but she was decidedly cool to Kelly tonight. No doubt she noticed the way Matt kissed her on arrival. The marriage might be over, but Linda would hardly enjoy watching her soon-to-be ex-husband paw a younger woman right in her living room. Kelly had always been uncomfortable with the way she was expected to kiss and be kissed by men she hardly knew at these affairs. It was like giving a bit of her soul away.

Now, where had *that* come from?

This stuff hadn't bothered her so much before she went to Ireland.

Before Conor, she had been half alive. She knew that now. For comfort, she thought of him now. The way he smiled. The way he talked. The way, when he touched her, it felt clean and right. What had he *done* to her?

She waited until three couples left, just so she wouldn't be too obvious, then she tracked down her father to ask if he was ready to leave. Of the two, it was usually her father she found more receptive in situations like this, mainly because he liked to play the role of indulgent father in public.

"Sure, honey," he said when she told him she was ready to go home. It was tacky to stay too late, anyway, as if you didn't have any plans for later in the evening.

Her mother frowned a little when they found her talking about golf to Matthew. This was another indication that Matthew's marriage was on the rocks. Usually Kelly's mother, as behooved the gracious consort, would have spent some time with Linda, a woman she had known for years. But Linda was about to become an ex-wife and therefore socially invisible until she found a new man. She no longer had any influence with her CEO husband, and so it was no longer worthwhile for Kelly's mother to cultivate her.

Connie plainly wasn't ready to leave, but she never contradicted her spouse in public. Kelly suspected it was part of a notarized agreement her parents had locked away in a bank vault somewhere.

"Going so soon?" Matthew said, putting his arm around Kelly.

"We had a lovely time, Matthew," Connie said.

"It's always a pleasure to see you," Matthew replied as his thick, slightly moist fingers idly kneaded Kelly's arm.

Kelly smiled sweetly and detached herself from his grasp. He made her feel shopworn.

"See you Monday, Matthew," she said. "Where's Linda? I want to say goodbye."

Especially since it might be the last time I see her.

By the time Kelly returned from Ireland, Matthew and Linda's divorce would be official, and Linda would quite literally disappear. Even if she continued to occupy this house while Matt went into the new condo on Lake Shore Drive, Linda and her husband would no longer be invited to the same parties. She would soon be supplanted by a younger woman, and her ex-husband's friends and business associates would hardly want to invite the middle-aged mother of his children to make everyone uncomfortable, like a ghost, at their parties.

Not that Linda would be missing much. She probably couldn't wait to kiss all these boring, self-centered people good-bye.

Kelly found her hostess alone in the kitchen, fussing over a plate of finger sandwiches. It seemed most of the guests were eager to disassociate themselves from the future divorcée.

"Lovely party, Linda," Kelly said, kissing her cheek. Well the *party* was lovely. The *people* made it boring.

"Thanks. Have a nice trip to Ireland."

"I will. Good-night."

"Good-bye, Kelly," Linda said wistfully. "Have a good life."

Unaccountably, Kelly's eyes filled with tears. For Linda? Or for herself? She got out of the kitchen before she made a fool of herself and ran right into Matthew. Of course, he had to fondle her arm a little more. Kelly wanted to scream.

"Thanks again for inviting me," she said lamely.

"I'll look forward to seeing you Monday," he said with an intimate smile that suggested they were planning a romantic assignation instead of a business meeting. "We'll talk. About Ireland."

Kelly gave him a suspicious look. Was there a slightly threatening tone to his voice? Kelly's blood ran cold.

What new plans did Matthew have for Whitlock Castle? And for her?

Nineteen

A hideous two days later, Kelly was on her way back ("Home!" sang the little voice in her heart) to Ireland. It was a cold, overcast April day in the Midwest. It would probably be just as cold and overcast in Ireland, but Kelly couldn't wait to get home, er, *back* to Conor and the castle.

Once she was in her seat, she snuggled into the comforting folds of the beautiful purple wool cloak.

Only seven more hours, the little voice inside her head sang.

She tried not to think of her meeting with Matthew.

He didn't paw her exactly, although he kept giving her those intimate smiles and implying that when the Irish assignment was over he'd like to meet with her privately and discuss the VP position. Crudely put, the implication was that if she performed well, she could count on his support. She came very close to telling him what he could do with the promotion, but when he started talking about the castle, Kelly bit her tongue.

He had been thinking about her suggestions for renovating the castle as a luxury hotel, he said, and decided perhaps he *should* rethink the idea of making the castle into a combination hotel and medieval theme park. He promised not to make any firm decision until her studies were complete.

It was victory of a sort.

The only thing was, she felt soiled because she didn't make it absolutely clear to Matthew in terms even *he* could understand that his attentions were unwelcome. She was afraid he would retaliate by destroying the castle.

Kelly awakened groggy and a little disoriented when the plane touched down at Shannon Airport. She had dreamed of Conor looking strong and clean and handsome, and Matthew looking relentlessly groomed and sinister, and her parents were in there somewhere, but none of it made any sense.

After Kelly stumbled off the plane and through customs, she gave a faint scream when someone came from behind and took her suitcase out of her hand.

"Conor," she sighed, grabbing his shoulders. He set the suitcase on the floor and wrapped his strong arms around her, looking surprised, but pleased, by her enthusiasm. He looked so wholesome and wonderful in his long-sleeved blue shirt and worn jeans, like an angel come to earth to make the world shiny and new after she had been immersed in all the subterfuge and dirty little deals at Corporate.

She had come away soiled.

But Conor could make her clean again.

She put both hands on the sides of his face and stretched up on tiptoe to kiss him as if her life depended on it. When they had to break off the kiss or turn blue, he laughed shakily and picked up the suitcase.

"Were you missing me, then, Kelly Sullivan?" he asked, "or are you just pleased to get back to our beautiful weather?"

It was raining, of course, but the sunlight was shining through the clouds. There would be a rainbow later.

"You have no idea how good it looks," she said, thinking even the concrete looked reborn.

Conor stopped walking and looked searchingly at her face.

"What is it?" he asked, looking concerned. "What happened to you in Chicago?"

Kelly could have wept with affection for him. He knew she was troubled, and he acted like someone who cared. No one else in her world was this sensitive to her.

"The castle might be safe for now," she said, giving him the good news first.

"That's . . . good," he said cautiously, still searching her face.

"It's *everything*. It *has* to be," she said vehemently.

Conor knew there was something else, but this was not the place to discuss it.

He put an arm around her shoulders and started walking again, loving the feel of her through the softness of the purple wool that had been his gift to her. Something was bothering her beyond the usual fatigue from jet lag, and he was going to find out what it was.

"We'll go to the cottage," he said, "so we can talk."

All the way to County Cork, Kelly kept clinging to his hand, and once she leaned over the gearshift and nibbled on his neck. His heart broke. She was like a lost child seeking affection and comfort. He'd seen this restlessness, this pain, before. Ghillie had been like this after she'd lost her place in the dance troupe. She had come to him then, wanting him to take her to his bed.

But he refused, knowing it wasn't really *him* she wanted. He would not take advantage of her confusion.

And he would not take advantage of Kelly's, no matter how much he had dreamed of having her willing and hungry in his arms. It would be hard to resist her. They had not made love since that one night, and he had craved her ever since.

Kelly seemed happy. She kept giving him sly, eager little looks. She thought they were going to the cottage to make love.

They were going to talk. Only that, he told himself

firmly as he tried to ignore the way her perfume filled his nostrils.

She was going to tell him what had happened in Chicago to send her into this reckless state.

Kelly took her index finger and traced a slow, languid line from his temple, to his ear, and then to his jaw and down his neck, causing his traitorous body to give a shudder of anticipation.

Why did he have to be so bloody noble?

"If you want to get there alive," he said in a voice that wasn't quite steady, "you'll be keeping your hands to yourself a bit."

To his relief, she settled back on her side of the car. When they stopped in front of the cottage, she was all over him again as soon as they were out of the car. He should probably have put a stop to it right away, but she slipped her arm around his waist, and he couldn't resist kissing the top of her head as they walked inside. Her hair was all soft and sweet-smelling, and her lipstick was smeared from kissing him. He could taste it on his lips.

Once inside the door, she pivoted against his shoulder and put her arms around his neck. She lifted her face to his expectantly.

Did he ever claim to be made of stone? All his noble intentions almost crumbled as he bent to taste those full, sensual lips.

Just one kiss, he told himself. He broke off the kiss, held her close for a moment more, and then he released her.

"Let me take this," he said, swirling the cloak off her shoulders so he could hang it on the peg by the kitchen door.

She misunderstood and started unbuttoning his shirt.

"Kelly," he said, laughing in his frustration. "We need to talk."

"Okay," she agreed, looking up into his eyes. "Later."

He covered her busy fingers with his hands and trapped them against his chest. She frowned and tried to free them.

"We'll talk now," he said.

Kelly closed her eyes and took a deep breath. When she opened them, the glazed look was gone. She bit her lip. For the first time, she really *looked* at him.

"Well, I see I've made a mistake," she said, sounding mortified. "I'm sorry. I didn't mean to embarrass you." She looked down at the floor.

"Kelly," he said softly, putting his hands on her shoulders. He bent his head so he could gaze into her face.

"Don't worry," she said with a shaky laugh. "I'm over it now."

"Well, I'm not," he admitted. "You make it hard for a man to think straight, but I can't be taking what you're so set on offering if I don't want you to hate me later. Something happened in Chicago. Something that worried you."

She looked so chagrined that he led her to the couch and pulled her down so he could cradle her in his lap. She put her head on his shoulder and gave a shuddering sigh, like a child who had been crying.

"It was so awful, Conor," she said. "The office. My parents. And old Matthew leering at me. He's getting divorced. He's always had kind of a thing for me, but I've been able to laugh it off because he was married. Now he's not going to be married anymore."

"What did he do to you?" Conor asked. He could feel the tendons stick out on his neck.

Kelly gave an unconvincing laugh.

"Nothing at all. He just implied that once his divorce was final, he'd like to get to know me better. And he kept touching me in ways that seemed impersonal but didn't feel that way."

"*Touching* you?" He'd kill the man with his bare hands!

Kelly shrugged.

"You know. Kissing me on the cheek at the party. Taking my arm if we're walking in the hall at work. Little things that sort of put his stamp of ownership on me. The usual stuff."

"The bloody blackguard," Conor said, holding her close and staring with hot eyes at the opposite wall.

"Well," she said, trying to sound cheerful. "At least the castle is safe for now. He hasn't completely ruled out the medieval-theme-park idea, but at least he's listening to my arguments in favor of keeping the castle intact and operating it as a luxury hotel. It's the best we could have hoped for at this point. I have his support for now."

Conor could tell she wasn't entirely happy about it.

"And what is the price of this support?" he asked, forcing himself to sound calm and controlled.

"Well, the implication was that I might have a personal relationship with him."

"Sleep with him," Conor corrected through gritted teeth.

"That is the implication," she admitted. "Funny, but I really thought I could do *anything* to become vice president. And when I got to know you and your family, I thought I could do *anything* to save the castle."

"No!" shouted Conor.

"Oh, don't get your shorts in a bunch," she said. "You said once I wasn't like *them*, and you were right."

"Thank God for that," he said, holding her close as if to defend her from blackguards like Matthew Lawrence.

"No. Instead I'll just let him think I *might*," she said huskily, "which means instead of being a whore I'm merely a tease. Like *that's* anything to be proud of."

"Quit your job," Conor said. "You can't go back there."

She gave a brittle laugh and kissed him full on the lips.

"You're so sweet, Conor."

"You're not making it sound exactly like a compliment," he told her suspiciously.

"It is, though. I don't give a rat's ass about being vice president anymore. But if I quit now, Matthew will put someone else in charge of the Whitlock Castle project—someone who won't fight for it. It might even be Bradley Kovacks, and this guy is a butcher in an expensive suit. I can't let that happen."

"It's not your battle," Conor insisted. "I won't let you make that kind of a sacrifice for us."

"A fate worse than death, you mean?" she asked sardonically. "No. I am not going to go to bed with Matthew Lawrence. It would give me great satisfaction to tell him so in terms even a jerk like him can understand, but I'm not going to let him wreck the castle if I can prevent it."

To Conor's regret, she got up and started pacing. He'd seen her like this before, as if the ideas were bombarding her so intensely that it was either move or be bludgeoned to death by them.

"The basic plan hasn't changed. When I'm finished, I'll have done such a thorough job they'll have to acknowledge the castle is too valuable an asset to destroy. And then, when he's committed to the idea of a luxury hotel, I'll look for another job."

She perched on the sofa next to him and he couldn't resist touching her hair.

"And what kind of a job would you be looking for, Kelly Sullivan?" he asked.

She smiled wistfully at him.

"I'd like to manage a hotel, like the castle. If it were mine—" she broke off. "Well, I started out in hotel management, but then I was promoted to Corporate and it was too good a deal to turn down at the time. Now I can start over. It won't be as much money or prestige, but managing a hotel is what I really want to do. You've taught me that."

She put her arms around his neck and twisted her body so he had no choice but to cradle her in his lap. He didn't have the control to resist her.

"What are you doing?" he said helplessly between frantic kisses as she started unbuttoning his shirt again.

"Seducing you," she said, looking a little desperate. "Please."

"This isn't what you want," he said, trying to get a grip on his sanity. The zipper to that short, hip-hugging plaid skirt was under his fingers, and he had to will them not to open it.

"Trust me on this," she said. "I do."

He stood up so abruptly he had to catch her elbow to keep her from tumbling to the floor.

"You really mean it, don't you?" she asked, looking shamefaced.

"Do you love me, Kelly?"

She felt as if he had put a gun to her head.

"If we just . . . do this, and it doesn't mean as much to you as it does to me," he told her, "then I'd be letting you use me."

Kelly sat on the sofa with a dejected thump.

"Just like old Matt wants to use me," she said. "God, Conor. Is that what you think?"

"It's all right," he said, kneeling in front of her and taking her face between his hands. "You're just confused and jet-lagged. I'll drive you up to the castle and fix you a cup of tea—"

"I do love you," she said. His heart turned over when twin tears pooled in her eyes and went down her cheeks. "I really do."

"That's the jet lag talking," he said, helping her to her feet. He didn't dare let himself believe it.

"It is *not*!" she said angrily, wresting her arm away. "Quit treating me like I'm unstable. I finally get the nerve to say it, right out loud, and you have the gall to *patronize* me."

Against his better judgment, he pulled her into his arms and kissed her until they were clinging to each other for support.

"Does this mean you've changed your mind?" she asked.

"No," he said. "It means if you're saying the same thing after you are yourself again, I'll take you up on it."

"Always the gentleman," she said sarcastically.

He looked longingly at the enticing short skirt and the long, long legs it revealed. Then his eyes went back to her face. Kelly pressed her hands to her bright red cheeks. Then, with hands that shook, she unzipped her skirt.

"What are you doing?" Conor cried out in alarm. He grabbed the waistband of the skirt to keep it from falling. She leaned close and threw her arms around his neck so their bodies were touching from breast to hip. "Ah, Kelly," he

said, closing his eyes. "This is not the best way of demonstrating you're in your right mind."

"Push me away if you don't want me," Kelly dared him,
resuming her task of unbuttoning his shirt. He was wearing
a white tee shirt under it. She almost smiled. "I'm exhausted
and jet-lagged. I'm no match for you."

"That's a lie the size of Dublin City," he said.

"I saw the way you looked at me just now."

"Heaven help you, Kelly Sullivan," he growled, letting
the skirt drop to the floor. "I tried to do the right thing. I'm
damned if I'll let you walk away from me now."

"Thank God," she breathed, sagging bonelessly into his
embrace. He lifted her free of the skirt.

The next thing Kelly knew, she was in his bedroom trying
to tear his clothes off. He was laughing, but his eyes were
hot. He stopped to pull his tee shirt off while she reached for
his belt.

"Slow down," he said, looking serious. "I don't want this
to be over too soon."

He kissed her mouth and then her eyelids. Then he
skimmed the sides of her breasts and her waist with his
hands.

"So beautiful," he breathed. "So beautiful and strong and
fine."

He took the elastic band of her panty hose and, kneeling,
slowly peeled them off.

With his teeth.

Her face burned as he pulled them free of her feet and just
stared at the dainty blue lace triangle of her thong bikini
panties.

"Ah, Kelly," he said, almost reverently.

He took the end of her turtleneck sweater and pulled it
over her head, filling his hands with her lace-covered
breasts.

"Blue," he said, kissing the rounded tops of them above
the blue lace bra. "My new favorite color."

She closed her eyes and shuddered with pleasure when he
sat her on the bed and knelt before her, kissing her breasts,

her abdomen, and her navel. All the time, his hands caressed her back and the smooth indention of her waist.

He hooked his fingers under the thong and kissed the flesh that emerged as he pulled it down.

"Conor," she sighed. "Oh, God." His tongue traced a slow path at the tops of her thighs where the skin was tender, but he didn't touch the throbbing heat so close to it.

He was driving her crazy.

Conor put his hand under her knees and lifted her onto the bed. Then he started kissing her again, lightly and teasingly, all over her body as he removed the bra. He laid his hand on her heated mound—only that—and she nearly came. He drew his hand up and covered her abdomen and then her navel. Her back arched and the hardening of her nipples was almost painful. He groaned and took one in his mouth.

Kelly plunged her fingers into his hair and writhed as he levered himself over her and slowly rubbed his body against hers as he kissed her face and shoulders. The light abrasion of his chest against her tender, swollen breasts and his hard erection against her thighs made her gasp with pleasure.

Just when she thought she couldn't stand it anymore, he abruptly left her. Her eyes opened in alarm, but he made a soothing noise and lightly touched her shoulder. She heard the drawer of the bedside table slide open and she realized that she hadn't even thought of protection. He returned to her, sheathed, and pressed apologetic little kisses on her face as he slowly sank into her willing softness.

He said her name over and over as he drove her to heights of pleasure so intense she thought she would die of it.

When the explosion came, they cried out in unison and held each other through the giddy, breathless laughter of release.

Kelly's body shuddered with the aftershocks as Conor leaned above her, smoothing her damp hair from her temples, and watched her lovely, flushed face.

She was so beautiful and responsive to him, but he didn't delude himself that she was his.

He kissed her lips and she responded with all the generosity and fire he always found in her. Then he kissed her warm, salty brow and sat up.

Kelly opened her eyes and found him sitting on the side of the bed. Kelly swung her legs around so she could sit beside him and touched his shoulder in concern.

"Conor?" she asked, moving her hand to his face. "Is something wrong?"

He moved his head away from her hand. She felt as if she had been slapped.

"This is the last time, Kelly," he said in a voice that sounded like death.

Kelly bit her lip and pulled the sheet around her to cover her breasts.

"That bad, huh?" she said, trying for a light tone.

"No," he said, looking at her with a sad, regretful smile on his face. "That good."

"Maybe it's the jet lag, but you're not making a lot of sense."

"You're the love of my life, Kelly. I can't do this again knowing you're going to go back to America in a few months and I'll never see you again."

Kelly picked her bra up off the floor and looked for her panties. Fortunately, Conor wasn't a flinger.

"So you think you're a one-night stand," she said huskily.

He looked her straight in the eye.

"Yes, I do," he said softly. "I know what happens once a girl gets used to the city. She may come to a place like this to heal after some disappointment, but when she's strong again, she'll go back to where she belongs without a backward look."

Kelly's eyes narrowed.

"You're not talking about me at all," she said, hitting him on the head with a pillow. "You're talking about Ghillie!"

He took the pillow and threw it against the wall.

"I asked you to marry me last time when we got caught by

Aunt Rose and Aunt Margaret. You behaved as if someone had asked you to marry a monkey in the zoo."

"I did *not!*" Kelly shouted.

"You did," he said quietly, capturing her wrists when she looked like she wanted to hit him.

"Well, that's not what I meant," she said, flushing.

"You said you loved me," he said, releasing her wrists. "But do you love me enough to live in this cottage with me, my aunts, and my father all crowded together?"

She sighed and rested her head against his shoulder.

"Why can't we just enjoy what we have while we can still have it? Why do you have to make everything so complicated?"

"It's not complicated at all," he said, his voice like lead. "Stay with me. Marry me. Or leave me be. I can't go on doing . . . this, when I know you're going to leave me and return to your big noisy city and your big important job."

"What about the castle? I told you what could happen if I leave Lawrence at this stage of the acquisition."

She saw her panty hose on the floor and tried to reach for them, but she couldn't quite do it without exposing her breasts. It seemed wrong to let him see her naked under the circumstances.

He gave her a smile with something of his old humor in it and handed the wadded nylon to her. Then he turned his back so she could put her underwear on. He pulled on his pants and went into the other room to get her skirt and shoes. By the time he came back, she had her sweater on. He picked up his shirt and turned his back to put it on. She slipped into her skirt and sat, steaming, on the other side of the bed. He turned around and sat down next to her.

Those legs, Conor thought longingly. He wanted to reach out and just trace them with his fingertips, those smooth thighs, the pretty knees, the elegant calves and dainty ankles. But he wouldn't half blame her if she slapped him.

"I owe you an apology," she said, surprising him. "You said you didn't want to, and I kind of forced you into it."

"Well," he said, giving her another of those smiles that made her breath catch in her throat, "I *did* want to. But it's hard to be loving you so much and knowing I'm not that important to you."

"Who *says* you're not important to me?" she demanded. She got up and started pacing. "God! I'm in no shape to deal with this. I need a cup of coffee." She was practically whimpering. "I've never been the love of anybody's life before. It's too much responsibility."

He had to laugh in spite of himself.

"Then the men in America must all be mad."

"I figured I'd finish up here and wave goodbye and you'd get over me. I thought *I'd* be the only one to suffer." She gave him the glimmer of a smile. "I guess I thought you would be my last fling."

"Your last *fling*? Before *what*?"

She made a helpless gesture.

"Before I settle into a solitary middle age, I suppose. I'm over thirty and kinda fat and I'm really past it. All the men my age are already married. And if they're not, they're looking for younger women to be their trophy wives. Even the older men are looking for someone younger."

Conor was absolutely stunned that she could see herself in that way. The memory of how her luscious curves felt under his hands was burned into his brain. He'd known this was the last time, and he'd taken time to memorize her body with his.

He wanted to drag her back to bed to show her just how desirable she was, but he wouldn't make that mistake again.

He had to have all of her, forever, or none of her.

"You are the most beautiful woman I've ever known," he said instead. "And I will never, ever get over you."

Her eyes went all soft, and she reached out to him.

"No," he said firmly, moving away. "Come along, now. I'd best be getting you back to the castle."

At the door he picked up the purple cloak and swirled it onto her shoulders. Then he fastened it at the throat and kissed her softly on the lips.

The last time, she thought, putting her arms around him and kissing him back.

Then he made a gesture toward the door to indicate she should precede him and followed her out into the misty morning.

Twenty

"*Kelly! Just the* lass we need," exclaimed Sean when Kelly and Conor walked in the front door of the castle. Ghillie had been leaning against the desk talking to him, and she gave them a speculative look that made Kelly wonder if she had just come by the cottage and seen Conor's car there.

If so, the hens at the Rosary Sodality would know all about it by nightfall.

"Don't be bothering Kelly with your big plans when she's just set foot in the door," Rose said briskly as she walked in with a teapot and cups on a tray. She must have seen Kelly's nostrils quiver. "Go up to your room, girl, and I'll bring some tea to you there."

"*Bless* you, Rose," Kelly said soulfully. She turned to Sean. "What big plans?"

"For the festival, of course."

"Da," said Conor, rolling his eyes.

"I'd love to hear your plans," Kelly said. "Maybe I can help."

"There's the lass," Sean said, giving his son a triumphant look. "These girls agree it would be a shame not to have the festival after all these years, don't they? Even though my dour-faced son doesn't want to be the Summer Lord."

"Conor!" cried Ghillie. "Of *course* you'll do it!" She gave Kelly a look that told her of Conor's refusal to cooperate must be all her fault.

"I've no time to be making a fool of myself pretending to be the Summer Lord," he grumbled.

"Well, how much work is it?" Kelly asked, helping Ghillie and Sean gang up on him.

"I have to get the cottage ready for Da and Aunt Rose and Aunt Margaret to move into. It'll cost too much, and June's the height of the tourist season, so we won't be able to get enough help from the village—"

"Bah! You've been listening to your Aunt Rose again," Sean said in disgust.

"What's wrong with the cottage?" Kelly asked innocently. "It looks fine to me."

Conor gave her a wide-eyed, incredulous look, and Kelly knew she was blushing.

Good move, bucket mouth!

Why don't you just tell the whole county you and Conor have spent the last half hour doing the wild thing at the cottage?

"Don't be an old Grinch, Conor," Kelly went on quickly.

"All right, all right! I'll do it," he said, throwing up his arms. "It's plain Aunt Rose and I are outnumbered."

Kelly already knew Margaret tended to puddle right up at the mere suggestion that they might not have a festival. By Kelly's calculations, that made it a tie—Sean and Margaret versus Conor and Rose. Kelly was touched that Conor apparently thought Kelly got a vote. Or maybe the deciding vote was Ghillie's.

"Good," said Kelly as Sean pounded his son on the back in his exuberance. "I'm going to go to sleep for about a week and I'll see you later."

As she took her suitcase from Conor, their hands touched and her breath caught in her throat when she looked into his eyes.

"Conor, there's business we need to discuss about the church jumble sale," Ghillie said a bit sharply.

Conor frowned and turned to Ghillie, so the spell was broken. Kelly trudged up the steps with her suitcase and carry-on bag, feeling as if her knees were jelly. She should be half dead from jet lag, but she had never felt so alive. Comes from being thoroughly ravished, she thought, reliving the experience slowly and savoring it like a lovesick groupie.

After this assignment was over, she promised herself, she would come to terms with how she felt about Conor.

She had no sooner changed into her nightgown and robe when Rose came to the door with her tea.

"Oh! You brought some of Margaret's biscuits," Kelly said, giving into impulse and kissing her on the cheek.

"I'll have you know," Rose said, trying not to look pleased, "that these I made myself."

Kelly bit into one. Suddenly she was ravenous.

"Thanks, Rose," she said, setting down at the little table by the fireplace and taking a long sip of tea. "Looks like you lost on the festival deal."

Rose accepted Kelly's implied invitation to sit and have a gossip.

"There's no stopping Sean when he has an idea in his head," Rose said. "Conor's a bit like him that way."

Kelly snorted.

"I noticed," she said.

"He's a good man and he'll be making some lucky woman a good husband."

Kelly raised her eyebrows.

"So, are you warning me off or telling me I should snatch him up?"

"He's got his eye on you, has Conor," Rose said carefully. "I've only seen him like this once before."

"And that's when Ghillie broke his heart," Kelly finished for her.

"You'd think a man with Conor's looks would have a different girl every night of the week, but not our Conor. Not that girls don't chase after him in a way that would make you blush."

"I don't doubt it," Kelly said. "He's a hunk."

"Is that what you say in America?" Rose asked, interested.

"Yes, and don't you tell him I said so."

"If you're the one he wants, the rest of us will have to be making the best of it. I'll leave you to your rest now," she said, and left.

Kelly felt the corners of her lips quirk up when she was gone. It was less than gracious, but in her own peculiar way Rose had just welcomed Kelly to the family.

"You're going if I have to put you on the bloody bus myself," Conor shouted, glaring down at Ghillie. She had her hands on her hips and was glaring right back at him.

"That I won't, Conor O'Meara! And don't be thinking you can give me orders just because you've known me since we were children."

Kelly stuck her head in the door.

"Excuse me, folks," she said brightly, "but the guests are starting to choose sides."

Ghillie started to tell Kelly where she could take her pushy Yank interfering ways, but Conor cut right across her.

"Ghillie has an audition in Dublin, and she's saying she's not going to go," he said.

"That's *wonderful*, Ghillie," Kelly said. "Of *course*, you're going!"

"Sure, and you'd like to see the back of me, Kelly Sullivan," Ghillie said, spitting fire. "It's not a private audition. It's an open audition, and there are only three places."

"And you'll get one of them," Kelly said confidently. "What's the problem?"

"I'm not ready. I'll *never* be ready. I gave all that up. I can't *do* it anymore, don't you bloody fools understand?"

"You looked like you were doing it just fine to me last week," Kelly said.

Ghillie rolled her eyes.

"Of course, I looked good to *you*, you ignorant Yank," she snapped.

"You looked good to me, too, and you won't be calling *me* an ignorant Yank," Conor interjected.

"No," Ghillie said, baring her teeth at him. "You're just a big, thick-headed clod."

To Ghillie's irritation, Kelly walked in and sat down on the sofa, for all the world as if she were a spectator at a play.

"Make yourself at home," Ghillie said sarcastically.

"Thanks. Now, tell me why you want to shoot yourself in the foot. Here's your chance, babe. Go for it!"

"That's what I've been telling her," Conor said. "Maybe she'll listen to you."

"Why should she?" Kelly asked, raising one eyebrow.

Ghillie shut her mouth with a snap since she had been about to say the same thing.

"Because I've talked to her until I'm blue in the face, and I've had enough of it." He turned to Ghillie. "You'll be on that bus for Dublin in the morning. I'll be by your house at half past seven to pick you up. Be ready!"

He stamped out.

"Damn you for an interfering, bull-headed meddler, Conor O'Meara," Ghillie shouted after him. She glared at Kelly as if she were trying to decide the best way to cut her to ribbons.

"Hey!" said Kelly, raising her arms in truce. "I just got here! Suppose you fill me in. It doesn't hurt to bounce it off an impartial person."

"Impartial," Ghillie snorted.

"Humor me," coaxed Kelly. "What is the worst that can happen if you go to this audition?"

"I'll be out the bus fare and I'll fail."

"Big deal. That's why they call it an audition. If you don't get a spot in the troupe, at least you will have tried."

"You don't know anything about it," Ghillie snapped, pacing. "Everyone will know where I've gone and why. If I come home in disgrace, they'll all know that, too."

"But if you stay home you'll never know if you *can* do it."

"I *can't*! I was cut from one troupe. What makes you think I'll get into another?"

"You were run-down and exhausted then," Kelly said matter-of-factly. "You'd been dumped by your fiancé and you weren't sleeping or eating right."

"Well," Ghillie said huffily. "It's nice to know my personal life is such a popular topic of conversation."

"Hey! I'm the one whose underwear is the talk of the parish, remember?"

Ghillie gave her the ghost of a smile. There was something kind of appealing about the Yank. She could almost like her if she wasn't going to break Conor's heart.

On the other hand, Ghillie thought resentfully, it didn't take Conor long to forget Ghillie when the Yank pushed her way into his life. Ghillie had run home from Dublin, ready to throw herself into his arms and settle down to marriage now that she'd had her career and the city had spit her out. But Conor wasn't after taking her back. She needed time to heal, he said, and he was right. She had shivered like a skinny dog most of the time when she first came home, and she tended to burst into tears at the least little thing that went wrong. Or went right. Strong, dependable Conor was at her side, encouraging her as she mended and healed.

She didn't know at the time she had already killed the seemingly boundless love he once had for her. He continued to treat her with a sort of brotherly affection, but as soon as he set eyes on Kelly Sullivan, he was gone.

Even while Ghillie was in Dublin being courted by city men, Conor's love and the village were always in the back of her mind as a pleasant place she could always revisit if she had a mind to. It gave her security. She knew it was selfish of her, but when she came home to find Conor still unmarried, what was she to think but that he had been waiting all this time for *her*?

All right. She could live with the idea that Conor didn't love her. As one who had been betrayed so recently, she knew that even the strongest tree can die from neglect. After being dumped by Morgan, Ghillie had an idea of how she had hurt Conor years ago, and she regretted it.

That didn't mean she didn't resent the bloody hell out of

the Yank who replaced her in Conor's affections, nor was she going to let the Yank boss her around like she did everyone else.

"God Almighty, look at you," Kelly said, grinning. "When I came in I thought you were going to tear old Conor apart with your bare hands. You've probably been eating like a horse since you've been back. And you don't get your kind of muscle tone from loafing around. You've been working out. You ride your bicycle all over the place, so your legs are in great shape. And I know damn well you dance half the night at the pub for free with the least encouragement. So, why don't you cut the crap and tell me why you don't want to go to the audition."

"That life is behind me now. I've said good-bye to it."

"Bullshit!"

Ghillie gave a little snarl of irritation.

"All right! If you *must* know, the man who jilted me is going to be there. He's a choreographer. We were going to get married someday. After the next show. After I became a soloist. After he got a new show. After we both made more money. Then, suddenly, I was thirty years old and he was spending all his time with a young dancer, one he took under his wing as he once did me. Next thing I knew, we were unengaged, and I was out of a job."

"Boy, that sucks," Kelly said with real sympathy. "And so you came running back to Conor."

"To my parents," Ghillie corrected. "To the village."

"Bullshit," Kelly said again. "Not that I blame you. Ol' Conor is some port in a storm. He *will* put you on that bus tomorrow, you know. When he starts talking in that 'Voice of God' tone, you know he's not going to budge on this."

Ghillie snorted. Did the Yank think she could tell *her* about Conor O'Meara's stubbornness?

"You'd be better off talking to the wall!" Ghillie said.

"There you go," Kelly said, standing up and having the nerve to put a sisterly arm around Ghillie's shoulders. "You've spent a few months at home letting your family and friends pamper you, and now you've got your strength back. Time to get back to work and reclaim your real life."

"I'll go, if only to have the lot of you off my back," said Ghillie, giving Kelly a hard look. She wiggled out from under Kelly's arm. "I need a cup of tea and maybe a few biscuits. If by some miracle I win a place in the troupe, I'll have to give up the sugar again."

With that, she stalked off to the kitchen, leaving Kelly shaking her head.

Conor walked in a minute later, grinning

"I just saw Ghillie. She bit my head off, but she's going tomorrow," he said. "I knew you'd make her mad enough to want to show us all."

"Glad I could help," Kelly said.

"Kelly, there you are!" Margaret said, bringing in a plate of cookies. "Isn't it wonderful? Ghillie's going to an audition tomorrow." She put the cookies on a table and turned on the TV.

Kelly helped herself to a cookie and kicked back.

It was good to be home.

Twenty-one

Connie and Donald Sullivan had an extremely poor opinion of Ireland by the time the car lurched to a stop and spewed them out on the street before Whitlock Castle.

"My sinuses," Connie complained, sniffing into a tissue. "So far the mother country sucks."

"Elegantly put," her husband said dryly. "God, the rain! So, this is what all the drunks back home were crying in their Guinness about."

They said this in front of the driver, who stiffened.

Touchy lot, these Irish, Donald thought as he paid the man the agreed-upon rate and added a decent tip, even though at the current rate of exchange the price of having their teeth rattled by the miles over bad road amounted to highway robbery.

A cold, wet, and expensive country. Nothing to get sentimental about here.

Connie and Donald were on a rescue mission. Their usually bright and resourceful daughter had somehow fallen under the spell of this impossible place, and they would be damned if they were going to stand back and let Ireland suck out all her vitality and promise. What they saw during their mercifully brief visit to the village only confirmed their opinion of Ireland. All the men they encountered had red noses, and their faces were lumpy, like potato skins. The women looked a little better—the young ones, anyway. But all of them dressed in clothes Connie would have been ashamed to donate to a thrift shop.

The thirty-something element in this village was decidedly scarce. No doubt they were either home caring for their many children under the age of six or gone to bigger cities.

Connie remembered her own mother, who always seemed wrinkled and ancient like an apple-head doll, even though she couldn't have been more than forty when Connie and Donald eloped, determined to find a better life for themselves than could be found in a poor Irish neighborhood in Boston.

"Nineteenth century," Donald decided, squinting at the castle. "Looks sound. Nice place, if you like the hysterical Gothic look."

Connie's heart swelled. Her Donald's business was architecture—huge, gleaming buildings that featured clean lines and functional space with that original touch of sleek perfectionism that was his trademark. Donald was tall, handsome, and he was always reaching for the stars. When she met him she was sixteen and he was nineteen, the oldest of nine children who had moved into the neighborhood to live with relatives after his family had been thrown out of their former home for nonpayment of rent. His father had not been good at holding down a job, and that was what came of it.

Connie's mother had sworn no daughter of hers would marry a lazy, good-for-nothing Sullivan, but Connie had seen something special in Donald the moment she met him. They shared a dream of leaving that dingy, depressing world, and they did it the day Connie turned eighteen and didn't need anyone's permission to marry. Donald by that time was twenty-one and his own master. He had no formal schooling in architecture, but he read books, and a strong, strapping young man had no trouble finding work at the construction sites in Chicago while he took classes at night and completed his education. It took him years, with Connie working first in a factory and then in an office.

The day Connie and Donald finally had saved the down payment for their own home was the second proudest day of their lives.

Their proudest was the day their perfect, blonde, laughing daughter was born.

There would be only one child. Not for Connie and Donald the shack full of hungry children they couldn't afford to support. Their daughter was going to have everything her parents didn't—a nice home she wouldn't be embarrassed for her friends to see, pretty clothes as good or better than the other children's, good schools, a fine education—all handed to her on a silver platter.

Kelly would have a career. A *splendid* career. After all that her parents had achieved coming from nothing, how could she fail?

Most important of all, Kelly would never have to be ashamed of the people she came from because Connie and Donald had made them disappear. It was quite easy, actually. Their parents and siblings all predicted they'd be back on their families' doorsteps, starving, for the godless city chewed up and spit out the young like olive pits. These brash, know-everything youngsters didn't need to think they could come back home for their parents to support them when they failed. It gave Connie and Donald immense satisfaction to prove them wrong. Neither had been back to the old neighborhood again, and if anyone was rude enough to ask about their origins, they were evasive. No one needed to know—especially Kelly—that they had family in a poor neighborhood in Boston.

They walked up the stairs to the castle and opened the front door, a little surprised by the size of the lobby. A cheerful woman about Connie's own age bustled about at the front desk.

There but for the grace of Estée Lauder, thought Connie.

"Good morning to you," the woman said. "Are you here to take rooms?"

"Yes," Connie said while Donald seemed preoccupied with an examination of the casement windows. "We've come to visit our daughter. Kelly Sullivan?"

The woman's face lit up like a light bulb.

"Ah, a lovely girl is Kelly. You must be so proud of her."

"Yes. We are," Connie said, feeling irrationally jealous of this stranger's obvious affection for Kelly.

"Margaret O'Meara," the woman said, offering her hand to be shaken.

"Connie Sullivan," Connie said after a slight hesitation. She gestured toward her spouse. "My husband, Donald." Donald turned at the sound of his name and smiled at the clerk.

"Ah, it's plain to see where Kelly got her looks," the woman said inanely.

Before she could go on with any more chatty observations, Connie quickly said, "Look, Margaret, it was a long flight, and we'd like to check in right away and see our daughter. Is she in?"

"Yes," the woman said, looking snubbed even though Connie had been perfectly polite and she *was* the customer. She turned and got a key off a peg. "I'll put you in the room across from Kelly's."

"Fine," Connie said, signing the register. "If you'll call someone to get our bags—"

"Right away," Margaret said. She went to a doorway. "Conor!" she called.

A very handsome man walked into the room and smiled at Connie. Dark hair, dark blue eyes, dressed in a light blue oxford-style shirt with a maroon tie and dark pants. Oh, God. This was going to be harder than Connie thought.

"Conor, here are Kelly's parents, Mr. and Mrs. Sullivan, come to stay with us," the clerk said.

At the sound of Kelly's name the wattage turned up and his already devastating smile became dazzling.

"A pleasure," he said, starting to offer his hand but thinking better of it, obviously, because Connie didn't offer hers first.

"Mr. and Mrs. Sullivan would like some help with their bags, Conor," Margaret said stiffly.

"Of course," he said. "You've put them in the room across from Kelly's?"

"Yes, and they'd like to see her right away."

"Of course," he said again, picking up all the bags. "Kelly didn't mention you were going to visit us."

"We wanted to surprise her," Connie said stiffly, not that her family's plans were any of *his* business.

"This way, please," he said, apparently noticing her reserve.

Conor felt a goose walk over his grave, as the saying went. Kelly's mother was every inch a fine lady from the crown of her perfectly styled red-gold hair to her cream-colored, alligator-skin shoes. She was wearing a lime green suit with ivory trim and fancy buttons on the short, double-breasted jacket. Her blue eyes looked through him as if he had no right to exist. They were clear and hard as ice.

"Donald!" Kelly's mother said sharply.

Her husband abandoned his inspection of the fireplace and came to the desk immediately, as Conor suspected he always did when his imperious wife summoned him. His shrewd green eyes examined Conor with quick intelligence.

"Donald Sullivan," he said, offering his hand.

"Conor O'Meara," Conor said, putting down a suitcase to reach for it. The older man's handshake was so firm Conor considered challenging him to a bit of arm wrestling to get the showdown out of the way. But these were Kelly's parents, Jesus pity the girl.

"Nice place," Sullivan said coolly.

"Thank you," Conor said, guiding them to the stairway.

He was annoyed that they didn't look impressed. He remembered how Kelly's eyes had shone when she saw it on that first day and felt sorry that such an imaginative woman had been born to a couple of cold fish like Connie and Donald Sullivan.

"Our lift is out of order," he said when both Sullivans raised their eyebrows. They exchanged a glance and led the way upstairs with Conor following like a lackey.

"Just along here," he said when they had arrived at the second floor. Connie was inspecting the place as if she were a prospective buyer. Conor opened the door to the room and stood back, although he knew better than to expect compliments.

It was a lovely room, although a bit smaller than Kelly's. The window overlooked the gardens, and the upper panes had a Celtic knot design adapted from the *Book of Kells* that most people fell in love with on sight. There were no flowers in the room as there would have been if they had made a reservation. But there was a nice fireplace with a marble mantel, lace curtains, and a matching lace bedspread. On a pretty bedside table was a statue of the Blessed Virgin with a little crown of pink paper roses on her head because it was May, her month. Mrs. Sullivan gave it an incredulous look.

"I hope you'll be comfortable," Conor said formally.

"We'd like to see our daughter now," Connie said in a tone of voice that suggested Conor was holding Kelly prisoner. "What is the extension in her room?"

Yanks, Conor thought with an inward sigh.

"I'm afraid we have no telephones in the guest rooms," he said.

Mr. Sullivan's shocked look vividly reminded Conor of the expression on Kelly's face when he gave her the same news that first day.

Before the older man could say anything, his wife gave a little huff of outrage.

"Donald!" she said, giving Conor an accusatory look. "There is no bathroom in here!"

"You're kidding," Donald said, looking around the room as if he expected to find a door they had overlooked. "Wait a minute! There's no TV! Unless—" He walked over to the wardrobe and opened the door wide. Conor knew from traveling that in fancy hotels the telly was hidden in the furniture, as if watching it were a secret vice. There was nothing in the wardrobe except some empty hangers for the guests' clothes. "Good God! I didn't expect cable, but no TV!"

"There is one in the guest parlor downstairs," Conor said, deliberately keeping his tone unapologetic. He turned to Connie. "There is a bathroom on this floor, of course, that the guests share."

Her eyes widened with horror.

"Oh, Donald," she said. "We couldn't possibly stay here."

She shuddered as if she had found rats nestling in the bed.

The Sullivans stared at each other for a moment, and Mrs. Sullivan lowered her eyes.

"You're right, of course," she said with a sigh, as if her husband had spoken. "We'd like to see our daughter now," she said to Conor.

Conor nodded and led the way to Kelly's room across the hall, but there was no answer when he knocked.

"She must be somewhere in the building," he said. "Aunt Margaret would have noticed if she left, unless she went out the terrace doors."

Conor heard a noise down the hall.

"Excuse me," he said, glancing down the hall to the open door of the loo. It was usually closed, unless—

He walked down the hall and peered inside to find Kelly on her knees before the toilet, scrubbing it.

"Hi!" she said cheerfully. "What's going on? Are you putting some more guests up here?"

She was wearing a damp white tee shirt that molded itself to her curves and a pair of baggy khaki shorts with lots of pockets in them. Her hair was a mess and her face was bare of makeup. She wiped some sweat out of her eyes and grinned at him. She looked so cute he wanted to scoop her into his arms and kiss her.

"Yes. Your parents just arrived," he said.

"Get out!" she said, giggling.

"I'm serious. They're here. In the room across from yours."

"Stop it," she said, still smiling as she gave the bowl another swipe.

When he didn't say anything, her eyes widened with dismay.

"Oh, shit! You're serious," she said. "Tell them I'm dead or something. If Mom sees me looking like this, she'll pitch a fit like you wouldn't *believe*!"

Conor made a helpless gesture of warning, but he was too late.

"Oh, shit," Kelly repeated softly as her parents appeared in the doorway behind Conor. "Hi, Mom!" she called out with a weak smile on her face. "Hi, Dad!"

Connie Sullivan looked as if she were going to burst a blood vessel, and her husband gave Conor a furious, accusing look.

"What . . . are . . . you . . . doing?" Connie said slowly, emphasizing each word in a tone of deep disapproval.

"Cleaning a toilet," Kelly admitted. Her chin was thrust out defiantly, and her eyes were flashing.

"Kelly has been kind enough to help us out a bit now that the tourist season has started," Conor said in a rash attempt to appease Kelly's parents.

"My daughter," Connie said haughtily, "has never cleaned a toilet in her life." She sounded proud of it, and she was. She had worked her fanny off for years so no daughter of hers would ever have to do manual labor.

"Grow up, Mom," Kelly said, rolling her eyes. "Of *course*, I've cleaned toilets. Do you think the little people clean my apartment?"

"Of course not," Connie said, frowning. "But naturally I assumed you had a cleaning service—"

"I do now, but I wasn't making that much money as an assistant manager so I did my own housework then. Besides, I did all these fun jobs during my orientation period at Lawrence, and you know it. A director of guest services has to know how it's done."

"That's different," Connie said, almost in tears at the sight of her beautiful daughter on her knees, dressed practically in rags, cleaning a bathroom used by *strangers*.

"What are you doing here?" Kelly asked.

"Nice welcome, honey," her father said humorously.

Kelly smiled ruefully.

"Sorry, Dad," she said apologetically. "Welcome to Ireland. You, too, Mom." She smiled winsomely at them, absently finger-combing her hair and making it worse.

Her mother winced.

"I suppose we should have called to tell you we were coming," Connie said deliberately. "Oh, that's right. No phones. We would have had to send smoke signals."

"There's a telephone at the front desk you're welcome to use any time," Conor interjected. Kelly's mother gave him a cool look. His jaw was clenched, and he looked as if he'd dearly love to give her and Donald a piece of his mind.

"That will be all," she told him, lifting her brows.

To her annoyance, he looked at Kelly, and a glance passed between them that struck terror in Connie's heart.

Her cherished, well-brought up, intelligent daughter was in love with this . . . this *Irishman*!

She was cleaning *toilets* for him, for God's sake!

Kelly gave him a reassuring little smile, and with a stiff nod at Connie, he left.

"Mother," Kelly said reproachfully, standing with a little wince. Her bare knees were reddened from kneeling on the floor, and repulsed by the sight, Connie looked away. "You treated Conor like a *servant*. I was never so embarrassed in my life."

"*You* were embarrassed? Just *look* at you! Cleaning toilets!" she said, just as if she had caught Kelly selling drugs or picking through garbage.

"Now, Connie," Donald said mildly. "It's been a long trip and we're tired. Let's rest up a bit and then we'll all talk."

"Oh, gosh," Kelly said. "I'll bet you guys need to use the

bathroom after all that. I'll just get out of your way. I'm all done now."

Connie stared after her daughter as if she had never seen her before when Kelly put her bucket and cleaning supplies in a little cabinet and scuttled out, stretching her back as she went.

Connie had not reared her only daughter to refer to bodily functions in conversation, not even indirectly.

She always knew something like this would happen if she ever came to this dismal country.

"If this place isn't a complete disaster," she said scornfully, following Kelly out of the bathroom and looking around the hall. "Art Nouveau and Art Deco and Greek Revival and God knows what else all jumbled together. And not even the most basic of creature comforts."

Kelly stared at her, openmouthed.

"How can you say that?" she said in amazement. "It's beautiful! Just because it doesn't have a telephone in every room and you have to share a bathroom, you can't call it a *disaster*! This isn't a five-star hotel yet. It's just a family-owned bed-and-breakfast."

"Since when do you clean toilets for strangers?"

"For pete's sake! For the first month I was here, I was the only one on this floor, and since I was the only one using it, I got into the habit of giving the bathroom a scrub now and then so Conor's aunts wouldn't have to climb up here and do it. It's no big deal. I also mind the front desk occasionally and help them serve breakfast to the guests if they've got a full house. Just to keep my hand in, you know."

"How nice for the O'Mearas. A free maid."

"Come on, Mom. Lighten up. You'll like it here if you give it half a chance. I'm really glad you came, even if we did get off to a bad start. Please. Freshen up. I'll bring you some tea and some of Margaret's prizewinning cookies, and you'll sleep off your jet lag and feel a hundred times better."

"Very well," Connie said. She gave Kelly a placating smile and saw her daughter's tense face relax.

"Good. I'll run down to the kitchen and be right back."

Donald opened the door to the bathroom and looked out at Kelly with a shocked look on his face.

"Kelly! There's no shower in here," he exclaimed.

Kelly gave him a weak smile.

"It'll be okay, Dad," she said with a sigh.

Kelly had to talk to Conor. She went downstairs and found him checking in some guests at the front desk. Feeling self-conscious, she tried to tidy her hair, but she knew it was hanging down in damp wisps. She started to leave.

"Please wait, Kelly," he said, smiling at the guests.

When the young couple went off cheerfully to find their room, he gave Kelly a crooked smile.

"What can I do for you?" he asked.

"Shoot me," she said, rolling her eyes, "before I die of embarrassment."

"The jet lag is a terrible thing," he said kindly.

Kelly hesitated, tempted to go along with this generous excuse for her parents' behavior.

"No. I'm afraid they're like that all the time," she admitted. "Did they say how long they were staying?"

"No," he said, his eyes dancing.

Kelly's shoulders slumped.

"I could disconnect the immersion tank," he offered. "A cold bath in the morning should send them on their way soon enough."

"No," Kelly said, laughing. She sobered. "I know I sound terrible—"

"Kelly, I've seen worse," he said. Kelly doubted it, but she let that pass. "And here we don't apologize for our parents. We accept them, and we do the best we can."

"You're right," she said. "I'll take them to the pub tonight for dinner. Who knows? Maybe it'll mellow them out a little." She looked down at herself. "I'd better take some tea up to them and change my clothes. I'm a mess."

She started to turn away, but he reached out and cupped the back of her head in his hand and kissed her.

"Thanks," she said gratefully, giving him a hug. "I needed that."

She peered at his blue shirt anxiously.

"Oh, God! I'm filthy. Did I get you dirty?"

"Never," he said. "Don't worry so much, darling. How much damage can they do?"

Kelly didn't have the heart to tell him.

The O'Mearas were such sweet people. They didn't *deserve* Kelly's parents.

Twenty-two

When they emerged from their room after sleeping off the jet lag, the Sullivans were outraged to find Conor O'Meara leaning over the front desk, laughing into Kelly's eyes. Her face was turned up to his, a heartbeat away from a kiss.

Connie gave a hiss of outrage, and the young couple broke apart, looking guilty, as well they might!

"We'll meet you at the pub later," Conor said to Kelly, nodding to Connie and Donald in greeting.

Connie's eyes narrowed.

Damn his eyes!

Conor O'Meara was wearing a pair of indifferently fitted dark slacks with one of the ubiquitous off-white, cable-stitched fisherman's sweaters so prevalent in seacoast towns. On his head he wore a jaunty little cap.

He should have looked pedestrian. Ordinary. Not worth a second look. Instead, he looked rakish and handsome.

"Be careful," Kelly told him. "Are you sure it's safe to be on the river after dark?"

"It is when *I'm* driving, love," he said. He gave Donald a cool look, as if in invitation for him to make something of the casual endearment.

"Well, you'll have your dad in the boat," Kelly went on.

"Mr. O'Meara has been visiting friends, and he's coming in on the bus tonight," she explained for her parents' benefit, just as if they cared how a bunch of losers from God-Knows-Where, Ireland, lived their lives.

Kelly was driving her parents to the pub in the O'Mearas' car, which was why Conor would have to collect his passengers from the Dublin bus in his boat. Kelly had no problem driving on the left side of the road, her parents knew. She had visited England and various islands in the West Indies many times both on business and on vacations with her parents. Connie and Donald had introduced her to most of the major cities and best vacation spots in the world over the years. The only country they hadn't visited was Ireland, not that anyone could class *it* as major.

The pub itself was exactly what Connie had expected, she thought, her nose wrinkling at the smell of nicotine hanging on the air. There was a live band tuning up, and the tables were all crowded together. Kelly was helpfully explaining all the items on the menu, just as if Connie and Donald hadn't had enough bland Irish cuisine in their youth to last a lifetime.

"Try the bacon and cabbage," Kelly said. "You'll love it."

Sure she would, Connie thought sourly. Soggy cabbage that had been on the boil so long it had no texture or flavor left. Greasy pork, served with the inevitable boiled potatoes and salt and pepper as the only seasonings.

Lovely.

Well, it looked about as safe as anything else on the menu, although it was likely to keep her up all night.

Connie went to exchange a pained look with her spouse, only to be annoyed to see him reach enthusiastically for a pint of Guinness Kelly brought to the table from the bar.

"Bacon and cabbage," Donald said cheerfully. He looked a little guilty when he encountered his wife's disapproving stare. "Well, I'll give it a try," he added in a more temperate tone to maintain the fiction that eating bacon and cabbage would be a new experience for him.

Kelly beamed at him.

"You'll love it. Trust me," she said.

Not as far as I can throw you, my girl, her mother resolved grimly.

"I knew some Sullivans when I was a lad out by Galway," a wisened little fellow said, seating himself uninvited next to Connie. "Would you be any relation?"

Donald gave him a slightly scared look. As a matter of fact, Donald's family *had* come from Galway. Fortunately, there was little likelihood any members of Donald's immediate family had visited since then, dirt poor as they had always been.

"Sorry," Donald said with a forced smile. "It's a bit too far back to tell."

"Hey, Dad," Kelly said, breaking off her conversation with a waitress. "That reminds me of something I wanted to ask you. What was your grandfather's name? I thought while I was here I'd try to trace our roots just for fun."

"He's been dead for years," Donald said evasively.

"Well, I know," Kelly persisted. "But if I had his name, it would help. Didn't your grandparents ever say where in Ireland they were from?"

"I was young when they died," Donald said through gritted teeth.

"Yeah, but surely you remember—"

"They were absolutely *nobody*, Kelly! Poor as dirt," Connie rapped out. "No one you want to know about. So drop it *now*! And stop embarrassing your father."

Kelly's mouth dropped open, and Connie's face burned as the muttering started up around her.

"Sorry I brought it up," Kelly said in a small, hurt voice.

Mercifully, the wizened little man left Connie's side and went to stand with some of the other fellows by the bar. They were all looking at Connie.

"Oh, here's the food," Kelly said, sounding relieved. "It looks good, doesn't it?"

Connie gave a depressed sigh. Yep. Bacon and cabbage hadn't changed since the days of her unlamented youth. Same soggy vegetables. Same boiled potatoes. At least she wouldn't have to suffer the indignity of eating corned beef with the cabbage, an Americanism that made a bad thing worse.

"You've got to try the soda bread. It's fabulous," Kelly said.

Fabulous, Connie thought derisively. *No, Kelly, dear.* Frango mints are fabulous. Paté de foie gras is fabulous. Escargot in puff pastry is fabulous.

Plain old Irish soda bread is *not* fabulous!

It didn't do Connie's mood any good to watch Kelly attack the unappetizing mess with all the finesse of a starving truck driver. Well, Connie knew who to thank again for her born-again Irish pride.

That Conor O'Meara, that's who!

Speak of the devil . . .

Connie had just asked the waitress to take her nearly full plate away when he showed up. Connie's mood improved when she saw there was an extremely beautiful redhead with him. The girl was elfin thin with porcelain skin and eyes of so pure a green Connie suspected she wore contacts.

"Listen, everybody," Conor's Irish baritone boomed out. The din from the band died out with a whine from the uilleann pipes. Conor grabbed the beautiful girl's waist and lifted her so she could stand on a chair. "Miss Ghillie O'Brien won the audition, and she's now officially a member of the Irish Dance Troupe in Dublin."

Cheers erupted as the dainty girl took a bow without overbalancing on the chair. Conor lifted her off in a graceful display of long legs and cotton skirts. She was soon engulfed in a crowd of well-wishers while Conor looked on proudly. Then, when it looked as if the girl would be some time answering questions, Conor wandered over to where Kelly was polishing off her meal and pulled a chair up for himself.

Connie had hoped to see Kelly look crestfallen at the sight of Conor paying attention to the beautiful girl. Instead, she had been delighted by the little announcement. Of course, that probably meant the girl, whoever she was, would be moving to Dublin, on the other side of the country from Conor O'Meara.

Damn!

Kelly's face was glowing as if it were illuminated from within by a lightbulb.

She leapt up from the table and accompanied Conor to the dance floor where she enthusiastically if clumsily performed a little dance to the applause of the spectators. Jeez. Five years of ballet lessons and she couldn't do any better than *that*, Connie thought in disgust.

"You must be Kelly's mother," a genial man said, bringing his pint of Guinness over to the Sullivans' table. Connie recognized him as the older man who had accompanied Conor and the beautiful girl inside the pub, but Connie hadn't paid much attention to him. He extended his hand.

"Sean O'Meara," he said.

Connie had intended to give him the brush-off, but it seemed he was the owner of Whitlock Castle, at least until Kelly's company took over.

"Connie Sullivan," she said, frowning a little as she took his hand. Apparently he didn't know a gentleman waited for a lady to extend her hand first, or didn't care.

Savages!

"Eh, your Kelly is a lovely girl," he said, his eyes twinkling. "Our Conor's quite taken with her. Don't they make a fine-looking couple, now?"

With a wave of his hand, he indicated the dance floor where Kelly was laughing up into Conor's eyes. The Irishman looked absolutely entranced by what she was saying. Then the music changed, and the beautiful redhead saucily maneuvered herself between them and laid claim to Conor.

Good, thought Connie, watching Conor perform an intricate little step-toe with the redhead. Against her will, Connie's toe started tapping. Despite everything, in sentimental moments Irish music could make her feel weepy. Conor and the redhead were as good as professionals.

"Now *there*," Connie said to Sean O'Meara, "is a fine looking couple."

Sean laughed.

"Conor and Ghillie? We all expected them to marry when they were young, but Ghillie went off to Dublin, and that was the end of that."

"They might get together yet," Connie suggested.

Sean shook his head.

"I thought so, too, but Ghillie has had a taste of the city now, and her heart will never rest anywhere else. Your Kelly, now. There's a match for my Conor."

"What do you mean?" Connie demanded with a nervous little laugh. "Kelly lives in the third largest city in the United States, and she thrives on it."

"Ah, that girl would thrive anywhere, so full of life and energy she is," Sean said fondly, glancing at the dance floor where some of the bar patrons were showing Kelly a new dance step. Connie could hear Kelly's laughter over the band easily. "I've no doubt she's a success in her important job in America, but that's not where her heart is."

Connie gave the man an annoyed look.

"I suppose *you* know more about my daughter than I do?" she asked in a voice calculated to squash his presumption.

"Well, if you can't see how happy she is here, I'd have to say I do."

"Nonsense," Connie snapped. "Kelly is a naturally cheerful person. She's perfectly happy in Chicago."

Never mind that Connie hadn't seen Kelly's face glow like this since she was a child on Christmas morning. How *dare* she be happy here, when Connie and Donald had sacrificed so much to make sure she would never know the backward, bumptious, claustrophobic, *poor* sort of life from which her parents had escaped.

Connie's shrewd eyes were not dazzled by the castle's faded grandeur. These O'Mearas were as poor as church mice in heart, if not in fact. They might be getting some decent money from the sale of the castle, but they'll hoard it away and live like paupers, just the same. Or squander it on drink. And Kelly, if she rashly marries Conor O'Meara will end up supporting the lot of them *and* cleaning their toilet to boot.

To Connie's extreme annoyance, Kelly came over to the table and tried to talk Connie and Donald into joining the group on the dance floor. Donald actually stood up, but fortunately he caught Connie's warning look and sat down again with some regret. Donald had been quite a fine dancer in his youth. So had Connie, for that matter.

"Party poopers," Kelly chided them laughingly before she went back to the dance floor and straight into Conor's arms.

"She can keep it up all night," Sean said admiringly, "Lord love the girl."

Connie gave Kelly a look that could kill. The girl's face was flushed as if she'd had too much to drink, and she was dancing *much* too close with that Irishman! When the dance ended, they came back to the table.

"It's time we got you home, Da," Conor said, clapping his father on the shoulder.

"I hate to see you cut your night short, boy."

"There will be other nights," Conor said.

"Actually, we'd like to go back to our rooms, too," said Connie, giving her husband a straight look when he started to object. The traitor was actually enjoying himself in this noisy, smoky, *tacky* bar! Another minute and he'd be out on the dance floor making a fool of himself. Connie stood, signaling an end to the discussion.

"Can you take Dad in the car with you?" Conor asked Kelly. "It's a bit cold for him out on the boat."

"I'm not a delicate old man to be wrapped in cotton wool," Sean huffed.

"You haven't been out of the hospital that long," Kelly said in an affectionate tone that made Connie's heart burn with jealousy and resentment. "Come on, now. Conor's right about this."

Chuckling, Sean let himself be persuaded by her pretty coaxing.

"Actually, I'd be glad enough to go home now," Ghillie

said, wandering over from the dance floor during a break in the music. "Is there room in the car?"

There wasn't, of course. The car was a tight squeeze for four. Five would be impossible.

"I'll go in the boat, then," Sean said.

"No, you won't," Kelly insisted. "You or Ghillie can drive the car and *I'll* go in the boat with Conor."

She looked so pleased with herself for having come up with this idiotic solution.

"Absolutely not!" Connie snapped, crossing her arms to signal she was making a stand here. "It's dark and it's probably going to rain. It's too dangerous for you to be out in a boat this time of night."

"Aw, Mom," Kelly wailed.

"She'll be safe with me, Mrs. Sullivan," Conor said quietly.

The *hell* she will, Connie thought, fuming

"Just you be careful with my little girl," Donald said, giving Conor a man-to-man look.

"I will, sir," said the young hero, putting his arm around Kelly and leading her out. At the door he took off his jacket and put it around her shoulders.

Every woman in the room practically swooned.

"Conor will take good care of your girl," Sean said cheerfully.

That's just what Connie was afraid of.

"They're not usually like this," Kelly said ruefully once they were outside the pub. "Sometimes they're worse."

"A bit overprotective is all," Conor said, scooping her into his arms for the treacherously muddy walk to where his boat was tied.

Kelly thought briefly of the first time Conor tried to carry her to his boat that long-ago day when she first arrived in Ireland.

To think she had made a fuss and made him put her down for fear he would drop her. She must have been crazy, she decided as she put her arms around his neck and held on tight. The cool mist felt good on her face, flushed from dancing, and Conor's jacket smelled of the sea.

"I could get used to this," she said with a sigh.

He stopped walking and kissed her.

"We could stop by the cottage," he suggested.

Kelly was tempted.

Boy, was she tempted!

"They'll know," she decided regretfully. "I swear they'll know. Mom will open the door when I sneak to my room with my shoes in my hand, and she'll see it all over my face."

"Just to talk," he coaxed. "I'll make some coffee. I won't lay a hand on you. I swore I wouldn't touch you until you put an end to this fling business and made an honest man of me."

"You didn't mean that," Kelly said.

"I did, yes."

They arrived at the boat, and he set her gently inside as he busied himself with the anchor.

"Tonight when we were dancing," she said, feeling embarrassed, "and then just now when you kissed me, I thought—"

"That I'd changed my mind? Decided to let you toy with me and be left behind while you go back to your city and your important job?"

She couldn't speak.

When he would have stepped back from her, she threw her arms around him and just held on for dear life. He held her tightly for a moment. Then he framed her face with his hands and forced her to look into his eyes.

"Don't worry about it now, love," he said, a little sadly. "We've time to sort it all out."

But they didn't, and they both knew it.

Connie looked down from her window over the gardens and saw her daughter lift her face to Conor's for his kiss in the moonlight. There was something so tender in the way he held her that Connie's determination wavered for an instant.

Conor stood still and watched while Kelly turned and walked to the house. The night fairly sizzled around him.

Then Connie thought about her beautiful daughter being buried alive in this backwater, bearing a dozen screaming children to this man, and cleaning his toilets.

Someday you'll thank me, she thought grimly.

Twenty-three

Kelly felt a bit guilty as she waved her parents off with more cheerfulness than was probably polite.

She was fed up with walking on eggshells, wondering what awkward thing her mother was going to say next. Her dad was just as bad. He kept looking at Conor as if he were a potential rapist.

Had her parents always been such snobs and prudes?

Kelly couldn't believe such behavior out of the modern mother who had startled her sixteen-year-old daughter by suggesting she go on the Pill just because a senior asked her to go to the prom. Of course, Mark's parents owned that showplace on the North Shore, and she supposed her mother considered him a suitable prospective husband for Kelly.

Conor, she made it perfectly clear, was not.

Too bad, Kelly thought furiously. She was too old to let her parents have a line-item veto over her love life.

Bless his heart, Conor was taking them to Shannon Airport in his car.

He probably didn't want to take any chances that they would miss their flight. She had rarely in her life been so annoyed with her parents. You want to talk about ugly Americans! At the moment it really scared her that their genes were in her body.

When the little car was out of sight, Kelly drew a deep breath and went into the kitchen. She must have looked as down as she felt because Rose held up a gloriously fat-glistened piece of bacon in invitation and smiled when Kelly gave a little moan of anticipation. Kelly opened her mouth like a baby bird so Rose could stick the rasher inside.

"You don't have to bite my fingers," Rose said with a dour smile.

"Hey! I can't be responsible if you get them between me and my bacon."

"Well, and it was lovely of your parents to pay you a visit," Rose said comfortably.

"And isn't it the Blessed Mary's own grace that we've seen the back of them," Kelly said, mimicking Rose's brogue.

Rose had to laugh.

"Sit down and we'll have a proper breakfast," she said. "The guests are all fed and out for the day, and no more are expected until this afternoon. Margaret's in the basement washing the linens." She shook her head. "How your parents can start the day with no breakfast but a cup of coffee and a piece of dry toast is a wonder."

Kelly snorted and savored the memory of her mother's horror when she was confronted with the shocking reality of bacon, eggs, sausages, and potatoes that first morning.

"Hey! I was the same way until I came to Ireland, and you guys taught me how to live," she said.

"Yanks," Rose scoffed tolerantly as she handed Kelly a filled plate.

"Good morning, my darling girls," Sean said as he came in and sniffed hopefully around Rose's skillet. Rose narrowed her eyes and made a gesture with her spatula to shoo him away from the stove.

"So, they're off then," he added, nodding at Rose when she handed him his bowl of porridge.

"Conor just left with them for the airport," Kelly said,

going to the pantry for the peanut butter, cinnamon, and her precious container of protein powder so she could doctor up Sean's porridge for him. Sean beamed at her, obviously enjoying the attention of both women.

Besides, he knew one of them would slip him a piece of bacon or sausage before the meal was over, the old devil, Kelly thought affectionately. She grinned when she saw Rose break a piece of white pudding in two and hand him a piece.

"Eh, Margaret would have given me a whole one," he said with a theatrical sigh.

"Get along with you," Rose told him.

It would be so easy to be part of this family, Kelly thought. Having her parents at Whitlock Castle sure pointed out the difference between their outlook on life and the O'Mearas'.

How am I going to fit into their world when this assignment is over, Kelly thought with a feeling of panic.

But, like Scarlett O'Hara, she'd think of that tomorrow.

Sean was talking about the festival, and Kelly entered into his plans with relish.

"We have a banner—where did we put the banner, Rose?" he asked.

"With the other things in the potting shed in the garden," Rose answered. "We'd best be getting it out and seeing if it needs pressing if you're determined on this foolishness."

"I'll fetch it," Sean said eagerly, getting up. To Kelly's horror, his face turned gray, and he clutched the table for support.

Kelly ran to ease him into the chair. Rose ran to his other side. One side of Sean's face went all wonky.

Omigod, omigod!

"I'll be all right . . . in a minute," Sean said. His words were slurred. Beads of perspiration broke out on his forehead and upper lip.

"You're going to the hospital," Kelly said.

"Conor has the car," Rose said, panicky, "and he won't be back from the airport until—"

"Go call an ambulance," Kelly told her, looking at Sean. "*Don't* make me have to start CPR," she told him sternly. "It's been a few years since my last certification."

"*What* ambulance?" Rose asked. "There's no ambulance."

"Shit! It's the boat, then. Come on, Sean."

Later Kelly couldn't remember how they did it, but between the three of them, Kelly, Margaret, and Rose managed to get Sean down the steps to the little dock and into the boat.

"Conor, if there's no gas in this thing, you're a dead man," Kelly said as Rose and Margaret settled Sean the best they could.

With her heart in her throat, Kelly pushed off and jumped inside the boat, gave the starter a pull, muttered prayers of thanksgiving as the engine roared to life and raced down the river.

When she got near the village she quickly tied the boat and ran into the pub screaming for someone to drive Sean to the hospital.

Later, Kelly didn't remember much about the wild ride. Sean was examined and installed in a room, and Rose and Margaret had been sitting with him for a few minutes by the time a wild-eyed Conor rushed in the door.

"Is he—"

"No," said Kelly. "He's resting now."

He closed his eyes and let out a long, pent-up breath.

"Can I see my father?" he asked the nurse at the desk.

"Certainly, you can," she said kindly. "We've got him on a respirator to help him breathe, but he's conscious."

"And I gave him a piece of white pudding," Rose said tearfully after Conor left to sit with his father and his aunts came back to the waiting room to sit with Kelly. Margaret put her hand on her sister's.

"Hush, now," Margaret said gruffly. "It would take more than a bit of white pudding to kill Sean O'Meara."

It was a kind lie, and they all knew it.

"If Sean wants a festival, we'll give him a festival," Rose

vowed. "I'll not say another word against it if he'll just live, please God!"

A little later, Conor joined them.

"He's sleeping," he said. "One of us should stay here with him. I'd like to, if it's all right with all of you."

"I'd like to stay, too," Rose said tearfully. "I'm the one who fed him—"

"Forget the damned sausage," Kelly snapped. "He'd have snuck the sausage and a couple of pieces of bacon, too, if you hadn't given it to him. So, enough with the guilt already!"

Rose looked as if she'd have something to say about that, but Margaret put her hand on her sister's arm.

"She's right, Rose," Margaret said.

Rose sighed.

"I know," she said grudgingly.

Conor shook his head slowly and smiled at Kelly. To her surprise, he took her hand and kissed it.

"What was that for?" she asked.

"For getting him here. Thank God you asked me to show you how to drive the boat."

"And his angels and all his saints," Kelly added with real devotion. "Are you ready, Margaret? I guess it's just you and me to get the rooms ready for the invasion this afternoon."

"Thanks, Kelly," Rose said meekly.

"My pleasure," she said, putting her arm around Margaret and leading her out. "It's a good thing Mom's gone because I'll be cleaning *lots* of toilets today."

By early afternoon the rooms were ready for the guests and Kelly was minding the front desk. She had bathed and changed into a business suit because today, of all days, the appraiser from a Dublin auction house was expected to arrive to go over the inventory Kelly had prepared so carefully and assign tentative values to the various furnishings.

Kelly reminded herself, firmly, that she was representing Lawrence, and she couldn't let her anxiety over what was happening at the hospital with Sean distract her from business. Margaret would relieve Kelly at the front desk when the appraiser arrived.

She glanced impatiently at her watch. Where *was* the guy? She just wanted to get the business over and done with. Conor had called once to say his father was resting and his doctors were optimistic that he would come home in a few days if he had no further problems.

The auction house representative arrived about thirty minutes later.

"Filthy bad roads," he said in cheerful apology. "What a lovely old building this is."

Kelly almost said "thank you" and had to remind herself it wasn't hers. She excused herself for a moment and called Margaret from the kitchen.

She introduced the gentleman and showed him to his room, for he would be staying several days.

"Let's get right to it, shall we?" he said genially. "I can't wait to see what treasures Whitlock Castle holds, and may I say we are honored that Mr. Lawrence has chosen us to handle the sale?"

Warning bells screamed in Kelly's head.

"The sale? *What* sale?" she asked. "I understood this was an independent appraisal for insurance purposes only."

"No. You must be mistaken. Mr. Lawrence assured me personally that the furnishings of Whitlock Castle are to be sold at auction prior to reconstruction."

He ran his hand over the carved wainscoting.

"The woodwork, of course, can be extracted and sold. I am confident that it would go for a pretty penny."

"Yes," Kelly said, feeling the blood drain from her head at the thought of this mutilation. "Perhaps you would like to start with this room. Here is the inventory I have prepared."

"Certainly," he said enthusiastically. "What a lovely fireplace! I'll just have a look at the ground-floor rooms this afternoon. You needn't accompany me. I see you have all the lists identified by room number on the floor plan. Splendid!"

"Well, then," Kelly said awkwardly. "I'll leave you to it. If you'll excuse me . . ."

I've got to get to a phone right away to find out what's up
with this sale shit!

"Matthew! How are you?" asked Kelly, forcing professional bonhomie into her voice when what she really wanted
to do was reach through the telephone wire and rip his lungs
out.

"Fine, Kelly. Fine. How's the Irish project coming
along?" he said amiably.

"Very well," Kelly said, slipping easily into the protocol.
"Absolutely. Matthew, I was just curious. The appraiser is
here, and he mentioned a sale. Did I miss something?"

"Yeah. Well, Kelly. We've decided to go with the medieval theme park after all. After everything's out, we'll do
a little superficial remodeling, throw some straw on the
floor, and we'll be in business."

"Matthew! You *promised*!"

"Well, it's nothing personal. Strictly business. We're having a bit of a cash flow problem here, and we can use a little
shot in the arm from the sale. The remodeling job is going to
be kind of down and dirty, and it won't look all that authen-
tic, but, hell, the bastards who stay there with the wives and
kids wouldn't know the difference, anyway, would they?"

He paused to laugh at his own cleverness.

"Listen, sweetheart," he continued. "Do me a favor and
keep an eye on those paddies, will you? I don't want them
carting all sorts of stuff off to their new place before the sale
is final."

"The contract stipulates—"

"I *know* what the damn contract stipulates," he said in a
voice that suggested he was gritting his teeth in a forced
smile. "Just keep an eye on the bastards."

Then he hung up on her! Kelly couldn't believe it.

And to make matters worse, she slammed down the phone
and looked up into Margaret's ashen face.

"It'll kill Sean," Margaret said flatly when Kelly poured
them each a cup of tea and sat down with a dejected thump
to confirm Margaret's worst suspicions.

"I'm afraid of that, too," Kelly said, burying her head in her hands for a moment and rubbing her weary eyes. "I had him convinced not to do it when I was in Chicago. What could have happened?"

"I don't understand," Margaret said. "When Mr. and Mrs. Lawrence visited us last year, they were full of plans to turn the castle into a luxury hotel. 'We won't change a thing,' his wife said. 'It's perfect as it is.'"

"That's probably the key right there. They're getting divorced. Unfortunately, the one keeping the company is an *idiot*."

"We can't tell him," Margaret said dejectedly.

Kelly gave a mirthless laugh.

"You're right about that. *Damn!*" She gave Margaret an apologetic look. She knew the sisters were shocked by her language sometimes, and she tried to tone it down in their presence.

"I think the situation excuses it," Margaret said wryly.

"I tried my best. I really did. And you can believe I'll continue to do everything I can to change his mind. I thought I had convinced him and the financial people and the marketing people with enough cost analyses to drown them in paper."

To Kelly's surprise, Margaret put a comforting hand on *her* shoulder.

"You're a good girl, Kelly," the older woman said soothingly. "And you've kept this inside yourself all this time, when I can plainly see how much you love the place."

Tears started in Kelly's eyes. She had not expected this depth of generosity and understanding from one of the people her company had wronged.

"Well, Conor knew, and he was helping me with finding local contacts for the restoration work I hoped the company would do instead of the demolition. He didn't want you or Rose to know about this because he thought you were upset enough with Sean in the hospital."

"We were, that," Margaret agreed. "To think of the two of you carrying this burden."

"Matthew told me the inventory and appraisal were for insurance purposes, and I believed him. He probably intended to sell the furnishings from the time he agreed to buy the castle, and I *helped* him."

Margaret was staring at her in horrified fascination.

"What a terrible person he is," she said. "How can you bear to work for such a man?"

"I'm beginning to wonder that myself."

"Well," Margaret said briskly. "I think this calls for drastic action."

She brought a crock full of her famous cookies to the table and plunked them in front of Kelly with all the aplomb of a bartender putting up a fifth of scotch for a patron in need of consolation.

"They're for the guests," Kelly said, remembering how Margaret had chased Conor away from the crock whenever he tried to sneak a cookie from it. "And with Sean in the hospital, who knows when you'll have time to bake more."

"Drastic times call for drastic measures," Margaret said grimly, crunching into one of the crisp, perfect wafers. She took one and held it in front of Kelly's lips. Kelly bit it, cupping her hands to catch the crumbs. When the first taste of brown sugar and butter exploded on her tongue, the tears overflowed and ran down her cheeks.

The fact that Margaret *comforted her* when no court in the world would have convicted her for yelling at her, made Kelly feel humble and undeserving.

"There, now, love," Margaret said soothingly. "Rose will have to be told, of course."

Kelly gulped and grabbed another cookie from the crock.

"*That* will be a pleasure," she said grimly. "Rose doesn't like me, anyway."

"Yes, she does; yes, she does. It's just her way. The most important thing is to keep this from Sean."

"Right. We'll just pretend everything is normal," Kelly said. "I can do that."

• • •

"All right," Conor said that evening after one thoughtful look at Kelly's determinedly cheerful smile of greeting. "What is wrong?"

Kelly's shoulders sagged, almost in relief. She had been keeping up an act all afternoon for the guests and for the appraiser. Unfortunately, this was the moment of truth. Conor was back, and he knew something was up. Rose was with him, looking weary, but not too tired, as usual, to come to full attention at the hint of a fresh crisis.

Before Rose could say a word, the appraiser, who had been admiring the black fireplace, approached wreathed in smiles. When Kelly reluctantly introduced them, he pumped Conor's hand enthusiastically.

"A splendid place, Mr. O'Meara," the little man said.

"Thank you," Conor said, a bit blankly. "I hope your room is comfortable."

"Perfectly, perfectly! My only regret is it's too warm to use the fireplace. I haven't enjoyed a coal fire for many years. Working here is like mining for buried treasure. It will be a glorious auction! I can't wait to talk to my office about the publicity."

"Auction," Conor said woodenly.

"Yes! September at the latest, I'm told, although Mr. Lawrence hinted at the possibility that it might come earlier. Well! It's a pleasure to meet you, sir. I'll just wish you a pleasant evening and proceed with my explorations."

With that, he gave them a general smile and toddled off.

Rose was looking at Kelly as if she'd love to give her a piece of her mind and was only waiting until the little man was out of earshot.

Conor just looked sad.

"It's not Kelly's fault," he told Rose, giving her a warning look when she turned accusing eyes on Kelly. "She's been working to prevent this for some time."

"I'm sorry," Kelly said apologetically. "I've let you down."

She would have said more, but a young couple with two children came to the door, and Kelly had to put her professional face on. She greeted the couple and looked up their reservations since she was the one standing behind the desk.

"I'll show them the way," Conor said, smiling at them. "Aunt Rose, Kelly, I'd like to see you in the family parlor when I get back."

"Okay," said Kelly. She looked into Rose's angry eyes and braced herself for the coming confrontation. Fortunately, Rose was too polite to let it rip in front of guests.

"Oh, wow! *Look* at this place!" the American woman exclaimed as she herded her children along in Conor's wake. "If you touch *anything*—anything at all—you *die*, get it?" she added grimly to her children.

"Come along then," Rose said to Kelly. "It's time you made a clean breast of it, young woman."

Kelly flinched at the anger in Rose's eyes, but she soon learned the anger wasn't for her.

"That boss of yours is a proper blackguard," she said darkly when Kelly had filled her in on the background. She'd save today's revelations for when Conor joined them. "And I'd like to send that little man snooping around our house about his business, I don't mind saying."

"He's just doing his job."

"Does Margaret know?"

"She overheard me when I called Matthew in the hope it was all a mistake."

"And when were you thinking you might tell us?"

"I *hoped* I wouldn't have to tell you at all. Conor and I decided we'd give it the good fight and tell the rest of you only when it became unavoidable. At that time Sean was in the hospital, and you were both worried sick about him."

Conor came into the family parlor and sat beside Rose.

"If Da hadn't had this new stroke, I'd be for telling him," Conor said, when Kelly had filled them in completely. "It's his house, and he has a right to know. But now . . ." He made a helpless gesture.

"I don't see how we can avoid telling him," Rose said, sounding bitter. "He's still got to act for this family with that blackguard Mr. Lawrence. It's bound to come up."

Kelly and Conor looked at each other wide-eyed. They'd almost forgotten something very important.

"I've got Da's power of attorney, and it's *my* duty to act for this family now," Conor said slowly.

"So you can handle the whole affair behind his back without him any the wiser," Rose said, clearly not liking it.

That made three of them.

Margaret and Rose had heard the news now, and neither had crumbled, even though their brother was clearly not out of danger. Conor's well-meaning impulse to protect them from the truth had been wrong. Kelly saw that now, and Conor did, too, if she wasn't mistaken.

"But we can't tell him now," Conor said. "Not until he's stronger. Maybe not even then."

"He'll know when the bulldozers line up at the front door, gunning their engines," Kelly said glumly.

"We can't keep it from him for too long," Conor acknowledged, "but can't we keep it from him until after the festival? He's talked of nothing else since he came home."

"Yes," Rose said, nodding her head. "Yes. Let him enjoy the festival, and may God forgive me for speaking out against it."

"After it's over, we'll suggest that we start moving things to the cottage," Conor said thoughtfully. "Once he's settled, we can—"

The phone rang. They exchanged anxious looks, and Conor sprinted for the front desk.

It could be the hospital.

But it wasn't.

It was Kelly's assistant with the news that Kelly's participation would be required in a conference call at 4 P.M. Chicago time—10 P.M. Irish time.

Kelly gathered her inner fortitude.

Just what she needed—a late meeting of the kangaroo court when she was already physically and mentally drained. But she could do it—project confidence and composure when what she really wanted to do was run amok all over Matthew's head with an ax. She *had* to do it. Obviously something happened to undermine the influence she had had with Matthew. If he decided to replace her on the Whitlock Castle project, there was every chance her replacement would be someone so eager to curry favor with the boss that he or she would cheerfully hack the castle to pieces before the O'Mearas' eyes without the least compunction.

The thought made Kelly's blood run cold. After she shared a silent cold supper with Conor and Rose, she sat for a long time in the Peacock Room, just memorizing the beautiful stained glass window as if it were the face of a beloved dying friend.

Twenty-four

"*You touch that* fireplace—you *breathe* on it—and you're a dead man," Kelly snarled at her least favorite coworker.

Bradley Kovacks raised his eyebrows.

"Kelly, old girl, I don't think you understand the situation. Matthew wants this thing chipped out of the wall and on a plane for Chicago by tomorrow. If you know what's good for you, you'll stop wasting time."

"Listen up, you slimeball! The contract stipulates that Lawrence doesn't move a candlestick until September. Just because Matthew has decided to throw a few thou at the O'Mearas to up the timetable doesn't mean it's official until they accept those terms."

"I don't believe this," Bradley said, trying to look shocked. The weasel knew damned well she wasn't going to let him cannibalize this fireplace. He was in Ireland on his way to Italy where Lawrence was in negotiations for a nineteenth-century mansion in Naples. Kelly didn't have any doubt Bradley put the idea of collecting the fireplace in Matthew's head so he could use it in his new condo. If Kelly refused—and Bradley had to know she wasn't going to let the fireplace out of Whitlock Castle without a fight— Matthew would naturally question her loyalty.

Bradley and Kelly both knew that executives who were disloyal stood about the chance of a snowball in hell of making VP.

"Look, Kelly, Lawrence Hotels plunked down a fortune in earnest money for this place. The O'Mearas owe him something for that money. What does it matter if the fireplace goes to Chicago now or later?"

"Well, for one thing," she said, hands on hips, "that money is in escrow, and the O'Mearas can't touch a dime of it until the sale is final. Matthew is entitled to *nothing* until then. The O'Mearas could sue his ass for this."

"But they won't," Bradley said, smirking. "Ever hear the expression, possession is nine-tenths of the law? Once we've got it, there won't be much they can do about it. Now, stand aside and let these guys do their job."

Kelly swept him and the clearly uncomfortable workmen a contemptuous glance.

"You are pond scum, you know that? You know very well Sean O'Meara is in the hospital and can't defend himself."

"All the more reason to do it now."

"No way! If the O'Mearas don't know their legal rights in this case, you can bet your ass I'll tell them."

"You won't do that," he said confidently, "because if you do, I win."

Kelly shook her head.

"Bradley, I'm sure you couldn't *begin* to understand this, but there are some things I won't do just to be VP."

He raised his eyebrows.

"You know, when it was obvious at the cocktail party the old man had the hots for you, I thought you had the promotion nailed," he said with a nasty smile on his face. "But you're playing right into my hands. It's going to take a lot of nooky, honey, to make the old man overlook this kind of insubordination."

Conor stepped silently out of the shadows and had Bradley by the throat before the last word was out of his mouth.

"Would you like to apologize to the lady?" His voice was

soft with menace. "Or would you rather have my fist halfway down your lying throat?"

"Forget it, paddy. You've about fifteen years too late to defend this little shark's virtue," Bradley choked out.

Conor started squeezing, but Kelly caught his arm to stop him.

"Don't dirty your hands on the jerk, Conor," Kelly said. "I *mean* it," she added when he gave her a look of disbelief. "Let go of him."

She could tell it was an effort, but Conor thrust Bradley away from him with a contemptuous gesture. Bradley had to do an awkward little dance to remain upright.

"Wise move," Bradley said with a sneer. "Come on," he said to the workmen. "Get to work. She talks big, but she's not dumb enough to piss away a fancy title over *this*."

"No," the obvious leader of the men said after exchanging glances with his companions. "We aren't after destroying property if there's some question about the ownership."

"Wise choice," Conor said with a sarcastic curl of the lip toward Bradley.

The workmen nodded and left, muttering vague apologies.

"Come back!" Bradley shouted after them. "Come back and do what I paid you to do!"

"You haven't paid us anything, yet, Yank!" the leader said. "You should be ashamed of yourself!"

"Damn paddies!" Bradley shouted. "I should have known better than to hire a bunch of stupid—"

"That's *enough*," Conor said in a tone of voice that struck Bradley to resentful silence. "Get out. Ordinarily I would offer a Lawrence employee a room for the night, but you can sleep in your car, for all I care."

"Who *is* this guy?" Bradley demanded.

"Conor O'Meara," Kelly said with a wry little smile. "Sean's son and acting interim manager. And this, Conor, is Bradley Kovacks, my coworker from Lawrence."

"The butcher in an expensive suit," Conor said softly.

"You bet your ass," Bradley said with a cocky grin.

"Get out of my house, Yank," Conor said, grinning right back and taking a threatening step forward. Bradley stuck his chin out and stepped up to meet him. Both men had raised their arms and balled their hands into fists.

"Hey! Time out!" Kelly shouted. "Have you guys forgotten there are *guests* here?"

"You're right," Conor said apologetically. Then, quick as lightning, he grabbed Bradley by the scruff of his neck, raised him almost off the ground so Bradley had to move with him to avoid being choked, and walked him to the door.

Jesus, how I'd love to smash the bleedin' fecker's teeth in, Conor thought, seething with a rage he could only control for Kelly's sake. The miserable little cur could thank *her* for the fact that his pretty face would stay intact for a while longer.

It was with great satisfaction that he threw the sputtering blackguard down the steps. At the bottom, Bradley got up and stalked away, favoring his right leg.

The workmen, congregated in a muttering little circle, looked warily up at Conor from where he stood at the top of the steps, coolly watching Bradley frantically start the rental car, accidentally kill the engine, and then, causing the car to lurch a little, speed madly away.

"He said his company owned the place," the leader said apologetically. "He showed us his business card, and—"

"And you didn't have any reason to question him," Conor finished for him. "He wouldn't have hired men from our village because they would know we have possession of the castle until after the tourist season."

"He's a bad one," the man said, shaking his head. Then he grinned. "Your woman with the temper wasn't letting him get the better of her, was she?"

"No," Conor agreed. He couldn't help grinning back. "She could have handled him without my help. I just wanted the satisfaction of throwing him down the steps."

The workman held out his hand, and Conor grasped it.

"We'll be moving along, then," he said apologetically. The men got in their car and drove away.

Conor went into the castle to see Kelly pacing agitatedly in front of the fireplace. She looked stricken when she raised her eyes. He took both of her clenched hands in his. He could feel them trembling.

"I should have stood back, wringing my hands, and let you mop up the floor with his face. *That* would have been the sensible, politically astute choice. But, no. I had to make my loyalties plain," she said. "The bad part is, I don't care. It felt *good*. I would have taken a poke at him myself if you hadn't come in."

"You've risked your career for us."

Kelly gave a half-hysterical little laugh.

"I've been risking it all along by consistently putting the castle and the O'Mearas ahead of my responsibility to Lawrence. I've worked for Matthew for ten years, for God's sake!"

She pulled her hands out of Conor's and started pacing again.

"And I've broken the cardinal rule—I've gotten personally involved with an interim manager."

Conor stood in front of her and trapped her restless hands in his again.

"And you regret that," he suggested, looking into her beautiful, distressed face. He wanted to kiss her so badly he could hardly stand it, but he knew it would be a mistake.

"No," she said with a half smile. "It's not just you. It's your father and your aunts and this place. These past two months have been the happiest of my life."

"Mine, too," Conor said. "Kelly, you were sent here for a reason. You belong here. Not just here in the castle, but in Ireland. With us. With me."

"*Me*? In Brigadoon? For keeps?" She gave a brittle laugh. "Can you *see* it?"

"I've been seeing it from the minute this pushy little Yank came in here and threw a fit because I didn't meet her at the airport," he said wryly.

"Liar!" she said with a reminiscent grin.

"Well, maybe not from the *first* minute," he admitted.

"Look. Nobody's died here. You stopped him from taking the fireplace. With luck, he won't try anything else because he was clearly in the wrong, and you didn't let him get away with it."

"You don't know him," Kelly said, rubbing her eyes. "God. I'm just so *tired*."

"Go to bed, love," he said, kissing her cheek. "You've fought enough battles for tonight."

She clung to him a minute and went.

A week later, the repercussions set in. Matthew's assistant called and told Kelly that Matthew had ordered her back to Chicago.

Just like that.

When she walked into the kitchen where dinner was just ending, all conversation stopped, and everyone stared at her, even Sean who was obviously in midstory.

"What is it?" he asked, concerned. "Your parents?"

"No," she said, smiling sadly. Sean was such a pure soul. Naturally he would think of danger to one's family as being the greatest evil that could befall someone, which was amazing considering he had actually met Connie and Donald Sullivan.

"I've been recalled. To Chicago," she said. She felt as if the dinner she had just consumed so appreciatively was turned to lead in her stomach. With very little encouragement, she might throw up. She didn't want to go—she *couldn't* go.

But she had to, and she would.

It's not as if there was any choice.

"You're going to leave before the festival?" Sean asked, looking crestfallen.

"My work here is finished," she said, managing to smile.

"I know what I'll do," Sean said, brightening. "I'll just call Mr. Lawrence and ask him to let you stay a while longer."

He looked so pleased with himself at this solution. According to plan, Kelly and Conor between them had shielded

Sean from Matthew's true nature, figuring it would be better to let him learn the awful truth after the festival. Kelly shuddered to think what would happen if Sean innocently called Matthew and asked if Kelly could stay longer as a friendly favor between business associates.

"No," Kelly said a bit too emphatically.

Sean stared at her in surprise.

"I'm really needed in Chicago," she said, trying to smooth it over. "He's probably got another project picked out for me, and some of my older projects are probably at the stage where they need some attention."

"Tomorrow, then," Sean said. "Well, lass. It's been a pleasure to have you with us."

Kelly was especially touched when Margaret gave her a jar of her famous homemade jelly to take home with her. The older woman's lips thinned when Sean jovially suggested that Kelly take one to Matthew, too.

She jumped about a foot when she turned on the light in her room that evening and saw Conor stand up from where he had been sitting on her bed.

"Oh, *thank* you," she said, clutching her heart. He had quickly put a hand over her mouth to stifle the blood-curdling scream that rose to her throat. "I didn't need those five years you just took off my life."

"I wish you didn't have to go," he said, taking her into his arms and kissing her.

When they broke apart, Kelly let out a long sigh of contentment.

"God, I needed that," she said as she rested her cheek against his chest. He kissed the top of her head. "I wish I didn't have to go, either. Is this a council of war, or what?"

"Or what," he said with a smile in his voice. "The war is over. We fought the good fight, and I tell myself I'm no worse off than I was before. The castle is still lost to me, and the fact that your boss is going to destroy it makes no difference in the end. I want you to know I appreciate all you have done for us."

"Yeah. I was a big help," Kelly scoffed.

"Here, none of that," he said, kissing her on the cheek. "You've made the past few months bearable."

"Damn it! It would have made money as a luxury hotel! Look how well you've done since the rest of the rooms were opened up on the second floor."

"*We've* done," he corrected her. "You more than any of us. You'll come back for the festival?"

"No," she said with a sigh. "It would be too painful. Besides, I'll probably be on another project by then."

She didn't add that it would cause an off impression at Corporate. She had already given Matthew cause enough to question her loyalty, and, besides, if she came back she'd have to leave Conor all over again.

God, she'd miss him. His smile. His touch. His sense of humor and fun. His strong arms around her.

"Conor? You know that promise you made about not touching me unless I agreed to stay? I don't suppose—"

"Christ, Kelly!" He broke away from her and turned away so she couldn't see his face.

"Well, there's no reason why—"

"Because it would kill me to let you walk away, that's why. Jesus, do you think I'm made of stone?"

Kelly hung her head.

"I'm sorry. I—"

"Besides," he added with a glimmer of humor, "it would be just like Da or Aunt Margaret to rap on the door to tell you something just when—"

Kelly shuddered.

"True," she acknowledged with a rueful smile. "You know, this is just as hard for me. I'll never forget you."

"Yes you will. You'll go back to Chicago and your fancy restaurants and your fast cars and your big-shot men with the oily smiles and their big bank accounts. You'll marry one of them and shudder to think you once had unprotected sex with a poor, lovesick paddy who—"

Kelly thumped him on the chest.

"Once?" she said indignantly. "*Once*? You obviously were not keeping count! Poor, lovesick paddy, my ass! Do you think I don't see all those chickies swarming around you? You'll get over me soon enough."

"You're wrong," he said seriously. "I will *never* get over you. I don't blame you for going back to your real life. I have nothing to offer you."

"Like I'm a helpless twit looking for a meal ticket," she grumbled.

Conor took her in his arms.

"I understand why you have to leave. You owe a debt to your employer, and your work here is finished. I would do the same. But you can come back to me. I hope you will."

Kelly felt humble and elated at once. This good and worthy man truly loved her. And she loved him. She knew it now, even though she couldn't live in his world or he, in hers.

The next day he took her to the bus stop. She insisted that he and the other O'Mearas were far too busy during the beginning of the tourist season to take her all the way to the airport.

It wasn't a private farewell. The pub across from the bus stop was full of locals and tourists. Kelly's fellow passengers watched Conor and Kelly with great interest, too.

Kelly wanted very badly to kiss him, but he had a closed expression on his face.

"Good luck, Kelly," he said softly when she picked up her suitcase and boarded the bus. When she got in her seat and leaned across her seatmate to look out the window, she could see him watching her from the sidewalk, silent when all around him were waving, blowing kisses, and shouting their good-byes. When he saw her watching him, he raised his hand in a sort of valediction.

Good luck, he had said.

Irish for good-bye.

Twenty-five

Okay, Kelly old girl, Bradley thought with satisfaction when he told Matthew that Kelly disobeyed his direct order to surrender the fireplace. *Let's see if you can get yourself out of this mess.*

He had handled things masterfully, manipulating events so he could go to Ireland personally to demand the fireplace, which virtually *guaranteed* she would refuse.

Bradley would have to be a fool not to know she hated his guts.

He thought he'd done the white-knight-caught-in-the-middle-of-an-awkward-situation bit with consummate skill.

Without being too obvious—and Bradley was a master at this—he dropped in little poison darts, so fast and deadly they would not register on Matthew's brain until they drew blood. Bradley subtly mentioned Conor, saying that Matthew should not misunderstand. There was absolutely no proof—certainly none that Bradley could see—to indicate Kelly was sleeping with the guy. But what else was he to think when she threatened to help the O'Mearas press charges against her own company?

Bradley was very kind and a bit patronizing. One would think Kelly would know better, but she *is* in her thirties and unmarried. Maybe the guy and his family have been work-ing on her insecurities. She wouldn't be the first woman to think with her emotions instead of her brain.

It would have given Bradley great satisfaction to see Matthew go into a towering rage, the kind that made the walls at Lawrence quake. Everyone walked on eggshells and talked in whispers after one of these rampages. At these times Matthew was capable of anything.

Even firing the fair-haired girl.

Instead, Matthew just looked annoyed, which would do the trick well enough.

Bradley had planted the seed. Now it was time to leave it alone so it could germinate in the dark.

"I'm sorry I had to be the one to tell you," Bradley said apologetically. "But I thought it would be better coming from me than from someone else."

"I appreciate that," Matthew said.

When Bradley was gone, Matthew gave a deep sigh. He knew Bradley's motives, of course, and didn't blame him in the least for trying to discredit Kelly.

However, Matthew already knew all about Kelly's unfor-tunate relationship with the O'Mearas. The previous evening he had dinner with her parents, and although they had tried to make light of the situation, they plainly wanted Matthew to recall Kelly from Ireland and the dangerous proximity of Conor O'Meara.

They needn't have worried.

Kelly had brains and ambition. She wasn't about to blow a potentially brilliant career over some big, dumb stud. Matthew wouldn't even mention that she had crossed the line in Ireland, and she'd be grateful—especially when he played his trump card.

So grateful, Matthew thought with satisfaction, that he'd soon have Kelly Sullivan exactly where he wanted her—in the expensive custom-designed bed of his expensive custom-designed condo on Lake Michigan.

• • •

It wasn't cold in Chicago this time when Kelly arrived at O'Hare, which made it worse. Kelly would have found the seductive warmth of the purple wool cloak a comfort as she endured all the noise and dirt and sterile efficiency that was her real life.

She was dressed correctly but uncomfortably in a suit that was a little too tight and shoes that pinched her feet more than they had the last time she wore them, testament both to Margaret and Rose's cooking and to wearing her Nike Airs almost exclusively the past month or so in Ireland.

Her former co-workers—the ones who used to greet her with smiles so huge their back teeth showed when she was the fair-haired girl—gave her small, neutral, tentative smiles that would be retracted the moment someone else approached. It proved as nothing else could that her butt was on the line here.

Julie, to her surprise, was sitting in her old station near Kelly's cubicle. Kelly figured she would have defected all the way into Bradley's camp by now. In this, apparently, she had done Julie an injustice.

"Hi," said Julie. "I'm glad to see you."

"Thanks," Kelly said cautiously.

"Here is the mail you need to deal with personally," she said, pointing to various stacks on Kelly's desk. "Here are the phone messages you probably should return right away. You have a management meeting at two o'clock and a team meeting at four. And we have a rally at 4:30."

"A rally," Kelly repeated blankly.

"Yeah. For the new computer system. Each department has a representative on the team, and they've been working with the consulting firm for weeks to figure out how to actually implement it, so we're having a rally to generate excitement."

Julie delivered this in a deadpan tone of voice.

"We'll have a presentation and refreshments," she added unenthusiastically.

"I thought Matthew was dead-set against the idea of a new computer."

Julie gave Kelly a strange look.

"But it was all on your e-mail. I made sure you got all the memos," she said.

"I haven't been keeping up with the e-mail," Kelly admitted. "Things were pretty busy at the castle. High tourist season, you know."

Julie was still looking at her strangely, and Kelly wasn't surprised. Tourist season at Whitlock Castle should mean nothing to the Director of Guest Services for Lawrence Hotels. Julie *would* stare, Kelly thought with grim amusement, if she could have seen Kelly scrubbing toilets and painting woodwork, happy as a pig in mud.

Kelly felt depressed. Was she ever, in her whole life, going to be that happy and fulfilled again? She muffled a shriek when her pager went off.

Kelly looked at the readout on the unit.

It read 223. The extension for Matt's assistant.

Kelly shrugged and called. Matthew wanted to see her in fifteen minutes. Fine with Kelly. It was going to be a bad scene, and she'd just as soon get it over with. She started sifting through her phone messages and tried not to think about what was waiting for her in Matthew's office.

As it turned out, it was the last thing she expected.

"I've decided to name you vice president," Matthew said as soon as they were alone at the small conference table in his office. "Congratulations."

Everything Kelly had worked her butt off for the past ten years was hers.

Just like that.

Kelly accepted the hand Matthew held out to her and gave it a firm shake. She couldn't think of a thing to say.

Matthew seemed delighted with her astonishment.

"You've never been a yes-woman, Kelly," he said in a tone of smug congratulations. "I like that."

Since *when*, she thought, biting her tongue.

"And you think out of the box. I know how you spent your time in Ireland."

"You *do*?" she asked, absolutely stunned as reminiscences of the hot passion she shared with Conor O'Meara flashed through her brain.

"Of course," he said, giving her one of those naughty-girl-did-you-think-you-could-pull-the-wool-over-my-eyes? looks. "You knew my wishes with respect to Whitlock Castle, but you completed your evaluation and made your recommendations accordingly. Very impressive. The fireplace thing with Kovacks was a test, by the way, and you passed with flying colors."

"Then you've changed your mind about Whitlock Castle?"

He smiled faintly.

"You've got more important things to think about than one project in Ireland."

He took two neatly labeled file folders from his desk.

"Ireland, Italy, and Tokyo were just the beginning. I'm looking at sites in Argentina and Brazil. With last year's collapse of the South American economy, there may be some bargains to be had there. I want you to study these and give me a report on your preliminary recommendations."

"Matthew," Kelly said carefully. "I'm overwhelmed."

He smiled and covered her hand with his.

Kelly withdrew her hand, careful not to do so in haste. Then she picked up the file folders and smiled at him.

"Thank you, Matthew," she said, keeping it crisp and businesslike. "I'll go over these tonight and have a report ready for you by Monday."

"That's my girl! It's great to have you back."

"Great to be back, sir," she lied.

Wasn't it just like Matthew to promote her to vice president now that her heart was no longer in it?

It was hard to get any real work done for the rest of the day because there was an endless parade of well-wishers at her desk to suck up now that she had *arrived*. All the tentative, cautious smiles of people willing to disassociate themselves with a corporate pariah were gone, and in their place were the wide, insincere grins of people wondering how they could parlay Kelly's new status into something for themselves. They were practically salivating.

Her triumph was further sealed by an invitation to play golf with Matthew on Saturday.

Golf.

The gods were crazy, as usual.

The rest of the afternoon passed like a near-death experience. Kelly felt as if she were outside her own body watching her new best friends schmooze. It was like their mouths were moving, but nothing was coming out.

Congratulations.

Well-deserved.

But what it came down to was, *What's in it for me*?

Kelly smiled and thanked them and wished they would all go away. Their groveling gave her little satisfaction. All these people were trying to impress her with the fact that they'd been on her side all along. Some said they were relieved she was given the promotion instead of Bradley and tried to ingratiate themselves with her by saying uncomplimentary things about her "competition" for the title.

"Bradley isn't my competition," Kelly said coolly to one well-wisher. "Bradley is a member of my team."

It wasn't true, of course, but it gave Kelly a sense of mean satisfaction to watch the weasel backtrack so fast he almost bit his tongue.

To Kelly's relief, Julie appeared with a big cardboard box and shooed everyone out.

"Sorry folks," she said without a shred of apology in her voice. "Moving day."

"Where am I going?" Kelly asked, helping Julie put her stuff into the box. She didn't care, really. She just wanted out of the claustrophobic goldfish bowl her department had suddenly become.

"Executive floor, babe. You're getting Linda's former office next to the great man himself."

"You don't have to do this," Kelly said, wresting the box away from Julie.

"Well, I'm thinking that if I suck up big time, I'll get to move upstairs with you," she said, looking a little sheepish.

Kelly gave her assistant a speculative look.

Of course.

A rise in status for Kelly would also be a rise in status for her assistant. In a sense—if Julie played her cards right—she had arrived, too.

Any administrative assistant in the company would give her two front teeth to be the executive assistant to a VP, and Kelly had the pull now to have any of them promoted to the position of her assistant if Julie screwed up.

Now that, Kelly thought wryly, was power.

She could command absolute loyalty as long as *she* didn't screw up.

"Wait! Wait! Wait!" Julie demanded with a scowl when Bradley walked by her with the speed and stealth of someone trying to get around a sleeping, rabid dog. Julie was seated in a neat, open office glowing with state-of-the-art equipment now that she had moved up in the world. She had a fax machine, her own color laser printer, and a brand-new PC still shrouded in its placenta of bubble wrap awaiting installation by the IS team.

It wouldn't be long until the techies were swarming all over Julie's workstation in their zeal to get her computer hooked up. Just another one of the fringes of being associated with the new VP, Bradley thought wryly.

Julie, of course, had not been aware that today would be the day of her triumph, so she hadn't dressed the part. She was wearing a blue pantsuit with a white blouse and not much makeup. Even so, she had a smug, confident look about her.

Bradley was willing to bet that tomorrow she would be wearing a pretty dress or suit, high heels, full makeup, jewelry, and perky hair, just as she had a few weeks ago when Bradley was paying attention to her.

A new job or a new man, the dress code was the same.

Bradley sighed.

He had missed those pretty dresses and the little pearl earrings. She'd be wearing them again soon, but gone forever were the innocent smiles of pleasure that used to light up her face whenever she saw him.

It just wouldn't be the same.

Julie continued to do his grunt work but only, she made it clear, because she was a team player. His every overture of peace was met with a cool stare or cynical smile.

Bradley figured Matthew's assistant or even Julie herself would arrange for a temp to handle Bradley and the other director's stuff until a permanent administrative assistant could be found for them to share. Bradley knew he couldn't expect an assistant of his own with all the budget cuts in progress.

For now, Julie was very much the dragon guarding the door.

"She's busy," Julie told him.

Bradley was accomplished at getting past officious secretaries, but he decided against turning on the charm. In her present mood Julie was likely to throw her coffee mug at him.

"I just need a minute," he said. "Who's she with?"

Julie ignored the question.

"Sorry. She doesn't want to be disturbed. I can have her call you."

Yeah. I'll just walk away, empty-handed, and wait to be summoned into the lady of the hour's presence like the rest of the peons. Still, it would be even more humiliating to sit and wait with his toes curled under his chair.

"Uh, Julie, I have this proposal—" he began.

At that moment, Kelly appeared at the door to her *huge* office, Bradley noted jealously, and ushered out the other Director of Guest Services.

"Bradley," she said with a tight smile. "Did you come to see me, or were you looking for Julie?"

"You."

"Okay. Go on in and sit down. I'll be right back. Julie,

keep an eye on him." She gave an artificial laugh and added insincerely, "Just kidding."

Her office had that new-house smell of fresh paint and new carpeting, and Bradley fought back his resentment. Surreptitiously, he glanced at her day planner, which was opened to the current month-at-a-glance page.

Golf with Matthew Lawrence on Saturday.

Shit!

Matthew hadn't invited Brad to join them, a sign that his star was on the decline.

He quickly sat straighter when Kelly came back in.

"What can I do for you, Brad?" she asked with a cool, professional smile.

"Just stopped by to offer my congratulations."

"Thanks," she said with a deadpan expression. "Was there anything else?"

"Uh, well. No, except . . ." He stopped.

"Except?" Kelly asked with raised eyebrows.

"Well, I was hoping you were free for lunch tomorrow."

"Sure, if I can bring my own food taster along," she said sweetly.

Not good. Oh, well. What did he expect?

"Aw, Kell," he said winsomely. "We're all members of the same team now."

"Yeah. Right," she said, looking amused.

Oh, she was going to enjoy this, all right.

"About 11:30?" he suggested, showing all his teeth. "T.G.I. Friday's?" He knew it was one of her favorites.

"Sounds good to me," she said, smiling. "I'll meet you in the lobby."

When he didn't get up right away, she cocked her head in inquiry.

"Anything else?" she asked.

"Well, uh, I've got this proposal going, and I was wondering if I could use Julie for an hour or so this afternoon."

"Julie's a human being, not an office machine," she said coolly. "Ask *her* if she has time to help you."

"Yeah. I'll do that," he said, getting up. So much for trying to get Julie to do his work without asking her directly. She'll probably spit in his face.

God. This was his worst nightmare: Reporting to Kelly Sullivan and having his treatment of Julie come back to haunt him.

Julie looked up when he stopped in front of her desk. He noticed her computer was hooked up and she was copying files from diskettes onto her new hard drive. The pixies from IS must have come while he was talking to Kelly.

"How can I help you?" she asked with a professional smile as if she were speaking to a complete stranger. It irritated the hell out of him.

"Do you have time to help me out with a proposal?" he asked.

She nodded absently.

"I'll be down later. All your files are still on the hard drive at my old desk because my replacement down there will need them. I'll give you a call when I've finished here, if you like."

"Yeah. Thanks. I'd really appreciate it," he said with real sincerity.

She didn't notice.

She just gave him a perfunctory smile and went back to her work.

Kelly spent the rest of the day mending fences and positioning herself.

It seemed strange to be isolated in her pristine office high above the floors where the day-to-day work was done.

She had had months to think about how she would structure the department when she was VP, how she could earn the trust and loyalty of the other directors she'd had to beat out for the promotion, how she'd use her new influence to make a difference in the running of the company.

So far, it was almost too easy, but she knew this was only the honeymoon period. Instead of high-grade polymers or plasterboard, her office furniture was made of real wood, and her file cabinet drawers rolled on smoothly silent rollers instead of clanking open and shut like the cheap ones in her old cubicle. There was a coffeemaker at Julie's workstation, presumably so Julie could make coffee for Kelly in the morning. It remained to be seen whether Julie would, in fact, cave into convention and brew it.

To her amusement, Kelly actually had her own bathroom. She grinned at the thought of the O'Mearas' awe at how far she'd come up in the world when she told them about it.

Conor.

God, how she missed him. She looked at her day planner. Three weeks before the festival. Politically, it was not a good time for her to be gone. Who knew what sleazeballs like Bradley could do to undermine her new standing in her absence? Moreover, Lawrence employees were supposed to give management at least a month's notice before they left for vacation.

But, hell. She was a VP now. She'd pull rank to get the time off if she had to. God knows she had accrued enough vacation time in ten years.

On the way home she rented *Michael Collins* just so she could listen to Liam Neeson's accent. Liam, though gorgeous, was no substitute for Conor, but he might help her through the worst of the withdrawal.

She should have been half dead from jet lag, but she was all keyed up. She put the videocassette in her VCR just as the phone rang.

Conor, Conor, Conor, she chanted in her mind, willing it to be him. If it wasn't, she promised herself, she'd call him, er, *them* just to let them know she had arrived safely and to thank them for their hospitality.

"Hi, honey!" her father's voice boomed across the line. "I hear we'd better start shopping for that BMW."

"Dad! How did you know? I was going to call you tonight," she said apologetically, aware she should have called her parents right away.

"I just talked to Matthew," Donald said. "Congratulations, honey! We're so proud of you. We'll pick you up on Saturday so we can go car shopping."

"Sounds great, Dad, but I promised to play golf with Matthew on Saturday."

"Well, we'll go later." Donald sounded pleased. "Golf with the CEO, huh? That's my girl! Is it just the two of you?"

"Looks like."

"All the better! Mom sends her love. She's out with a client tonight."

"I'll give you a call Friday night when I find out when we're golfing. Thanks for calling, Dad."

She hung up the phone and went back to Liam.

Conor, she thought with a sigh. He was so far away from her now.

A BMW.

It all seemed so shallow. All day, her restless eyes searched in vain for genuinely friendly faces and humor and beauty. Her sleek, modern, tastefully decorated apartment was a mockery after having lived in Whitlock Castle. As for humor, there was plenty of joking around the office, but it was all a little mean. God, she'd sell her soul for a little honest *craic* instead of all this poor-spiritedness.

But, hey! She was a VP. She could, as the jargon went, effect positive change. She had the influence to save Whitlock Castle for the present. It would have to be enough. She would go to Ireland for her vacation. She would see them all again. Then she could return to her real life and hollow success.

"You're going to be on vacation during the company picnic?" Matthew asked in a shocked voice.

Missing the company picnic was Simply Not Done, especially by a brand-spanking-new vice president.

"I'm afraid my plans have been made for some time," Kelly said. She knew better than to use the word "sorry." That implied the issue was subject to negotiation, which it definitely was not.

She had to go back.

She had to see him again.

She had to know whether what she felt for him was real. If it wasn't, she would go on with her life.

If it was, she would *still* go on with her life, but at least she would have had that week.

No way was she giving *that* up so she could do the frigging three-legged race with old Matt.

"Well, you're welcome to participate if you change your mind," he said, making it clear from the tone of his voice that if she was the smart girl he took her for, she'd reconsider. "So," he added a bit too casually, "where are you going?"

"Just a little trip to see friends," she said evasively, "but I promised, and I wouldn't feel comfortable backing out at this stage."

She could tell he didn't think much of this excuse. But she could hardly admit she was heading right back to Whitlock Castle to spend the hot, steamy midsummer nights with Conor O'Meara and say good-bye to the castle before Matthew Lawrence got his pudgy, slightly moist hands on it.

Twenty-six

"Home, home, home," sang the little voice in Kelly's heart when the plane touched down at Shannon. After O'Hare, it looked so sane and welcoming.

Ireland in the spring rain was beautiful.

Ireland in June was positively glorious. Her eyes drank in the splendor of the sun shining on cobalt blue water and lush green fields during the bus ride to the village. The happy chatter of her fellow passengers and the music of their lilting voices brought tears to her eyes.

"Conor, Conor, Conor . . . home, home, home," sang her heart.

Don't think about what happens after this week is over, said her head.

When the bus lurched to a stop in the village, Kelly got off and stretched her cramped arms and legs. She hadn't told the O'Mearas she was coming. She hoped they had room for her. It would seem odd staying at Whitlock Castle as a guest.

It was the first day of the festival, and Kelly's stomach was pleasantly full of butterflies. She'd see him tonight. She waved when she saw Ghillie step out from the faded canvas canopy by the pub.

"What are you doing here, Yank?" Ghillie asked with narrowed eyes as she approached Kelly.

Ghillie looked good. She was even more sleek and beautiful than she had been a few weeks ago. Every inch of her body radiated confidence. She wore a cropped sleeveless top that showed off her well-developed arms, and the short drawstring skirt made her legs look even longer than usual. She had "city" written all over her.

Funny world.

"I came to the festival," Kelly said, refusing to let the redhead put her in a bad mood. "Is that okay with you?"

"Don't give me that," Ghillie said. "You just want to get Conor all stirred up again."

Kelly forced down the little thrill of pleasure she felt at just hearing his name.

"I came to the festival," Kelly repeated.

Ghillie shrugged.

"If you say so." Her eyes turned furious. "But don't you hurt him, damn you."

Kelly raised her eyebrows.

"You're one to talk."

"I was young and stupid," Ghillie said. "You don't have that excuse except maybe for the stupid part. That remains to be seen."

Kelly couldn't repress a smile. Despite everything, she kind of liked Ghillie. Even though she and Conor had lost their virginity together.

"Do you want a lift to the castle?" Ghillie asked. "We both know you can't wait to get there."

Oh, why pretend?

"Sure. Thanks."

"I've got Conor's boat," Ghillie said, grinning. "Hang onto your stomach, Yank."

If ever a man felt like a jackass, it was Conor O'Meara.

It was full dark on Midsummer Eve, and all day little flashes of heat lightning had crackled in the air. The aging American hippies staying on the second floor had disap-

peared at dusk and were probably capering naked somewhere out in the dark beyond the village in a peculiar attempt to celebrate the summer solstice.

They couldn't feel more exposed than Conor did now.

The things he did for his family.

He was wearing a tight pair of black pants, and that was
about it except for his shoes and the magnificent set of
Celtic jewels his great-grandfather commissioned from a
local artisan when he presided as the Summer Lord over the
first Midsummer Eve festival more than seventy years ago.
Every O'Meara head of the family had appeared as the Summer Lord in an unbroken line since that time, and in all those
years none of them had died of embarrassment, Conor told
himself. So maybe he would survive, too.

What made him feel even more self-conscious was the
knowledge that *she* was out there somewhere. He hadn't
seen her yet because by the time he got back from Cork
with the new tractor part she was sleeping off the jet lag and
he could hardly burst into her room with all his family
about.

The courtyard had been draped in boughs and lit with
candles in wrought-iron holders. A carefully watched bon-
fire burned in a steel ring. One year a pair of crazy tourists
actually tried to jump over it in a misguided attempt to enact
a Celtic ritual. He remembered how Kelly and his aunts had
put their heads together over the decorations. Everywhere he
looked, he saw her handiwork.

Naturally, she would want to see the festival.

She wasn't necessarily coming back for *him*, he told himself.

Conor took a deep breath and stepped out into the darkness of the courtyard. When he was in place before the
flower-draped great chair from the dining room, William
MacNamara and his father lit the petrol-soaked fagots on either side of the chair. To those farther away from the front of
the courtyard it would look as if he had just suddenly appeared from the air like magic.

He heard a collective gasp from the gathered crowd and

then wild applause, just as if the Summer Lord didn't mate-
rialize this way every year.

Feeling like a bloody fool, he stood up and rapped his
staff loudly on the wooden board set up in front of the chair
for this purpose.

"Let the festival," he declared, trying for a deep, hollow
tone, "begin."

There was more applause as the band began playing a
stately dance tune. He stepped onto the floor of the courtyard.

Damn, it, he thought, *where the bloody hell is Ghillie?*
Ah, here she was, all red curls bouncing and heels clicking
as she danced up to him and took his hand.

It was all rehearsed, of course. The crowd applauded and
shouted Ghillie's name because she always put on a good
show. Even so, he almost missed the first step of the dance
because he suddenly glanced at the front of the crowd and
she was there with her eyes sparkling in the firelight and her
lovely, voluptuous body clothed in a one-shouldered, softly
draped gown in a brilliant shade of peacock blue. Long silver earrings glittered at her ears, and matching etched silver
bracelets in a scroll design adorned each shapely arm. Like
most of the spectators, she had adopted vaguely Celtic-
inspired dress for the occasion.

"Jesus. Stop mooning over the Yank and pay attention,"
Ghillie muttered in disgust through the bright smile fixed on
her face.

Fortunately, Conor had little to do but present her. The
dance was easy compared to some of the others, thank God.
Otherwise he would probably fall flat on his face after he
tripped over his tongue.

Kelly stifled the feeling of jealousy that made her want to
pull all of Ghillie's luxurious red hair out by the roots when
Conor put his arms around her waist and Ghillie looked
adoringly up into his eyes.

God, he was magnificent! On both forearms he wore
twisted silver bracelets in a traditional Celtic knot design
set with winking stones that flashed blue and purple and

red and green in the firelight. Around his neck was a hammered-silver torque set with a huge blood red stone. His belt was curved black leather studded with silver. On the front was a mythical creature—a dragon or a gryphon, probably—with moonstone eyes. He wore an etched silver coronet on his dark hair with a single cobalt blue stone in front.

Ghillie was wearing a short black dress with green trimming around the square neckline. The skirt was lined in matching green fabric and gave the audiences tantalizing little glimpses of rich color whenever she twirled or leapt in the movement of the dance. She looked sleek and sophisticated next to Kelly and all the rest of the women in the audience, who suddenly looked like rejects from *Xena, Warrior Princess*.

Now that she felt like an overdressed cow, Kelly thought she'd look for an unconditionally admiring audience. Sean O'Meara was in his glory, sitting in the twin of the Summer Lord's chair, flanked by his sisters as he clapped his hands in time to the music and joked with a small crowd of well-wishers.

"And here's our lovely American friend," he said, clasping Kelly's hand. "Sure, and don't you look beautiful tonight?"

"Thank you, Sean," she said, grinning. "Looks like a great turnout."

"Always is," he said, looking smug. He looked toward the castle. "We're sending the old lady out in grand style."

He looked around with a comical frown on his face.

"And what is wrong with the young men, I'd like to know, that none of them have asked you to dance? You! Patrick O'Brien! Ask the lady to dance!"

A smiling red-haired man stepped forward and reached for Kelly's hand.

"To *this*?" Kelly asked incredulously, looking at the dancers performing what looked like a complicated square dance with no caller. She took an involuntary step back. "Forget it!"

"Come on, give it a try, why don't you?" the red-haired man said. "It's not as hard as it looks."

With that, he pulled her into the dancers and Kelly improvised madly to imitate the steps.

Conor and Ghillie, of course, were showing off with some fancy footwork at the front of the line.

"Any relation?" Kelly asked, gesturing with her head toward Ghillie when she and her partner came together.

"My twin sister," he said, grinning as Kelly stood stock still and stared at him, searching for a resemblance.

"Aye, but isn't it a pity she got all the beauty in the family and left me with this homely face?" he asked mournfully.

Kelly had to laugh. He was as handsome as his sister was beautiful, and he had to know it.

He gave her a little nudge to get her going again.

"We're all mad proud of Ghillie," he said. "Are you going to let her take your man away?"

Kelly gave a sigh. Did everybody in the place know why she was here?

"I don't think you can call him mine," she said, looking over at Conor as he laughed at some remark of Ghillie's. "Some would say she saw him first."

"He's yours, all right," Patrick said, grinning. "Did you see the look he just gave me when I put my arm around your waist? I'd better get you over there, or he'll be putting his fist through my face."

"Hey! What are you doing?" Kelly cried out when he quick-stepped her right up to Conor and Ghillie.

"Here you go, boyo," Patrick said cheerfully as he spun Kelly straight into Conor's arms. "Come along, Patricia," he added to his sister when she gave him a killing look. "It's time you had a partner who was worthy of you."

"Lovely! Where is he?" Ghillie said, looking around.

Her brother took her hand and stepped effortlessly into the dance, improvising some steps that had some of the watchers applauding and his fellow dancers scowling because he interrupted the patterns.

Ghillie responded with a staccato little flurry of steps that brought cheers.

"Ah, Kelly, I've missed you," Conor whispered as he put his arms around Kelly and led her into the darkness at the edge of the courtyard. She put one warm, soft hand on his bare chest and closed her eyes.

"Looking good, Conor. *Feeling* good," she breathed.

"I hear you got your promotion. Congratulations," he said as he kissed her temple.

"Uh, thanks." She moved her hands to his biceps and drew him closer. "Look. Do you think we can go somewhere?"

"Absolutely," he said, gently mocking her Midwestern accent. "But not yet."

The band had switched to a waltz, and Kelly felt her face flush with heat when he led her back into the crowd of dancers.

Kelly had waltzed with Conor before at the pub, but not when he was bare-chested like some primitive Celtic god.

Michael Flatley, eat your heart out.

She turned her face into his bare shoulder and tasted his flesh. It was salty and arousing, like the endless sea.

When the lovely dance was over, Conor drew her into the darkness beyond the courtyard. Once out of the festival-goers' sight, he broke into a run. Kelly picked up her skirts and ran by his side, laughing as he circled the castle and went in the front door.

He obviously didn't want anyone to see them go inside, which meant he had wicked intentions.

She hoped.

He took his time leading her up the tower stairs with only the courtyard torchlight reflected in the windows to lead them.

"You are so beautiful," he said, pinning her arms against the wall at one point and leaning in to kiss her.

When he stepped back, she wrapped her arms around his waist and hugged him, tasting him by kissing his chest.

"Better not be starting that now," he said with a shuddering sigh of pleasure. "We have a long way to go, and I can't promise I'll last the whole journey if you don't keep that teasing little tongue of yours to yourself."

"And you with your big, greedy hands all over me," she chided in a mock Irish brogue. When they got to the door of the lord's chamber, he kissed her once more just to torture them both a little.

God, he'd missed her. He badly wanted to devour her, as if he were a hungry beast that had been unsatisfied too long. He needed her like his lungs needed air. Had he vowed not to make love to her again until she promised to marry him and stay in Ireland?

He had been a fool.

Tonight, right here in this room, he would convince her they belonged together.

Even if they could never do it here again.

If he failed, at least he would have tonight.

He had made his preparations carefully in the hope they would be needed. As Kelly watched with heavy-lidded eyes, he lit the cathedral candelabrums he had dragged into the room that afternoon and savored the way her face grew luminous in the romantic light of all those banks of fat white candles.

Conor led her to the window where the pastel glass glowed in the candlelight. The sheers from the partially opened window fluttered cool against Kelly's heated skin, and the bed was turned down to reveal embroidered ivory linen sheets. Roses from the garden perfumed the sultry air around them.

Outside the darkened window, bright little pulses of heat lightning split the sky, feeding the tension that grew in Kelly's body as Conor's gentle, reverent hands explored the fabric along her bared back. He kissed her neck, the sensitive place just behind her ears, her damp temples, and she shuddered with pleasure. She turned in his arms with a muffled sob and threw herself into his arms, turning her face up to his for a kiss. He devoured her lips hungrily and pressed her pliant body tightly against his.

His hands kept roving along her back and at the sides of her waist until he abruptly broke off the kiss and held her at arm's length.

"What kind of a dress *is* this?" he asked, his face a picture of frustration.

Kelly stared at him stupidly before she caught on.

"And you an engineer," she chided him. She reached down to where the dress was wound about her body. "It's very clever. It's just all this fabric, see, and these long tie things you can drape around to make different, uh—"

Conor's clever fingers made her lose her train of thought. He had gently peeled her hand away from the tied fabric and finished unwrapping the folds of the dress himself, very slowly with his lips on hers.

When the vivid blue fabric dropped to puddle around her ankles, Conor was reminded of an alabaster goddess rising from the waves of the sea as Kelly's body emerged in a smooth, strapless silken garment the color of a ripe peach. It cupped her full, straining breasts smoothly and then fell straight to her ankles. He pulled her close until her breasts were pressed against his and kissed her while his hands sought the hooks that stopped him from exploring the rest of her lovely skin.

He released the top hooks first and freed her breasts into his caressing hands. He bent his head and took one into his mouth as he freed the rest of the hooks. Kelly's back arched as he allowed his lips to descend, kissing her and tasting her until he reached the smooth indention of her waist. He could feel her taut muscles contract with sensual tension under that soft, soft skin.

He took a deep breath for control, stood, and put his forehead against hers.

"It's hard to go slowly when all I want to do is—" he broke off and let her strapless garment slide all the way off her hips, leaving her in a pair of lacy peach-colored French-cut panties that bared her hipbones and long, long legs.

"Perfection," he sighed, taking her lips again.

Then he scooped her up in his arms to carry her to the

bed. Kelly, deliriously grateful, placed adoring little kisses on his cheek and jawline. She held on with one arm and caressed his muscular shoulder with her free hand. She was burning for him. If she didn't have him *now*, she was going to go up in flames.

As soon as he put her on the bed, she was busy peeling down the waistband of his pants. The heavy leather and silver belt hit the floor with a loud *ka-chunk* that made them both laugh. She ran a caressing hand down his abdominals and had the satisfaction of feeling him shudder under her touch.

His body was magnificent. Her greedy hands grasped his hips and caressed his thighs. When she released his engorged organ, it sprang free and stood perfectly erect. Kelly felt a little dizzy. She cupped his muscular buttocks in her hands and lowered her head, nibbling delicately. The next thing she knew, she was flat on her back and Conor was kissing her fiercely and deeply with his swollen organ burning a frantic path across her sensitized flesh. She parted her legs and tried to capture him.

He got up from the bed and silenced her with his lips when she tried to protest. One hand continued to caress her writhing body while his other hand opened the bedside chest.

Condoms, she thought dizzily. When he put his knee on the bed, she took the little packet in her shaking hand.

"The hell with this," she said with a hysterical little laugh as she tossed it over the side of the bed.

"Kelly!" exclaimed Conor, shocked. He would have reached back into the dresser drawer for another, but Kelly was having none of it.

"Come here," she said, rising up and grasping his shoulders. "I want you inside me, no safety net. No barriers. Just you."

"Be very, very sure," he said through gritted teeth.

In answer, she took him into her hand and pulled very, very gently. With a low growl, he pinned her to the bed and entered her in one powerful stroke. Then he withdrew and entered again, over and over. The building pressure in her belly and the friction of her pebble-hard breasts against his chest had been enough to make her explode; every inch of her flesh had been sensitized and throbbing for release before he entered her. Now she was mad for him.

Kelly wrapped her legs around his waist and gasped when he gripped her buttocks and drove harder. Faster and faster he went, and Kelly heard little snatches of inarticulate, passionate words as the tension suddenly burst and her senses shattered.

Kelly gasped for breath as the almost unbearable pleasure burst upon her. Shards of light illuminated her closed eyelids. Then his explosion came, powerful and hot, filling her with heat and unbelievable pleasure.

She couldn't speak.

She couldn't think.

She could only feel. She had gone limp and spent, but she felt passionate tears start in her eyes when Conor gathered her tenderly in his arms and very carefully rolled over so she would be on top. She lay cuddled against his chest and wanting nothing more in this world but to lie here, like this, with him forever.

Conor's breath was still coming in ragged gasps, but gradually his breathing evened out. Kelly was falling into a pleasant doze when she felt Conor's body stiffen. She started to lever herself up, but he crushed her against his chest with his encircling arm.

"Not yet, love," he said tenderly as he kissed her temple. "Just let me hold you a while longer."

First the passion, and then this unbelievable tenderness.

After a while, Conor sat up and gave Kelly an apologetic caress.

"We'd better go," he said regretfully.

"Conor, I—" Kelly began. He silenced her by putting one finger over her lips.

"Don't look so troubled, love," he said. "I only wanted tonight, and if that's all you can give, I have no right to demand more."

She nodded, her heart full. Then she started looking for her clothes while he looked for his.

"Uh, Kelly," he said, looking embarrassed. "What you did . . . when you threw it away . . . if you should find yourself—"

"Pregnant?" she asked, guessing what disturbed him.

"Yes. You'll tell me, won't you? Even though you don't want us in your life."

Us. Him and their child.

Kelly was shocked.

"How can you ask that?" She was hurt that he thought she would keep something like this from him.

"You wouldn't . . . get rid of it, would you? Because you don't want the father? I would take the child. You wouldn't be bothered with either of us again."

He was staring into the flames of the candelabra tree.

"No. No. No. How can you *think* I'd do such a thing?" she asked, putting her arms around his neck. "If we've made a baby tonight, I will love and cherish it."

She gave a long, shuddering sigh.

"You must think I'm a real bitch," she added, feeling dejected.

"No. Never," he said, kissing her as if to nullify the ugly word. It lay between them, like something obscene in this beautiful room still rosy with the glow of their lovemaking. "God, Kelly. I don't know what I'm saying most of the time when I'm with you. I'm sorry. I have no right to be bringing it up."

"Oh, Conor," she said, resting her head on his shoulder. "You have every right. Understand that. I would *never* destroy a child of my own body, no matter what. Children are precious and sacred gifts, even if they are a bit awkward if you're on a heavy career track."

He still looked troubled. As troubled as she felt.

"I wish we could stay here, just like this, forever," she said, horrifying herself when she realized she had said it right out loud.

"Me, too. Come, love," he said. "We have to go before we're missed."

He kissed her and pulled on the black pants.

"Or, at least before we're missed for too long," he amended.

He had dressed himself, found Kelly's sandals and panties for her, and snuffed out most of the candles by the time she struggled into her strapless slip. Her fingers were clumsy.

"What is it, love?" he asked in concern.

"I can't remember quite how I had this tied," she admitted ruefully as she struggled with the seemingly impossible folds of the dress.

"Let me help," he said teasingly. She slapped his fingers away.

Kelly couldn't help laughing.

"Funny how it seems to expose more of me than it covers up with your so-called help," she pointed out. He kissed her neck as he brought one of the long ties over the opposite shoulder. To her amazement, he had found the key to making the one-shouldered look work.

"Hey! You've done this before," she said in mock reproach.

He laughed down into her face; his eyes were sparkling with mischief.

"I'm good with my hands," he said, demonstrating in a way that made Kelly's knees start to buckle. "You've said it yourself."

Then he stepped back and left her to secure the dress.

"It's not easy to see what I'm doing," she said. "Let's hope this thing holds together, or the jig is up."

They remade the bed with the fresh sheets Conor had ready.

He'd definitely thought of everything, it seemed, even the condoms in the bedside table.

Kelly had certainly put the whammy on *that* good intention. Was it the heat of passion, or did some part of her want to be tied irrevocably to Conor?

Twenty-seven

Conor and Kelly stepped into the sultry night just in time to watch a long, black limousine disgorge its well-dressed passenger.

Matthew Lawrence's eyes went straight to their joined hands.

"Matthew! What are you doing here?" Kelly said, forcing a smile to her lips. "Matt, this is Conor O'Meara, the interim manager. Conor, my boss, Matthew Lawrence."

"The question," Matt said coldly, completely ignoring Conor, "is what *you* are doing here, Kelly."

Conor's fingers tightened on Kelly's when she would have freed her hand.

"Welcome to Whitlock Castle, Mr. Lawrence," Conor said, matching Matthew's cool tone. "We're having a festival in the courtyard tonight. Would you care to join us?"

"Absolutely," Matthew said grimly.

Conor pulled Kelly along with him to lead the way to where Sean was holding court with his sisters, and Kelly could feel Matthew's eyes burning holes into her back.

Kelly had to admire the smooth way Conor pulled off the introductions, considering that he was shirtless and wearing more jewelry than a Las Vegas showgirl. He had to be caught off guard by the way Matthew was sizing him up, but it didn't show.

For the rest of the evening, Kelly sat with Sean and Matthew, hoping to forestall any conversation that might upset either of them. Sean, oblivious to her discomfort, kept Matthew supplied with Guinness. Matthew was in senior-statesman mode, being genial and gracious and radiating quiet power. It was one of his best acts.

Matthew insisted he wouldn't dream of putting the O'Mearas to the inconvenience of finding him a room in the castle for the night. He already had a room at a comfortable inn near the airport. He agreed amiably with Sean that Kelly was a pretty and intelligent girl who would make some lucky man a fine wife. He even smiled when Sean slyly hinted that Conor spent more time at the castle when Kelly was in residence.

All the time, goosebumps were rising on Kelly's skin. She knew that soft, controlled voice. Matthew was very, very angry. She knew very well he hadn't decided impulsively to come to Ireland to pay a courtesy call on the O'Mearas. He came to find *her*. This was going to be very, very bad.

The absolute mother of all taboos at Lawrence was being caught in bed with a member of the interim staff on the facility grounds. Matthew was a little demented, but he wasn't stupid. He knew very well what Kelly and Conor had been doing alone in the castle when he arrived. *Everybody* at the festival probably knew.

Margaret and Rose were setting out food. Kelly squirmed. Ordinarily she would have been quick to lend a hand, but she didn't dare leave Matthew sitting alone with Sean for fear of what he might say to him.

Meanwhile, Conor danced with one female after another; he didn't give Kelly a second look. He probably thought he was easing the pressure off her with her boss, and he was right. It would have been even more awkward if he had hung around, making it clear that Kelly was his date, more or less, or implying subtly that Kelly needed *his* support to deal with her own boss. Even so, the sight of Ghillie laughing up into Conor's face so often made Kelly want to grit her teeth.

Matthew finally straightened and smiled apologetically at Sean. He held out his hand.

"Sean, it's been a pleasure," he said. "Kelly, why don't you walk out to the car with me?"

"Certainly," Kelly said, smiling uncomfortably. This was not going to be pretty.

Once they were both seated in the back of the limo, Matthew gave a brave smile and a sigh of disappointment.

"Kelly, Kelly, Kelly," he said, chiding her gently.

Oh, God. He was going to be *kind*. She'd rather he yelled.

"That's quite an . . . unusual costume. A Celtic princess, are you?" There was just the slightest edge of contempt shading the amusement in his voice. He did this *so* well.

She would not start babbling and apologizing. She would *not*.

"Something like that," she said, forcing her voice to play it lightly. "It was the last festival the O'Mearas would have, and I thought it might be fun."

"Perfectly understandable," he said in that maddeningly amused tone again. "Well, they're nice people. Salt of the earth. It's no wonder you started to identify with them, especially the good-looking son. Nice fashion sense, too."

"So, are you going to tear off my epaulets or something?" she asked with an arch smile. "Demote me to the mail room? Tell Mom and Dad?"

He laughed.

"No." He gave her another of those smiles she did not trust. "You're on vacation, after all. But Kelly, you are far too valuable to the company to concentrate so much of your effort on one project. Mentally you have not made the transition from Director of Guest Services to Corporate Vice President of Guest Services. I had agreed to let you see the Whitlock Castle project through, but I've decided that was a mistake."

Kelly held her breath. She did not dare say one word or

she might start pleading with him. That would only harden his determination.

"Therefore," he said, giving her a severe look just in case she was thinking about objecting, "I am assigning Brad to finish up your work on Whitlock Castle."

Omigod, omigod. The absolute *worst*-case scenario. Bradley would bully the O'Mearas. And he would think nothing of gutting the interior and throwing the furnishings on the antiques market to ingratiate himself with Matthew.

"He'll be happier with one of his nature girls," Matthew said almost kindly. It took Kelly a minute to realize he was talking about Conor. "Someday you'll thank me for this."

Jeez. He acted like he was her father, and he was sending her to summer camp to get her away from a horny fifteen-year-old boy after he caught them steaming up the windows of his car.

"Am I grounded?" she asked, forcing herself to smile.

Matthew gave that unnerving, kindly laugh again.

"Would it work? No, seriously. Enjoy your vacation, but be back in the office by four o'clock next Monday to debrief on the Whitlock Castle project before Bradley and the team. Make your best pitch to persuade Bradley and me not to do what we wanted to do in the first place. Fail to convince us, and—" He drew his finger across his neck. "It's your shot, babe. Succeed or fail, your involvement with Whitlock Castle is over at the end of the day on Monday. After that, you'll concentrate on your responsibilities to Lawrence as a whole."

"Matthew, I—"

"Kelly?" he said in gentle reproof. "Let there be no misunderstanding. I would be completely within my rights to order the demolition at once, and I will if you fail to present yourself in Chicago for that meeting."

At last, Kelly was permitted to see the anger.

"I'll be there," she said.

"I could have you terminated for having a sexual relationship with an interim manager, or do you deny what I saw this evening?"

"No. I don't deny it." She was not ashamed of loving Conor, and pretending she was would be the worst kind of betrayal.

"Wise," he said. "That relationship must come to an end once you come to Chicago. You *do* understand this?"

Hypocrite. If I had been seeing you *on the side, that old policy wouldn't mean a thing.*

"I understand," she said out loud.

"That's my girl," he said, putting his hand over hers. "Enjoy your little fling. Get it out of your system."

Like he was doing her a favor.

"Come back to Chicago ready to *work*," he continued grimly. "Don't throw your career away on some big, dumb stud who will keep you barefoot and pregnant for the next ten years and probably hit you around a bit on the side."

"He's not like that," Kelly blurted out.

"They're all like that, babe," he said smugly. "This place seems to mean a lot to you. If you want it to stay in one piece, you'll be in Chicago on Monday and give it your best shot—then you'll stay the hell away from Conor O'Meara for good."

"I'll *be* there," she said again, letting her smile harden along the edges.

Matthew patted her hand.

"I know you will. You're too smart to let your hormones ruin your career. See you Monday, Kelly. Get your head and your legs together between now and then."

"Nice cheap shot, Matt," she said, gritting her teeth.

He turned his back on her to look out the window.

It was dismissal. She opened the car door and got out.

Even though it was warm and humid outside, Kelly felt a chill when she stepped out of the air-conditioned car.

When the limo pulled away, Conor materialized from the shadows. She had the absurd idea he had been watching the whole drama, ready to intervene if she needed him.

Her would-be white knight.

"Are you all right?" he asked.

"Yeah. Peachy," she said sarcastically.

Conor was looking at her as if he expected her to scream or explode or something.

"He's taking me off Whitlock Castle."

"He knew exactly what we were doing. It was all over your face and probably mine as well," he said ruefully.

"That pretty much describes the situation. As you know, it's against company policy to become intimate with a co-worker, *especially* a member of the interim staff. I could be fired for this. Instead, he's going to turn Whitlock Castle over to Bradley Kovacks. Jesus, this is my worst nightmare."

She gently shook Conor off when he put his hands on her shoulders.

"I'm to get you *out of my system*, like you're a bad drug or something. He threatened to gut the castle, Conor, and he'll do it if I don't shape up and be a good little VP. I've got one shot at convincing Matthew, Brad and the bean-counters to call off the bulldozers. If I fail—*Hello*, Euro Disney!"

Conor looked properly horrified.

"Don't worry, Conor," she said, patting his arm. "I can fix this. I *have* to fix it."

"And what about *us*?" he asked quietly. "Are you after fixing that, too?"

"There *is* no us. That's his number-one demand. Not now. Maybe never. God, Conor, don't look at me like that."

"So, am I to wait for you, or forget you?" His voice was tight and a little cruel.

"Forget me, if it's easier," she said, feeling a tear leak down her cheek.

"Easier," he scoffed. "Jesus."

She didn't blame him for stalking off, even though her whole body cried out for the comfort of his arms around her. Ghillie met him just as he was about to turn the corner and disappear from Kelly's sight. Ghillie looked up into Conor's eyes. Then she put her arm around his waist, gave Kelly a poisonous look, and steered him away from the evil Yank.

• • •

Kelly's eyes were still puffy from crying herself to sleep when she heard the soft knock on her door. She had been crying herself to sleep every night since the festival. You'd think she'd be out of tears by now. She was still in her robe, but her work day had begun. The bed was littered with all of the printouts she'd made since she came to Ireland. She had to give the best presentation of her life, and she had to do it in less than a week.

She figured her visitor would be Rose or Margaret. She pulled her robe together in a show of modesty when she opened the door to Conor. He was carrying a steaming cup of coffee in front of him like a peace offering.

"It's a little late for that," he said with a sad, reminiscent smile.

Heat rose to Kelly's face as she took the coffee from him.

"Thanks," she said, her heart in her throat.

"I came to apologize for—God's truth, I don't know what I came to apologize for," he said with a shaky laugh. "Kelly, you've been shut up in here for three days. You've eaten practically nothing. Come to breakfast in the kitchen. Go out in the garden for a little while and get some fresh air."

"Conor, I—" she began, shaking her head.

"I promise not to bother you," he said, staring at the opposite wall. "I won't talk to you. I won't even *look* at you. Please. We're all worried about you."

Kelly's eyes filled again. She was so touched by their concern. She'd stayed away from them so long because she tended to leak tears at unexpected times. She thought she might be having a nervous breakdown, and she refused to let them see it.

She suddenly realized she wanted a bath. She wanted to see her Peacock Room. She wanted to get out of this robe. After Monday, she might never see the O'Mearas or Whitlock Castle again.

"You're absolutely right," she told Conor. "Get out of here so I can get dressed. I'll be right down."

She gave him a friendly hug.

"Thanks, big guy," she said. When he held her close for a

moment as if he didn't want to let her go, she gave him a thump on the shoulder. "Now, scram!"

On Sunday night she hooked her laptop up at the front desk and went through her presentation for the O'Mearas while Conor clocked her time with a stopwatch.

"Time," she called over Sean's, Margaret's and Rose's enthusiastic applause. There was no reference in the presentation to the possibility of turning the castle into a medieval theme park. This was her best-case-scenario proposal for a luxury hotel, and she had poured her heart and soul into it.

"Fifteen minutes, three seconds," Conor said. "God, but you're a brilliant woman."

It was going to be the best presentation of her life. And when it was over, Whitlock Castle wouldn't be hers anymore.

She brought herself up short. The castle had *never* been hers.

Conor had never been hers.

Her intentions had been so good, and she almost brought about the castle's destruction.

As for Conor, all she had brought him was unhappiness. He didn't have to say a word for her to know it.

"Here, I'll help you," he said as she gathered her materials and her equipment.

"Oh, you don't have to bother—" she said quickly.

"It's no bother," he said. He picked up the laptop case and projector screen. Sean, Rose, and Margaret had melted away as if at some signal from Conor. "You don't have to be afraid to be alone with me, Kelly. I'm not going to force myself on you."

"Oh, Conor," she said in a long, shuddering sigh. She put her hand to his cheek, and her heart broke at the way he closed his eyes as if to memorize the touch of her skin. "I know that."

Embarrassed, he turned away and motioned for her to precede him to the steps. When they got to her room, he put her computer where she indicated and took her in his arms.

"I guess I lied," he said as he kissed her.

She knew she should push him away, but she kissed him back instead. God, he tasted good. Her lips tingled with relief. He hadn't kissed her since that night in the tower, and her whole body had craved him ever since.

This wasn't fair to either of them.

Even so, she couldn't quite seem to break the death grip she had around his neck.

"You're not going to come back, are you?" he asked.

"Honest to God, Conor. I don't know. I can't deal with this issue now."

"An *issue*, is it?" he asked, sounding offended.

"I have to focus completely on that presentation tomorrow. You *know* what's at stake. I can't allow anything or anyone to distract me. Not even you."

"I guess you've had your fling," he said, smiling ruefully.

"I was *wrong*, okay?" she snapped. "You're not a fling. But I can't let old Matthew have his way with Whitlock Castle without doing everything I can to stop it. Whose side are you on, anyway?"

"Yours," he said. "Yours, always. I'm sorry." He stepped back and held his hands out to indicate his harmlessness. "I won't touch you again. Not until you're ready to come back to me."

"Hey! No pressure *there*," she said, trying to smile.

"Maybe your boss is right, and you'll be thanking God for a narrow escape once you're back in Chicago. Maybe I'll be thinking the same."

"Do you believe that?" she asked.

"No," he said. "I don't believe *I* will."

She made a growl of absolute frustration.

"You'd better go. Tomorrow will be a long day for both of us."

"Good night, love," he whispered. Then he was gone.

When Kelly walked down the stairs the next day, it was as if the past four months had never happened.

To Conor she looked just as perfect and remote as she had the day she first came to Whitlock Castle.

She was wearing another of those expensive suits, this one in bright blue linen with white trim at the collar and cuffs. Her beautiful legs were encased in white stockings and neat white shoes. Every hair was in place; she had gone to Cork to have it trimmed at an expensive beauty parlor. He had liked the way it had grown a bit shaggy at the edges as if in invitation for a man to run his fingers through it. He remembered the way she used to roll her eyes and blow her bangs out of the way with an exhaled breath to make Aunt Margaret laugh.

She was leaving him. Her luggage was lined up by the door. He followed her outside and put it in the trunk of the car. There was nothing more to be said. Aunt Rose, Aunt Margaret, and Da came to the door to give her a hug.

Conor's fingertips itched for the softness of her cool, fragrant skin, but he knew it would be madness to touch her.

"You'll call so we'll know you arrived safely?" he asked.

"I will. I'll go straight to the office from the airport, but I'll call you from home tonight to let you know how it went."

He nodded. He didn't trust himself to speak. She was talking about that presentation again, as if Whitlock Castle was the only thing between them.

Maybe it was.

He had no right to expect more from her. He couldn't promise her the life she was used to. He couldn't even promise her the life *he* was used to once the castle was gone.

She wouldn't let him give her a proper lift to the airport. Kelly insisted that he drop her off at the bus stop. She would make it to the airport perfectly well on her own.

And she would. Kelly Sullivan didn't need anything or anybody to get where she wanted to go.

They said little in the car on the way to the village.

At the bus stop, they shook hands. Actually shook hands! It was unbelievably awkward.

"Good luck," he said solemnly.

"Thanks. You, too," she said, looking sad for a minute. Then she was all brisk and businesslike as she handed her luggage over to the bus driver for storing away and carried her computer case up the steps. Once inside, she waved at him from her window once, and then she turned away as the bus pulled smoothly into the road.

Conor had chores to do. The immersion tank was acting up again, and more guests would arrive that afternoon. But instead of getting in his car and heading back to the castle, he stood and watched her bus until it was out of sight.

Twenty-eight

The city of Chicago unfolded below Kelly like an illustration in a pop-up storybook. It seemed about that real to her. She went through all the airport stuff with her head in a fog, totally focused on her presentation. There was something almost comforting about the impersonal cacophony of hundreds of voices speaking in scores of languages, the indifferent attention of the airport employees, the silence of the taxi driver as he drove her to her apartment.

Ireland was so full of life and color that it *forced* her to look at it and to listen to the animated voices of its children.

Right now, Chicago was just what she needed. She was on a mission. All the turmoil in her mind over Conor could be put on hold in Chicago.

She dropped off her luggage at her apartment, freshened up a little, and made sure her suit was still presentable. It would not do to give the presentation of her life in a wrinkled skirt.

When she got to the office, everybody looked at her as if she were newly risen from the dead. No one spoke to her beyond a civil greeting. Kelly was important now. Vice presidential. By virtue of her promotion, everybody from the receptionist to the maintenance guy who scuttled out of her way with the floor polisher respected her space. The staccato echo of her high heels on the Italian tile underscored her sense of mission as she crossed the reception area and ascended the stairs to the executive floor.

Julie actually stood, as if for the queen, when Kelly approached her.

"Welcome home," Julie said formally.

Home? Nothing had ever felt less like home than this.

"Thanks," she said. "I have a presentation in thirty minutes, so please take messages if anyone calls. Except Matthew, of course."

"Of course," Julie said with a tight smile. It looked painful.

Kelly sighed.

Stay focused, she told herself.

She had just read through her notes for the presentation when the phone rang at Julie's workstation.

"Ms. Sullivan is not available at the moment," Julie said pleasantly into the instrument. "May I tell her who called?"

"No, I'm afraid that isn't possible. Your name, please?" Julie added in a stronger voice after a short pause to listen to the caller.

Kelly dove back into her notes, almost tuning out Julie's voice until her assistant, who was more than a match for the random persistent caller, said the magic word.

"Mr. O'Meara. As I told you, Ms. Sullivan is not available—"

"Julie! *Julie!* Transfer that call to me!" Kelly ordered.

Julie looked up from the phone, frowning. Kelly knew she *hated* it when Kelly said no calls and then made *her* look like an officious witch by taking the call anyway. Julie continued to scowl as she transferred the call. Well, Kelly didn't need to worry about Julie's oppressive genuflecting anymore, at least not until she got over her snit.

"Conor," Kelly said into the phone, not bothering to filter the warmth from her voice. Hearing his voice was going to wreck her concentration. She didn't care. "Hi! I just got here. Look—I've got the presentation in a few minutes. Can I call you back when it's over?"

Silence.

"Conor?"

"Kelly." His voice had unshed tears in it.

"Conor, what is it?" Kelly asked as goosebumps raised on her skin. "Your father?"

"Yes. He had a stroke after you left and he's in another coma. They don't know if he'll make it this time."

"Oh, my God," Kelly breathed. "I'm so sorry. Is there anything I can do?"

"It helps to hear your voice. I'm sorry. I thought your presentation would be over by now—"

"Never mind that."

"Did you know your friend Bradley Kovacks was going to send that antiques appraiser here today with the workmen who construct crates for merchandise?"

"Oh, my God," she said, closing her eyes. "The appraiser didn't mention the sale to Sean, did he?"

"He did, yes. Da collapsed an hour later. I was at the farm, or I'd have taken the man aside first."

"Oh, God. Conor, please believe I had *no* idea—"

"Kelly, love. Of course I know that. I have to go. The doctor just came into the waiting room to talk to us."

"I'll call tonight," Kelly promised, near tears as she returned the phone to its cradle.

"Julie, see if Matt's in, will you?"

Julie nodded. Then she looked up, startled, when Matthew walked past her and into Kelly's office. He closed the door behind him.

"Sean O'Meara just had another stroke," she said, fixing him with an accusing stare.

"I'm sorry to hear that," Matthew said pleasantly, although Kelly knew he couldn't care less.

"I suppose you knew the guy from the auction house was going to show up at the castle with workmen to construct the crates today. It was a done deal from the beginning, wasn't it?"

"Now, Kelly," he said in gentle reproof. "I've taught you better than that. *Nothing* is a done deal until it's done. Whatever we decide later, there's no reason why we can't sell some of the higher ticket items to ease our cash flow. It's called *business*, honey."

"Don't . . . call . . . me . . . honey," Kelly said, giving him a look that should have turned him to stone. "You let me believe there was a chance to keep the castle intact."

He raised his eyebrows.

"In theory there was a chance your presentation might convince me. Or even Bradley. Bradley reports to you now. You might find a way of convincing him it would be more healthy for him to play this your way. I doubt it, though. He's pretty unhappy about losing the promotion, and he can hardly take it out on me. I, of course, have let it be known that the idea of an auction to ease our cash flow would please me."

"So Whitlock Castle is just a playing piece in the power struggle."

"That's all it's ever been." He gave her a fatherly pat on the shoulder. "In general, I am pleased by the way you handled yourself on this assignment. Your model for Whitlock Castle as a luxury hotel will come in handy for other projects. It was genius, exactly the caliber of work I've always known you were capable of. Now it's time for you to focus on higher and better things. *All* of our projects deserve your attention, not just one. You have to think global."

"Out of the box," she said grimly.

"Exactly," Matthew said, apparently pleased that she was catching on. He stood and opened the door. "Now. You've got ten minutes. I'll see you in the conference room."

"What are *you* looking at?" Kelly snapped at Julie, who just happened to be standing by when Matthew walked through the door.

"Hey! I'm just an innocent bystander. I wanted to know whether I'm in or out for this meeting."

"Hell, come on in," Kelly said, making a helpless little fluttering motion with one hand. "Sell tickets. It's going to be the performance of my life. Afterward, I might just kick the snot out of Bradley Kovacks. I'm feeling kind of mean right now."

"Sounds like a plan to me," Julie said with malicious glee.

Kelly gave a great presentation. Everyone said so. But in the end, she might as well have stood up there and recited the phone book. It made about that much difference.

Bradley wasn't even there. He was on his way to Ireland to give Conor O'Meara his ultimatum. Matthew wanted the O'Mearas out of Whitlock Castle by the end of July and was willing to pay an amount equivalent to the O'Mearas' projected revenue from the castle for the last two months of the contract.

This was an offer Kelly knew Conor couldn't refuse. The O'Mearas were burdened with debt from repairs to the castle over the years and Sean's hospital bills. Conor had gone through his father's financial records after he was given power of attorney, and it hadn't been pretty.

"It was a good show," Matthew said amiably as she packed up her laptop.

"Thanks," she said with an impersonal smile.

"How does Cancún sound?"

Kelly raised her eyebrows.

"Are we buying another property there?"

"No," Matthew said, taking her elbow to move her away from Julie, whose head popped up like a cork out of a champagne bottle at the mention of Cancún.

What now, Kelly thought as he steered her into his office and closed the door.

"Kelly, I'm concerned about your mental state. Obviously, you need to put this Irish thing behind you," he said. "I've decided to send you to Cancún. You can meet our people out there. Play some golf. Clear your head." He gave her a faint smile. "Come back next week ready to kick butt."

Kelly locked her jaws together. It was either that or spit on him.

Matthew picked up an expensive letter opener and turned it over carefully.

"Kelly, now that you're a VP, I think I can tell you this in confidence. The cash flow problem is a bit more urgent than I've indicated to you and the other officers."

Kelly stared at him.

"Frankly, we need this sale of antiques from Whitlock Castle to save our butts. It was extremely expensive for us to buy out Linda's share of the business. We can finance the purchase using some of the other properties as collateral. Fortunately, the Irish property is worth far more than we're paying for it, thanks to the fact that Sean O'Meara insisted on using his family solicitor from the village to handle things from his end instead of hiring a more qualified solicitor from one of the bigger cities. With an influx of cash from the auction, we'll be fine."

"I understand," Kelly said.

"I was sure you would," Matthew said, looking relieved. "So, how about it?" When Kelly gave him a blank look, he said, "Cancún."

"Cancún," she repeated. "Sure. Why not?"

Matthew looked at the backs of his hands.

"If I can shake myself loose at this end, I might join you there over the weekend. We haven't played golf for a while. Now that you're a VP, you won't have to let me win."

"I've *never* let you win," she said scornfully.

"Thank you for that," Matthew said. "Why don't you go home and start packing? The ticket will be waiting for you at the airport tomorrow evening."

"Great," Kelly said, forcing enthusiasm into her voice.

Then she got out of there before she said something unforgivable.

Cancún. Jeez.

Could he *be* any more obvious?

But Kelly didn't have time to worry about old Matt and

his power plays. As soon as she got inside her apartment, she raced for the phone.

"Margaret!" she said, relieved that someone answered. "How is he?"

"Kelly!" Margaret exclaimed, her voice brightening. She had sounded so weary at first. "There's been no change. He's pulled through worse."

She was saying it more to herself than to Kelly, and they both knew it.

"How are the rest of you doing?"

"As well as can be expected, thank you." She paused. "It's Kelly," she said, obviously talking to someone else at her end. Her voice was muffled, apparently from covering the mouthpiece with her hand.

"Kelly."

Conor's voice.

For a minute Kelly couldn't think of a thing to say.

"Bradley's going to try to force you to move out early," she blurted out. "Conor, I didn't know. Honest."

"Of course, you didn't," he said, sounding shocked that she thought he could believe such a thing of her. "How did your presentation go?"

"It went okay, but I might have saved my breath. It was a done deal. They want the sale to go through as soon as possible, and they're going to make you an offer you can't refuse."

"We'll see about that," he said harshly. "I have to go."

"Oh. Good-bye, then."

"Good luck," he said, and hung up.

Kelly was left staring at the receiver, a little stunned by Conor's abruptness.

Well, what did she expect? The man had important things on his mind.

Kelly was late for work, but no one would say a word.

She was *somebody* now.

Julie's elevated status had moved her to new heights of efficiency. She did everything but click her heels together as she gave a brief resume of all the calls Kelly had received, who wanted to see her, what had been handled already by Julie, what could and what could not wait.

No personal chatter. No joking.

When Kelly entered rooms from now on, conversations would stop not because they were about her, but because Kelly was one of *them*. Not that she would see her former co-workers that often now that she was enthroned in seventh heaven.

It was four o'clock in Ireland.

Was Sean still in a coma? Was he dead? Had he awakened? Was it any of her business?

Kelly stiffened her spine, then she got up from her desk to go to her first meeting. She had a job to do, even though her heart was no longer in it.

By the end of the day, she had picked up the phone a dozen times to call Ireland but chickened out as soon as she heard the dial tone. Now that Bradley was on the spot, the last thing any of the O'Mearas probably wanted was to talk to anybody from Lawrence—especially her.

Almost five o'clock, thank God.

She had been edgy all day, and she had to keep a hard clamp on her emotions to keep from laughing giddily or bursting suddenly into tears like a mental patient in the series of meetings she attended. In an hour she would be on the way to Cancún, ostensibly to touch base with her staff there and rest up after "the Irish thing," as her boss so delicately put it.

She'd go because she was on thin ice, and she knew it. But she wasn't going to go to bed with Matthew Lawrence. One had to draw the line somewhere, even if one had drawn it too late.

She jumped when the speaker on her phone suddenly came to life.

"Kelly! In my office! Now!" barked Matthew's voice.

She exchanged a wide-eyed stare with Julie, who had been putting some files away in Kelly's office.

"On my way," said Kelly, giving Julie a *what now*? look.

Matthew was pacing like a caged lion and snarling into his speaker phone.

"She's here," he said to whoever was on the other end of the line. He motioned Kelly to a seat.

"Hi, Kell," said Bradley's amplified voice. "Glad you could join us." The sarcasm in his voice didn't quite disguise the panic. "Your boy Conor is pulling the plug."

For a moment Kelly's disoriented brain gave a cry of distress at the thought of Conor unplugging his father from life support. But only for a moment. The decision to let Sean O'Meara pass gently from this earth would hardly have Matthew's shorts in a bunch.

The cry of distress must have escaped because Matthew gave her an almost approving look.

"That's right," he said grimly. "He's backing out of the deal."

"But—he can't," she said. "He'll have to pay the penalties for backing out. His creditors will close in. He'll go under."

"What do you expect from a stupid mick?" Matthew said contemptuously. "Forget Cancún. You are going to Ireland tonight to talk some sense into your boyfriend."

"I can handle it from this end," objected Bradley, who obviously hated the idea of being bailed out by a woman, especially *her*.

Matthew ignored him and turned to Kelly.

"*Don't* fail," he told her. "Is Julie still here? My assistant's gone for the day. Julie can try to get you a ticket on Aer Lingus tonight. If she can't, you can fly standby. I don't care what you have to say or what you have to do. Sleep with him, if you have to. But make sure Conor O'Meara goes through with this sale."

It was the moment of truth.

Fail, and she was dead meat. Matthew wouldn't demote her right away because that would make *him* look as if he had made an error in judgment, but eventually she'd find herself at the bottom of the ladder again, crawling up.

Succeed, and she would have solidified her position with Lawrence and made Bradley the Butcher look like an incompetent stooge. It was plain that Brad had bungled the job. Kelly could prove her superiority by making sure the auction that would save Matthew's ass went through.

It's not like Conor had a hope in hell of holding on to the castle if the sale *didn't* go through.

"You'd better get going," Matthew told her.

"Sorry boss," Kelly said coolly. "No can do. Conor has made his decision. *I* am not going to talk him out of it."

Matthew's expression turned nasty.

"You *will*, Kelly, if you know what's good for you. I made you vice president; I can unmake you just as easily."

"Fine. I hope you boys will be very happy together," she said, including Bradley in her valediction.

"Where the hell do you think you're going?" Matthew demanded, grabbing her arm when she would have left the room.

She pushed him away with so much force that he staggered and had to grab the top of his desk to keep from falling.

It felt great!

"To clean out my desk. I'm history," she sang.

"You can't do that!'"

"I just did."

Kelly flew standby on Aer Lingus after all, but she paid her own fare, thank you very much.

Talk about burning your bridges.

Matthew would make sure she would never work in *this* town again. Or in this industry.

Her parents would probably never speak to her again—if she was lucky. She could imagine what they'd have to say if they did. Angry as they probably would be with her, though, at least she could depend on them to close her apartment, sell her furniture, get rid of her car, and forward the money to her. She hoped there would be a last check from Lawrence. If not, oh *well*!

Nothing like bungee jumping without a bungee.

She didn't take much with her. For all she knew, she'd be sleeping off her jet lag in someone's car. Thank heaven the

Irish didn't believe in locking their doors. Most even trustingly left their keys in the ignition.

Kelly wouldn't blame the O'Mearas if they didn't exactly welcome her with open arms.

Conor was talking on the telephone at the front desk when she carried her luggage into Whitlock Castle. His face went utterly still when he saw her. He hung up the phone rather abruptly with a promise to ring the caller back.

"How is your father?" Kelly asked.

"Awake, thank God."

He walked around the desk, but stopped about two feet away from her. His hands opened and closed as if he wanted to touch her but didn't dare.

She knew exactly how he felt.

"If you've come to talk me out of keeping the castle, you can save your breath," he told her.

"Gutsy move, O'Meara," Kelly said admiringly. "Not very sensible, but gutsy."

"I know that," he said, smiling wryly. "None of us will be able to retire until we're in our nineties. If then."

"Yup. That's the way I see it, too." Going for broke, she threw her arms around his neck and kissed him.

He started to protest, but then he gave a long sigh and kissed her back.

"Love, I've nothing to offer a wife," he said, carefully putting her away from him.

"Sorry to hear that. Can you use a manager, then?" she said. "This is your golden opportunity to get me cheap because I quit my job today."

He stared, started to smile, and then he grew serious. It was a beautiful thing to watch.

"Are you *mad*? I'd have to pay you in—" His hands made an agitated little arc. "Hell. Porridge, maybe."

"I accept," she said happily. She felt so alive. "Conor, my man, Whitlock Castle is going to make money hand over fist."

He threw his head back and laughed.

"You're as mad as I am," he declared. He swept her into

his arms. "You'd better marry me after all, love, and heaven help you."

He kissed her and gave her a cocky grin.

"Lord, I'd love to see your mother's face when you tell her."

Twenty-nine

A month and a half wasn't much time for planning a wedding, but Kelly, always the astute promoter, wasn't about to turn down a perfect opportunity to use her marriage to Conor to put the international hospitality industry on notice that the new Whitlock Castle was open for business.

As long as they were working without a net, anyway, Conor and Kelly decided to do it up big. Every room in the castle was ready for occupation except for the tower room. Kelly had immediately appropriated it for herself and Conor as their future living quarters. She cashed in her 401(k) account to pay the O'Mearas' legal penalties for backing out of the sale of Whitlock Castle to Lawrence Hotels.

The past month had been spent in an orgy of painting and refurbishing. Whitlock Castle's days as a bed-and-breakfast were numbered. It would continue to be operated as one through the fall, close over December and January, and open in late February as a full-service luxury hotel. In between fittings for her wedding gown in Cork, Kelly was up to her neck in interviews for staff.

She was working fourteen hours a day and loving it because Conor was working right along with her.

The only thing that marred her happiness was the thought

that the bride's side of the aisle would be filled with travel writers and other industry professionals instead of family. Her mother hung up on her when she called to tell her about the wedding.

Rose, Margaret, and Ghillie rode to the church with Kelly in Conor's car. All three had been surprised to be asked to be Kelly's bridesmaids. Kelly figured Ghillie was entitled to be in the wedding as a consolation prize for not getting Conor. Rose and Margaret protested that they were too old to be in the wedding party, but Kelly pointed out that they were her best girlfriends in Ireland and she wanted them.

These days, Kelly pretty much got what she wanted around Whitlock Castle.

Ghillie was wearing a gorgeous green chiffon floor-length gown with bright pink roses in her hair. Rose's and Margaret's outfits were really mother-of-the-bride suits, and they didn't match. Margaret's was pink, and Rose's was her favorite shade of ice blue. Both were silk.

As for Kelly, she was wearing a traditional floor-length gown with embroidered illusion pointed sleeves and a cathedral-length veil with a little crystal tiara. Once, she would have thought thirty-three too old for the whole gown-and-veil bit, but, what the heck, she was only doing this once. Kelly's eyes misted when she saw Conor's big grin as he waited with his father, Ghillie's brother, and William Mac-Namara, the chicken guy, at the end of the aisle.

Conor had thrilled Kelly by volunteering to wear a black tuxedo for the wedding, and he was so handsome he took her breath away. The other three men wore their Sunday suits and had probably been slagging him about the tux all morning.

Now *that*, she thought, grinning back at him, was true love.

Ghillie, Rose, and Margaret were almost at the altar when the organ music changed and Kelly took the first step forward. To her surprise, her parents stepped up to join her from where they apparently had been waiting on either side of the arch inside the doorway.

"Pardon me, miss, but I heard you might have an opening for someone to walk you up the aisle," her father said, looking unsure of his welcome.

"Dad!" Kelly cried, hugging him. "Mom!" She hugged Connie, too. She was so glad to see them.

Her dad offered his arm, and Kelly took it. When her mother dabbed at her eyes with a tissue and would have walked away to sit alone, Kelly grabbed her arm with her other hand.

"Hey!" she whispered huskily. "Where do you think *you're* going?"

So, Kelly was escorted to the altar by both her parents.

"Did you know they were coming?" she whispered to Conor when her father had handed her over to him.

He grinned.

"Da rang them up when he got out of the hospital. I don't know what he told them, but the next thing I knew they were coming to the wedding. They wanted to surprise you."

"This *rocks*," she said, smiling into his eyes.

"There's more. Most of the people on the bride's side of the church are your relatives. Your parents have spent the past month tracking them down on the Internet."

"What?" Kelly turned around and Conor took her arm.

"You can meet them later," he said, stifling a laugh.

"Oh. Yeah," she said sheepishly.

DO YOU BELIEVE IN MAGIC?

MAGICAL LOVE

The enchanting series from Jove will make you a believer!

With a sprinkling of faerie dust and the wave of a wand, magical things can happen—but nothing is more magical than the power of love.

☐ *SEA SPELL* by Tess Farraday 0-515-12289-0/$5.99
A mysterious man from the sea haunts a woman's dreams—and desires...

☐ *ONCE UPON A KISS* by Claire Cross
0-515-12300-5/$5.99
A businessman learns there's only one way to awaken a slumbering beauty...

☐ *A FAERIE TALE* by Ginny Reyes 0-515-12338-2/$5.99
A faerie and a leprechaun play matchmaker—to a mismatched pair of mortals...

☐ *ONE WISH* by C.J. Card 0-515-12354-4/$5.99
For years a beautiful bottle lay concealed in a forgotten trunk—holding a powerful spirit, waiting for someone to come along and make one wish...